ONE IN THE
CHAMBER

ALSO BY ROBIN PEGUERO

Novels

With Prejudice

ONE
IN THE
CHAMBER

ROBIN PEGUERO

GRAND
CENTRAL

New York Boston

Copyright © 2024 by Robin Moses Peguero

Cover design and illustration by David Litman
Cover copyright © 2024 by Hachette Book Group, Inc.

Hachette Book Group supports the right to free expression and the value of copyright. The purpose of copyright is to encourage writers and artists to produce the creative works that enrich our culture.

The scanning, uploading, and distribution of this book without permission is a theft of the author's intellectual property. If you would like permission to use material from the book (other than for review purposes), please contact permissions@hbgusa.com. Thank you for your support of the author's rights.

Grand Central Publishing
Hachette Book Group
1290 Avenue of the Americas, New York, NY 10104
grandcentralpublishing.com
twitter.com/grandcentralpub

First edition: March 2024

Grand Central Publishing is a division of Hachette Book Group, Inc. The Grand Central Publishing name and logo is a registered trademark of Hachette Book Group, Inc.

The publisher is not responsible for websites (or their content) that are not owned by the publisher.

The Hachette Speakers Bureau provides a wide range of authors for speaking events. To find out more, go to hachettespeakersbureau.com or email HachetteSpeakers@hbgusa.com.

Grand Central Publishing books may be purchased in bulk for business, educational, or promotional use. For information, please contact your local bookseller or the Hachette Book Group Special Markets Department at special.markets@hbgusa.com.

Library of Congress Cataloging-in-Publication Data

Names: Peguero, Robin, author.
Title: One in the chamber / Robin Peguero.
Description: First edition. | New York : Grand Central Publishing, 2024.
Identifiers: LCCN 2023046058 | ISBN 9781538742464 (hardcover) | ISBN 9781538742488 (ebook)
Subjects: LCGFT: Political fiction. | Thrillers (Fiction). | Novels.
Classification: LCC PS3616.E3534 O54 2024 | DDC 813/.6—dc23/eng/20231002
LC record available at https://lccn.loc.gov/2023046058

ISBNs: 9781538742464 (hardcover), 9781538742488 (ebook)

Printed in the United States of America

LSC-C

Printing 1, 2024

For women.
For my mamá,
eres amada, y eres suficiente
(you are loved, and you are enough).

"This is for you, Patty."

ONE IN THE CHAMBER

OO

DIE ON THIS HILL

You aren't born a killer. You don't gradually become one, either. One minute, you're not, and the next, you just are. Like your first time having sex. Just as thrilling. Just as awkward. Nothing much changes but the label. You're still you. But now, you're a quote-unquote murderer. You played God and took a human life.

It's entirely natural, but it still shocks people. Some people want other people dead. We visualize our goals, and we achieve them. Shouldn't that be celebrated?

You wish someone wanted *you* dead. Not that you have a death wish. You're too self-involved for that, and suicide is so gauche. You just wish you were that important to someone. It's a compliment really: to have given another person's endpoint more than a passing thought. To decide *for* them that today is enough. And not just today, but at this very minute, their contribution to history should meet its unceremonious finish. High flattery.

You're welcome.

You have the senator's warm blood on your hands. In the darkness, it looks and feels like microwaved fudge. It smells like pennies. Like copper Lincolns. The decedent would have loved the comparison to the Great Emancipator.

You're free now, Senator.

The crackling of the television whines in the background.

"…The news desk is now able to project the winner of the presidential election. Having netted Iowa's six electoral votes by a razor-thin margin, we can declare that the forty-seventh president of the United States will be…"

One of your knees digs into the thin government carpet while the other hovers inches over the body. You don't shake. You're at remarkable peace. Like a coroner, you pore over your victim, head to heel. You memorize the details. You want the moment etched into your conscious mind. Why shoot a deer if you can't admire its fallen carcass? You don't need its permission.

The newly dead don't undergo a transformation. They look like—at any moment—they might flip over, stand up, and walk right out of there. You watch precisely because you wonder if this might happen.

Death is just a silencing. You much prefer people that way.

You're silent, too. You have so much to say, but it would fall on defunct ears. At the periphery stand a few eyeballs ensconced in shadows. Weaklings stunned silent. See, some people want other people dead, and they make good on their wishes, but they can't stomach it afterward. You feel the saddest for them. Even the deceased has taken this development gracefully. You don't hear them bellyaching.

You have so much to say, but not to those who stay on the sidelines. And you're not the type to talk to yourself. You're not crazy. That would be too facile an excuse. So is "evil." What even is evil in a non-egalitarian, capitalist society that leeches off the labor of the least among us and wages perpetual war with untold civilian casualties? That isn't a criticism—*you're no socialist! No peacenik!* It's merely a descriptive matter. There are no good guys or bad guys anymore. Just guys. And girls. And the sixty-one other genders, of course—*you're no bigot!* All of them looking out for number one.

What you are is a rational actor. Murder is a perfectly rational enterprise. Governments do it. Even the greatest, oldest democracy in the world engages in it. Or something like that. You're no history major.

The doors to the committee room fly open as armed men in boots and tactical vests burst in. You stand and raise your bloody palms in the air. You finally begin to shake.

You shout over the commotion.

"They made me do it!"

01

THE GENTLE MAN FROM IOWA

We hang the petty thieves and appoint the great ones to public office. —Aesop

I dressed myself in my father's hand-me-down beige suit on a late August morning. The cuffs fell short. The shoulders were tight. The tip of my fat yellow tie hit just above my belly button. I parted my gelled hair to the side. I settled my tortoiseshell glasses on the bridge of my nose. I applied aggressive globs of acne treatment to a patch of emerging redness.

My roommate—the formless mound of bedsheets in the corner—stirred.

The curtains shrieked against the metal rod as I swept them open, directing bright sun onto him. The mound bellowed a string of curses.

I walked off campus to the main road and waited for the bus, leaning up against a deep green light post, parked beneath potted lavender flowers suspended in air. The post left a film of dirt down my right arm. I spent the ride slapping my suit sleeve, drawing looks from riders, including a man in tattered clothing muttering to himself.

I got off at Union Square, dodging taxicabs and slamming my hard black soles against asphalt in a sprint toward the Senate side of Capitol Hill. The long walk—even under the shade of elms—left me coated in sweat. Summer was sticky and suffocating here. It was a lie that the city had been built on a swamp, but it still felt that way.

I slung my jacket over my shoulder for the last few paces. Before entering the Hart Building—the most modern of the three Senate office spaces—I stared at the Capitol Dome in the near distance. The sun distorted its surface, giving it an ethereal, wavelike appearance.

It looked more majestic in person than it did on TV. My chest puffed out in pride at making it here. I was there to change the world. We all were.

I stepped into frigid air-conditioning and stood beneath the doorway vents for a beat, audibly moaning. The Capitol police officer at the metal detectors cleared his throat to get me to cut it out.

A senator wearing an identifying pin on his lapel cut the line, striding around and past the magnetometers. Looked like he never got checked for weapons. The officer, who like his colleagues had memorized the faces of all 100, let him by with a smile.

I wandered the marbled floors, watching professionals my age speed-walk the halls in a controlled chaos. Many baby faces in full suits and Dupont Circle haircuts with bulging backpacks strapped to their backs, big enough to fit their egos. The skylit atrium poured sunlight on them so they were literally aglow. The month-long August recess featuring vacations and slimmed-down schedules had ended. Everyone was back in their Sunday best after weeks of strolling into Congress in jeans and chucks.

I arrived at my intern orientation on the minute, with not a second to spare. Exact counts were important to me.

Shelly, the twenty-something intern coordinator, stared at her phone and droned at me.

"Iowa Senator Bill Williams is the president pro tem, the oldest and most senior member of the Democratic Party. But that doesn't mean he isn't plugged into our generation. He's inspired a sort of underground fandom. You've seen the TikToks?"

She didn't look up.

"Of course you have. They call him 2 Bills. Get it? 'Cause his name is William Williams. It's totally catching on. Sort of like a Notorious RBG thing. May she forever rest in power."

She glanced down at the résumé in front of her.

"You're a Hawkeye?"

"Just graduated."

"Then we're only a year apart. How was the game in Ames this year? That finish was wild, wasn't it?"

My smile was tight. I was no good at small talk. I'm a killjoy like that.

"'Wild' is a good word."

"How was everyone feeling afterward? I can only imagine."

I swallowed long. She waited for an answer.

"Actually, I don't follow football."

She frowned and looked down, speaking to her hands.

"I was talking about basketball."

She returned to her phone and finished her rote presentation. She led me to the ID processing room. I didn't smile for the picture.

"Oh, shit. I forgot. Don't laminate that yet," she warned the middle-aged black woman behind the counter, who rolled her eyes but paused. "Senator Williams is the chairman of the Judiciary Committee. Did you want to work out of the personal office or—"

"The committee," I said fast.

"You sure? You won't get face time with the member."

"Fine by me."

Bills are born out of committee. It's where things happen. Personal offices are for the grunts. It's all skinny paychecks and stress headaches. Unlike most of my peers here, I didn't care to be seen. I much preferred to blend in. It's why I walked on the balls of my feet. It made the least amount of noise.

I looked surly in my ID picture. Underneath my square face it read, "Cameron Leann—INTERN, US SENATE JUDICIARY COMMITTEE."

I was raised on modest means by my withholding mother and doting grandparents. We were working middle class, and not middle class the way 70 percent of Americans call themselves middle class, but true-blue paycheck-to-paycheck, penny-pinching, clipping-coupons-in-the-grocery-aisle middle class. One big health scare away from bankruptcy. Mom was the type who let me steal small stuff, shielding me from detection as I shoveled candy into my mouth from those troughs of bulk goods by the pound.

Dad made his cameos in my life every now and again, but the disruption he wrought outweighed the marginal benefit. He was a drag, an anchor on the family, so we tolerated him only in small doses to keep from going under.

Mom and Dad together didn't produce much good in the world, except for maybe my baby brother, Nathaniel, younger by seven years. When I felt homesick and lonely those first few days in the capital, I mostly thought of him. How I hoped to make him proud. How I hoped he might not recognize me now: suited up, shit together, shoulder-to-shoulder with the most powerful people in the country. I was a new man here.

I operated on a highly routinized system. I ate the same breakfast every morning: two hard-boiled eggs and one glass of 2 percent milk. I counted daily calories (2,750) and steps (10,250). I religiously jerked off three times a day at designated hours. Once in the shower. Once after the lunchtime lull. Lastly before bed.

That first week brimmed with nothing. Like a stray, I'd roam from desk to desk of permanent staffers, flashing idle hands and puppy-dog eyes. *Will work for attention*, they read. Other, more industrious interns had already come by and snatched up the research project or the memo-writing assignment: Brad had arrived an hour early each day; Katherine had scheduled her coffee chats weeks in advance; Jackson played lacrosse with the chief-of-staff's son.

"We'll find something for you to do," they'd say. "You can always help answer phones."

I'd let the phones reach the eighth, ninth, tenth ring. As I said, I didn't like talking. Instead, I sat at a computer, refreshing news site after site until my pointer finger turned purple. Then, I went home.

At night, my roommate tried to ask how my day went.

He was a try-hard. From the first day we met, he was chatty and overly familiar, as if two grown men sleeping inches from each other meant we had to become fast friends. It was too summer camp, too inorganic.

I wasn't there by choice. I just had no money.

So I'd shrug and say, "I have to shit."

I'd stow away in the bathroom, sitting on the toilet seat and checking my phone until I saw the light under the door go out. Only then would I slink out to my bed, rub one out in deadly quiet, pray, and fall asleep.

One morning, a young white staffer asked me to cover his meeting with the top brass of an advocacy group so he could take an extended lunch. I took one look at the gray-haired adults waiting for him in the lobby and declined.

"Won't they be offended to be babysat by a kid like me? I know nothing about the semiconductor industry," I said.

"Neither do I. You think I can do shit for them? I'm twenty-three. Just nod as they talk your ear off. They know the game. They're just happy to be away from their desks."

By Friday, I had settled on the idea that coming here had been a mistake. One big waste of time.

But that all changed when I met *her*.

I had nearly missed out. I was headed to a secret self-session when I crossed paths with Shelly. She had rarely dropped in on me in the week, and even as her eyes scanned the length of me, there was barely a hint of recognition.

"Capitol tour. Rotunda. Now."

Her order just floated behind her as an afterthought.

I considered ignoring it. Congress was out of session—senators famously don't work on Fridays—and I had my mind already on the weekend. But this was my first assignment of interest. I would finally learn how to lead tours. I grunted, whipped around, and followed along.

The Rotunda was full of natural light and tourists. Noise echoed off its sandstone walls, so that tens roared like hundreds. At the eye of the cast-iron dome was a faraway fresco: George Washington ascending to heaven, flanked by women. Sun poured in from windows out of reach, lining the perimeter. Massive paintings of countless white men in wigs and stockings—in varying states of standing, sitting, talking, *founding*—outfitted the walls. Bronze and marble presidents on pedestals loomed as tall as giants. Noted racist Andrew Jackson was the most gallant among them with permanently windswept hair.

In the center, dwarfed by the majesty, was *her*.

Her hand hung off her hip. Her high-heeled, red-bottomed shoes pointed inward. (I couldn't tell you the brand, but I knew it meant she was better than me.) Her updo had loosened, spilling streams of blonde into her face, prompting her to intermittently blow them away. Her cheekbones were high but full, and she had a prominent chin. Her eyes were big, blue, and nestled deep in her sockets like turquoise quartz sparkling in rock. She pulled at an invisible chain on her neck, groping herself until she made her pale skin red. I caught myself staring at her bony sternum.

She pulled the crowd closer with a wave of her hand. She gave a shouty introduction. I missed her name. She pointed lazily as she spoke, indicating generally without precision. Her hands were notably small.

I swore she kept looking at me. I'd know because, even as others turned to study the room, I studied her. Her eyes never landed on me longer than a flash. They would float away, dutifully far not to rouse suspicion. But inevitably, they'd return, before flitting off again. Her eyelashes were long and moved in a hummingbird bustle.

She led our tour group away. I walked at her periphery, shoulders pulled way back and trying to stand taller. Inside a room of crimson drapery, gray columns, and rows of cherry wood school desks arranged in a semicircle, she came alive.

"This is the Old Senate Chamber, site of the famous caning of Senator Charles Sumner," she said, grinning. "The hot topic of the day? Whether my great state of Kansas would enter the Union as a free or slave state, tipping the balance of power in the lead up to the Civil War. Antislavery Republican Charles Sumner had some choice words for his proslavery colleagues: calling one a nameless animal and telling another that slavery served him like an ugly harlot."

She leaned in and lowered her voice.

"Apropos of nothing, Congressman Preston Brooks—who was apparently boys with one of these slavery apologists—took offense. He made his way across the Capitol, all the way from the People's House to the Senate Chamber—right here—and struck an unsuspecting Sumner repeatedly in the head with his metal-topped cane. It was a vicious attack that left Sumner bleeding profusely onto the Senate floor and critically wounded, but Brooks walked right out, detained by no one. Each became heroes to their respective factions. But Sumner had the last laugh. He recovered and went on to serve another eighteen years in the Senate, whereas Brooks died soon thereafter at the hardy old age of thirty-seven."

She shared in the light laughter. Her incisors were uncommonly sharp.

"And, of course—the ultimate victory—after catastrophic war, the scourge of slavery was finally tossed into the waste bin of history. Anyone able to tell me, perhaps a fellow Kansan among you, on which side—free or slave—did the state ultimately enter the Union?"

I fired off the answer unthinkingly. I was at least pleased with the depth of my voice.

"Free."

She turned to me and held her gaze. She didn't say anything at first. She just looked at me. Through me. Others turned to curiously peer at me, too. See what had stopped her dead in her tracks. I didn't blink or breathe. My chest was too tight for air to pass through. Gradually, the muscles in her face softened and a smile poked through.

"Rock chalk, Jayhawk."

At the end of the day, I tossed off my jacket, rolled up my sleeves, and slouched onto a retaining wall just outside the Hart Building. I shut my eyes and baked in the sun for a bit. At the sound of feminine laughter, I peeked out of one eye.

Our tour guide was standing to my left, opposite a young-looking white girl and guy sharing a vape pen between them. The two were mirror reflections: standing at identical heights, boasting pouty pink lips and sandy red hair, and wearing powder-blue suits and bored expressions. I didn't catch myself staring. But the tour guide did.

"Free-Stater!"

She walked over, motioning for the smoking pair to follow.

Out shot her hand to my eye level. Her fingernails were a chipped pink.

"Liz Frost. Senator Dale Whitehurst's office."

They all introduced themselves that way in DC. Their full names followed immediately by what they did and for whom. A walking, talking LinkedIn profile.

I accepted her hand. It was warm and fit in mine wholly.

"I'm Cam."

She squinted, but not one line appeared on her unblemished forehead. She had not let go of my hand.

"Erm, I work for Judiciary," I finally added.

"Ah, 2 Bills," she said, letting go. "These are the Blum twins: Isla and Scoop. They're college interns in my office. Juniors at the University of Kansas."

Isla and Scoop gave matching half nods before returning to their phones and e-cig. I was as equally uninterested in them. I turned back to Liz.

"What do you do for Senator Whitehurst?" I asked.

"Staff ass."

"Excuse me?"

She laughed. She did so in bursts, not continuously like most people.

"You're new here, aren't you?"

"First week."

"It's what we call staff assistants. You know, answer phones, greet visitors, handle tours, supervise interns—basically the little bitch of the office. You're an intern?"

I nodded.

"How old are you?"

I considered lying.

"Twenty-two."

"You look older." She said everything in a half taunt, hardly suppressing an impish grin. "I'm twenty-four. So you're from Iowa, not Kansas?"

"Yes, Iowa. Small town. Farm country."

She squinted again, making her eyelashes dance. Her mouth opened and shut, as if it were testing out but ultimately rejecting a bold statement. It lurched out of her anyway.

"You have Chinese in you, Cam?"

I felt itchy heat rise to my cheeks.

"I'm sorry?"

"You look vaguely Asian to me. You know, smallish eyes. No offense. You're still cute."

My upper lip twitched. Scoop raised his eyebrows and smirked into his phone.

"So cringe," Isla murmured.

Gross was more like it. But I gave it a pass. Everyone's a little bit racist.

"Just plain white. Irish actually," I said through gritted teeth.

She shrugged.

"You make friends yet?"

I coughed, although I didn't need to.

"Well, no. I have a roommate. But yeah, no."

"That's what's great about DC. We're all transplants, searching for a connection. You can come here and reinvent yourself. Become an entirely new person."

There was intensity in her eyes and then, abruptly, warmth.

"Our friend Randy has a swanky pad nearby. We were just heading there to meet up with some friends. All of them work on the Hill. Wanna join?"

Isla looked up from her screen to indiscreetly roll her eyes at Liz.

"Sure, I'll tag along."

On the walk, as soon as we stepped off the Capitol complex, south past the main Senate buildings, the dome, the main House buildings, and into the million-dollar residential Hill neighborhood, the twins switched out their vape pen. Skunky sweet-smelling smoke wafted from this new one. I must have made a face.

"Weed's legal here. Just not on federal property," Scoop said.

He offered me a hit.

"I don't smoke."

It didn't take long for Randy's row house to come into view. It was a three-story brownstone topped by castle-like cones. A perfectly manicured rosebush bloomed to the side of its entryway steps, and a gleaming white Mercedes was parked out in front.

"Fuck," I muttered. "This all him?"

"Basically. His uncle's back in the state. Away most weekends. So it's just him most of the time," Liz said.

She led us down the side alley toward the back and down a series of stairs into the basement. The inside was just as lush: renovated kitchen with steel-topped appliances, masculine black and brown leather décor, a sweeping sectional couch situated around a massive flat-screen TV bolted to the wall, and a California king with silk sheets in the corner. Four other people were inside.

"Honey, I'm home!" Liz belted out.

"Who's the new kid?"

I didn't register who had asked it.

"Another stray Liz has charitably taken in," Isla said.

My eyes focused first on the black man nearest to us, standing before an open refrigerator door. He was towering: easily over a half-foot taller than me and wide, noticeably built like a brick wall under his partially splayed open button-down. His skin was so black, it shined, and he wore a high and tight fade above a nicely symmetrical face.

Liz jogged into his arms. The two kissed lengthily. She had to get on her tiptoes to reach him.

"Baby," she purred.

He was her boyfriend. She had a boyfriend. My chest deflated.

I strode up with an inflated smile and offered my hand. He gave me his. It swallowed mine. I initiated a hand slap and back pat.

"I'm Cam. I intern for the Judiciary Committee."

"Charlie James the Third. I'm Senator Scott Denton's body man."

"You're a Republican?"

It flew out of me. I'm sure my cheeks turned red. At our age, being progressive was reflexive. I'm not even sure I chose it. I had always been. Being siloed in congressional offices with like-minded people, you forget exactly half of the folks walking past you are on the other team, most of them as young as you, too. But almost never black.

Charlie chuckled, but it was Liz who answered.

"His boss is a RINO," she said. "Moderate, pro-choice Republican from swing state North Carolina. We give Charlie a pass. Don't worry. He's woke."

Charlie winced. Being around Liz apparently meant ignoring the screwy remarks she slipped in every now and again. Pretty girls get away with things like that. I found it refreshing. She was admirably carefree. The sting of offense was short-lived and all that remained was intrigue.

"You played football, Cam?" Charlie asked.

"No. I didn't play any sports."

Charlie's forehead wrinkled.

"Well, you look it. Broad shoulders."

"I'm an Iowa farm boy. Lots of baling hay."

"Huh. I guess you *are* a little short for it."

I widened my smile, baring teeth. I didn't appreciate the barb.

"Charlie played Division I ball," Liz said. "He was quite good at it at a place where football is religion. He was a literal god on campus who could do no wrong. But we know better, don't we, Charlie?"

She caressed his clean-shaven jaw, capping it off with a pinch that appeared to hurt a little too much.

"You drink beer, Clark Kent?" Charlie asked, extending a frosted can to me.

"Clark Kent?"

"Yeah. You got the dark hair. You got the glasses. You got the Iowa farm boy thing—"

"Superman's from Kansas, Charlie. Not Iowa," Liz said.

I accepted the can.

"I do drink beer. Thank you."

Scoop stretched out his hand for one.

"You're not twenty-one yet, kid," Charlie said. "Ask me in a couple months."

Scoop smiled in earnest for the first time, revealing a slight gap between his front teeth. I had known him for only twenty minutes tops by that point, but lightheartedness was so antithetical to his essence that he looked like a different person. Charlie threw an arm around his skinny shoulders and rustled his hair before handing him a beer despite his teasing.

Liz detached herself from Charlie and—in a move that accelerated my heart rate—planted her palms on top of my shoulders.

"Let me introduce you to the rest of the gang."

A man with slicked-back hair and a beauty mark on his cheek was rolling a joint on the couch. He stood to greet me.

"This is Chuy," Liz said. "That's Mexican for Jesús."

"I'm from Ecuador. Not Mexico. Our group is a rainbow coalition—as diverse as the Hill gets," he said. I noted that he was just as fair-skinned as Liz, and he looked moneyed. "My government name is Jesús Lavandeira. But it's true: you can call me Chuy."

He pronounced "Ecuador" correctly, not like a gringo, and he sang his name in a perfect Spanish accent. He wore a tailored herringbone suit that hugged him, a floral pocket square, and a series of rings, one sporting a purple gem. One, but only one, of his fingernails was painted black on each of his hands. It was the middle finger.

"Oh, and my pronouns are they/them."

"Cool. Mine are he/him," I said.

Chuy's eyes widened.

"I like this one. You done good bringing him around, girl."

Liz laid her head on their shoulder.

"Chuy's the highest ranking of us all. They're the legislative corre-spondent for Senator Abby Kelley from California."

"It's a fancy way of saying I write constituent letters for the crone."

"I've heard stories about her," I said. "Yelling. Cursing. I read some-where she doesn't let junior staffers look her directly in the eye."

"Yeah, she's a real bitch," Chuy said, before sitting back down, cross-ing one leg lazily over the other.

Liz next brought me to a white man tinkering with the TV. He was lanky and dressed in casual seersucker with floppy brown hair that fell into his eyes.

"This is Randolph Lancaster. He works for his uncle, Senator Chris Lancaster from Connecticut. What are you on now, Randy? Your third year as an intern?"

"Fourth. But who's counting?"

"Your uncle, no doubt," she said.

He grimaced.

"That asshole wouldn't say a word. I know where the bodies are bur-ied," he said, turning to me. "I didn't catch your name, bruh."

"Cam. Your place is chill."

"Thanks. Where do you live?"

"The dorms at Georgetown. It's a shoebox I share with another guy. But it's funded housing, so I can't complain."

He and Liz shared a pregnant glance.

"We don't have one of *those* in our little Benetton ad," he told her, smiling.

He meant poor. It was humiliating.

"You single, Cam?"

I stuttered. "Oh. Uh, yes. Single."

"Bet. We can cruise together. Chuy isn't the best wingman for land-ing chicks. I'm more likely to score him ass than the other way around."

"*Them*," Liz corrected.

"I love you, Chuy, and you know I'd kill for you, brother. But you've got a dick. And I know this because when you get me drunk, you try offering it to me—"

"One out of eight straight men try a same-sex experience these days!" Chuy chimed in.

"—so you're a *he* to me, unless and until it comes off."

Randy planted a lengthy kiss on Chuy's cheek. Chuy looked unnerved.

"That's a Greenwich limousine liberal for ya!" Chuy hollered, sweeping their hand across their body theatrically.

In a normal voice and directed at me and my stunned look: "Ignore the performative transphobia. Queers love Randy. And he loves the attention. He's a textbook narcissist. Forget gay or straight: he's a Randy-sexual."

"Randy is a rake," Liz added.

"Pardon her old-woman vocab. She's obsessed with Victorian Era romance novels. You know, lady porn," Randy said, hand shielding his mouth for effect, although the volume of his voice carried normally.

I struggled to hide a chuckle.

"He's the oldest of us all," Liz continued with a sly smile, "but he's a professional intern who puts his efforts solely into bedding the women of his intern class. Inexplicably, he's usually successful."

Randy bowed. I found the performance charming. He was all show.

"You're not a virgin, are you, Cam?" he asked.

"No," I said too forcefully, reflexively looking at Liz. "Why? Do I look it?"

Randy shrugged.

"No, I suppose not. Maybe just like a missionary, socks-on, jackrabbit sex with a long-term girlfriend kind of guy. But Charlie's taken and Scoop's a child, so I'm sure when you chill out, you'll do just fine for my purposes."

As punctuation, he reached over and loosened my tie for me.

"Go easy on him, ya'll. He's a sweet boy," Liz said, winking at me.

She pulled on my forearm—making the hairs stand at attention—and brought me lastly to a white girl on the other end of the couch. She was a blonde, like Liz, but of a browner hue, and freckles populated her nose and cheeks. She stood and hugged me. She left a natural scent like ripened bananas behind.

"This is Lisa Stoltz. She's the press assistant for Florida Senator Sandy Grunwald-Santos."

Lisa found me attractive. I could tell by the way she flagrantly avoided eye contact and how the rates of her blinking and breathing shot up by milliseconds. When she finally spoke to me, the skin beneath her freckles turned bright pink.

"Nice to meet you, Cam."

Everyone took up a spot on the couch. Liz and Charlie cuddled directly across from me, within my field of vision. I sipped my beer slowly. Randy had left MSNBC on.

Chuy lit up their joint and passed it down the line. Liz inhaled and left the smoke trapped in her lungs for a while. No one declined a turn. It made its way to me.

"Clark Kent doesn't smoke," Scoop said, sneering.

It was clear the twin looked up to Charlie. Imitating him was how he expressed his fondness, down to the unfitting nickname the lineman had bestowed on me.

I watched Liz as she emitted smoke out of her nostrils like a dragon.

"I'll take a hit," I said.

I puffed and did not exhale until my eyes watered. It hit me immediately: light-headedness and relaxation. My legs shot out from my body as I pleasurably sank into the couch.

"That's some good shit," I said.

There was hooting and applause.

"How do you like it so far on the Hill?"

I didn't know who asked it. I had been staring at my own hands.

"Honestly, I hate it," I said, chuckling. "I'm not doing anything. Sitting around with my thumb up my ass all day."

I was part of the generation raised on *The West Wing*. You come to Washington to do big things: work on policy, hobnob with hotshots, leave your old, unremarkable life behind. Save the world in forty-two minutes or less. People say it's more like *Veep*, but I wasn't even getting that. I was stuck still watching the commercials.

"Your supervisor is Shelly, right? She not giving you work?" Liz asked.

I shook my head.

"Come to me next week. I'll take care of you. All of our bosses work together on the Committee. That's how we became friends. The press has even given them a nickname: the Gang of Six. Nothing gets passed in the Judiciary Committee without the green light from the Six. Media whores, the lot of them."

I had heard a little about the fabled Six. At a time of unified government—when the Democrats enjoyed majorities in the House and Senate and occupied the White House—they had positioned themselves as a thorn in President Bob Stevenson's side. Watering down his criminal justice bill. Outright killing his pass at immigration reform. Confirming nominees to the judicial bench at a fast clip, but stalling those without the clout to promise them anything in return.

Vice President Kiara Jones was facing a strong challenge from Florida Governor Chad Thornton for the presidency, in no small part due to the Six's recalcitrance.

Liz was playing with her hair while she lay on Charlie's chest. The joint made a second round.

"But we all hate it here," she continued. "That won't go away—with work or without it. Members are overgrown children. No matter your title, we're all just personal assistants, subject to their whims and tantrums. It's demoralizing."

"Big facts. Senator Kelley is a terror. Everything you heard about her is true and tenfold," Chuy said. "You know, she once chucked a stapler clear across the room. Thank God it didn't hit me. I'd have sued the ill-fitting pantsuit right off of her."

"Senator Grunwald isn't cruel. She's kind," Lisa said in a monotone, as if the weed had turned her into a zombie. "But she works like a bull. And that means you have to work like a bull, too. No respect for your time. No respect for your own ambitions, your own life. The woman wants to be president so badly, she can't see anything or anyone else."

"Her black husband's hot, though," Liz said.

"He's *Hispanic*. But, Liz, my girl, you clearly got a type," Chuy said.

I sulked quietly. A type *not* me.

"My boss works us to the bone, too," Liz said. "Ever since 2 Bills went off his rocker, Whitehurst has been playing shadow chairman. He can't wait until 2 Bills croaks so he can take over. Did you guys see the chairman's recent interview? He forgot the question within seconds of being asked it. The rumors of cognitive decline are finally hitting the mainstream media. It won't be long before a pressure campaign calling for his retirement begins. And Whitehurst—his *beloved* mentee—will be secretly behind it all. Coward."

"Charlie's got it the worst," Scoop said.

A few of them shifted uncomfortably in their seats.

"Why's that?" I asked.

No one dared answer for Charlie. We all just waited awkwardly to see if he would oblige.

"I'm Denton's token black," Charlie finally said, nose flared. "Trotted out to help siphon off just enough black votes from the Democrat to win reelection. Failed college football star becomes Morgan Freeman to this white man's Miss Daisy, chauffeuring him from event to event. Yessir, Massa Denton. Right away, Massa Denton."

The quiet lingered for minutes.

"Who's Miss Daisy?" Isla finally asked.

The tension deflated into laughter.

The TV resounded more crisply once the ebullience ended.

"...the right-wing militia group's plans were thwarted after the FBI intercepted communications planning the kidnapping and execution of several government officials. The eight men—all with ties to white nationalism—have been apprehended and could face federal terrorism charges..."

Randy chuckled.

"Idiot boomers," he said. "Our generation would know better than to plan it over any electronic medium. It'd have to be done all in person. Even cell phones can be bugged by the government."

"It's always these right-wing nuts also," Chuy said. "So predictable. The government is watching their every move. But they wouldn't see it coming from liberals. Can you imagine? If a bunch of progressives resorted to violence like that? They might just get away with it."

I had been listening to them but staring only at Liz. She looked adrift, with a twinkle in her eye and a soft smile. I found it alluring—and chilling. She felt the heat of my gaze and locked eyes with mine. She didn't pull away. We just stayed like that, even as we continued to speak.

"You guys really hate your bosses?" I asked.

She nodded, almost sadly, almost solemnly.

"Even you, Randy? Your own uncle?"

"I can't stand the prick," he said immediately. "Nothing I do is ever good enough for him. I'd want nothing more than for him to vanish off the face of the earth. Wish it'd been him who died and not my dad."

Liz and I were still watching one another, barely blinking.

I wanted to be liked by them. They were all so cool and self-possessed. Exactly the type of DC personalities you dream of getting in good with. The ones who know where to find all the best receptions with open bars and heavy finger foods to get around the ethics rules against free sit-down meals. Big-city energy. Not backwoods trash like me.

I tried out a joke.

"Then why don't you kill them?"

My voice trembled on the way out. I was expecting a marked reaction. Likely laughter. Maybe horror. But I was met with surprising forbearance. No one stirred. Liz just nodded softly.

"Maybe we will."

ELECTION NIGHT

Charlie had his elbows on the table and his large hands cradling his head.

"Who suggested it first? I can't really recall. I know it wasn't me. I'm a black man in America. We don't make jokes like that. And it was just a joke. We had a good laugh about it. It was just a stupid, stupid joke. I see that now. Not funny at all. Just stupid, stupid, stupid, stupid, sssssttttuuu…"

His voice faltered.

"Cam? It wasn't his idea, I don't think. He didn't say much of anything that first time. He never says much of anything."

He peered at his reflection in the giant mirror opposite him.

"Is someone watching us from behind there? Are you recording this? Aren't you supposed to tell me if you are?"

Tears sprang to his eyes.

"Can I call my mama now? She's going to be so pissed at me. I wasn't supposed to end up here, man. I was supposed to be better. I was supposed to be the good one. Fucking white girls. Mama told me they'd get me in trouble. She told me to stick to my own. But I didn't listen. I never listen. I want to go home. Back to North Carolina. Back to my mom's. Can I go home now, Officer? Please."

02

DRIVING MR. DENTON

Liz made good on her word. The Monday after that first hang, she poked her head into the cubicle crammed with committee interns.

"Free-Stater, you open?"

I nodded and leapt to my feet.

She strutted down the Hart Building hallways, leading me to the underground tunnels that connected the buildings in the Capitol complex. I tried my best at keeping up but remained always just a few steps behind. I didn't mind. It gave me the opportunity to watch the full length of her.

"What are we getting into?" I asked.

"Not 'we.' It's Charlie who needs the help. His boss, Senator Denton, asked for an intern-slash-gofer to staff him at an event today."

I grumbled. A favor for her *boyfriend*. Of course. She half turned to me, eyebrow raised. I wiped off the discontent and beamed.

"Thank you for thinking of me."

"No problem, Cam. We're *friends* now. We look out for each other."

She stressed the word "friends." I nodded along.

We walked to the Russell Office Building, the oldest of the Senate offices. Outside a door and plaque labeled "Senator Scott Denton: North Carolina" stood Charlie, clad in a conservative black suit, white shirt, and solid-primary-colored tie.

Senator Denton was an old-school iconoclast who repeatedly bucked his party seemingly for the thrill of it. His politics were indiscernible outside of compromise as an end in itself and worshiping at the altar of almighty bipartisanship. No first principles whatsoever.

Before noticing us, Charlie had been looking into the face of his wristwatch.

"One strapping gofer, as requested," Liz said in greeting.

"You brought me Clark Kent."

He sounded as thrilled as I had been. The corners of his mouth dipped downward.

"Denton prefers men—*white* men—at public events, doesn't he?"

She said it through a mischievous smile and twinkling eyes, but Charlie nodded in earnest.

"Keep up. We're late," he barked at me, marching off. I had to double his speed to match the strides of his long legs. We walked outside to an older-model champagne Honda Civic sitting in the employee parking lot. I pulled up to the passenger-side door.

"Denton sits there," he said in a baritone.

It took me embarrassingly long to process what he meant and pivot to the backseat. The inside of the car was surprisingly messy: binders, loose paper, notepads, ties, socks, and size 8 dress shoes littered the floor. I had to sit with my feet propped up on hills of clutter, boosting my knees up to eye level.

When the engine sputtered on, hip-hop music blared. Charlie swiftly lowered the volume.

"I like this song," I said.

"You would. You all do."

We drove up to the Capitol dome and sat in park as Charlie kept his eyes locked on the side doors. I did the same. Charlie must have texted him. Within a minute, a white man of shorter-than-average height, coal-black eyes, aquiline nose, and thinning gray hair emerged. I recognized him from TV as Senator Denton.

Charlie switched off the music for NPR before the senator pulled open the passenger door and hopped in. Denton didn't acknowledge me. He didn't even address Charlie. We just peeled off in silence. Almost immediately, the senator was on his cell phone, talking loudly into the receiver.

"I'm in the car...Some fringe pro-family, evangelical group. You know the sort. Sons of the Confederacy or some shit. Cotillions, long-barrel shotguns, closeted homosexuals, and generations of inbreeding...Top of the list? Blowing up the gay agenda. You got to play the hits. No one comes to hear the new songs...The hot topic right now is Title IX reform. That's the focus of the talk. You know, keeping trans kids off the field—who the fuck knows why—and better protections for students accused of rape in schools. Now that I can get behind. These poor boys get no due process, worse off than a common street dealer getting off on technicalities. Sent right back to ravage their ghettos. But one mere accusation of rape, and the boy's crucified. No facing your accuser. No high burden of proof. Just a girl's word."

It sounded so reductionist coming from him. These were real people, caught in real crosshairs—not caricatures. He was a walking, talking minstrel show.

I felt Charlie's eyes intermittently peek at me from the rearview mirror. I kept my own glued to the window, feigning inattention.

The senator was uncharacteristically quiet for a period, mumbling noises of agreement, as if he were just waiting—like Double Dutch—for his chance to jump back in. The soothing voice on NPR filled the vacuum.

"Breaking this hour: NPR news can now confirm, the Chief Justice of the Supreme Court has died at the age of eighty-seven."

"I've got to go," the senator said, poking at his screen—his long nail tapping it wildly to end the call—and letting the phone fall to his lap. "Charlie! Turn that up."

Charlie obeyed.

"This vacancy in the highest court of the land comes just sixty-four days before the nation votes for its new leader. Unpopular outgoing president Stevenson, at the end of his statement offering condolences, announced his intention of sending the Senate a nominee, citing recent precedent of a quick turnaround to confirm the last associate justice before an impending election. As expected, Democratic presidential nominee Kiara Jones has called for swift confirmation hearings for the unnamed nominee from her party, while the Republican nominee, Chad Thornton, has denounced the president's plan as an end run on the will of the American people. Once there is a nominee, the power shifts to the Senate Judiciary Committee, where the infamous Gang of Six—Senators Williams, Whitehurst, Denton, Lancaster, Kelley, and Grunwald-Santos—can play kingmaker. It's said nothing gets past the committee without the express say-so of the Six."

The senator clapped his hands. The slap of his bones made me jump.

"Let's fucking go!" he yelled.

His phone rang to the tune of the "Battle Hymn of the Republic."

"Dale," he answered. That'd be Liz's boss, Senator Whitehurst. "It's going to be a shitshow with Bill at the helm. It should be you, Dale… I'll have to vote against the eventual nominee, but we should send a slate of candidates to the White House today…Sandy will be a pain in the ass, but she's a freshman senator. She'll let the old men do the talking if she knows what's good for her."

Charlie pulled up to the National Mall. Denton opened his door and swung a leg out onto asphalt.

"I can accompany you, sir," Charlie said. "I can leave the intern to watch the car."

Denton turned his eyes on me for the first time. He made his choice in seconds.

"This is a conservative group, Charlie. It wouldn't look right. You understand."

Charlie sent an open palm toward the backseat.

"Binder!" he ordered. "The blue one."

I scrambled to pull it out from under my feet and hand it to him. Charlie gave it to the senator.

"I pulled together some talking points, sir. As you know, reforming Title IX is of particular interest to me. Your Judiciary counsel reviewed it."

Denton was flipping through the pages, shaking his head, wrinkling his nose.

"Where are the talking points Matt wrote?"

Charlie shrank in his seat.

"They're in the back of the binder, sir."

The senator tore out Charlie's pages and laid them softly on his chest.

"Stick to what you're good at, son."

Denton flashed him a tight smile, tossed the binder onto my lap, and stalked off, leaving the car door wide open. I stared after him through the window.

"You slow or something? Follow him!"

Clutching the binder, I stumbled out of the car and caught up to the fast-walking senator. We weaved through crowds of tourists, none of them aware there was an elected official in their midst. He was just another old white guy in a suit.

It was just us two. No protection between him and the masses other than myself. It was terrifying and exhilarating. I could see the beads of sweat forming and rolling down his neck, which I could reach out and easily wring if I wanted. I could smell his old-timey aftershave. I could see the smattering of dandruff dusting his shoulders.

We pulled up to a crowd gathered on the green. He traversed the perimeter, walking directly onto the stage even as a speaker was mid-speech. That speaker didn't even finish his sentence. He caught sight of the senator and flowed abruptly into an introduction. Denton pried the binder from my hands. I stood off to the side as he stepped up to the mic and flipped open his talking points on the lectern. They were only a crutch. He barely looked down at them.

As he spoke, I watched the crowd. Mostly men. Red faces in camouflage, trucker hats, and flag-inspired attire. Lots of creative salt-and-pepper facial hair. Children on shoulders wearing gun iconography on their tiny shirts. The donor class—donning suits and expensive watches or clerical collars and Bibles as props—were interspersed throughout, cheering at all the same applause lines as their coarser brethren.

I recognized them. They were my people. My neighbors in flyover country. But I didn't understand them. They looked like artifacts from a time capsule. Times were changing, but they were not, and the world was passing them by. It was frustrating.

Denton was full-throated: protecting the nuclear family and stemming the expanding definition of gender and sexuality.

"What even *is* a demisexual?" he cracked.

Such low-hanging fruit. Was it this easy to appease the base? Pick a minority and lay into them? I guess we all enjoy feeling part of the dominant group, if we can swing it. There's comfort in numbers.

I spotted a few skeptics in the crowd, shaking their heads, pointing their thumbs, rumpling their faces. Put off not by the message but by the messenger. Denton was a lifelong bachelor, which inspired widespread, bipartisan belief that he was gay. But no men had come forth with tawdry stories of down-low trysts—not on message boards, not on the pages of checkout-aisle rags. Beltway insiders were convinced the man was merely asexual—one of the many recent lexical additions he railed against—or had successfully stifled all latent sexual impulses in naked pursuit of power.

People make everything, always, about sex. Freud would have a field day.

At some point, Denton gestured behind him to a distant Lincoln made of limestone across the reflecting pool, drawing a tortured connection between freedom of religion and the enslavement of flesh-and-bone people. He *loved* Lincoln.

"Lincoln was a Republican," he reminded them. "Not a lot of people know that."

Everyone knows that.

I was daydreaming when I heard sustained applause. Denton was done. He was beaming, on a high. He walked off the stage, handing me the binder. We marched off. A gaggle of reporters intercepted us. A microphone was shoved in his face.

"Are you open to supporting the president's nominee to the Supreme Court, Senator?"

Stragglers from the crowd joined, leaning in to hear the senator's answer.

Denton smirked and started toward the car again, as if he intended to bypass the inquiry. But he stopped himself.

"I can tell you this: a nominee who doesn't support a major overhaul of Title IX is dead on arrival. Big Brother needs to get the heck out of regulating the sex life of kids on college campuses."

Others shouted follow-up questions, but their voices crashed against one another in cacophony. Using his outstretched arm as a rudder, parting the sea of implorers before him, he sprinted away. I followed in his wake.

Charlie had not moved from his spot. As we entered the car, he cranked up the air-conditioning and waited for direction. The senator sighed loudly, a balloon noisily deflating.

"I'm fucked," he said.

He twirled his finger in the air. Charlie reacted by shifting the car into drive and accelerating off. The senator's phone resounded, but he let it ring. He sat slumped in silence, against the backdrop of his phone's constant buzzing. Under the shadow of the Capitol dome, Denton stepped out.

"Oh, and Charlie boy, can you pick up my dry-cleaning and drop it off at my house before returning to work?"

Personal errands like these were prohibited by ethics rules. Charlie nodded anyway.

The senator indelicately tossed his keys into the vehicle, hitting the dashboard, which shot them down to the passenger-side floor. Charlie reached over to retrieve them as his boss walked away.

"You can get out here."

He was talking to me but staring at the steering wheel. The idling engine sent trembles through the car.

"I'll join and help you. If that's all right."

I had felt bad for swooping in and stealing his job. For being just another white face at the right time. And Shelly wouldn't miss me. She was too self-absorbed and us interns too lowly for her to notice I was gone.

Charlie looked into the rearview, his big brown eyes scrutinizing me. The ends of his lips curled slightly upward but only briefly. He sent his eyes darting away.

"Move to the front then. I'm not your Uber."

I stepped out of the back and into the passenger seat. Charlie sped off, revving the engine and making the tires shriek. He tossed off his tie and threw it over his shoulder into the mess. I did the same. He switched back to "urban" music at a deafening level. The car shook from the treble and bass.

"This your car?" I yelled over it.

He nodded. "Had it since school. Charles James the Second gave it to me."

His father was apparently in the picture. That surprised me.

"Is that common? To use your own car?"

Charlie snorted.

"Yes. This gig doesn't come with perks. I make pennies."

Judging by the bling on his wrist, he didn't need a fat paycheck. My wrists looked naked in comparison.

Charlie pulled up to the officer's booth and rolled down his window. The elderly white man inside said something, but the music drowned him out. Charlie didn't bother turning his head. He flashed him the credentials clipped to his waistband, pulling long on the elastic string, and left it there until the officer lifted the boom barrier.

"The man knows me. And still, he asks for my ID every time."

"Maybe he asks everyone for it. Maybe it's just his job."

He rolled his eyes at me.

"He doesn't. It isn't."

We drove to Chinatown. It was small. Other than a traditional Chinese archway and some characters slapped onto storefronts, it barely read as Asian. Most of the establishments were American chains. Most of the pedestrians were black.

Charlie read my mind.

"Not many Chinese around these parts anymore," he said. "Leave it to Denton to track down the one Chinese-owned Laundromat still around. My man likes his races to specialize along historical lines."

He couldn't find parking. He pulled up parallel to the dry cleaners and turned his hazard lights on.

"You like Chinese food?" he asked.

"Who doesn't?"

He swung his long finger at the restaurant a few doors down. His nail was neatly filed down and shiny.

"That was the meeting place for John Wilkes Booth and his co-conspirators. Now it serves bomb egg rolls and plays classic R & B hits from the nineties. DC's wild, ain't it?"

Charlie placed a wad of cash and a claim ticket in my hand.

"Pick up Denton's suits. Then get us two orders of the shrimp egg rolls. You're not Jewish, are you?"

"No."

"I'll wait here and make sure we don't get towed."

I walked into the cleaners as wind chimes announced my presence. I approached the elderly Asian man behind the counter and slipped him the ticket. His deep smile wrinkled the sides of his eyes and his forehead. He began speaking a foreign language—lyrically, speedily.

"I'm sorry. I don't understand what you're saying."

A teenage boy came racing out from the back, shouting him down in the same language. He softly shoved the elder to the side.

"Sorry about that," he said. "My gong-gong isn't supposed to talk to clients. I don't know what got into him."

The man retreated to a sewing machine nearby, head hanging low.

A twinge of guilt squeezed my heart.

The boy pulled the senator's clothes from a rotating garment conveyor. "You work on the Hill?"

I didn't answer out of confusion at first. He helpfully pointed at the ID fastened to my waist.

"Oh. Right. Yes."

"Fancy," he said, eyebrows arched. "Oppose gentrification, OK? It doesn't just shove out people. It shoves out culture."

Ma-and-pa stores like these—like the alteration shop my grandpa used to own—are the economic engines of this country. I liked the boy's sentiment, but I shrugged. Who cared what I thought?

"I'm nobody."

"A nobody closer to a somebody than we are," he said, gesturing to himself and the old man.

I nodded, smiled, and inserted a couple of dollars into the tip jar.

"Thank your grandpa for trying to help me."

I walked over to the restaurant. An Asian woman in a sparkly vest attended me. I ordered the egg rolls to the tune of Boys II Men in the background. As she began to turn, I ran my finger down the paper menu beneath the glass-top counter, stopped at a familiar item, and called her back.

"How are your scallion pancakes?"

"Delicious."

"Add an order of those, too."

I returned to the car with my hands full. Charlie reached over and opened my door from the inside. I hung the suits from the grab handle and sat the food on my lap. It was too warm for my thighs, but I just left it there and didn't complain. He appeared impressed that I had successfully returned.

"Good man," he said, before speeding off.

We headed to drop off the senator's laundry in Alexandria, Virginia, which didn't take longer than twenty minutes. Neoclassical architecture gave way to suburban greenery. Charlie pulled into the driveway of a midsize, one-story home on a sweeping plot of land. When we stepped out of the car, the sun was high, and the air was muggy. We retreated fairly quickly to the inside.

Senator Denton's foyer was spacious and minimally furnished, but the wall opposite the door was cluttered with art, tapestries, tchotchkes, pottery, and sculptures. Lots of colors, patterns, pouty lips, aggressive noses, head wraps, and clay masks—decidedly African. *Exotic.*

Charlie caught me staring. The display was off-putting.

"Africa as fantasyland. As a faraway idea. In the abstract. Fitting neatly on a white man's entryway table," he said.

"Big yikes."

He nodded and waved me into the kitchen.

We pulled up two stools to the island in the center and dug into our bags of food. He stood and opened the drawer in search of dishes. I wagged my finger.

"These containers double as plates."

I unfolded the take-out box, breaking the sides down until it lay flat.

"Lots of Chinese spots in small town, Iowa?" he asked.

"Everywhere, man. It isn't Bumblefuck."

Charlie drowned his egg roll in duck sauce. I had mine plain.

"I've never tried these," he said, opening the container with the pancakes.

"A slice of flaky heaven."

He tore into one and bobbed his head approvingly. He reached into his pocket and tossed a set of bulky keys onto the countertop.

"These are digging into my leg."

There had to be more than a dozen keys chained together.

"Quite the collection. Like a school janitor's," I said.

"Being elected senator opens a lot of doors."

"Like what?"

He singled out a key. "The Senate gym." He selected another. "The lockers at an exclusive, members-only country club. Negroes merely tolerated." A third: "The doors to the committee room."

"Aren't those always open?"

"Not after hours."

"Why would he need to go in after hours?"

"It's where he goes to think. Sometimes in the middle of the night. He just sits in the dark, in his seat."

"You ever consider slipping into the committee room after hours yourself?"

I finished chewing and swallowed a bite. I looked up from the food at his wide face. It took him a while to match my gaze.

"For what?"

He was smiling but his eyes were smoldering, on fire. I had piqued his interest.

"To catch him off guard."

All the muscles that his shirt just barely contained were taut. I was perfectly still.

"And why would I want to do that?"

I shrugged, looked away, and resumed eating.

"To show him your work. At a time he might be more receptive. In his downtime. Away from the busyness."

His stiffened body relaxed.

"Right."

I felt his eyes finally abandon me.

"I'm a field Negro. Not a house one. Does not matter the time of day. That ain't changing."

"Race is a big thing for you, huh?"

He looked amused.

"It's a big thing for everyone else. I'm just a mirror. I didn't know from birth I was black. I had to be told I was. I had to learn it. You always know you were white?"

What an odd question. Others had always seen me that way. It had seeped into my bones like osmosis. There was no one moment it dawned on me. Race was obvious, wasn't it? We all know it when we see it.

"Yeah, I guess so. It's pretty mindless," I said finally.

"Well, mine's on my mind all the time."

"Sounds exhausting."

He laughed lightly.

"There we agree."

We were done eating. We wiped our hands on napkins in silence, but he lingered and didn't get up. I waited for his lead. He crossed his arms so that his muscular forearms pressed up against the fabric of his shirtsleeves. His nostrils flared.

"Promise me you'll tell me if you fuck my girlfriend."

My mouth fell open to protest but no sounds came out. I blinked repeatedly. I almost chuckled, but he was dead serious. I felt laid bare. Was I so transparently slavish to my most shameful, base desires? The dark, ugly recesses of your mind are meant to remain private. You would never act on those thoughts. At least, you'd like to think so. Had he seen something in me that proved otherwise?

I cleared my throat to make way for words.

"Charlie, I would never—"

"Just promise me, will ya?"

His tone left no room for equivocation. I agreed, stiffly nodding along.

He collected the keys from the table and stood.

"Let's hang his suits and get out of here."

I followed him into the sparse master bedroom. A queen-size bed was propped against the wall: wooden headboard, immaculately white sheets. Affixed above it was a crucifix. Nothing else adorned the walls. A window faced the stretch of field behind the home. The room had a private bathroom, a closet Charlie opened and left the clothes inside of, and a striking metal door, dead bolted, opposite the bed.

"What's that?" I asked, chin pointing to the door.

"I haven't a clue. It's locked."

"Good thing you have the key."

We stared at each other for a beat. Adrenaline warmed my chest. I knew a thing or two about the sinful things men kept locked away.

He fished the keys out of his pocket and walked over, staring at them in thought. I walked up beside him. He fingered each key, settling on a vintage one reminiscent of a warden's. He looked at me again, briefly, before he inserted it into the lock, twisted it—sending a riffling sound echoing—and pulled the door open.

We were greeted by a wall of heavy, humid ancient air.

It was a cellar. A flight of wooden steps descended into a dim room. Charlie hesitated, but eventually, he dipped his head and walked down. I followed, even as my heart was knocking up against my rib cage. I could not see what lay ahead of us. There was so much quiet, even my thinking shut off. Time felt frozen. We reached the floor level, but it took a minute for my eyes to adjust. Although rectangular windows lined the top of the walls, they were soot-ridden, leaving the room blanketed in darkness.

I reached out to a wall of ragged, sharp rock. It was scratched, lacking pattern but intentionally so, as if a wild animal had dug its nails into it in a frenzy. Beside it were more deliberate markings. Straight vertical lines grouped into fours and a diagonal fifth cutting across them. I counted them. There were forty-four. I felt a sense of dread that was nearly out of body, like I was watching myself in a horror movie and I desperately wanted to cover my eyes. I shivered even as I was sweating.

Charlie made an indescribable noise. It was a guttural sound, a hybrid shout and groan but short, as if choked off.

He was crouching, trembling. He had picked something up off the ground, and he had it in his hands. They were chains. They led to restraints, just large enough for wrists and ankles, others large enough for necks. There were dozens of them bolted to the floor, clear across this rear wall. I stepped closer, leaning over Charlie, to view framed black-and-white photographs nailed to the wall above the shackles.

The people standing side by side in them—some of them children— looked all the same. The same rough, weather-beaten sacks of clothing. The same deadened eyes. The same gleaming black skin. My own skin was crawling at the sight of our vile history. The racist enslavement of human beings preserved like a museum exhibit for no one in some guy's basement. I felt dirty.

Charlie surged to his feet and darted up the stairs. I ran after him.

He had tossed open the bathroom door and fallen to his knees in front of the toilet. He lost his lunch. I massaged his back as he did, surprising myself with the showing of warmth. It had poured out of me unconsciously. I wasn't affectionate with people this soon. I wasn't affectionate with men much at all. Blame my dad. Charlie accepted my touch. I couldn't begin to imagine how wrecked he must have felt.

He was slow to get up.

"He lives on a fucking former plantation."

"I'm so sorry, Charlie."

The car ride back was quiet. His eyes were red.

"What kind of man seeks out such a place for a home?" I asked. My chest felt heavy.

He kept his eyes on the road.

"A dead one."

He dropped me off at the Hart Building.

"You're not returning to work?" I asked.

"I have to go see about a locksmith. You know, in case I have committee business after hours."

We exchanged a long look. I nodded, shut the car door, and walked away without another word.

At the end of the day, Liz checked in on me.

"How'd it go?"

The intern cubicle had emptied. She sat in a chair, kicked her feet up on the desk, and laid her phone down.

"Denton gave his speech without a hitch."

"I meant with Charlie."

"Oh."

I stared at my computer screen and moved the cursor around aimlessly.

"I guess we bonded."

I cringed at the inadvertent pun.

"Good," she said. "I want you two to become friends, Cam."

I looked over at her and smiled.

"Me, too."

I turned to the old bulky television in the corner tuned to CSPAN.

Chairman Williams—bald, liver-spotted, and bloated—was presiding over a hearing on the rise of domestic terror threats. He spoke haltingly, reading from sheets of paper that shook in his wrinkled grasp.

"The fate of regaining a woman's right to choose rests in that man's quivering hands," Liz said.

"He makes a good case for term limits."

Her phone vibrated. The screen read, Dale Whitehurst. She answered, but she barely spoke, appearing tense until the call ended.

"I thought you were just a staff ass. The senator calls your personal cell directly?"

Her light eyes looked hollowed out, vacant.

"He makes it a point to have the cell of *every* young woman in the office."

It seemed inappropriate to me, but she said it so blasé. I wrinkled my forehead as if to ask, but she didn't expound.

Instead, she got up and walked over to exit, turning back to me with an arm up against the doorframe.

"The gang is getting pizza at the trendy spot down the street. You down?"

The *gang*. I could be part of the *gang*.

I hastily shut off the computer and stood in reply.

The others were already there when we arrived. Isla and Scoop, on their phones, didn't acknowledge me. Lisa waved politely. Chuy smiled. Charlie jerked his chin upward. Randy threw an arm around my shoulders when I sat down beside him.

It felt nice to belong. It was clear that we all had our roles: Liz, Randy, and Chuy prattled enough for the rest of us, while Charlie, Lisa, and I served as their wordless laugh track, and Scoop and Isla comprised the Greek chorus, intermittently lifting their eyes from their devices to insert a dry quip. There was an equilibrium, a balance, and I fed off the rhythm.

I think they liked how easy it was to project and graft onto me whatever it was they loved about themselves. I was a blank canvas in that way, and there was nothing narcissistic people liked more than a mirror reflecting back on them. There was no shortage of self-love in DC. Everyone's favorite subject was themselves. Sometimes, they let slip out ridiculously privileged and well-heeled thoughts, but I found it as fascinating as watching a different species of animal interact at a zoo. I suffered their lack of self-awareness in engrossed silence.

In a moment when the conversation fractured along pairs, I tried to engage Scoop, who had noticeably not warmed up to me yet. I peered over his shoulder.

"What's got you so rapt?"

I meant for the inquiry to come off light, but I could tell it sounded accusatory, mocking. His glare indicated he agreed.

"Cap Hill So White," he said.

"Huh?"

"It started off as a site for Hill staffers of color to gripe about their shit treatment at work. But as with everything, it's been appropriated by the whites. So now, it's just a general collection of anonymous stories about horrible work conditions here. Pretty funny stuff."

"You know you're white, right?"

"BCE. By cosmic error."

The entry presently on his screen—up-voted by hundreds—read:

> **Dear #CapHillSoWhite:**
> **my boss makes me pick up his dog's shit and meal**
> **prep for him at his home, guess who doesn't wash**
> **their hands in between, lol**

"That's sick," I said.

Scoop's clucking was deep and staccato. It made him sound stupider than he actually was.

43

"Deadass."

"Can't that be traced back to him? Or her?"

"The post deletes in twenty-four hours."

When dinner was over, and we were about to leave, Charlie sauntered over to me, surprisingly, and gave me his hand.

"Cam," he said in valediction. Not Clark Kent. His tone and expression were sober, but he looked at me kindly.

I accepted his hand. I felt him transfer cold metal—a key—between our warm palms. We were accomplices. I liked that.

That night, in bed, I pulled up Cap Hill So White on my phone.

> **Dear #CapHillSoWhite:**
>
> **My boss says he's a "history buff," and that's why**
> **he dresses up as a Confederate soldier in those VA**
> **civil war reenactments. But I know his kink is to wrap**
> **himself in the Stars and Bars and shout "The South**
> **Will Rise Again!" during climax. My brothers and**
> **sisters in Christ: He's not even trying to hide the white**
> **sheet anymore.**

ELECTION NIGHT

Randy had his fingers interlaced neatly in front of him.

"No one broke in. I think it was open. Yeah, everything was open. Why? Did someone say otherwise?"

He swept a strand of brown hair behind his ear and relocked his hands in secular prayer.

"What *about* security? How would I know? I don't recall seeing any-one. There was an election happening. The networks were closing in on a winner. The focus was elsewhere. Everyone was saying there might be widespread protests if Chad Thornton won—down at the White House, at the RNC, at his hotel. Not on the sleepy Senate side. It was a ghost town."

His lower lip trembled.

"No, I'm not cold. I just need something to take the edge off. I guess a nip of bourbon is out of the question?"

He laughed, all by himself, and became grim again.

"Is my uncle all right? Is there a way I can see him? You know, just one more time. One *last* time, I guess. Is that possible? Might you arrange that for me, please?"

03

THE COUSINS LANCASTER

I was eating my lunch on the retaining wall outside the Hart Building when Randy strolled up. He wore a pair of black shades, a handsome Italian gray suit, an oxford dress shirt, and designer loafers. He had his brown leather messenger bag strapped across his chest, just now arriving to work midday, and he held a coffee drink in each of his hands.

"Bro, what are you doing out here alone, eating this sad-sack lunch?"

He tossed off his sunglasses. He had dark, entrenched circles under his eyes, and the red veins in them were bulging. It looked like he hadn't slept.

"Just chilling."

He picked up half of my sandwich from the Tupperware, holding it away from him as you would a grenade.

"Mayonnaise sandwiches with the crusts cut off? You're so white bread, dude."

It was not just mayonnaise. It was banana *and* mayonnaise. But I *had* cut the crusts off. He threw the half in his hands into the plants behind me. I shot up in protest.

"Relax. I know a place with great hot wings. I'll take you there. If we're going to be pussy hounds, we need to start going on hunts together."

He whirled around and started again toward the building. I followed.

"Then why are we going inside?"

"Getting reinforcements."

As we walked to the underground tunnels, I texted Shelly that I had found work to occupy me for the rest of the afternoon. Per usual, no answer. We hopped onto the Capitol subway train, a string of windowed cars humming as it glided down a straight-shot track toward the Dome with stops at the main office buildings along the way. A senator and his aide stepped in after us. He smiled.

"Hey there, Randy. Tell Chris I'll join him for a few holes on Sunday."

"Sounds good, Senator. He's been working on his swing."

"But it's still shit, isn't it?"

"It's still shit," Randy said, laughing. "Make sure you put some money on it."

"Thanks for the insider information," he said, winking.

"Of course. Just don't tell the SEC."

We stepped out at the seven-story white-marble offices at Dirksen, one of the three main Senate buildings, leaving the senator on the train headed to the Capitol.

"Kyle's Mormon," Randy said, pointing at the train speeding away. "But I've seen him stumbling drunk. Good friend of my uncle's. I've known him since I was little."

We walked up to the doors of the Judiciary Committee, where the senators conducted their official business in a claustrophobic room that looked bigger on TV. It was shut, and a Capitol police officer—an older black man with prominent moles on his face and a modest paunch—stood patrolling the hallway just outside it.

"Here you go, Stan," Randy said, gifting him one of the coffee drinks. "A little afternoon pick-me-up."

"No cinnamon, right?"

Randy turned the drink in the elder's hand to show the sticker printed on the side: "Pumpkin Spice Latte. NO CINNAMON." Randy's own said the same, minus the customization.

"Great. I'm horribly allergic. Even a sprinkle will give me the runs. Thank you kindly, sir."

"I got you. When I found out we both have the tastes of a basic teen-age white girl, I knew I had to look out for you."

Randy bowed before departing.

"Stan works the graveyard shift. Posted right there in front of the committee room overnight. He gets a day shift once a week, so I try to bring him a caffeine kick on them."

"He must trust you."

"I wouldn't slip him anything. He's not my type," he said, chuckling.

"But it'd be easy to mix up the drinks. Make a mistake."

Randy stopped and extended his arm across my chest to stop me. He frowned, but it looked unfamiliar on him. His facial muscles just didn't appear comfortable moving that way.

"But I wouldn't want to hurt him."

We didn't speak. Randy looked impossibly young. It was his eyes that glinted like a child's. They were awash with sadness. It was clear that Randy was a sensitive guy, that he felt everything in excess. Like a toddler. It was what made him so appealing. Even in this split second, he boasted an emotional range that on my most vulnerable day I could never match.

Just as suddenly as the look had come, he got rid of it, and his jocular self-assurance took root.

"Speaking of which, take a sip of this."

He held out his drink to me. I smirked but took a swig. Randy was a touchy guy. It was how he showed affection. There was an offer of intimacy in sharing his same cup that I didn't want to reject. I grimaced as I swallowed the warm liquid. It was spiked with bourbon.

"Now we're talking!" he said, cheering, and trying to ruffle my hair but the gel had hardened it beyond mobility. He patted my back, perhaps as a means of wiping off his damp hand, and we proceeded down the hallway. He brought me to his office, leading me past a door whose plaque read: "Senator Christopher Lancaster: Connecticut."

But first he unclipped my ID and stuffed it in my pants pocket for me.

I shuffled my feet uneasily. A man had never reached into my pants before, but Randy observed few boundaries, personal or otherwise.

"Follow my lead," he said.

A group of young staffers were congregated in the front lobby. A white woman was behind the reception desk, fielding a phone call and tapping on her keyboard furiously. The two white girls hovering around her turned to face Randy and squealed at the sight of him. Sitting in chairs against the wall were other interns—two boys and a girl, looking bored. One had his head rolled back and his eyes shut. I could hear light snoring over the girls' commotion.

"You made it," one said, giggling.

"Tiffany, Carly, this is my cousin, Cam Lancaster."

I whipped my head to the side and bore into him. He kept his focus on the girls.

"Oh, another one," the other girl said. "The senator your uncle, too?"

"Yeah. My Uncle Chrissy."

Randy beamed, seemingly tickled by the flourish. I had said it sarcastically, but the girls didn't seem to pick up on it.

"He's a zaddy," she said, loud enough for the room's occupants to hear. "His nephews aren't too bad on the eyes, either."

I had to stifle laughter. I had not met women like them in DC: flighty, unsubstantial. The flirting was so over-the-top and immediate. It hardly felt genuine, but Randy didn't seem to mind. All of us were performing lies for one another anyway.

"Want to go for a ride with the Lancaster boys?"

"We have to ask Priscilla."

On cue, the staff assistant at the desk ended her call. She turned hostile eyes on Randy. Her lips were a straight line.

"Pris, might I take these young ladies off your hands?"

"For what?"

"In service to the great people of the State of Connecticut, of course. Servicing two of them in particular," he said, gesturing to us two. I felt my face grow hot. Priscilla rolled her eyes.

"Would it matter if I said 'no'?"

He approached and leaned against her desk. He collected her hands in his. His tone was solemn.

"It matters to me a great deal what you say. You know that."

The Randy-coaster had dipped again. Judging by the emotion in his tone, it struck me that the two must have had a thing of their own.

"Go on, Randy. I'm sure the senator wouldn't expect anything less."

Dear #CapHillSoWhite:

My boss lets his degenerate nepo baby go hog wild during the work day. Junior must have the goods on him.

As we walked out of the building, the girls lagged a few paces behind, whispering between themselves.

"Carly's for you," Randy said to me. "Been there. Done that. She's a bit of a starfish in the sack, but the body's on point."

"Which one's Carly?"

"The young one."

"That's not helpful. How *young* are these girls?"

"Old enough. Legal."

I shook my head.

"Who cares? You're twenty-two," he said.

"And you're twenty-seven."

He shrugged.

We piled into Randy's white Mercedes. His vanity license plate read:

"FUCBOII." When he pulled out of the employee parking lot and up to the security booth—manned by the usual elderly white man—the boom barrier was lifted for him, credentials unnecessary.

Randy drove recklessly. He rolled down the windows and had to shout at the girls in the backseat over the sounds of burnt rubber and wind.

"You girls excited to vote for Jones?"

"Hell yeah! First black woman president," said Carly, the raven-haired one.

"*Half*-black," said Tiffany, the brunette.

"There's no such thing. One-drop rule, Tiffany. Crack open a history book once in a while, girl."

I clutched my own knee to keep from calling them dimwits.

"It'll be our first time voting, too."

Randy grinned at me. *Barely* legal.

"Behind that charming Southern drawl, Thornton's a fascist pig," Carly said. "Did you know he's against Plan B? Says health care plans shouldn't have to include it because it's a quote 'abortifacient.' What a moron."

"If that comes to pass, I'll run an underground clinic right out of my house," Randy said. "My apartment is already stock-full with Plan B. I'll be a modern-day Harriet Tubman."

The girls applauded. The Underground Railroad into his pants. I smiled to myself.

We arrived at an establishment with no windows, neon lights, and the outline of a woman's shapely body adorning the awning. It was a strip club.

"I thought you were taking us to a wings place," I angry-whispered.

"Garden of Eden Gentlemen's Club *is* a wings place. They're consistently rated number one."

"And these girls are going to want to be here?"

"It's the premier spot for the politically connected. The president's cokehead son comes here. They'll be honored."

"Can they even get in? I don't have a license, you know."

"Cam, I'm Randolph Evarts Lancaster. No one is ID'ing any of us."

He was right. He fist-bumped the bouncer, said something charming that I couldn't hear, and pointed to the three of us before we were ushered in and set up in a darkened back corner booth. It was fancier than the typical club—boasting floor-to-ceiling mirrors, velvet ropes, plush royal purple carpet, and glass chandeliers—but it had that undercurrent of tawdry sleaze inherent to the trade. Other than the naked girls making their rounds, it was largely empty.

Randy ordered bottle service and several baskets of their famous wings.

The vodka bottle they brought was obscenely large.

"It's not even one p.m.," I said.

"What's your obsession with numbers?" he asked, tearing into a chicken drum. "Age. Time. You know, numbers are just human inventions, right? The Egyptians, I think. We existed for millions of years without them."

It was another number—*money*—that allowed him to enjoy these spoils, but I kept the thought to myself.

It was jarring: to see his hands and mouth covered in sauce so dangerously close to clothing undoubtedly worth thousands. I felt soaring anxiety just waiting to see if a drop would fall and sully them.

Women would approach us every other minute with offers of lap dances—sounding like fast-talking car salesmen filtered through baby voices—but I turned them politely away. Randy partook liberally. He didn't even bother wiping his hands. He accepted a dance from a black woman—mixed probably, *half*-black as Tiffany might say—and left her body, including parts otherwise private, coated in orange. It was nauseating, and degrading, and fascinating all at the same time. He had marked her as his. She had the autonomy of a paper napkin. And yet here I was, drunk off a Jesus complex while envying the power he flaunted. He did tip her generously, though.

Tiffany was game for it all. Carly was more reserved. She still drank too fast, tossing aside the two thin black straws in her cocktail and electing to swig right from the glass. It left a constant film of pineapple juice above her lip.

"Why not sip out of the straws?" I asked.

"It's bad for the environment. It's critical we reduce our carbon footprint, don't you think?"

I crumpled the features of my face together, collecting the dozen or so wet plastic straws she had left littering the table for emphasis, but she just laughed.

"You don't look like your cousin," she said.

"He got the tall and skinny genes."

"No, not that. I meant you don't dress like him."

I suffocated the embarrassment beneath an easy smile.

"I don't like wearing my wealth on my sleeve. My mother taught me to be humble and not showy. She married into the Lancaster name after growing up in a poor family in Greenwich."

"So inspiring," she said. "Also, there are poor people in Greenwich?"

At some point—two-thirds of the bottle through—Randy invited me to the bathroom.

"I don't need to go," I said.

"Neither do I."

The bathroom was among the darkest I had ever seen. I doubt I'd be able to see my own dick in my hand at the urinal. It had no stalls, just an open toilet in the corner. Privacy was a low-order luxury at an establishment designed for men to share in collective arousal.

He removed a vial from his inside jacket pocket and tapped it against the sink counter, loosening two clumps of white powder that he straightened into lines with his Senate ID.

"You try blow before?" he asked.

"No."

"It's no big deal. Like a shot of espresso. Plus, it's powder. The legal penalties are radically less severe than those for crack. Thank you, white privilege!" he sang.

He handed me two of Carly's forsaken straws, which he had swiped from the table.

"Go ahead. Recycle. Reuse. Save the whales or something," he said.

I held the straw in my hand for a while. Randy was quiet. I could not hear him breathing. I didn't want to turn him down. He was showing me a good time, and I was no ingrate. My manhood was on the line, too. So much of being a man was constructed in public. In moments like these.

I dipped down and snorted a line, shooting the powder up with as much power as I could muster. My brain smarted. I threw my head back. When I returned to Earth, I let loose a whoop and hopped in place. Randy was wide-eyed.

"You took that like a pro."

He seized the two straws from me and treated himself to the second line. His nose twitched for seconds after like he was a rabbit. We stood in front of the mirrors. Both of us had a single nostril caked in cocaine. We burst into staccato laughter, wiping off the remnants before returning to civilization.

Hours rolled by quickly after that. I ventured from my well-worn spot: chatting, dancing, and taking shots. No chasers, no mixers for me. I don't do empty calories. A woman gave me a lap dance as Randy tipped her throughout. Then Carly gave me one. It was embarrassing, not sexy, but before it ended, we were making out nonetheless. I felt her pineapple mustache wetting the patch of skin above my lips. It was a sacrifice I was willing to make in exchange for getting to keep my hand planted on her ass.

When we exited, the sky was a tableau of orange, pink, and cerulean. No one was fit to drive. But no one was fit to care, either. Randy drove no less cautiously under the influence.

The revelry was ongoing after reaching Randy's home. We imbibed, smoked, and jammed out to way-too-loud music. By the time darkness fell, we were holed up on distant ends of his couch, making out with our respective dates to the sound of the first presidential debate playing on the TV. It was very DC of us.

"Vice President Jones, press reports have the final three contenders for the Supreme Court winnowed down to three men: two of them white. Do you and the president fear that the country is not ready to elect its first black woman president and install a minority woman to the Court at the same time?"

"That's preposterous, John. The president is committed to nominating the most qualified individual—period. Because the composition of the Supreme Court isn't a game."

"How about that, Governor Thornton? The chief justice was a staunch conservative who authored the opinion overturning a woman's right to an abortion. The president has an opportunity to swing the political makeup of the Court to the left. Should he feel compelled to choose a moderate, centrist nominee given the views of the justice he would be replacing?"

"John, the president oughtta lay off entirely. This ain't his seat. It belongs to the American people, and certainly not the wacky, socialist left lookin' to raise taxes, give government handouts, provide abortions on demand, and ram their godless, secular, pseudo-science down our throats. Chief Justice Warner was a protector of life—of that innocent, itty-bitty baby in the womb. Heartbeat as early as five weeks. Feelin' pain as early as twelve weeks. And Key-ahhhh-ra ova there says you can kill it without blinkin' an eye."

"It's vice president to you, Governor," she said.

"Well, you can call me Rick. I'm just a backwater boy from rural Florida."

"*You were born in Manhattan,* Rick, *and you have degrees from Harvard and Yale. Come on! This is the problem,* John. *The other side lives in a world of its own cynically crafted lies, and it's irresponsible. Plots on the lives of elected officials—mostly by your friends on the far right,* Governor—*they're being foiled on a daily basis. And you're using dog whistles. Won't you tone down the racist rhetoric before someone gets killed?*"

"*Uh-oh, looks like the woke police is out to get me. I'd be afraid y'all would arrest me if your administration hadn't defunded the police and confiscated their guns. This is what America would look like under a President Jones. An erosion of our Anglo-Saxon, Judeo-Christian values replaced by...by God knows what! Constantly callin' good, hardworkin' Americans racist if they don't say what's politically correct. The whole coun-try'd get canceled.*"

"*Governor, did I hear you right in using the word 'replaced'?*" the mod-erator asked. "*Are you alluding to Replacement Theory, the white suprema-cist view that the country is growing unfortunately browner and blacker?*"

"*There goes the left-wing media, everyone! I don't know nothin' about this 'theory.' When I was a boy, schools taught us real history. Not this Crit-ical Race nonsense the liberals want to use to indoctrinate our children. Why not ask the vice president about* that *theory? How she wants to teach boys and girls as young as age five that they're racist?*"

"*But first, Governor, will you disavow white supremacy? Will you tell people who believe it that you do not want their votes?*"

"*I will accept a vote from anyone who wants to vote for me. Anyone who thinks the liberals have gone too far in changing the DNA of this coun-try. Anyone who wants to reclaim power from the coastal elites and return to traditional, old-fashioned morals. We're tired of being shut down. Of being told we have nothin' worthy to say because we're white, or we're men, or because of what our ancestors did a long time ago. I will not forsake anyone just because they live in the heartland, or they pray to Jesus, or they believe that marriage is between one man and one woman. If you and the rest of the left-wing media think that half the country is racist, then so be it. I will be their voice if no one else will."*

It felt icky to hook up to the soundtrack of an American fascist. Randy must have thought so, too.

"Shall we retire for the night?" he asked.

I came up for air at the sound of his voice. The girls agreed and left for the bathroom together.

"Take Carly to the room on the second floor. I'll stay with Tiffany down here," he said, pointing to his bed.

I had a nagging feeling, dulled and buried beneath the layers of booze and blow but still there.

"They're drunk and high," I said in protest.

"So are we. So who's taking advantage of whom?"

My mind felt foggy, but any answer I might supply—even in my right mind—felt inappropriately essentialist. We were men, and men were always in the wrong. It felt silly to say aloud, so I shrugged it off.

I escorted Carly up the darkened stairs to a room of medium size and wood-paneled walls. It did not look lived in. We fell onto the neatly made bed, rolling on top of it as we kissed. We settled with her on top. We undressed ourselves in a mad dash. Moonlight and shadows hit her body at all the right angles. She looked like she had been charcoal sketched by a gifted artist. I felt lascivious panic rev up inside me like an engine.

"What language is that?"

She was caressing the spot above my heart, between my shoulder and pectoral, where I had been tattooed. Branded.

"Um, Sanskrit."

"What does it mean?"

"Fire."

That kindled her passion. She was biting my lip, and her nails were digging into my shoulder. We snowballed up to the point of union, but I hesitated right before.

"I have to tell you something: I'm not a Lancaster."

"I know."

"You do?"

"I know everything there is to know about that family. There were only two brothers: Randy's uncle and his late dad. When he died, it dominated the local news. Chris Lancaster was driving the car that crashed into the ravine."

"And you still want to do this?"

Here she broke into a wide smile laced with pity. She suddenly looked years older.

"You're strong enough to pick me up and throw me onto the bed. That's all that matters right now."

I grunted, forcefully flipped our positions—tossing her on her back—and pushed forward.

Randy was right. Carly barely moved. But it was more than just being passive. She was transported elsewhere. Her body became an empty vessel. Her eyes lost focus, so they weren't looking at me but past me, through me. Her mouth fell slightly open. The charm on the end of my neck chain—a golden cross—twirled above her, its shadow making the sign of the cross. Her body only moved with my thrusts. I felt myself become noticeably harder inside of her.

My hands migrated to her throat. I wrapped my fingers around it, joining them at the nape, and pressed my thumbs down on her larynx. I increased the pressure slowly and rolled my head back, descending into moans. My eyes twitched, directed at the ceiling, as a tingling surged from my groin upward, enveloping my body.

I wasn't taken out of it until I felt intense pain—a burning—on my arms. She was clawing into me, drawing blood, thrashing her limbs and flopping beneath me. I released her immediately. She erupted into heaving.

"Too hard! I couldn't breathe!" she said amid fits of hoarse breathing.

"My God! Sorry! So sorry. Fuck. I'm awful. What's wrong with me?"

I gave her space, curling up by the headboard, knees tucked into my chest and arms encircling them: a boy chastised. When she was breathing normally, she crawled over, laying a hand on my biceps.

"You didn't hear me? I was telling you to ease up."

I shook my head vigorously. Something deep, something primal had taken over. She saw it scared me just as much as it had scared her. Her eyes softened.

She felt bad that I hadn't finished. So she went down on me, and we fell asleep after.

I awoke the next morning to severe head pounding and a booming voice.

"Young man, young lady: what are you doing in my bed?"

Senator Lancaster had a full coif of silver hair that swept across his forehead and dropped a lock down right above his thick eyebrow. Like Superman. He looked hefty in his suit—not fat, not buff, but somewhere in between, meaty but soft—and his face was full, with expressive lines, not wrinkles, adorning it. He was a rugged patrician.

I rocketed up in bed but not to my feet, ashamed of my nakedness. Carly did the same, somehow both sitting up and sinking deeper into the covers.

"Uh, Randy, um, sent us here."

He inspected us—hands crossed in front of him, rolling luggage beside him—stone faced and unspeaking.

"Randolph!" he eventually yelled. Loud but monotone.

Before departing: "Come down decent. Do not exit my home. The last thing I need is the sighting of a young girl emerging from it at this early hour."

We dressed silently. I wore my slacks and messily tucked in my shirt, leaving my blazer and tie hanging off my forearm and my shoes in my hands. In the basement, Randy and Tiffany were in similar states of sloppy re-dress. Randy—trying hard, nearly straining, to appear perfectly unfazed—remained shirtless, arms extended behind him, palms flat on his silk sheets. He had a tattoo of his own perpendicular to his sternum in black ink reading: "Tankerhoosen."

The senator moved methodically, dialing several people on his cell phone, directing them in no uncertain terms, and slipping cash out from his wallet. He handed the hundred-dollar bill to Tiffany.

"You girls can leave out the back. There are loosened fencing boards that lead to the rear neighbor's yard. They're aware you're coming. Don't disturb them. Just walk around the side of their home to the street behind this one. A driver will be waiting for you."

They started off, and I tried following. The senator laid a heavy hand on my shoulder.

"No, son. You stay. I want to chasten Randolph in front of his friend."

I slumped onto the edge of the bed beside Randy.

The senator stared at his nephew. He took a long time collecting his thoughts and forming his words, forever a cautious politician even in the privacy of his own home. The wordless suspense perhaps served as punishment itself. My own pulse was thrumming under my skin.

"I didn't know you were coming back today, Chris," Randy finally said first. "Your scheduler doesn't share a damn thing with me."

My heart fluttered at the informality.

"And still, you direct your friends to my room. To my bed. Such an effete way of acting out. Like a dog pissing in the corner. Be a man, Randolph."

Randy jumped to his feet. He squared his shoulders. He stood just taller than his uncle.

"I won't hold back, Randolph. If you want to go, I'll beat you into submission like I should've a long time ago. Do not test me."

Randy shrank, deflating a few inches.

I was filled with secondhand shame. This wasn't discipline. It was humiliation. Strip us of the money and the material possessions, and we're all the same. The words could've easily come from the lips of my own dad. Deep down, I think I heard them in his snaky voice.

"It reeks of booze and drugs in here. No doubt you spent your work-day self-indulgently. You court nothing but ruin. Part of me waits for the day you offer me relief, and I read in the paper that all of your excesses have inevitably led to your death."

"Aw, I love you, too, Uncle Christopher."

"It's no longer funny, although it does border on parody. You're a caricature. And as you grow older, my patience wears thinner."

"Then send me away, why don't you?"

"As much as I'd love it, I can't do that. I promised your father—"

"Keep him out of this!" Randy roared, finger in his uncle's face. "You don't get to mention him. You don't get to invoke him to lecture me."

The senator sighed.

"How long will you persist in trying to hurt me?"

"Forever. Always. Until my last breath—or yours."

"Very well, son. You continue being a fuckup. I'll continue pretending I see the potential in you to change."

"I took after you, Uncle Christopher. You were the fuckup. My father was the better man, wasn't he?"

Randy had receded to my side. He appeared enervated and near tears. His voice was shaky. The senator nodded.

"That he was," he said, eyes shining. "And I can't help but think, if he were alive, he'd be incredibly embarrassed of you, just as he was embarrassed of me."

Randy collapsed on the bed, noisily letting loose the air within him.

"Sober up and drive your friend home. Take the day off from work. No one wants you there anyway."

He left. Randy lingered in his supine position. I was afraid he might never speak up, leaving us in limbo for hours on end. Nothing felt proper to say. I tried anyway.

"Tankerhoosen?"

He sat up and rubbed his chest, over the skin emblazoned with the word.

"It's where my dad died. Arthur Lancaster: popular state attorney general and expected candidate for national office before his untimely death. Tankerhoosen became synonymous with the scandal. That's what the media called it anyway."

After a while, he hadn't picked the thread back up. So I pushed.

"When did it happen?"

I remembered the story, but I wanted him to share it with me. I wanted us to feel close.

He gave me a sideways glance but answered.

"I was in high school. My uncle was a nobody at the time. Scratch that—he was a drunk. His older brother was beloved and accomplished. They were driving back from a nighttime fundraiser out in the north-eastern part of the state. My uncle crashed the car, and it fell over a cliff. Into a ravine. Into streams of water from the Tankerhoosen River. My uncle climbed out, scathed but alive. And then, he disappeared. He didn't report the crash for four whole hours. He told us he was blacked out. That he was disoriented. That he was scared. The Lancaster name can't be tarnished—no matter what—so we kept all of that in the family. My dad died on the way to the hospital. I didn't get to see him."

"That's awful."

He was silently crying now.

"How does one become a senator after that?" I asked.

"Memories aren't long in politics. He got community service and a suspended license on charges of leaving the scene of an accident. He cleaned himself up. Got sober. Waited a few years. Reformed his image. Ran on picking up the mantle of my dad's legacy, pursuing his lost life's purpose. He now absolves his guilty conscience by bribing and barely tolerating his brother's only son."

He wiped his face, shut his eyes, and interlocked the fingers of both hands on top of his head.

"You know I dream of burning all of this down…"

"I get that. It's only stuff. Material goods. It doesn't guarantee happiness."

"…with him inside," he said, turning his whole body toward me. "I've dreamt of lighting a match. While he is sleeping upstairs. Leave the gas stove on. Maybe slip him half an Ambien. The drug has a half-life of about four hours. You know, so he wakes up during the fire. Too late to get out, but enough to be aware of his fate. Enough to know it was me."

I swallowed hard the lump in my throat. He was smiling. It faded as he looked away. When his eyes returned to me, they were fixated south of my face.

"You're bleeding."

I looked down to see patches of blood had seeped through my shirt, up and down my arms. I rolled up my sleeves to inspect the gashes.

"Damn, bruh. I didn't take you to be so rough in bed," he said, grinning, his tone climbing in pitch. "You're a beast. A real lady-killer."

I flinched. That really was an unfortunate phrase.

"Coke given you the jitters?" he asked. "I'll brew you some coffee before we go."

"Isn't that counterproductive?"

"You'd think, but it helps. Fools your brain or something."

He walked over to the kitchen and turned a knob on the stove. The igniter clicked. The gas hissed. The whoosh of the fire consuming it brought me great comfort. I exhaled along with it, evacuating all tension.

ELECTION NIGHT

Liz was frantic. Her quaking hands were everywhere—in her hair, in her face, wiping tears and spreading streaks of mascara.

"I don't know (*sob*) what happened. I had (*sob*) nothing (*sob*) to do with it. I had no idea it would lead to *this*."

She leaned forward in her seat, arms splayed out on the table.

"Call me Frost—all my good friends do. Did you talk to Cam? I don't really know him too well. I just met him, in fact. We weren't awfully close. I didn't have him over for dinner or anything like that. And I never understood what his deal was, you know?"

She reached for her heart, clutching her chest, and her voice drew down to a whisper.

"What were my motivations? I had none. I had nothing against the senator. This was just a breakdown in communication. It all got out of hand. It snowballed into tragedy. And I regret playing a role in any of it. But I am innocent."

She froze in place.

"I'm not in any trouble, am I? Do I need a lawyer? 'Cause I did nothing wrong here. You believe me, don't you?"

04

VULTURES CIRCLE
IN BROAD DAYLIGHT

We were in line at the bustling Dirksen Café, where everyone—staffers and tourists, lobbyists and senators—grabbed a midday bite amid meager lighting, dingy carpeting, and gloomy-gray, load-bearing columns.

Randy had tattled to Liz about my al fresco, party-of-one homemade lunch breaks, and she insisted I join the gang at the Senate's counter-service restaurant instead, even if I continued bringing food from home. The same sandwich Randy had so inelegantly tossed into the dirt grew more embarrassing every day. No one else brought from home, and the lines were so long, I managed to finish my food by the time any of them first sat down at the table. I didn't know what to do with my hands, so I folded them in front of me like a schoolboy. It was the feeling of being a free-lunch kid at the popular-kids table all over again.

So I began ordering a soup, the cheapest item on the menu. Liz caught on.

"Choose any of them but the Senate Bean," she said. "It's on the menu every day out of tradition. Can't guarantee a fresh batch."

I paid in cash that first time. By the second time, Liz leapt in front of me at checkout.

"Put his soup on my tab," she told the brown woman at the cash register.

I protested at first.

"You're doing me a favor," she said. "I get points on my card. Plus, you're an unpaid intern. And we're Democrats. We're all about redistributing wealth. If they're going to call us socialists, might as well make the label fit."

On this day, Liz was playfully prodding me from behind in line, laying her head on my shoulder and squinting to read the electronic menu screen ahead.

"My eyesight's getting worse," she whined.

"Want me to read it to you?"

Instead, she swiped the glasses from the bridge of my nose and nestled them on hers.

"No, I need—" I began but cut myself short.

She pursed her lips together.

"These aren't helping at all."

"My prescription's low."

A white man with a full beard approached us at our table, tray in his hands, folders wedged under his armpits, and eyes in a panic.

"Liz!" he said. "Glad to have run into you. The committee room is bare today—tumbleweeds are blowing by—and DJW is up on the dais. When the camera pans over to him, no aides will be sitting behind him. We just need bodies there, ASAP."

She dropped the chicken finger in her hand.

"Bodies plural? May I bring this committee intern with me? He doesn't have a real job to tend to."

He looked me up and down.

"Yeah, sure. He's good-looking enough."

"I thought Washington was Hollywood for ugly people?" she asked.

"True. It's not much of a compliment."

When he left, she gathered our uneaten items for disposal.

"Everything's always an emergency for Adam. I swear neuroticism is a prerequisite for job advancement here. At least it wasn't the chief of staff. All those guys are egomaniacs. Come on, we've got to rush."

She gripped my forearm, and I winced, resisting her pull. It was still tender from the slashing Carly had given me. Liz didn't ask. She just grabbed my hand instead, and we sprinted down the halls, weaving in and out of foot traffic.

Her hand was soft. I couldn't stop fixating on the touch. I felt my own calloused, rough-patched version rub up like sandpaper against hers. I worried it would become unmanageably sweaty, and she would slip out of my grasp. That I would lose her. She was staring at me as I drifted in obsessively long contemplation a step or two behind her.

"You know Lisa likes you, right?" she asked.

Rushing blood rouged my cheeks.

"She doesn't know me."

"What's to know? You're hot. You're shy. You're quiet. Just like her."

She dropped my hand at the threshold to the committee room. We entered quietly and hewed to the wall, making our way past the gallery and sitting behind the senator to the left of Chairman Williams. Senator Dale J. Whitehurst had perfect posture, sitting upright, back straight in his chair. He wore his mostly black hair combed backward. Only his thick sideburns and the hair around his temples were gray. Reputation of the city notwithstanding, he was objectively handsome: tall, fit, square-jawed, naturally tanned, and dimpled. Right out of central casting.

He and the chairman were the only two senators present.

"Before I turn it over to the esteemed gentleman from Kansas, I wanted to note an anniversary of sorts," 2 Bills said into the microphone. "Exactly forty years ago, Senator Whitehurst got his start in Washington working at my office. That isn't awfully well known. Dale was a fresh-faced intern, and I was just a freshman senator—with a lot more hair, of course."

Whitehurst chuckled affectedly.

"But I knew back then how incredibly bright and impressive he was. When he called me up many years later to tell me he was running for Senate, I was first in line to send him a check and endorse him. And as we sit here today—colleagues on this august committee, on the verge of voting through a new chief justice and shaping the Court for generations to come—I can think of no better partner and friend to do it with. The floor is yours, Senator."

"Thank you, Chairman," Whitehurst said. "And before I begin with my prepared remarks, I just want to say: as soon as the president announces a nominee, which I understand is imminent, I have zero doubt you stand ready to lead this committee with great verve and *clarity.*"

That was shade. Liz reached over to squeeze my thigh. I could see my eyes bulge on the screen overhead, broadcasting to the world our two faces behind Whitehurst's.

When the hearing ended—and 2 Bills slammed his gavel limply to adjourn—Whitehurst rolled his chair over to us. My stomach tightened as I looked away.

"Lizzy, back at the office get Denton on the line, will you?" he said, winking. "Make sure you document it. Thanks, dear."

He laid his meaty hand on her shoulder. He didn't turn to me whatsoever. He rolled back, stood, and walked off in a hurry, past a tortoise-paced 2 Bills with his hallmark cane. Liz jumped up.

"Follow me," she said.

We remained a few long strides behind Whitehurst. Tourists looked at him, confident he was someone important, but didn't bother him. In all likelihood, they couldn't identify him by name. Washington was Hollywood if it were filled with D-list actors: only vaguely familiar.

"Lizzy?" I asked on the way.

"Only he calls me that."

"Do you like that?"

"It doesn't matter. *He* likes it."

Dear #CapHillSoWhite:

Bro. My boss keeps calling me the wrong name.

[Anon] is the *other* black guy in the office. Hey, at

least there's two of us. Tiny victories.

We trailed the senator past the familiar sign reading, "Senator Dale Whitehurst: Kansas," and into a lobby of eggshell maroon walls. He disappeared into the heart of the office. Liz plopped down at the front desk, shooing away an intern filling in for her.

When it was just she and I, she shut and locked the front cedar door.

At her computer, she opened a spreadsheet listing a series of phone numbers. She highlighted the one beside the name Scott Denton.

"You have access to every senator's personal cell number?"

She nodded.

"Why lock the door?"

"Whitehurst has me record his conversations with senators. He's paranoid like that. I have hundreds of tapes locked away in this drawer here. From hours-long strategy sessions to a quick 'Meet me in the committee room.' He wants a record of it all, in case anyone tries back-stabbing him. DJW will drive the knife into you first. So by his instruction, I hit 'Mute,' listen in on the line, and turn on my trusty recorder."

"I take it the senator on the other side has no clue?"

"DC has a one-party consent rule. Legally, he doesn't need their permission. Linda Tripp did it to Monica Lewinsky before we were born but from Maryland: two-party consent. That was her mistake. You gotta outsmart the feds."

"Let me get this straight: you have hours of Whitehurst and other senators speaking. So you could edit their words, stitch together what you'd want them to say, call up a senator, and have him or her do whatever was directed?"

Her smile was soft and dreamy, bordering on sensual.

"In case I have a knife of my own to drive into someone, eh?" she asked.

On speaker, she dialed the highlighted number. A familiar voice—loud and brash—responded.

"Senator Denton, Senator Whitehurst is on the line for you. Are you available?"

He grunted in the affirmative.

Liz patched him through and hit record.

"Dale, you fucker. Just caught the tail end of that hearing. Bill was really slobbering your knob, huh?"

"Charming."

Denton belly laughed.

"Don't be so uptight, my boy. The man has no teeth so it'd probably be a good one."

"Scott, there isn't much time. Bill is intent on calling the White House today. Sandy's been in his ear. He wants to speak on behalf of the Six. And he wants to push for Loughlin."

Judge Loughlin, one of the three names floated to fill the Supreme Court seat. Liz's face lit up and her eyebrows danced. We were eavesdropping on something good.

"Loughlin? That commie?" Denton said. "There's no way you'd keep your caucus together. The centrists will break away. He won't even get out of committee. And I can't be associated with him whatsoever—not even a whiff of his pinko scent can waft my way. Understand? Plus, he's a no-go on Title IX reform."

"*You* made that a live issue. Not the rest of us. It was an unforced error. You know it's Sandy's pet project."

"I know. That bitch. Bill has a total hard-on for her. Metaphorically, of course. I'm sure the corpse can't actually get it up anymore."

"You know, for a virgin, Scott, you sure do have a gutter mouth."

"Fuck you, Dale."

"Ultimately, I'm not sure I can wrench the call from Bill's trembling hands. We may have to learn to live with Loughlin. He's apparently the White House favorite. He's a white man. Vice President Jones prefers it. She's convinced she'll lose if there's another black face in the news. The country isn't ready. It's too much, too fast."

"So that brings us back to Guttenberg," Denton said. "He's Jewish. Your side loves that shit."

Judge Guttenberg, the centrist pick who might just be a secret Republican.

Liz was beaming. Fun clung to her like lint.

"You're being unserious. Stop bringing his name up," Whitehurst said. "He was thrown into the top three for show. As a fake nod to bipartisanship. Can't say with certainty he's even pro-choice."

"So it has to be Wright. He's the blankest canvas. The least political."

Judge Wright, the lone black man among the three.

"He wrote that dissent on the DC Circuit criticizing Title IX. Sandy would flip," Whitehurst said.

"It's a fringe issue, Dale. I shouldn't have thrown kerosene on it, but it has a short shelf life. It will be drowned out by the excitement of nominating the first black chief justice. That black skin is like armor. Even Sandy won't be able to penetrate it. She married a black herself for Chrissake!"

"Even if Bill let me make the call, how am I supposed to convince the White House of Wright? The vice president is personally opposed. We need a bargaining chip. I'm not threatening to tank Loughlin. I won't do that to the president of my own party weeks out from an election. It's career suicide."

Denton was so quiet, and the line was devoid of even ambient noise, it sounded as if the call had dropped.

"Scott?"

"Tell the White House I will vote for Wright," Denton said.

"You'll vote for the nominee from the opposing party? This close to an election? Are you mad?" Whitehurst asked.

"Everyone knows I support returning to *Roe*. That already makes me a unicorn in this party. And I famously work with five other Democrats on the committee. Voting for such a historic first will help me with the blacks. He fits the bill on the red line I myself drew on Title IX. I'll tell my colleagues that I saved them from a Chief Justice Loughlin. We're in the minority. We can kick and cry and pointlessly shout bloody murder as President Stevenson appoints the most lefty chief justice since Earl Warren—or we can have a seat at the table and get a moderate in return. I think it's brilliant. Tell them I'll declare my 'yea' vote as soon as he's announced, and they get a confirmation that is bipartisan by at least one."

"What about the rumors about him?"

Liz and I shared a quizzical look. We didn't know about any rumors.

"Those type of rumors take down Republicans, not Democrats. His skin is as black as Teflon—"

"Teflon's a plastic. It's colorless," Whitehurst said, sighing.

"Whatever. You get me. Nothing will stick. He's untouchable."

"And what do I tell Bill?"

"Who cares? Lie to him. He'll forget what you said by morning anyway."

The senators ended their call. Whitehurst directed Liz through the phone.

"Get me Bill, Lizzy."

She pushed "Stop" on her recording device. She flipped out the mini black cassette, labeled it by name and date, opened the bottom drawer to her desk with the turn of a key, and tossed it indiscriminately into a pile overrun with others. She put a blank tape in, dialed a new number, and pushed "Record." A female answered—"2 Bills doesn't know how to use a smart phone," Liz explained to me—and got the elder chairman on the line.

When his voice filled the receiver, it resonated loudly.

"Who is this?"

"It's me, Dale."

Silence.

Eventually, as if the word weren't English: "Dale?"

"Yes, Bill. Dale Whitehurst."

"Oh, Dale, yes. I was just talking about you. I was singing your praises to Sandy. She dropped by with some carrot cake—my favorite."

"That's nice, Bill. Have you made the call to the White House yet?"

"What call?"

"About the nominee."

"Was that supposed to be today?"

"Yes, Bill."

"You think I can just call the president directly?"

"It needs to go through the chief of staff. Remember I gave you her number?"

"We're all very excited about Loughlin. You, too, Dale?"

"He's a sharp legal mind."

"Sandy thinks so, and I agree. He's a safe bet. If we tell the White House he has the support of the Six, it should push him over the top."

"Scott won't support him."

"Well, of course he won't. He's still a Republican, Dale. Did you forget that?"

Long pause.

"Silly me. Are you sure you don't want me to make the call?"

"Oh, but I was so looking forward to chatting with Bob. I haven't spoken to him since the convention."

Longer sigh.

"You won't be speaking directly to President Stevenson."

"I won't?"

"No, Bill. We're calling the chief of staff. She and I served in the House together. And I think she might receive our push in the best light if it comes from me. We don't want to look like we're telling them what to do."

"No, we don't want to do that. And it's a foregone conclusion at this point, isn't it? Everyone says it's going to be Loughlin."

"That's what I'm hearing."

"We just want to get in before it's announced. So we can say we supported him early on. You can't really mess that up, can you?"

Whitehurst masked a groan through a cough.

"I'm grateful for the opportunity."

"You deserve it, Dale. You know, I'm sure leadership will make you chairman when I finally retire. I think you're *almost* ready."

"Thank you, Bill."

"But we're gearing up for reelection in two years over here. Did you know my internals are still pretty high? And I think I have another six years in me. I feel great, Dale—just as I did forty years ago, you know?"

"Undoubtedly, sir. I should go make that call now."

"Of course. Give Bob my best regards."

Liz's hands flew to the sides of her head. It was adorable. The old man was losing it.

We heard a click. Whitehurst was still on the line.

"Eat shit and die," he said.

A dial tone followed. Liz ended her recording.

We let out some pent-up laughter. I was giddy with adrenaline. Everything she did, she did with adventure, teetering on the exciting edge of danger. It was intoxicating.

"The things you must overhear," I said. "I'm sure you have the ammunition to ruin his career."

"I wouldn't do that."

"I thought you hated him?"

"It's complicated. It's more of a love-hate relationship. It changes by the day."

"And today, is it more love or is it more hate?"

She didn't answer. She just smiled to herself.

"Come over for dinner tonight," she said.

Just like that. She hopped from topic to topic with the whimsy of someone light and unburdened. I wished I could be that unbothered all the time.

"To your apartment?"

"Uh-huh."

"Will Charlie be there?"

"Nuh-huh."

"Won't that upset him?"

"Why would it? We can talk about you asking Lisa out."

"Right."

That was disappointing.

I spent my early evening thinking hard on what to wear. Liz had only seen me in professional clothing. What a man wore in his down-time said a lot about him. My roommate noticed.

"You got a hot date tonight, man?"

"Your ramen's done," I answered.

I choose dark jeans and a collared short-sleeve shirt that fit snugly around my biceps.

I transferred from the bus to the Metro. Her place was a short walk from the U Street station. It was a newer-model, high-rise luxury apartment building with a concierge. Hers was on the top floor. My ears popped on the way up.

I knocked on her front door. It was Lisa—not Liz—who opened.

I couldn't quite form a sentence. I felt caught red-handed, despite doing nothing wrong. Her hair was pulled up, and she was in sweats. Color flooded her cheeks.

"Cam, what are you doing here?"

"Liz invited me."

"Oh."

She turned around and yelled.

"Liz! Cam's here!"

She disappeared inside, leaving the door ajar. I invited myself inside and joined Lisa on the couch. I smelled garlic and onion sautéing from the kitchen. We didn't say anything at first. She was barefoot, each toe painted in a fresh coat of pink. I remember thinking she had pretty feet, followed instantly by shame.

"Do you cook?" I asked.

"Huh?"

"I only cook the basics—you know: eggs, pasta, rice. Was wondering if you were the same."

"I'm more of a baker. Can whip up a badass cake."

I smiled. She was goofy under all that stoicism.

"I didn't know you and Liz lived together," I said.

"Rent's expensive in the city."

I frowned. This penthouse had to be a pretty penny even split two ways.

"This place is nice. Very spacious. The room I share with another dude is about the size of this living room. This a 2/2?"

She nodded.

"How's work?" I asked.

"The boss is manic. We're all sitting on pins and needles waiting on the White House announcement of the nominee. I think the comms director has drafted three different rollouts. She's literally losing hair."

Her voice was as taut as the strings on a violin. I felt a glut of sympathy and the protective—but brotherly—desire to talk her down.

"I have a hunch it may be Wright."

"It won't be. If it is, the next few weeks will be torture."

Liz hadn't told her what we overheard. We shared a secret—just the two of us.

"Your senator hates him?"

"He's not good for Florida families. That's how we talk in comms. It isn't personal."

"You from Florida, too?"

"Unfortunately."

She made her cracks while expertly avoiding eye contact. It made me pursue her eyes all the more obsessively.

"I tolerate it just fine," she said. "There are pockets of sanity. You got Iowa pride?"

"Why?"

"Because it's your home state," she said, brow furrowed.

"Oh. Bet. It has its redeeming value. We voted for Obama twice, you know."

"Talking heads say Jones has no chance there now."

"We'll see. If she wins it early, the night will be over."

"From your nice lips to God's ears."

She turned a deeper shade of pink. My heart picked up as I looked away.

"One of you play piano?" I asked.

Tucked in a corner was a sleek black baby grand piano. Lisa shook her head.

"It's decorative."

An *$80,000* decoration.

I sauntered over to the bench, sat, and dragged my fingers across the keys. I shut my eyes to assist with recall and launched into "Ode to Joy." I struck ivory with increasing fervor, bobbing my head to the melody. My fingers glided with ease. My breath came in short. I was floating back, back, back—away from there, somewhere familiar, back to the place where I was young. Lonely and longing for attention. Before romantic touch. Before you realized the possibilities of life, of something other than the family forced on you by fate. Before you knew you could choose your own family. Choose love. Before you knew how it felt—once chosen—to lose that, too.

Oh, Katie. I hadn't thought of that name in these city limits.

I ended my song abruptly. I whirled around.

Lisa was on the edge of her seat.

"You're teary-eyed," she said. "That was beautiful."

"I haven't played for fifteen years."

"And you still remember?"

"I don't let go of things easily."

Liz appeared from the kitchen, a bowl of pasta with red sauce in each of her hands. If she overheard the music—and she must have—she didn't mention it. She set the food down temporarily to get us drinks.

"Milk," I requested.

"With dinner? With pasta? Are you a sociopath?"

"Just Midwestern."

Once poured, she handed me the glasses to hold.

I had suspected she set the whole thing up for Lisa and me to get to know each other. She hadn't.

"Let's eat these in my room," she said.

I nodded slightly in Lisa's direction, before following Liz down a hallway and into her bedroom. Very little of her walls were left uncovered. There was no central color scheme. The décor looked like patchwork, and the room wasn't particularly neat. One wall was made up of just book shelves and rows of worn-out spines. She closed the door behind us. She set one of the bowls and a fork on her desk, before plopping down cross-legged on her bed and unceremoniously began digging in. No napkin. Steadying the bowl in her open palm.

I sat at the desk and began eating.

A little black cassette tape—like the ones she stashed at work—sat beside her desk lamp. Scrawled across the top in marker were the words "Burn after Playing." My eyes kept returning to it.

"This tastes great," I said. "You a big cook?"

"Only when I'm looking to impress."

"Well, *I* already find you impressive."

"Is that right?"

"The senator calls your personal cell. You get to listen in on calls where historic deals are being hashed out. It's remarkable, your proximity to power."

I felt special even holding her attention.

"Is that what you want, Cam? To be close to power?"

Of course. I wanted to be a nobody a whole hell of a lot closer to a somebody than the rest of the nobodies back home.

"I don't know what I want honestly," I said instead.

"You'll find your purpose here. You'll grow into it. We all do. The city has its way of revealing it to us with time."

"I don't know about that. Has Randy found his purpose?"

"Sure. He's a star that's burning out. What's it called? A supernova, I think. Not all purposes are noble."

"What's yours?"

"Oh, a girl's got to keep her secrets. I'll let you know once I fulfill it."

"You're enigmatic."

"Woman as an enigma. Common female trope."

"I'm sorry. Was that offensive?"

"Naw. Better than being called hysterical. A little mystery never killed anyone."

She looked like she was chewing on something other than food. A thought. A revelation.

"Long term, I'd like to open a used bookstore. You know, one of those quaint, cozy three-floor walk-ups in Eastern Market. Spiral staircase. Stacks of yellowed books to the ceiling. Organized chaos. A hideaway. A sanctuary. Not a very DC ambition, I know."

"Sounds...perfect."

Only she could have a dream so uniquely her and off the beaten path among the carbon-copy politicos. Nothing she did was usual.

There were picture frames on her desk. None of them featured Charlie.

"How long have you and Charlie been dating?"

"You sure you want to spend our time talking about Charles James?"

"Sure. You want us to be friends, right?"

"Not even a year."

"Is it serious?"

"'Serious.' I don't like that word. A eulogy is meant to be serious. A relationship is meant to be fun. It's 'solid.'"

"He certainly takes it seriously."

"What do you mean?"

"He warned me not to sleep with you. Actually, he just made me promise to tell him if we did."

She laughed.

"You know what they say, 'Never trust a man with two first names.' Pay him no mind. He was just trying to be alpha. If you and I had sex, I'd tell him myself."

"I don't understand."

"We can have sex with other people. We just have to tell each other about it afterward."

My mouth fell open. She laughed harder.

"Don't act so shocked," she said. "Do they not have these arrangements in Iowa?"

"You just seem so cool about it. I wouldn't have expected that."

"I don't think we're built for monogamy. I read some evolutionary biology shit about men spreading their seed for species survival and genetic diversity. I used to think it was just a bullshit theory written by men to excuse their bad behavior. But women do it, too. I saw it in my mom. And in myself, too. Ugh, a girl's worst nightmare: becoming her mother. I fucking *hate* my mom."

She was nervously twirling the same string of spaghetti with her fork.

"I hate my dad," I offered.

Her eyes snapped up. Her decadent smile spread across her face like the Cheshire Cat's. It was probably the first intimate thought I had volunteered, and she loved it.

"Are you just like him?"

I tried to answer, but I got choked up. I could only solemnly nod as our eyes locked in a piercing gaze.

"Not sure why Charlie felt the need to ward me off. I'm apparently not your type."

"Don't listen to the others. I don't have a type."

She set her empty bowl on the nightstand and crept up closer to me, teetering on the edge of her bed. She reached out and wiped sauce from the corner of my mouth with the meat of her thumb and slurped it up. It threw me off balance. Everything she did threw me off balance.

"Now let's talk about Lisa."

"You're really pushing that, huh?"

She shrugged.

"Can't be worse than those one-night flings with the girls Randy dredges up for you."

My face turned the color of the sauce.

"I wouldn't want to mess things up," I said. "With the group. With you. She was here first."

Lisa was *fine*. Just fine. She was no Liz.

"If it doesn't work out, I'll back you. But it won't end horribly. You're not an asshole."

"You don't know that."

"Oh, but I do, Cam. I *know* you. Trust me."

She swung her legs off the edge of her bed. Her shirt slid down her left shoulder, baring the blade.

"With how many men have you stepped out on Charlie?"

"We're back to that? Now you're being naughty, Cam."

I stared at my shoes.

"Just the one," she answered. "And who uses that expression anymore? '*Stepped out on*'? You're a geezer in a toned body."

"You compliment me a lot."

"Does that make you feel entitled to something?"

"Not entitled. Just confused."

"Good boy. Only an invitation is an invitation. It isn't cumulative. It's either there or it's not. Understand?"

"Copy that."

"You able to sit still in your confusion? Find peace in not resolving it?"

"I guess I don't have a choice."

She clicked her tongue against her teeth.

"It must be so hard for a man. Never quite sure from all the women in his orbit which do and don't want to fuck him."

I laughed. She didn't smile.

"You going to explain those scratches?" She was gesturing toward my bare forearms.

"Rough sex," I said, giddy, almost drunk off her frank talk. "But I suspect you already knew that."

"Randy likes to talk, but it isn't gossipy. He's just a golden retriever. Everything excites him."

"His uncle was none too happy."

"He never is. Watching him makes me sad. He's the narrator from *The Tell-Tale Heart*. Haunted soul, that one."

"You need a soul for that. He's a cold man. Heartless."

"I have nothing against the senator," she said, lying supine on the bed. "They both have demons they're exorcising in ways that clash. None of it is healthy."

My eyes swept back over to the tape and remained there.

"Does Whitehurst want to be president?" I asked.

"Don't they all?"

"Is 2 Bills in his way?"

"I'm sure he thinks so."

"Might one of his knives be reserved for him?"

I looked over at her. She had sat up, and her eyes had followed mine to the desk. She kept hers locked there.

When I left Liz's room, Lisa was still on the couch, curled up, eating ice cream, and watching TV. I walked past her at first but returned before reaching the front door.

"Would it be cool if I took you out sometime?"

It felt like something I was supposed to do. It wasn't manly to turn down the advances of a perfectly attractive woman. Standards were for women and gay men. Only eunuchs rejected easy sex. And there was nothing more important to a man than to prove something functional hung between his legs. It's why insurance companies will forever cover Viagra.

She straightened her posture. She set the carton down on the coffee table.

"On a date?"

"Yeah, on a date."

"Um, sure. That'd be cool."

I shot her a small smile, gave a slight nod, drove my hands into my pockets, and left.

ELECTION NIGHT

Lisa had her palms on her lap, pressing into her thighs, sweating onto her skirt.

"A tape? No one played a tape for me. I don't think I've even seen a cassette tape in real life. I'm only twenty-four."

She was stiff, glued to her seat and immobile. Even her eyes conserved their blinking, tearing up merely at the strain of holding them unnaturally open.

"Cam and I dated. I wouldn't say he was particularly into me. He was obsessed with someone else. Or maybe it was just his manner. He was either awfully guarded or plain boring. He once told me, 'You want me to peel back my layers, but you'd be disappointed if after all that work, you find nothing there. Just emptiness.' It kind of freaked me out. But he was always timid. He would never hurt anyone. Not *intentionally* anyway."

Her emotionless eyes began to shake.

"Was I in charge of the guest list? Sure. But I was always going to let my friends in: on or off the list. It was the one perk of helping set up the viewing party. Oh, you mean the senators? Was there one the boss didn't invite? Yes, there was one. How did that name end up on there anyway? Oh, that I can't quite remember."

05

OLD BOYS' CLUB

On the morning the nominee was revealed, I diverted from my normal course from the bus stop, choosing a longer route that sent me by a home with an elaborate, blooming garden out front. I had seen it on trips to Randy's house. I knelt down on the sidewalk, scuffing the knee of my light-colored trousers, and clipped off a handful of white lilies. I stuffed the flowers inside my jacket.

I arrived late to work. The energy within the building was electric: the chatter was louder, the rushing about speedier, and the hallways busier and disorderly. Half of these staffers were Republicans and yet—despite it being a monumental occasion for the opposing party—fight-or-flight instilled in them a commensurate spike in adrenaline. No one was funereal. This is what we came here for.

The intern cubicle was uncharacteristically empty. I grew restless after half an hour. The lilies were flattening up against my chest, crushed by the skin and bone draping my heart. They would not make it to the end of the day. I texted Lisa, the only one of the gang who reliably responded to me with punctuality. She did again, offering to rescue me from the monotony.

She was waiting for me outside the doors to her office—a short walk and a floor up from mine. She swung open the glass doors, beside the customary wall plaque reading, "Senator Sandra Grunwald-Santos:

Florida." Without greeting, I pulled the flowers out and handed them to her. Her brown eyes lit up.

"I saw these on my walk to work and thought of you."

It was what Good Guys do.

It was what my grandpa did, the original Good Guy. Every Sunday morning, before she woke, my grandpa brought my grandma white flowers.

His motivation was pure love. Mine was pure virtue-signaling.

"That's sweet. Thank you."

Lisa leaned in and planted a kiss on my cheek. My hand briefly grazed the small of her back.

"We'll get to that. For now, it's Armageddon. Come watch the world burn with me in the Fishbowl."

She led me inside, past the lobby and to a center room surrounded by glass walls and filled with three giant flat-screen televisions set to the same famously right-wing cable news channel. She sat me in an office chair in the corner, invisible and unacknowledged by a press operation of four in full chaotic tilt. She emptied out a mug holding pens, filled it with water, and placed the clipped flowers inside.

A fast-talking Democratic strategist on-screen was spinning the nominee's rollout, eyes intermittently dropping down to the out-of-frame talking points he desperately needed for his full-throated embrace of a person he knew nothing about.

"President Stevenson has chosen in Judge Frederick Wright a man of unimpeachable accomplishment. He has served on the prestigious DC Circuit of Appeals since the last Democratic administration. He is known for his even-keeled temperament befitting the highest court in the land. Not since Thurgood Marshall has an appointment generated so much buzz."

"But, Chuck, does he have the votes from the progressive wing of your party who had pinned their hopes on a more liberal candidate? This was a

surprise pick that contradicted all of our reporting that Loughlin was a lock
as recently as last night."

"The progressive wing of the party will fall in line because of the stakes.
We are a notoriously undisciplined party, but now just isn't the time for
interfamily squabbles. The first 'yea' vote for Judge Wright has already
come forward—and it's a Republican! We have a real shot at a bipartisan
confirmation that won't distract the country from rejecting the nativist,
racist, and corporatist agenda of Governor Chad Thornton and giving Vice
President Jones the promotion she deserves."

I turned my attention away from the segment and to my surroundings. The communications director, Reina, who appeared to be in her
late thirties—white, but with accented speech that made me think she
was Hispanic—vacillated between fielding phone calls and editing a
document on a word processor.

She was speaking so brusquely to the person on the other line that it
struck me only belatedly that she was speaking to the senator.

"You can't appear tepid...He's a former prosecutor, just like you...
You can't say that. Not in enemy territory....You're voting for him anyway. What's the point?"

Reina slammed the receiver down when she was done.

"SGS is on in thirty minutes," she said. "We need to send the talking
points to the recording studio *now*."

The only man—race also white, wearing a boot on his injured left
foot—swiveled to face her in his chair.

"Which one of the dozen versions do we send?"

"Find the least committal—you know, the one that says a lot but
nothing at all—and send that one. I'm out."

"What do you mean you're out?" Lisa asked.

"I'm not staffing her. My kid's home sick from school, and I haven't
slept. So I'm leaving. SGS needs a steady hand. She needs someone still
afraid of her. She needs a 'yes' man. And I don't do that."

"I'm disabled. I literally can't keep up with her," the man said.

"Then a 'yes' *woman* will do. Lisa, you're up."

Reina pointed to the fourth staffer—also white—a female as animate as the plants adorning the room, so almost certainly an intern.

"You'll stay behind by the phone to make last-minute changes to the text, and there *will* be changes; there always are."

"Who will roll the senator's briefcase? It's heavy and unwieldy, and you'll need your hands free, Lis," the man said.

"Cam can do it," Lisa said, pointing at me.

It appeared to be the first time anyone had genuinely taken notice of me.

"He's an intern out of the committee. Majority staff."

"Works for me. Off you go. *Now!*"

On our way out, a tall, lean black man in his early forties stopped Reina by the elbow. He had a bouquet of flowers in one hand and a bottle of champagne in the other.

"Mr. Santos," she said breathlessly to her boss's husband.

"Morning, Reina. Do you know where Sandy might be? She isn't picking up her phone."

She led him in the opposite direction from where Lisa and I were heading. On the way, Lisa became increasingly nervous, obvious from her rigid walk and vacant eyes, barely acknowledging me at her side. It freaked me out.

"This is a big fucking deal. I must stay attentive. I must stay disciplined," she said to herself.

She didn't sound human. I reached out and massaged her hand for a beat. It was sweaty.

We waited for the senator right off the subway, at the bottom of the escalators leading up to the Capitol. When Senator Grunwald-Santos appeared—looking young and smaller than she did on TV—it was hard to place her as a member, but for the two male staffers—also white—trailing her and the perfectly pressed turquoise skirt suit she wore that commanded attention.

It was a relay race. The elder staffer was buzzing in her ear, and then we relieved him as Lisa picked up the counsel seamlessly, handing the senator a printout of the talking points and a red marker, indicating to me that I should sub in for the younger staffer pulling an overstuffed black rolling bag behind him. He gave me a look I couldn't quite read, abandoned the bag noisily, and vanished like his counterpart.

I rushed to catch up to the women, who had already begun their hurried march to the recording studio. Its lobby was a heavily carpeted, softly lit room of warm color that led to a dark, narrow hallway with soundproof glass booths to our right, featuring senators seated in front of banal, single-tone backdrops.

The senator bloodied the pages handed to her in red marker in seconds.

"Reina thinks I'm drawing unwanted attention to myself. What do you think?" Grunwald-Santos asked, walking, reading, editing, and conversing all at the same time.

Lisa paused before speaking.

"I think you should stand by your convictions. Why else come to Congress if not to follow your conscience?"

The senator nodded slowly.

"I like that," she said. "Load these up to the teleprompter. We're on in how long?"

"Minutes, Senator."

Grunwald-Santos walked into a booth. As technicians miked the senator up, Lisa was on the phone with the intern, speedily conveying the last-minute edits in an adjacent control room. I grabbed a seat in the darkness. The senator checked her teeth in the television screen displaying her image, and the news crew across town was patched through to conduct a sound check. The edited script was sent and loaded just seconds before the intro music played and the anchor introduced her guest.

"Just weeks before America votes, the outgoing president seeks to install a new chief justice, Judge Frederick Wright, in an abbreviated and some say rushed Senate confirmation process. Joining us live is Senator Sandy Grunwald-Santos, a Democrat on the Judiciary Committee in her freshman term and member of the Gang of Six, an informal, bipartisan group of power brokers serving on that committee. Senator, welcome to 'Stay Right, America!'"

I loved how sacrosanct it is to stay on the right on DC escalators if you're content being stuck in one place. You walk on the left if you want to move forward. But the hosts and their conservative producers didn't seem to get that. Neither did the scores of tourists getting inevitably barked at for flouting the convention every day.

"Thanks for having me. This is a historic day. Weeks before I believe this country will elect its first black woman president, the administration has nominated a highly qualified and undoubtedly brilliant man to the Supreme Court. I am thrilled that my young black son can see himself reflected at the highest levels of the American government. Judge Wright's story—growing up working class and on food stamps in Inglewood and now serving with distinction on the federal bench—is the American Dream. But this is a lifetime appointment. We were elected to advise and consent, and I am taking that responsibility seriously. I am open-minded and excited about Judge Wright's nomination, but I am duty-bound to scrutinize his opinions—including his Title IX jurisprudence around sexual assault on campuses—that do cause me some concern. I look forward to meeting with Judge Wright and having my concerns allayed so we can proceed with his momentous nomination and confirm the president's pick."

"How do you have a deliberate process when the president is ramming this nomination through?"

"Your viewers remember the last Republican president nominated and got confirmed an associate justice on a much tighter schedule—"

"—But this is for chief justice. Shouldn't the American people have a say first?"

"They did have a say: when they elected President Stevenson to a full term."

"Your Republican colleague, Senator Scott Denton, announced his support for your party's nominee. Why not follow suit?"

"Senator Denton can speak for himself, but it would not have felt right or respectful to this process to have made up my mind before it has even begun."

"Are you worried that the concerns you have raised from the left will be seen as disloyal from members of your own party?"

"Firstly, I don't see the protection of our kids on college campuses as a left or right issue. Secondly, why else come to Congress if not to follow your conscience?"

Grunwald-Santos was beaming, but as soon as the bright lights dimmed over her face, she dropped the saccharine mask. She unhooked her own microphone and darted off. Lisa gesticulated wildly at me before leaping out of the control room in hot pursuit. I reached them in mid-stride.

"Cancel my ten," she said. I glanced at my phone. It was twenty till eleven. "I need to call Bill, Dale, and Scott. Tell their staffs it's an emergency. I'm sure they'll be eager to chat with me after that interview. You know how to set up a video conference for me?"

"Yes, Senator."

"Good. I need to see their faces when they lie to me. Was anyone in the office looking for me before this?"

Lisa began shaking her head, but my synapses fired off before I noticed it.

"Your husband," I blurted out.

The senator came to an abrupt halt. She was peering down at her feet.

"What's he doing in town?"

Lisa's eyes smoldered at me. I looked away from their heat.

"He had flowers with him."

The senator snapped her eyes up at me. My face burned.

"Oh."

Her stare softened.

"Thank you. You work for me?"

"No, ma'am. I intern for Chairman Williams."

"I'm quite fond of Bill. He's a good man to work for."

She picked up her stride without warning. We followed her back to her Hart Building office. As we made our way past staff offices and cubicles, a man with grays in his hair—race also white—joined our ranks, likely the chief of staff.

"I'm taking some work calls for the next hour. Do not disturb," she warned him.

"But who's staffing you?"

"Lisa will do it. I don't need anyone else for this."

She reached the door to her personal office, waving in an initially paralyzed Lisa. I stopped myself outside the doorframe alongside the chief of staff, setting the rolling bag upright.

"You, too. Get in here," the senator told me.

I tripped briefly over my feet but made my clumsy way in. The senator shut the door behind us three.

The oblong office was sprawling, with a single mahogany desk the very width of the room anchoring one end, a vast swath of carpet and nothing else in the middle, and several chairs, a round table, and a giant TV screen at the other end. I rolled her bag up to her desk and slunk away to a seat in the corner farthest from her.

Lisa fluttered about, setting up the senator's computer and making calls. The senator gazed upon a vase of fresh flowers sitting at the center of her desk beside a sealed bottle of Prosecco. She read the accompanying card aloud.

"'Go make history. Yours, Dom.'"

I looked at a painting of four historical figures strategizing—one of them Lincoln, none of them women—hanging off the wall behind her desk.

"Lincoln was drawn posthumously, after his assassination," Grunwald-Santos said. "I love Lincoln. But then again, who doesn't?"

She approached me with a notepad and pen in hand.

"Take note of everything Chairman Williams says and only him, will you? They'll be the only things I'll know to be true."

It didn't take long before four squares appeared on the screen, three of them populated by men—Senators Williams, Whitehurst, and Denton—and the one woman, Senator Grunwald-Santos. Lisa joined me on the far side.

"Gentlemen, thank you for taking my call on such short notice."

"You've had a busy morning, Sandy," Denton said.

"You watched the interview?" she asked.

"My staff briefed me about it. Something about announcing a vote for confirmation this early being *disrespectful* to the process."

"I was talking about myself, Scott. And it isn't every day that a Republican is first in line to support a Democratic nominee. You trying to sink his nomination?"

"Not at all. Just following my *conscience*."

"It's one thing to say you're an open vote or that you have questions in need of answers, Sandy," Whitehurst said. "It's another matter entirely for you to do it on the Republican propaganda channel."

"I can't afford to preach only to the choir," she said.

"You aren't winning any center-right folk with your sexual assault bullshit," Denton said. "You're positioning yourself for a future Democratic presidential primary. Get off your soap box, hon."

"Children, enough fighting," Williams said. "Sandy won't do the nominee any harm. She'll vote for him in the end and win plaudits from progressives for pushing him left. No harm. No foul."

"Bill, I must ask, did we push for Loughlin as planned?" she asked.

"Dale made the call. You managed to fuck that up, son?"

The question lingered without answer. Whitehurst was so still, it appeared as if his connection had frozen.

"I guess I did," he said finally. "We're just senators, after all. We can't tell the president what to do. Especially when he knows we'd vote for any nominee he throws at us anyway. It's our own damn party."

"But it isn't Scott's. I *am* curious about your hair-trigger endorsement this morning," Williams said. "I don't get it. What could you possibly get from announcing a 'yea' vote this early?"

Denton was chewing deep into his lip.

"I wanted to be on the right side of history," he said.

"Now *you* get off it, Scott," she said. "You're a white supremacist, for fuck's sake."

"A *gay* white supremacist?" Williams asked, scrunching his wrinkled face.

"I'm not gay, Bill," Denton snapped.

"You're not?" Williams asked. "I didn't know that, Scott. What *are* you then?"

"We're off topic," Whitehurst said. "Scott made our jobs easier. He stuck his neck out for us, and we should be grateful. Sandy made our jobs harder. Is it *you*, in fact, who is trying to sink this nomination?"

"That DC Circuit dissent was atrocious, misogynistic trash," she said. "You all know how much the issue means to me. Is that why you brought it up to the press, Scott? To mess with me?"

"Not everything's about you, Senator Nobody," Denton said. "No one even knows who the hell you are."

"But you're voting for him, right, Sandy?" Williams asked.

It was her turn to take her time.

"I haven't made up my mind."

The men shifted their bodies in their seats visibly on-screen.

Williams pouted his lips and let them noisily flap like a pair of purplish rubber bands. He swept his trembling hand through the wisps of whatever hair still sparsely sprouted from his scalp. He threaded his fingers over his distended belly. He turned his eyes directly into the camera, black pupils swallowing his irises so they appeared to be giant saucers of muck.

"Now that's going to be a problem, little lady," he said.

"Bill…" she began.

"I like you, sweetheart, but you *will* pay your dues. I haven't built a forty-year career here—and amassed the influence that I have—just to have a newbie tear it all down. Do not get too big for your britches, and certainly not over a softball, fringe issue like women's lib—not when there are real, kitchen-table matters at play—or I will relieve you from the committee. There are plenty of others—just as telegenic, just as *pretty*—who are eager to take your place and fall in line. Am I clear, young lady?"

My chest ached from holding in my breath. Men were men were men—even the progressive ones. No title could undo what centuries of conditioning had wrought. Lisa was pallid, looking anywhere but at her boss. The senator looked small in her seat, shrinking into it. Her eyes were glossy, and she pulled her blanched lips into two straight, parallel lines.

"Crystal," she said.

"Trust us, Sandy. We know best."

The call ended mutedly. The senator didn't say anything at first. Lisa and I didn't dare move.

Dear #CapHillSoWhite:
I hate the way my boss speaks to others. In public,
he's all charm. But put him in front of people who
can't do much for his career—like us, his foot-rest

servants—and he's the nastiest soul I've ever come across.

The senator let out a sigh and walked over to me, extending her palm to accept my scribbled notes. I had censored out the belittling parts. She appeared to notice and like that, smiling to herself as she read.

"This is impressively accurate," she said. "You caught every word. How did you do that?"

"I've been told I've got a good ear. Strong echoic memory, they call it."

"What's your name?"

"Cam."

"Well, Cam, if Bill doesn't hire you after your internship, you should apply here."

"Thank you."

"You, too, Lisa—you did great today. What's your title with us again?"

"Press assistant."

"You deserve a promotion. How'd you like to be deputy press secretary? It means a lot more responsibility. A lot more work. You up for it?"

"Definitely, yes."

"Let's start with preparing for my one-on-one meeting with Wright. Put together a dossier, including every press mention of him, down to his birth announcement if we can find it. And I'd like you to take over planning the Election Night victory party from Reina. She's not in the best of spirits lately. Invite all of your friends. We should start sending out invitations to the senators and the press soon. Get it on their calendars."

She walked back to her desk, collected a packet of stapled papers, and picked up the champagne. She shoved the bottle into Lisa's hands.

"Take this. Celebrate your new title. And here's the guest list for the party. But you can scratch him off," she said, pointing to the sheet for Lisa to see. I didn't catch the name. "He's a snake in hiding. Do you know what farmers do to snakes hiding in their sugarcane fields before harvest?"

Lisa shook her head.

"They burn them alive."

After we left, Lisa said something about meeting up later. I waited in my cubicle as twilight darkened the sky, but I received a text message from her calling it off soon thereafter. She had skipped lunch and planned on working into the night.

I ordered a pizza to the southern entrance of the Hart Building and headed up to Lisa's office. It was empty but for her, typing away at a computer in the Fishbowl. She jumped and whirled around at the sound of my voice.

"Figured I'd bring the date to you. You really should eat."

Courting a girl was a competitive sport. You don't take "no" for an answer. At least not the first "no"? Right? I think.

She relented, nodding and clearing papers so I could set down the greasy box. We dug in with our hands. She was ravenous, tearing into a slice and scarfing it down without concern for how it looked or how messy her hands got. I liked that.

I reached over to collect the bottle of champagne sitting on her desk.

"Shall we pop this sucker open? Celebrate your promotion?"

"Sure, but it isn't much of a promotion. I spoke with my chief of staff. No raise. Just an excuse to load me up with more work."

The cork shot off with a bang. The champagne bubbled out and over, spraying Lisa in the face. I apologized.

"It's only the first date, Cam. Don't you think it's a little early for that?"

I gave her a crooked smile and cocked my head to the side.

"Was that a come joke?"

"I'm not a prude. Just a woman of few words. You'll see."

I poured us champagne into two plastic cups and slugged down half of mine in a sip.

"That call was dramatic AF," I said.

"She's tough. She can handle it."

"You admire her?"

"She's what I'd like to become. This promotion brings me one step closer. She was a big-time prosecutor in Miami. Saw her on TV handling high-profile murder cases. I volunteered for her campaign for Senate right after she announced. My abuela loved her for being a strong woman. She voted Democrat for the first time just for her. I drove her to the voting booth."

"Abuela?"

"That means 'grandma' in Spanish. I'm half-Hispanic. Cuban, actually—a Jew-ban, I like to say. I don't mention it much because I look plain white, and I don't want people to think I'm taking advantage. You know, just checking a box or something. That probably doesn't make much sense to you."

"No, I understand," I said. "You close with your abuela?"

"It's cute when you say it like a gringo," she said. "Yes, she practically raised me. Mom wasn't mentally or emotionally present. Dad was working at his law firm all day and night. So it was just she and I in her one-room efficiency in Hialeah. She's a big Republican. Aversion to socialism and all that—even as she collects her Social Security checks without a hint of irony. But voting for the senator gave us a special bonding moment. I'm forever grateful to SGS for that."

"Grandparents are cool," I said. "Mine would just sit and hold hands at the dining room table in the morning. Not saying a word. Just sit and beam and bask in the sunlight, totally in love. Like out of a book or something."

"What about your parents? I don't hear you talk much about them."

I often watched my grandparents in awe, but my mother did not. She would stare from the kitchen and not exactly scowl, but the ends of her tiny mouth were an impossibly straight line, dipping neither down nor up. Her eyes were brimming: full of weariness, and resentment, and self-pity. My dad had never shown her such admiration, and she took it out on everyone else, including me.

At least Dad was away enough that I could imagine he was a better man than he ended up being. I lapped up his short-lived stints of fatherhood like a love-starved puppy. I became just another person rejecting Mom, who had stayed, for the man who had turned her into a shell of a person in the first place. That is, until I stumbled upon the skeleton in my dad's closet and was faced with the depths of his depravity.

"Oh, you know, just traditional Anglo-Saxon Protestant emotional repression," I finally said. "Nothing special."

I finished my cup and poured myself another.

I draped her hand with mine.

"Lis, I like you."

It's what I wanted to feel. It's what I knew she wanted to hear.

She wasn't as elated as I figured she would be.

"I didn't think that was the case."

"Why not?"

"I thought you were maybe too into someone else."

Was I that easy to read? The skin of my neck became itchy. I swallowed what was left in my cup in a gulp.

"Oh?"

"Well, you did have a night out on the town with Randy."

"That man has no discretion, does he? Did he tell everybody about that? I'm not like Randy."

"I know that. Don't listen to me. I just don't handle compliments well. They're hard for me to believe. I like you, too."

My heart thrummed in my chest. I felt blood rushing below my belt.

I was swept up in the moment. I leaned in for a kiss, and she recipro-cated. She tasted of pizza, but it was nice, long, and sweet. When she reached for the back of my head, clutching my hair, and her tongue began to dart into my mouth more aggressively, I pulled back and planted a conclusory peck on her lips.

The dreamy look in her eye produced a veiled panic in me. She was falling, too hard, too fast.

"I liked that," I said, despite my ambivalence. It's what they would say in the movies.

"Me, too."

A week later, I received a morning text from Charlie inviting me to lift weights with him after work. It was the first message we had ever exchanged privately, just us two. Despite myself, I got excited. He inspired envy in me: I resented him, I wanted to be him, and I wanted to be liked by him. I packed a change of clothes in a bag and, that eve-ning, waited for him outside the doors to the Senate staff gym.

He acknowledged me with a head nod but nothing more. I followed him inside.

For half an hour, we didn't say much to each other. He would grunt and launch into an exercise using free weights. While he rested, I picked up his same pair of weights and completed a set. In between heavy breathing and swilling water, I read on his sweaty face begrudg-ing respect and surprise that I was able to match his numbers. It was the primitive way of the world to prove yourself at physical feats before opening up on a deeper level. It was how I showed him I was strong enough to be trusted.

After a strenuous set that left me red-faced, huffing, and hunched over, hands resting on my knees, he finally addressed me in a full sentence.

"I'm glad you're dating Lisa."

I chuckled. A shackled-up man was a nonthreatening man.

"It's early but going well."

He doubled over, touching his toes and halving his giant body. I used the moment to be courageous.

"How are you and Liz?"

By the time he grew back to his usual height, he was smirking.

"Consistent. She has her periods when she's away, when she's distant. But when she's present, she's all in: affectionate, attentive, giving—almost too much. As if she's making up for the gaps in her love. She's like a drug, intoxicating and addictive, and I'm hooked, as much during the high as during the withdrawal."

"That was poetry."

"I was an English major."

"Why not pull her closer to you then? She told me about your open arrangement. Commitment has a way of placating unsure girls."

"I'm no good at that. I fail at being faithful, and I don't like failing at anything."

"But it must be hard sharing her. I take it you're no good at that, either."

He shrugged.

"It's all theoretical anyway. She hasn't tried it out yet."

I wrinkled my forehead.

"Females are that way," he continued. "Loyal to a fault."

I winced. At a gut level, I knew what he said was off-putting, but I was more upset that he got to talk that way, unreproached, and every word from white men was put under a microscope. His people liked to refer to women that way: *females*. It sounded clinical, almost alien, like a foreign species—not human. The thought metastasized into speech before my filter caught it.

"You all like to use that word: 'females.'"

"We all?"

His voice had dropped an octave.

"Football players."

His smile was impeccably white and wide.

"You know, as a kid, I once told a white friend of mine I had a thing for blondes. I remember seeing him rack his brain, like it didn't compute, until he finally said, 'So, like RuPaul?' He was being earnest. He just couldn't imagine me dating outside my race. I still think about that a lot. I wonder if lots of people are that way. And I feel guilty for dating white women."

"Why's that?"

"My community is skeptical of it. Especially black women. It feels like rejection. Maybe indicative of some self-loathing. White men aren't wife-ing up black women at the same rate. Leaves them with a smaller pool of suitors. It's no fun when your dating is made political."

"I'm sorry. That's shit. No one should get a say in other people's relationships. I dated a religious girl once. Pastor's daughter, in fact. Felt like the whole congregation, Jesus, and the saints were in bed with us."

Charlie laughed loudly, turning heads.

"You can be funny. Who knew?"

Just then, images of Judge Wright appeared on the multiple screens hanging from the gym ceilings.

"You proud of the Wright nomination?" I asked.

"Brother's a house Negro. As palatable to the whites as possible. But in his rearview mirror is the motherfucking law, like the rest of us."

"Isn't that a Jay-Z line?"

"Forgot. You're a hip-hop buff," he said, rolling his eyes. "Anyway, he's good on due process rights for men accused of terrible things on college campuses. So I'm a fan."

"You told Denton that issue was important to you."

He was looking past me.

"Did something like that happen to you at school, Charlie?"

I wanted to hear him talk about it: the injustice, the unfair treatment. I wanted him to know a view like that was safe with me.

He just lifted a thick finger, gesturing behind me.

I turned to find a middle-aged man within feet of me. Dressed down in a baggy T-shirt and shorts above his hairy knees, he was unrecognizable at first. My nervous system—in the way my pulse quickened, skin tingled, and little hairs lifted—nonetheless detected alarm, even as my mind remained foggy.

"Young man, do you mind spotting me?"

He asked but he must have been unaccustomed to noes, because he didn't wait for an answer. He stalked off and waved me over.

I stalled but eventually unglued my feet from the floor.

Senator Whitehurst pulled himself under the bar as I stood behind him, and pumped himself up, squeezing his eyes shut and jiggling his legs before lifting the bar. He heaved and spat at every rep, sending spittle flying out of him.

At the end of his set, as his arms grew unsteady above him, threatening to buckle, I wrapped my hands around the bar and helped lift it.

But my eyes were on his bobbing Adam's apple; they were on his windpipe.

If I just let go, the weight would crush it. It would choke him. The thought made me smile.

By the end of the third and final set, his elbows locked. The bar rolled from his palms to his fingers, threatening to fall down on his neck. I didn't help right away. My arms stayed pinned to my sides.

His eyes were teary. So were mine.

He let out a pitiful gasp, like air escaping a tire through a dime-size hole. Finally, I swooped down, collected the bar, and set it on the rack with a clang and rattle. I cursed under my breath.

He didn't wipe off the equipment before walking off. He just threw a bill—a *tip*—onto the bench. It was five dollars. It was a Lincoln. I left it there. Whoever cleaned up after him could have it.

ELECTION NIGHT

Chuy rapped their ringed fingers on the table, emitting a cacophony of sound that reverberated in the small, vacuous room.

"Sorry. I'll stop that."

They sat on their hands instead.

"Please don't call me Jesús. Only my niñera ever called me that. She was hardcore Catholic. I go by Chuy."

Chuy bit into their lip, hard enough to taste copper.

"You found *what* in my home? Voodoo dolls? They're not dolls. They're just art. It's cultural. Nothing sinister. No, one isn't missing. How did you get in anyway? Don't you need a warrant for that?"

They sat up in their chair, revived.

"Cam's precious. He always treated me with respect. That isn't usual for a nonbinary person like me. Or from a cis-masc person like him. I'm mostly male presenting, so people don't take my gender identity seriously. Not even close friends. Cam always did. He made me feel seen. I'd defend him to the ends of the earth. I'd kill for him. That's…a poor choice of words. I hear it now."

Their shoulders sagged.

"I came here on a plane, Officer. Not by boat. I'm a naturalized citizen. That can't be taken away from me, can it?"

06

BLOOD OATH

I often walked the halls of Congress without purpose. There wasn't always something to do. I had to get my steps in somehow. And it was good for people watching. There was a rhythm, a harmony in the bustle. The tourists were a slow stream, gawking at the minutiae. Lots of old-timey cameras strapped around necks. Lots of socks in sandals. Lots of Asians. The staffers were river currents, twisting and bending in between mountains of shoulders. Lots of senior-junior pairs, children being led by slightly older children, tethered by fast-slung conversation like out of an Aaron Sorkin screenplay. At times, I got caught up in the buzz and swelled with self-importance, but it all felt too performative. Like we were putting on a show but really only for ourselves: a self-contained ecosystem that ran off ego.

Every now and again—like a shooting geyser disrupting the flow—there was a member sighting.

I was riding the escalator down when a voice boomed behind me. "Move!"

I whipped around. Senator Kelley was a tall white woman with short-cut spiky black hair and light-colored eyes. The tautness of her fair, blemish-free skin belied her advanced age. She was striking, handsome even. Her arms were spread like Moses before the Red Sea. Her jarring image and growled demand sent me sputtering. I tried leaning into the men riding beside me, before realizing it didn't open up enough space, so I bounded down the steps gracelessly instead.

At the bottom, Kelley charged past me, leading two aides—a white man and Chuy—down a corridor. Chuy nodded at me with contrition in their eyes and moved on. I followed them out of curiosity and boredom, maintaining a discreet distance still within earshot.

Kelley had a glass award in one hand, some trinket no doubt gifted to her by a fawning special interest group at an event, and papers in the other. She flipped Chuy around, pressed the papers against their back as a makeshift desk, and noisily dragged the pen across the page.

"This line is *stupid*," she spat out.

Then, softer: "It's a serious letter. Can't be too saccharine. I'm told our phones are ringing off the hook about the Wright nomination: eighty-five percent in favor, but a vocal minority of women expressing hesitance. Let's tone all of this drama down. And you keep forgetting the Oxford comma. Didn't they teach you that in school?"

She handed them the papers and walked on.

The other man—holding her giant purse—handed her a phone.

"It's Senator Grunwald-Santos," he said.

She snatched the phone from his hands.

"Sandy! To what do I owe the pleasure?" She half turned to Chuy, miming the placement of a finger down her throat and rolling her eyes clean into their sockets, only whites showing. The trio hopped onto a subway train. I stopped in my tracks, pausing. When the bells chimed, presaging the doors shutting, I made my choice and surged forward and inside. The wind of the whipping doors swept through my hair, and my foot got caught in between. I tore my foot out from their jaws and stumbled backward onto the bench opposite the senator's.

The three of them watched me, wide-eyed. I looked away until I felt their glares subside.

"Respectfully, sweetie, this isn't my battle...I can't do that...I'm his home-state senator. It would embarrass him...Don't take the boys so seriously. It isn't worth blowing up our allegiances…It's futile. The seat is his. Don't make waves."

She tossed the phone into her bag. The shriek that lurched from her yawning mouth, like an anaconda unhinging its jaw, raised the hair on the back of my neck.

"What does my having a vagina have anything to do with it?" she barked at no one. Her aides were looking everywhere but at her. Apparently, tantrums were to be left unacknowledged. "She tried to pull that girl-power bullshit on me. Yet when she wants something from the boys, she bats her eyelashes and bakes her cakes and turns up the charm to an eleven. When it doesn't work, she cries sexism, and tries to rope me into political suicide. No, thank you. You can jump off that cliff all your own. I'm no lemming."

My face felt flush.

The doors swung open at the Russell Office Building. Kelley leapt up and out. Her aides followed.

"Condescending bitch!" she shouted, neck red, veins bulging, and spit collecting at the corners of her mouth. She chucked the award at Chuy's body. Their arm shot out, but it—and the whole right side of their body—went unnaturally limp as the award hit the pavement and shattered. Chuy fell to the ground, landing with a thud among shards of broken glass. I jumped out of the train and knelt down to their side.

A ring of bystanders formed. Kelley shoved shoulders aside to peer down at us.

"You all right," she said. More of a directive than a question. Willing the fact into existence.

"Yes, I just slipped," Chuy said. "I'm fine."

"Judge Wright is waiting on me," she whined. "I have to take Tom with me. But go see the attending physician. And just leave the glass there."

She and her purse carrier deserted them.

Dear #CapHillSoWhite:
my boss is hemorrhaging staffers left and right, the
senior ones don't make it past three months. the
tantrums, long hours, and low pay scare all the real
adults away. (one woman is literally losing her hair!) but
he makes us all sign NDAs, so no one is fairly warned
coming in. at this rate, i'll become chief of staff by 25,
lmao.

The crook of Chuy's hand was sliced open. I unknotted my tie from my neck and wrapped it tightly around their wound. Blood soaked through the paisley pattern.

"It's a hideous tie anyway," they said. We laughed.

"Are you able to walk?"

"Why wouldn't I?"

They said it with a sarcastic laugh, but there was something deeper. We locked eyes. Theirs were pained. It wasn't from the cut.

"Because you didn't slip," I said. "I watched your arm and leg give out. You don't have to tell me why. But I want to help you get to a doctor if I can."

"I'm not paralyzed, but my right side's numb. It's tingling bad."

"Then lean on me, and I'll get you out of here."

"You sure? I can hardly put any weight on it."

"I'm stronger than I look."

I helped them up, flung their arm around my shoulders, and walked them to First Aid.

The doctor saw Chuy immediately. She reviewed their file and then looked at me.

"I'm going to be asking questions about your condition. Would you like him to wait outside?"

"No, I think I'd like my friend to stay," Chuy said.

Chuy told her this was a flare-up. That they hadn't had one in over a month. That they were regularly taking their medication. She asked if Chuy was experiencing an uptick in stress. They answered with the saddest pair of brown eyes I had ever seen on a person.

She offered Chuy a steroid injection. The needle was horrifyingly long. I grabbed their uninjured hand and held it while Chuy was doubled over. They just stared at my hand, surprised, but they did not let go. The doctor cleaned the gash, surgically glued together the skin, and dressed it. Chuy was able to walk on their own in minutes. They were medically cleared and released in under an hour. I accompanied them back to their office.

"I have MS," Chuy said on the way.

"Will you be OK?"

"Well, I lied to her. I've been skipping some of my drugs. It's stupid and vain, but they make me lose my hair. I've been trying out some alternative treatments like aquatic therapy. I'm such a fucking idiot."

"No, you're not. I think you're brave. All of that was scary to me, and you handled it like a man. Oh, I'm so sorry—like a champ, I meant."

I felt him looking deeply at me as we walked side by side.

"Is someone close to you queer, Cam? I'm impressed by how much you know."

"I don't need to know someone to be knowledgeable."

"I guess I just figured you had a gay little brother or something— some sort of connection, something that makes you relate."

"I also don't need to be related to someone to relate."

A pool reporter and cameraman were outside the doors labeled "Senator Abigail Kelley: California," filming the senator and Judge Wright standing awkwardly shoulder to shoulder. Judge Wright was a man of average height and deep brown skin with a thin layer of closely shaved white hair dusting his scalp, a dimple cleaving his chin, and his gut extending past his belt buckle. We joined her staffers and his handlers comingling behind the lens just as he was departing, taking the media crew with him. Kelley made a beeline to Chuy. She squeezed their shoulder blade.

"How are you feeling, sweetie?"

I didn't recognize the voice as hers. It was syrupy and simpering.

"I feel fine. They patched me up."

They lifted their gauzed right hand.

"I'm sorry you missed the meeting with Judge Wright. I know you were excited to sit in with Tom."

"I was. But that's OK. He'll give me the rundown. I'll read his notes. I'll draft a new template letter."

"Honey, no. Go home. Take the rest of the day off. Recover."

"But won't you need help preparing for the confirmation hearing?"

"Someone else will pick up the slack. You shouldn't be working—not in your *vulnerable* condition."

They nodded.

"We're good, aren't we, Chuy?"

"Yes, Senator."

"I really do have butterfingers. It just completely slipped out of my hand. A total mindless accident, right?"

"Yes, Senator."

"Good. Feel better, sugar."

She strode off. Chuy watched the spot she had occupied—now just empty air—for several seconds.

"That was nice of her," I said.

"She's like an abusive boyfriend. It's always sweetness and love and compliments after a bout of mistreatment. It's how you stay hooked. You endure the beating for the high her affection gives you afterward."

"At least you get to go home."

"Yes, rewarded with being left out of everything. I don't even think I can drive my hobbled self home."

"Do you *all* own cars?"

I then lowered my voice, which I had shot off louder and more cutting than expected: "I can drive you home."

I didn't mean to judge Chuy. I liked them. There was a vulnerability to them in need of protecting. I wouldn't tell them this, but they did remind me of my brother: joyful but sensitive. Quietly haunted behind a mask of humor. I might look like the men who disappointed them growing up, but I wanted more than anything to subvert those expectations.

We walked out of the building and to their hybrid Toyota Prius. The back bumper was covered in stickers: "EQUALITY" in rainbow-colored lettering, "A Woman's Place is in the White House," "Vote Jones," "BLM," "ACAB," and "Trans Rights are Human Rights." They tossed me the keys, and I got behind the wheel. We were heading to their home in Alexandria, Virginia, not far off from where Senator Denton lived.

Upon turning on, their car speakers blasted Spanish power ballads.

The car rode smoothly. The engine shut off at every red light, squelching its purring. It accelerated without effort.

"You're a speed demon," they said.

"Is it making you uncomfortable?"

"No. It's exhilarating."

Not long after crossing into Virginia, a cop previously obscured by bushes pulled behind us, flashing their reds and blues. I jumped in my seat.

"I don't have a driver's license," I said in warning.

"What? Why?"

"Never got one."

"Great public transit in Iowa or something? Pull over."

We waited on the side of the road for the patrolman to appear. He was white and tall, wearing blue reflective shades and a blond crew cut. I lowered the window after he tapped on the glass.

"License and registration?"

I handed him the papers Chuy had withdrawn from the glove compartment, as well as their ID. He stared at it.

"Where's yours, sir?"

I couldn't see his eyes. Only my own unsure reflection.

"I don't drive. I was just helping out my hurt friend."

Chuy waved their ailing hand.

"What's your status, Jesús?"

He stressed the first syllable interminably, pronouncing it Heyyy-Zeus.

"Excuse me?"

Their pitch was high. Chuy thought he meant HIV. The officer froze in place, expression hidden behind his opaque lenses, but his jaw was clenched.

"Your immigration status? You have papers?"

"Oh."

I saw their body relax from my periphery before tensing again.

"Is that appropriate to ask me? I'm an American citizen."

I panicked at how cross they sounded. You didn't ask law enforcement questions.

"We work for Congress," I blurted out.

His blond eyebrow rose above his sunglasses.

I noticed that the black-and-white American flag stitched to his uniform had a thin blue line across it.

"For Republicans," I added unthinkingly.

He stepped back five paces and theatrically tilted his head at an angle, as if to gawk at the car's bumper and the messages adhered to it.

"I doubt that," he said once he'd returned. "Do you know how fast you were going, sir?"

"I don't. I'm not used to this car and the location of the speedometer."

He used the pen in his hand to tap on it within the dashboard.

"See? Right where it says zero: big and blue. I found that pretty fast," he said. "I assume you also weren't aware that going over eighty-five miles per hour is a criminal misdemeanor in Virginia. That means I can take you to jail today."

My heart's acceleration climbed to match that of my driving.

"No, sir. I didn't know that. I'm not from here."

"But your friend knows better, doesn't he?"

My hands—glued to 10 and 2—began to sweat. He had to know he was scaring me. Is that why he did it? Was this his midday entertainment?

The officer looked down at their ID again.

"Not an organ donor, eh, Jesús?"

"Gays aren't even allowed to donate blood, sir."

His lips curled into a slight smile. He seemed to like it when we fought back.

"What's your name, Mr. Republican?"

"Cameron Leann."

"So if I were to search that name, I wouldn't find any outstanding warrants or anything like that?"

"No, sir. You won't find a thing under that name."

The fear that he might try consumed my every thought. Severe discomfort nestled itself in my bladder.

"And where were you boys heading?"

"Home. Doctor's orders," Chuy said.

"It's a nice neighborhood. Big, expensive houses," he said, reading the address off the card. "Head there slower. Understood?"

Our nods were aggressive.

He returned our items and left. The relief—like a sneeze or a long piss—was orgasmic.

"You're not a very good liar," Chuy said.

I didn't respond as I drove off slowly.

Chuy's home was two stories of red brick, gray paneling, white columns, and giant windows facing west. It was quite adult. Inside, it boasted high ceilings, lots of natural light, model-house cleanliness, and modern décor.

"You own this?" I asked.

"I rent it. Or better said, my parents rent it for me."

Chuy made their way to the kitchen. They popped open a bottle of red wine and poured two glasses.

"It's still morning," I said.

"And what a morning it's been!"

I brought the wine to my lips. It was sweet, strong, and syrupy. It ran slowly down the sides of the glass when set upright after tilting.

"The more alcoholic, the slower it runs," they said. "That's what they taught me at sommelier class. You should join. There's even opportunities for you to make some money on the side if you need it: bartending Hill events."

"Do I look that hard up for cash?"

"I'm sorry. That's not what I meant. I just know it's tough working here—in this city, unpaid—if you're not loaded. It's aristocratic, and it's wrong."

I didn't need the pity, but I appreciated the sentiment.

"I'm just busting your balls," I said. "Wait, so you'd be able to serve members alcohol? Get them liquored up? Slip one of them something stronger, something incapacitating maybe?"

Chuy swished their wine.

"Hypothetically, of course," I added.

Chuy sniffed the wine and shrugged.

"Hypothetically, I could spike a glass of wine with crushed muscle relaxants. You know, to keep any more heavy objects from flying at me at the hands of temperamental senators. Hypothetically."

They puckered their lips and sipped.

I paced the adjacent dining room.

"So your parents are loaded? Your word. Not mine."

"They're diplomats. They do well for themselves."

"And all of this space is just for you?"

"Yes. It's wild. There's a library. Even a billiard room. Not all of it goes to waste. We got it mostly for the studio. Prepare yourself. It's giving *extra*."

They directed me down a hall to an expansive room of concrete floors, a vaulted roof, and workshop stations of bleached wood tables, paints, brushes, clays, and glues. Projects in various states of completion littered the room, from vases and sculptures to portraits and sketches. Laid against the anterior wall was a six-foot-tall wooden cross: sanded down, treated, and bolted together. Flathead nails were hammered into the spots where a crucified man's hands and feet would go.

"You're an artist?"

"I fancy myself one, sure."

"These are incredible."

I toured the room, running my fingers down the different textures of the art. A row of papier-mâché figures that stood just below my waist caught my attention. There were six of them. Four graying men in suits—one of them bald and portly. I couldn't identify the set until I pored over the two women. The likeness of one in particular—spiny haired and statuesque—was immediately recognizable. These were avatars of the Gang of Six.

"What are these?"

"They're called años viejos," they said, pulling out a phone and showing me pictures of dolls lining street corners. "In Ecuador, as we approach the New Year, you'll see them on sale: representations of cartoons, superheroes, even politicians."

They stopped their scrolling at an image of myriad identical Thornton dolls.

"Hated American presidents—or in this case, a would-be American president—are popular. At midnight, as the old year ends, you set your año viejo ablaze. You burn them. In effigy."

I turned my body toward Chuy.

"You ever think of setting any of them on fire?"

Their eyes looked forlorn and distant.

"The dolls or the people they represent?"

"Either."

He smiled, but I didn't.

"Only when I'm angry," they answered.

"You've been treated like shit today. Aren't you angry?"

Chuy polished off their glass in a gulp.

"Not enough."

"You show the others your art?"

"No. It's embarrassing. You're the first."

"I don't make you feel embarrassed?"

I moved closer. I felt special. Let behind the curtain. Seeing them as a person, stripped down and bare. Where our emotional core lives. I liked what I saw there. Great pain but great resolve, too. Like they were easily hurt and easy to hurt you back just the same. Like me. We felt bonded.

"No. You don't, actually."

"You tell the others about your MS?"

"No. I'm insecure about it."

"But you told me."

"I did."

"Then I guess it's my turn to tell you my insecurity," I said, settling close beside them so our shoulders bumped. "Sometimes, I think people don't see the real me. They see themselves. They see my father. They see nothing at all. Heck, sometimes *I* wonder who I really am. If there's any heft to me. If I'm just skin-deep. If I matter at all. Does that sound silly?"

I looked up at them with a shy smile. Their cheeks turned pink.

"No. Sounds *deep*, actually. You do matter, Cam. The more I get to know you, the more I feel like I see you, the real you."

"This stays between the two of us?"

"Of course. As long as mine does, too?"

"You have my word."

My eyes swept over a sharp-point palette knife.

"You have more than my word. You have my blood."

I dug the blade into my right palm, watching Chuy and only them as I did. The serpentine line I inadvertently drew looked like a crooked "S." Blood seeped through the surface wound. Chuy yelped.

"Are you a psychopath?"

"Maybe."

I offered them my bloody hand.

"Blood brothers—er, gender-nonspecific siblings?"

Chuy shook my hand with their gauzed one. Mine smarted, but I didn't wince. Or look away from their eyes.

"Brothers it is," they whispered. "Did you really just cut up your dominant hand to make a point?"

"No. I'm a lefty. I'd never put my jerking-off hand out of commission like that."

Chuy chuckled.

"Oh, you're sinister."

"What?"

"That's what people used to think about lefties. The word 'sinister' comes from the Latin for 'on the left side.' I needlessly studied it in school. Many languages conflate the two words. I think that includes the Irish—their word for left-handed means 'crooked, deficient,' something like that. You're Irish, right?"

I nodded.

"And you've branded yourself now," Chuy continued. "It's why we raise our right hand when we're swearing an oath. Did you know that? In olden times, if you committed a crime but were granted leniency, they would brand your right hand with fire. There was no reliable way of keeping track of criminal records back then. So the next time you were in court, a judge would see the marking and know you shouldn't be shown mercy a second time. A closeted Republican I was hooking up with told me that once. How's that for pillow talk?"

Chuy leaned in, grabbed and flipped up my marked hand, and whispered as if they were sharing a secret.

"What crime did you commit in your past life, Cam?"

It was a joke, but I looked away.

"We all have things we keep to ourselves. What I can say is that I haven't been shown much leniency."

They laughed and slapped a hand on my back.

"Let's get that bandaged for you, big guy."

Lisa texted me one morning while I sat listless in my cubicle.

She's asking for you, it read, followed by a shrugging emoji. Come over? She meant the senator.

Lisa and I hadn't spent much time together outside of work. She had been slammed with preparing the senator for her private meeting with Wright. The extra hours without extra pay felt exploitative to me, but Liz—and everyone else for that matter—seemingly found it typical.

"You worked so hard for this promotion, girlie. You deserve it," Liz had told her, hugging her close.

I had smiled emptily, but deep down, I felt like everything on the Hill was a pie-eating contest where the prize was more pie.

I visited Lisa daily at the Fishbowl, helping her out in whatever ways I could. It's what you did when you were sweet on someone. Grunwald-Santos noticed. She would stop by briefly and smile at me. She would make small talk.

The thought that she might ask for me—and by name—sent pangs of electricity shooting up and down my body.

Her office was abuzz. There was media spilling out the front doors, far more than the one camera and one pool reporter covering the meeting with Kelley. These were casual, getting-to-know-you meetings—as light and unserious as the participants wanted them to be—but the media was treating this like the Yalta Conference. I could hear the repeated click of flash photography, the shouting of questions, the shuffling of bodies maneuvering through the byzantine office layout and in between one another. I waited outside, unable to pierce through the crowd.

Lisa came and got me from an unmarked side entrance.

"Through here," she said, pulling me in.

She led me to the heart of the office. We emerged on the other side of the senator, the judge, and their aides with the press in tow. Grunwald-Santos pulled up to the door to her personal office, turned to the onlookers and said something too low for me to hear, which drew laughter, and ushered the judge in. Her chief of staff followed behind him. She scanned the crowd, caught sight of Lisa and me, and walked over.

"In you go," she told her.

At me: "And I'll need my stenographer."

She drew close, bringing her lips within an inch of my ear.

"But be discreet."

I felt her breath on my skin. It tingled.

We trailed her inside. One moment, there was pandemonium, and the next, as she shut the door to the world, there was peace. Perfect silence. The senator and the judge sat opposite one another at the far-side table. The aides—three of us, three for him—sat in chairs lining the wall, trying to be as inconspicuous as the wallpaper, barely breathing. From her chair, Grunwald-Santos twisted herself to hand me a notepad. I pulled a ballpoint out from my jacket pocket, settled the paper on my crossed-over left leg, and—once the talking began—made only slight, subtle movements with the pen.

Judge Wright had collapsed into his chair, a slackened version of himself: slumped, legs manspread, hands on his belly. The senator's spine remained straight. She was on the edge of her seat.

"Lots of fuss. Bet you're not used to it?" she said.

"No, Senator. Judges are usually pretty anonymous."

"Call me Sandy, Judge."

"Call me Freddy, Sandy."

"How have your meetings gone?"

"It's all a bit of a blur, but I've enjoyed them. Everyone's polite."

"Even the Republicans?"

"Especially the Republicans."

"Probably balancing out the venom they'll spew your way in a few weeks."

He shrugged.

"We won't have a problem with you on *Roe*, will we?"

"It was settled precedent for fifty years."

"That's not the answer you gave the White House, is it?"

He paused long.

"I assured President Stevenson that the Constitution guarantees Americans the right to privacy that extends to the reproductive health decisions made between a woman and her doctor."

"But you won't be saying that in the hearing?"

"No."

"Understood. You don't believe we're bound to the original intent of the Framers in interpreting the Constitution, right?"

"The same men who considered me three-fifths of a person?"

She smiled. He didn't.

"How *would* you approach constitutional interpretation?"

"Like I do the Bible. There are principles undergirding the text. There is a spirit in the black letter. There are new, modern challenges it does not address, but its values can be gleaned. It is a living, breathing document that maintains its relevancy in an evolving world."

She stared out the window. She looked bored.

"I'm a Democrat-appointed judge being nominated by a Democratic president and presented to a majority-Democrat Senate weeks out from an election in which a right-wing candidate has at least a fifty-fifty shot of winning. You won't get any surprises from me, Sandy."

"Then we should discuss my true reservations."

"You're going to go hard at me for my Title IX dissent?"

That damn dissent again. Those poor boys on college campuses given fewer rights than a murderer facing death row.

"I stand by it. I am a fan of due process," he said.

Her eyes narrowed. She leaned forward.

"So am I, Freddy."

"But not for teenage boys?"

"Young men. Let's not infantilize them."

"We're both former prosecutors. We held ourselves to a high burden of proof. We embraced it."

"These aren't criminal proceedings. No one's liberty is at stake."

"But a *young man's* lifelong reputation *is*. His future. His education. His career. Many times, his athletic prospects. The prying eyes of everyone on campus and beyond. The consequences are just as severe."

"And what about the girl?"

"*Young woman.* Goose, gander, right?"

She was staring at her hands now. Almost like he wasn't there. Like she had tapped into a scripted tirade born from her gut.

"The looks she must get," she said. "The skepticism, the knee-jerk disbelief. The documented dip in grades. You and I know the rape conviction rate is abysmal. It's a steep legal climb, and I get that. I *honor* that. I *embrace* that. But when we're talking about holding schools to account, when we're talking about the slightest bit of courtesy—changing class schedules or dorm assignments to get her a sliver of peace—the standard can't be insurmountable. They shouldn't be shut out in the courtroom *and* in the classroom, facing dual proceedings that are futile. A fait accompli."

"We're talking possible expulsion—"

"You know they're not getting expelled! They're getting promoted!"

Her voice was shaking now. She had scooted to the edge of her seat. Her raised volume had visibly reinvigorated our attention, as if our faces had been hit with cold water.

She continued: "They're playing in Saturday's big rival game, peers cheering them on, teachers padding their GPAs, boosters throwing heaps of scholarship money at their feet. All while she watches and sits in her trauma."

"But she watches in relative anonymity," he said. "The young man never faces his accuser. We did away with the Salem witch trials for good reason. There is a Sixth Amendment. There is a Confrontation Clause. She isn't even in the room when his lifelong fate—at the tender age of eighteen, nineteen, twenty—is decided, when he's forever branded an offender."

I felt torn, involuntarily nodding in agreement with the judge but moved by the woman's power and passion. She was transcendent.

"You would have her relive her trauma? Sit before him and recount what he did to her in painstaking detail and *twice*—both in a court of law *and* to school administrators. *Just* to get some accommodations. *Just* to get some accountability."

"I won't subscribe to a presumption of male guilt. It's as plain as that."

It was definitive. There was a period at the end of his statement. He was done debating.

She fell back into her chair, relaxing her muscles. A faint smile was plastered on her face.

"Well, congratulations. Today's dissent is tomorrow's majority opinion."

"There's that pesky advise-and-consent thing to get out of the way first."

"Oh, that show? It's pre-scripted, Freddy. It's a drama, but it isn't a thriller. We all know how it ends. I'm looking at the next chief justice of the Supreme Court."

They stood and shook hands. The aides leapt to their feet. The rustling nearly drowned out their final exchange, but I strained my ears to listen.

"Don't hold your fire next week, Sandy. I can take it."

"Never have. Never will."

She approached me and grabbed the notepad. Our hands grazed.

"Start putting together our questions for the hearing, Lisa. Use his arguments against him. He'll dress it up in legalese. But let's boil it down as bluntly as he put it today: This is about protecting men."

She squeezed my arm.

"Good job."

I stared after her as she approached the exit alongside Judge Wright. I reverted my attention to Lisa. She had been watching me watch her.

"She's mind-blowing," I said.

"I didn't take your politics to be so left leaning."

"The content was bullshit, but it was argued beautifully. She's a force."

Lisa nervously laughed through a frown.

Grunwald-Santos and Wright paused at the door and flashed each other a look. Then they donned their facades—placid smiles and unyielding eyes—as the doors swung open.

The flashing lights of celebrity were warm but blinding.

ELECTION NIGHT

I laid my palms face up on the table. Like an offering. Like I was Jesus. Dried blood was still caked on them. Bathed, baptized in the blood. *Do this in remembrance of me.*

"May I wash my hands? No need to swab them for DNA. I've got nothing to hide. The blood belongs to the senator. I'll cop to that right now. I got it all over me on a foolish impulse to resuscitate."

With the nail of my thumb on the left hand, I began to chip away at the coat of red on my right. There were droplets of white paint on them, too.

"Wrong place. Wrong time. Led astray and manipulated. I just wanted some friends. I just wanted to belong. But I didn't want any of this. Surely they've all told you that. How I had no dog in this fight. How I had no cross feelings—toward them, toward anyone. Certainly not toward the senator. You've heard of Iowa nice, right? That's me to a T."

The curdled shavings rained down onto the table as I clawed myself raw.

"Officers heard me say what? Oh, that isn't possible. Because I didn't *do* anything. I can promise you that."

I drew fresh blood. It streamed down from my right hand.

"Oh, my middle name? It's Eli, sir. Why do you ask?"

07

THE TIGHTEST ROPE

I met Randy and Liz at a coffee shop for an early-morning pick-me-up on the unseasonably cold early-October day that Judge Wright would face the Judiciary Committee. The town felt seized by the uncanny calm that preceded calamity.

"This it?" Liz asked, running a hand down the length of my thin fleece jacket. The move warmed my quaking insides. "It's below freezing, Cam. Don't you have appropriate clothes from those brutal Iowa winters?"

Liz was decked out in a heavy, puffy down jacket, with a mane of Inuit faux fur serving as a hood and shoaled in a pink scarf. Randy wore a leather bomber lined with sheepskin and a thick cashmere sweater underneath.

"We're a hardy bunch," I said.

"A *poor* bunch," Randy murmured through clenched teeth in Liz's ear, but I overheard. It got a chilly reception from Liz, who shot him a look, but I just smiled. I was too embarrassed to say anything. Maybe to compensate, he shot over to my side, wrapped his arms around my hip, and nestled his head in the crook of my shoulder. He smelled of expensive cologne and whiskey.

"I've missed you, buddy. Ever since you got with the missus."

Liz unwrapped her scarf and snaked it around me.

"Better. Chuy tells me you're secure, so your masculinity won't be threatened by the pink."

Did they all just talk about me when I wasn't around? Like I was a freak, a different species worth scrutiny and study?

"These climate-denying assholes will use today to reject the existence of global warming," Randy fumed. "Calling it 'warming' was a huge marketing fail. Climate volatility—now that's more like it. How else can you explain the overnight frozen tundra that cropped up outside?"

We ordered our drinks at the counter. Liz and Randy rattled off a dizzying series of adjectives—"skim," "soy," "nonfat," "double shot," "mocha," "foam," "whipped," "salted caramel," "drizzle," "two pumps," "stirred"—but mine was straightforward: "black."

"I don't know if that's giving me hot-man or serial-killer vibes," Liz said of my order.

I whipped back around to the barista.

"Add cinnamon, please. Extra cinnamon."

Randy's eyes twinkled.

Warmed by the cups in our hands, we began our trek to the Senate side. The frosty wind was whipping in our faces. It burned. Walking in a single file, barely uttering a word, we passed by the Supreme Court, that majestic high-column, long-stair edifice of marble. Penned in by police were protestors near its steps, huddled masses yearning to screech free.

Their posters—in varying degrees of good spelling—depicted gore: the underdeveloped limbs, eyes, and skulls of fetuses extracted from the womb. Scrawled beneath the pictures were warnings of baby holocausts, eugenics, female infanticide, and population control of communities of color. A sea of Chad Thornton red buttons and hats littered the crowd. There were some men but mostly women.

"Wright is wrong!" they chanted.

I locked eyes with a spectacled gray-haired woman who was huffing so loudly that her sallow skin was turning purple. As I approached her side, I didn't turn away—the polite thing to do. I couldn't. She captivated me. So much hate in so little a frame.

She paused her yelling. Her lip curled.

When we were parallel, she reached out and clasped a fistful of my scarf.

"You a baby killer, son?"

I froze. Maybe pink on a man somehow outed me as a liberal. Perhaps she had seen something in my eyes, something dead inside, something that conveyed little respect for life.

Liz answered for me.

"Only every time he forgets to pull out," she said, wrapping her leg provocatively around my hip and sticking her tongue out for emphasis. My hand darted down to the small of her back reflexively.

The woman grimaced and mimed the sign of the cross. We walked off.

Another demonstration raged outside Dirksen, where the Judiciary Committee would convene. These protestors were exclusively male, decked out in camouflage, biker's leather, Merlin-esque beards, and the color yellow. They weren't chanting. They were eerily silent. They lined the sides of the walkway leading up to the doors like guards without arms, staring down staff as we entered. DC famously banned guns from public places. A Chief Justice Wright would undoubtedly safeguard such a restriction. Their hands lacked weaponry, but their fingers formed an OK sign, a widely known nod toward white supremacy.

Some of the men in their ranks were unmistakably brown-skinned.

"It's the color coordination for me," I whispered.

"They're Buzzer Boys," Liz said. "As in, raising the alarm that time's up for white Western civilization because of growing multiculturalism. They wear yellow. I think it's a bee thing, too. You know how they say the world dies off once bees do? It's some sort of tortured analogy to white demographic decline. Very convoluted stuff. Lots of mixed metaphors and brains too small to disentangle them."

"What kind of alt-right paramilitary group chooses to call themselves 'boys'?" I asked.

Their display was pathetic. I didn't feel intimidated; I felt sorry for them.

"They're incels, Cam," Randy said. "You can't make it make sense. That's what lack of sex will do to you."

Inside, the three of us headed to the committee room. We all had a role to play in the hottest show in town. Mine was minor, but I felt fired up and special at being in the front row to history. Shelly corralled us interns into a darkened cloakroom off to the side of the dais that she called the "bullpen," keeping us at the ready to undertake menial tasks at senator or senior-staff command. She looked like an off-Broadway director: notepad in lieu of a clipboard, airpod in one ear tuned to CSPAN in lieu of a headset. Isla and Scoop sat cross-legged at the rear of the pack, scrolling through their phones like Gen Z zombies. They nodded at me in perfect sync without tearing their eyes from their devices.

Randy sat in the crowd in a seat reserved for VIPs. Liz sat down behind Whitehurst. He winked at her as she did. Lisa was already sitting behind Grunwald-Santos. My girl was ironing out the invisible wrinkles in her skirt. Chuy was sitting behind Kelley, whose nose was studiously in a binder. Charlie was standing against the wall by the committee doors.

The chairman gaveled in the session. Even as the gallery hushed, the buzz heightened. Electricity crackled through the air, undetectable by eye or ear. It was palpable.

The scripted pageantry that followed subdued the thrill. As 2 Bills spoke—behind glasses as thick as the bottoms of mason jars—he barely lifted his eyes from the loose-leaf pages containing his prepared remarks. The content and delivery were as riveting as melatonin.

The ancient Republican ranking member, Senator Johnny LaRue, next injected drama with a Southern twang. He raised hell: apocalyptic visions of express abortions on street corners, the laziest generation living high off the hog on unemployment checks or inflated minimum wage, and mandated vaccination chips implanted in skin doubling as the mark of the beast. But even then, the histrionics felt tired. He could have written it—and his staffers likely had—long before a nominee was chosen. It was red meat, traditional bogeyman tactics ripped from the pages of the Book of Revelation. Just plug and play wherever the wheel of liberal jurists landed.

Next, the guest of honor, Judge Wright—risk aversion come to life—was just as tedious in his statement, invoking apple pie, baseball, rock 'n' roll, and a few allusions to the black American experience sprinkled in for insulation. His speech was laced with so many contemplative pauses that it inspired tedium. It felt tactical. No news could spring from a voice so monotone.

Hours of questioning would follow, in order of seniority, alternating between the parties. The chairman was fawning.

"The historic nature of your nomination—what will it mean for your sons and boys like them?"

Senator LaRue was prone to meandering soliloquies that featured folksy sayings everyone speculated were improvisational.

"We didn't have socialism in the days of Moses. Can't skin a cat and call it a rat now, can we? Now tell me, Judge: did you read Karl Marx in college?"

> **Dear #CapHillSoWhite:**
> **My boss is a Bible thumper who sounds like Foghorn Leghorn. But after dark, it's all hookers and key bumps of coke. He's a hypocrite, but I help him maintain the charade, so what does that make me? His pimp?**

The energy in the room shifted when it was Denton's turn. The second Republican in seniority—and the only professed "yea" vote in either party—had drawn considerable intrigue. The gallery woke up from their collective naps to perk up, lean forward, and listen.

"Let's get the elephant in the room out of the way. I plan on voting for you. I'm crossing party lines. I've faced my fair share of scrutiny for that decision, so I'd like to use my time explaining my thinking."

Wright tilted his large head forward.

"Elections matter. Some on my side of the aisle point to supposed irregularities in the last contest—namely that our guy lost, and we plumb didn't like that—and pretend that Stevenson isn't the president. But he is. And with that comes power. This is his seat. His to fill with a man—or *woman*"—he snuck in there, rolling his eyes instinctively over to Grunwald-Santos—"of his choosing. Someone of like mind. The president is a liberal. So it's of no surprise *that* is who he has chosen: a liberal. No offense, Judge."

Light laughter followed. Wright didn't budge.

"I expect that when Governor Thornton wins, he, too, will appoint like-minded men and women who share my views. If you don't like the direction the Court is heading under a Chief Justice Wright, then vote! Earn the right to appoint judges who will read the damn document as it is and not imbue in it whatever fad legal theory is lately ascendant in socialist academic circles. No offense, Judge."

Nervous rumblings this time outnumbered laughs. Wright was stone.

"But until then, I won't whine myself into irrelevancy. It could've been a whole hell of a lot worse, friends. The names floating out of this White House were some of the most radical, activist candidates I've ever seen in my career. At least this man isn't predictable. He's bucked his party before. We know his thoughts on the rights of the accused against the woke, lynch-happy mob. It's written in ink. He's on the record."

"Point of personal privilege."

The voice from stage left was so soft spoken, Denton almost started up again, undeterred, until he belatedly registered the interruption, and he whipped his sights over to the Democratic side.

"The gentleman from Connecticut is recognized," 2 Bills finally said after prolonged silence. His eyes had been shut, and he didn't bother opening them. His arms were crossed over his chest, so he looked like a mummified corpse speaking from the Other Side.

"Does the senator from North Carolina refer to the judge's dissent in *John Doe v. Regents of the Catholic University of America*?" asked Lancaster, Randy's uncle.

That damn dissent.

Denton's mouth formed a perfect O.

"Chris…" he began, voice faltering. "Yes, but this is highly irregular."

Eyes in the gallery were darting around in confusion. The senator was speaking out of turn. The highly orchestrated show was coming undone.

"So was your lurid string of words evoking Civil Rights Era mob justice, but I digress. You won't mind if I clarify a few things for the record?"

Lancaster rarely spoke and not in such sharp terms. At least in public, he was meek.

Denton's eyes were hot coals, but his jaw shut noisily.

Randy scooted to the edge of his seat. His uncle intoned from deep in his belly, so the back row could hear. He was going to grill the judge on the facts of that damn dissent. Perhaps try to sink his nomination. Pierce through the prescripted, manufactured drama and get at the live, crackling Truth.

"The majority in *Regents of CUA* were hardly the torch-bearing left-wingers you've made them out to be. Same for the bishops at Catholic University. I would know. I've been denied my fair share of communion for being pro-choice. No worry—the wafer's no gourmet treat," he said to laughter. "The rectors at Catholic sought to fairly and soberly adjudicate serious allegations of rape. They heard from the girl. They heard from the boy. They used the same standard from civil courtrooms across this country: preponderance of the evidence. Who do you believe more? This was Mr. Doe's third time facing allegations of sexual misconduct. *Third.* After a process that took *months*, Mr. Doe was expelled. But for those months in limbo, the girl walked the halls with her rapist. They lived in the same dorm! They even shared a class together. She had to drop out of it and bear an incomplete on her permanent record—all because they could not move him without due process. And Mr. Doe ended up at another school, playing ball, hardly tarred and feathered and run out of town in shame."

He swung his eyes toward Wright. He had been pontificating, sweeping his gaze across the gallery for effect. But now, he turned his sights like lasers on the man at the center.

"Judge, you called that painstaking process, quote, 'a kangaroo kiddie trial shrouded in secrecy, dressed up in the trappings of law, but lacking in any real substance.' Really?"

Denton stammered in reply for him.

"My memory is getting foggier with age, but I don't recall yielding my time to Senator Lancaster. The gentleman from Connecticut is out of order."

"Let the judge answer," Grunwald-Santos interjected.

Her eyes were sparkling, and the corners of her mouth were pulled slightly up, only just suppressing a beaming smile.

"Now you, too?" Denton asked, slamming his open palm on the table. "This has become a circus!"

"You're no stranger to a hot bench, right, Judge?" Grunwald-Santos asked. "You treat your litigants to it on a daily basis. There's no reason the stuffiness of Senate parliamentary procedure should get in the way of an honest conversation. Senator Lancaster is asking if you still view the process so derisively as when you wrote those words?"

"Chairman," Whitehurst said in a steady voice, pivoting to his right. "You must regain control of this hearing."

Williams's eyes snapped open. At first, he blinked profusely, looking dazed and wildly about, as if he had nodded off and could not recall where he was. He gradually settled and turned his whole body—not just his head or eyes—to Whitehurst and stared. Thirty full seconds— an eternity—passed before he spoke.

"I *am* in control, Dale."

His chair groaned under his considerable weight in shifting back to Wright. It was the only sound in the committee room.

"Please answer the question, Judge."

Wright separated his clasped hands, cleared his throat, looked downward, and—in his characteristically deliberate manner—addressed the firing squad.

"The question before us in *Regents of CUA* was a narrow one. The plaintiff argued that the university, which receives public dollars, violated his due process rights under Title IX and the Constitution by stripping him of a material benefit—his spot in his class, his scholarship, his career prospects—by too low of a standard of proof: fifty percent plus a grain of sand. The majority found that standard adequate. I did not. I found that the clear and convincing standard of proof was more appropriate. That is not as high a standard as for a criminal conviction, wherein liberty is at stake. But it isn't as low as a civil judgment, where only money is at risk. It is a reasonable middle ground. I respectfully dissented, and my esteemed colleagues carried the day."

"But you went farther than that, didn't you, Judge Wright?" Lancaster was grinning now, baring his incisors like a wolf licking his chops. "You lambasted the whole process. All but compared it to throwing a bound woman into the bay to see if she floats."

A few hoots and hisses spilled out of the crowd. I looked to Randy, seemingly suspended—frozen—in anxious anticipation.

Whitehurst flashed a stern look to an unresponsive 2 Bills.

"The process Mr. Doe faced would be unfamiliar to any lawyer who's spent even a day in an American courtroom," Wright said. "For one, it's a black box, held entirely behind closed doors. Secondly, there is no cross-examination. The testimony from the complainant faces exactly zero scrutiny. This was important in Mr. Doe's case, as the US Attorney's Office declined to pursue criminal charges because of the complainant's credibility issues. The same story that led to his expulsion apparently could not withstand inspection from a jury of his peers. Thirdly, the accused does not get to hear what he is being accused of: live, in person, and in her own words. The alleged victim is sequestered, testifying before the disciplinary panel and no one else. Lastly, he is afforded none of the rights that are hallmark to American legal tradition: no right against self-incrimination, no presumption of innocence. He is afforded the opportunity to hire counsel, but he or she is less a defender in the traditional sense and just an advisor. These are not trials, only echoes of trials, skeletons of trials lacking meat on those bones, and I do not see how a fair observer can disagree as a descriptive matter."

It was Denton's turn to flash the whites of his crooked teeth.

"Well put, Judge," he said. "My colleagues bristle at my invocation of civil rights, but isn't it true that the rights restrictions of Title IX disproportionately affect students of color? Mr. Doe himself was a black man, wasn't he?"

"That is right."

I caught sight of the twitch in Charlie's jaw muscles.

Grunwald-Santos leaned into her microphone.

"That's because—just like the criminal justice system—whites face better outcomes and lighter punishment," she said, hair flying as she shook her head. "That doesn't mean we equalize down: less account-ability for perpetrators, fewer accommodations for survivors. The opposition to Title IX isn't about race! It's about gender. I've heard my colleague from North Carolina refer to Title IX as 'reverse discrimina-tion.' You don't approve of that language, do you, Judge?"

"Those are not the words I would use, no."

"I would hope not. It's language ripped straight from the men's rights movement. The girl in *Regents of CUA* was raped and somehow she's the privileged one!"

"Allegedly raped. Recall that Mr. Doe was never criminally charged," Denton said. "See, that's the problem when due process goes out the window. It's immediately 'believe women.' Who even needs a trial when a sentence of public shaming is doled out on her word alone?"

"The prosecutor called it a 'credibility issue' that the victim's boy-friend was black," Grunwald-Santos said. "He called that a *bad* fact. Because the jury would hear the white victim had a *thing* for black men like Mr. Doe and suspect she cheated and cried rape to hide the infidel-ity. What do you think about that, Judge?"

"I want to be clear: I did not and still do not have a position on the *outcome* of Mr. Doe's cases," Wright said. "He very well may have deserved the fate meted out to him by the bishops at Catholic. What I found inadequate was the *process*."

Lancaster jumped back in.

"But it seems to me that outcomes *are* important, and they do weigh heavily on you," he said. "In John Doe, you see a young man irrepara-bly harmed. I see a young man who was merely moved for the peace of mind of the victim. Don't you think which one we see speaks to what we value?"

Denton snorted.

"You would think, Chris, as much as you've seen the inside of a court-room yourself, you might not be so blasé about tarnishing reputations."

Heat visibly rose to Lancaster's face. Only his tightly pressed lips were colorless. Randy's heavy-lidded eyes shot down to his feet.

"Chairman," Whitehurst tried again, his tone this time imbued with more alarm. "I move for a return to regular order."

Williams kept his eyes shut.

"Answer the question, Judge," he bellowed.

"What was it again?" Wright asked.

The laughter from the gallery—raucous and over the top—was more tension release than humor induced. Lancaster, whose face had not yet regained its usual pallid hue, appeared disinclined to repeat it.

"Let's put it this way," Grunwald-Santos said instead. "Don't you think given the gravity of the allegation and the potential threat the perpetrator posed, a preponderance of the evidence standard is more than fair when the consequences—*reasonable* accommodations for the victim, no loss of liberty for the accused—are not as dire? His accuser put herself out there—coming forward, inviting scorn and suspicion, swearing under oath."

Wright's answer was economical.

"So did Emmett Till's."

The disquiet that followed felt like a veritable period to the abnormal affair. I watched all of the tension in Grunwald-Santos deflate. Lancaster's lips were stretched into a slight smile, like a vanquished foe impressed with being bested. The panic behind Whitehurst's eyes had settled. Denton was smug. All looked sapped of their energy. The fight was over.

"Does the gentleman from Connecticut yield his time back to Senator Denton?" 2 Bills asked.

"I will shortly. But allow me first to express where Senator Denton and I agree," Lancaster said. "Barring anything unexpected, Judge, I, too, will be voting to confirm your nomination. It's not just the historic nature of your appointment, although I swell with pride at the accomplishment. It's that I agree that the stakes are high. We face an unprecedented danger in the possible election of Governor Thornton—the most autocratic, bigoted, and science-denying candidate for president to date. And unlike the last one to hold that unholy distinction, he's far smarter and more qualified to successfully enact his retrograde agenda into law. And I am convinced—even if you and I disagree on the margins—you will protect the rights we hold sacrosanct. I can only hope our discussion today has softened your recalcitrance to Title IX. That was my only aim. But I do not think I am being too presumptuous when I say: you will be the next chief justice of the Supreme Court, Frederick Wright. Congratulations, and Godspeed, sir."

A few spectators, a cross-section of staffers, VIPs, media, elected officials, and the part of the public willing to wait in an hours-long line, began to clap. Wright cracked a smirk beneath his veneer of stoicism. Lancaster joined in the applause.

A white man with cruel eyes and a snarled lip stood up amid the crowd. He was just a few rows back from Wright. He was shouting, and he wore yellow.

"Let the tree of liberty be refreshed with the blood of patriots and tyrants!"

He had a mound of white powder in his outstretched hand. He sucked in his breath loudly and blew, sending the snowy dust in a plume toward the judge. Wright had turned to him at the sound of the tumult, so the wayward particles had leached onto his face, blanketing his black skin in clownish white.

"Die, monkey!"

My addled mind focused only on the shrieking. There was so much shrieking. And running. There was a tornado of limbs spinning before me. I felt rumbling beneath me, as if the building were shaking, but it was just hundreds of people springing to their feet at once. Bodies were bunching, slamming into one another as they darted to the exits.

One woman fell to the ground, covered her head, and began weeping. I stood in place, wobbly on my feet. I had to grip the walls to keep from falling. I didn't know where to go. But I knew I wanted to go and protect someone I cared about.

I surged out from the cloakroom. I ran up to the dais, behind where Lisa, Liz, and Chuy had been sitting ducks. Williams was scrambling to rise and reposition his substantial weight on his cane. I was a foot away from him. I could have kicked that cane out from under him. It would have gone unnoticed in the chaos. It could have easily been accidental. I imagined him spilling forward, the soft of his neck striking the side of the table on his way down.

I darted past him to Liz, where my instincts led me.

She was glued to her seat, seemingly paralyzed by the commotion. Only her eyes moved, sweeping across the deteriorating scene.

"Come."

I tugged her out of the chair and began to usher her away, but the obvious exit was crowded, and a scrum of police was forcefully removing the resisting offender in that direction.

"Emergency exit's this way," she said, withdrawing from my hold and leading me by the hand.

Her knowledge of the building was expert. She bobbed and weaved down hallways and staircases, at times against the current of frenzied staffers.

"No doubt they're locking the building down," she said, manically checking her inbox for the inevitable notice from Capitol police. "I'm heading to an exit manned by an officer I know."

"Won't he just turn us away?"

"Not me. He'll do as I say."

As we neared metal detectors and doors to the outside set in an alcove, she released my hand and batted it away. The young uniformed man with a skin-fade haircut and a tattoo sleeve poking out from his shirt rose from his stool to greet her. His gold-plated name tag read "Pvt. Gomez," and his hand shot up to cradle her elbow.

His partner was posted in the hallway, directing the traffic to shelter in place.

"What's happening?" Private Gomez asked.

"A protestor disrupted the hearing," she said, hoarse heaving swallowing her words. "He attacked Judge Wright. He blew some sort of chemical, some sort of residue at him. Anthrax? I don't know. I need fresh air."

The light drained from his eyes.

"It's a Code Red, Liz. No one's allowed to go anywhere."

"I'm asthmatic and claustrophobic. I'm hyperventilating here. I don't want to draw resources away from the emergency, but if I don't get outside, you'll need to call the paramedics for me anyway. Please, Ernesto."

Her hand was on his chest now.

"And him?" he growled.

I felt the strongest déjà vu. Like all the times a girl had begged a club bouncer to allow in boys like me alongside her. Liz was quick-witted, and she always had an answer, but not this time.

"I'm Senator Lancaster's nephew, Private," I said finally, needlessly adding bass to my voice.

I let it sit, but it soon struck me that I needed more.

"Our place is nearby. The senator will be evacuating there. He's asked me to meet up with him. I'll bring Liz. So she can lie down. So she can settle and recover."

He eyed me for a long time before the tension in his body fled him and his expression softened.

"Yes, sir," he said, unlocking the doors behind him.

Liz squeezed his shoulder blade on the way out.

It wasn't until we were met with frigid, blustery air that I realized neither of us had our coats. We were braving the elements in our work wear, and neither of us lived close.

"I need a drink," she said. "Let's go to Bull Moose."

Naturally, she was no longer heaving.

"Isn't that the Republican hangout?"

"You're learning. Yes, it'll be crowded with sad fucks from the morning, morose about losing the Supreme Court for a generation and seeking solace from the bottom of a bottle. Perfect atmosphere for us to lift our—*and* imbibe—spirits."

The walk to the House side of the Capitol was arduous. Our teeth were chattering by the time we stepped beneath the bar's burgundy awning and into its dim interior. We passed white bro after white bro, shooting dark liquor and swilling light, domestic beer beneath black-and-white photographs of Teddy Roosevelt. Lots of unironic mustaches, sockless penny loafers, and seersucker. One Viking-looking fellow wore pastel shorts and flip-flops. The skin of his lower half, like his hair, was raw red.

"I will never understand white men's compulsion to bare their legs and feet in public, no matter the temperature," I told her.

"Your people, no?"

"No." I chuckled. "It's amazing that these folks vote the same as the Buzzer Boys out there. So different, so much the same. What accounts for that?"

"Cognitive dissonance."

"And selling your soul for tax cuts for the wealthy."

We sat ourselves at the bar. Liz ordered for us.

"Two Macallans. Neat."

I cocked my head to the side, smiled, and squinted. So strong, so early.

"What?" she asked. "Let's warm up our insides. Put some hair on your chest. You don't have any, do you?"

"Why do you say that?"

She was teasing me. Trying to emasculate me.

"You don't strike me as particularly hairy. I can't tell if that's natural or by design."

How a taken woman could be so flirty never failed to surprise me. I didn't feel bad for Charlie, just relieved at my good luck.

But she was right.

"Genetic. I'm pretty smooth all over. Can't really grow facial hair. Comes out patchy."

Our drinks arrived. We toasted and clinked our glasses. We maintained eye contact.

"No seven years of bad sex!" she insisted.

I slurped down half my pour. My gums and temples smarted. The drink made me lose some filter.

"Is Ernesto hairy? Or smooth all over?"

She smirked, shutting one eye and pointing her finger at me.

"See, why do I think you're insinuating something inappropriate about me there, Free-Stater?"

"You two just seemed close. Touchy. He does what you say, even to the detriment of his job. He the one stray fuck you told me about?"

She grimaced.

"Can't conceive of a woman's worth to a man outside of using her body, huh?"

She was no longer smiling. Her spine had stiffened, and she had her back to me, looking conspicuously away.

"Hey," I said softly, laying a hand on her.

When she turned to face me, she was chewing her lip and her eyes were glistening.

"I'm sorry," I said. "That was shitty of me to say."

I wished I hadn't said it. Playful banter didn't come naturally to me. I understood why, from my mouth, women just didn't trust it. My eyes were too deep-set, my brow too protruding, and my jaw too square.

"I helped Ernesto's little brother get a congressional nomination to a service academy. Air Force, I think it was. He's a Kansan. The boy was heading in the wrong direction. His brother owes me now."

A visible chill ran through her and—as if it were a curtain lifting off her veil of melancholy—she reanimated, donning her traditionally sly, taunting demeanor. She finished her drink.

"No matter. No worry," she said. She leaned up on the counter, cleavage pouring out from her blouse. I silently cursed myself out for noticing. "Barkeep! Another round."

I didn't like hurting her.

"Liz, you can get angry with me. I don't want you brushing off the offensive things I do or say. We can go deep. That's how you get closer."

She was a person worth knowing: beautiful, and smart, and so fun, and a force that moves through the world as if she owns it. I couldn't help but want to see more.

"But I *don't* take you seriously, Cam."

It was my turn to look away, pained. I realized that I was pure amusement to her. Nothing more. She collected my hand in hers.

"Why take any of it to heart? You're one of the good ones, right?"

With her gaze and touch, she was reassuring, but her tone felt sarcastic.

"*Are* there any good ones?" I asked.

"Just gay or dead."

"Gays can be assholes, too. Don't put them down by raising them on sham pedestals. It's infantilizing."

"My bad. Just dead, then. Grim outlook for you, eh?"

My eyebrows shot up, but I shrugged.

"We're all immortal as long as we're alive," I said.

"Like *For Whom the Bell Tolls*," she said to herself, looking away.

"Another book reference. You have—what—hundreds of them in your room. You do a lot of reading, huh?"

"The posters on my wall were of playwrights and novelists—Ellison,

Baldwin, and Hughes—not boy bands. I had a mother more preoccupied with herself than with me. I had to find something to get lost in. I chose stories," she said. She had dropped the light and airy veneer.

I knew a thing or two about mothers more in love with themselves than their children. It struck a sad chord with me that made me feel alive, that made me feel seen.

"What do you like about them?"

I moved in closer, hopped up on adrenaline at her show of sincerity.

"I guess I didn't like myself very much. Or the world around me. At least while you're reading, you could be someone new," she said.

"I like that. Sitting in someone else's skin."

We scrunched our faces at the same time and laughed.

"That sounded far creepier than I meant it," I said, hands up in my defense. "Forgive me. I'm no good with words."

"You recognized Hemingway. I'm impressed. Wasn't sure you could even read," she said.

And there it was. She had slipped off the earnestness like a layer of clothing and reverted to needling me. It was clearly where she felt most comfortable.

"Why do I get the feeling you try to bait me into anger? Like you want to see how far I'd go."

"I court danger."

"You think I'm dangerous?" I asked, hopeful. I wanted to be *something* to her other than utterly banal and fodder for mindless flirting.

"You aren't until you are. Time tells all," she said.

"You said you knew me."

Her laughter was loud, musical, and sprung from her gut. I'm sure I wore my annoyance like a flashing neon light. Her hand landed daintily on my knee.

"*You* don't even know who you are, Cam."

She rapped her nails melodically on my glass.

"Now keep up. Can't let a girl drink you under the table. Unless you're trying to get me to take advantage of you under there."

I emptied the contents of my glass down the gullet, just as two fresh ones were placed in front of us. There was no toast this time.

"How's Lisa? She safe?" Liz asked.

She swished the liquid in her glass.

"Oh."

My hands darted to my pants pocket. She knew I hadn't looked at my phone. She knew I hadn't the faintest clue. She had asked anyway.

Fifteen unread text messages.

I scanned them quickly and sent an anodyne response.

"She's fine. In lockdown."

Liz must have texted Charlie long ago. There was the difference between us two. She was a good person.

I asked the bartender for ice. Liz raked her hair with her fingers and just watched me, silently, until she heard the cubes plopping into liquid.

"You're flushed!"

She stroked my cheek and followed the trail of red down my neck to the top of my chest exposed by loosened top buttons.

"A buildup of acetaldehyde. From the drinking," I said.

"Right. More genetics."

Her fingers lingered at my sternum.

"How's Lisa care for your slick-like-a-seal body?"

"You sure you want to spend our time together talking about Lisa Stoltz?"

"Yes. She should be on *one* of our minds."

I knocked back my drink until ice hit my teeth. I ordered another round.

"She wouldn't know."

"About your thoughts?"

"About my body."

She gripped my forearm and emitted a squeal.

"You two haven't consummated your relationship?"

I shook my head.

"It's not all I'm after, you know. I'm being respectful," I said.

She snaked her head until her unblinking, wide-eyed gaze pried my eyeline to hers.

"She's been busy. Her boss is demanding," I said.

She placed her hands on her lap like a schoolgirl.

"Her period's been uncooperative. Poor timing," I said.

In truth, I hadn't tried. I wasn't feeling it, and Lisa was beginning to notice.

Liz raised her palm to halt my protestations.

"We'll work on it, babe."

"We?"

"Just leave it to me. She and I are both Geminis."

"I don't need your help getting laid."

She leaned in and whispered, although no one else could hear us over the music.

"But won't it be a lot more fun that way?"

A white man sat down on the barstool to the other side of Liz. He said something, she giggled, and they shook hands. He continued chatting, without so much as a glance my way. He had a swoop of cascading brown hair for a hairline, like an Alabama Crimson Tide quarterback, and a youthful, doughy face. I rinsed my third scotch like mouthwash, stood up, and shoved myself between them.

"She's with someone, dude," I said.

She was tickled by this display. It was written in her eyes.

He was aghast, stubby-fingered hands in the air.

"I wasn't hitting on your girlfriend."

"He's a journalist," Liz said. She didn't elaborate.

"So?"

"He was asking me about the assault. Trying to get a firsthand account."

"Why us?"

He pointed at the IDs clipped to our waists. Mine was bright and embarrassing intern red. To read hers—lying perfectly on her upturned butt cheek—would still have required leering at her body.

I unclipped my ID and hers and stuffed them in my pocket as they taught us to do when out in public.

"Don't mind my boyfriend. He never learned to share," she said. Her hand on my chest alerted me to its taut, puffed-up state. "Join us for a drink. We can't comment officially, but we can gossip. Give you some background."

Luke Russell worked for a step above a rag. Neither a tabloid nor *WaPo*, but somewhere in between. It had recently published a kindergarten assignment from Wright where he noted in admirable penmanship for a five-year-old what he wanted to be when he grew up: Robin Hood. Unserious right-wingers spun it as early socialistic tendencies.

Bereft of the prospect of scoring, Luke was exceedingly dull. He talked mostly about himself. He overused speech crutches: beginning every other sentence with a long, humming "um." He scrolled endlessly on his phone, even while he was speaking. It was his job, he explained. He got paid to be insufferable among company, I guess.

He was a lightweight. After just one drink—a Bay Breeze—he was sweating, slurring, and spilling secrets.

"Early testing has indicated, like, it was just flour. No harmful chemicals detected. Ummmmmm, much more racist symbology than bioterrorism."

He was the type to use the word "symbology" over "symbolism."

"The man is being interviewed by the FBI in a windowless room. Ummmmmm, with those giant two-way mirrors, you know? Like in the movies. It's, like, idiot—never talk. They're not there to help you.

Ask for a lawyer. Ummmmmm, I'm shocked he was taken in alive. But really, I'm not. Now, if he had been a black man…"

He didn't finish his thought. He formed his short fingers into the shape of a gun and mock fired, sound effects and all.

He was the type to form his fingers into a gun and mock fire.

"The Dems are in high spirits now, but in twenty-four hours, they won't be. A bomb is dropping tomorrow. Ummmmmm, who knew there was something to all those rumors? It will blow Wright's candidacy right out of the water."

When he grew bored of hearing himself talk, he left us his business card and stumbled away.

"You were awfully possessive of me for someone who doesn't, in fact, possess me," she told me afterward.

"No one possesses you."

She appeared to like that.

"Would you hurt someone for me, Cam?"

I gave her the answer I thought she wanted.

"No."

She appeared not to like that.

"Bummer."

Luke had been an inebriated truth teller. Not long after waking the next morning, while I nursed an acute hangover with eggs and a glass of milk, I heard a newsbreak float over from my roommate's too-loud headphones.

"Doesn't this deal with your job?"

He tore them off his ears and cranked up the volume.

"…*The shocking allegations—a veritable October Surprise—threaten to sink the Democrats' only opportunity to confirm a Supreme Court nominee in under a month…*"

I wasn't going to share in this moment with him. Wordlessly, I slipped my own headphones over my ears—for effect, they weren't connected to anything—and returned to my breakfast.

ELECTION NIGHT

Scoop's hands were in his pockets, his right rolling a bullet fragment compulsively between his fingers.

"I never liked him."

His left was cupping his scrotum, a comforting impulse of his since infancy.

"Clark Kent—he was just trying too hard. And then trying too hard not to look like he was trying too hard. It just seemed phony. Duplicitous. That's a good word. I'm a superstar at vocab. I do the *New York Times* crossword on the reg."

He withdrew his left hand and, despite himself, sniffed his fingers.

"There was rage there, seeping beneath the calm. He rarely let it out. But I saw it. If you were looking—like *really* looking—there it was, in plain sight. I'm an awful good judge of character, mister. Like you: you're here to help me, not hurt me. I know that. Black lives *do* matter—my best friend's black—but I support the boys in blue, too. Only the feebleminded are unable to hold the two views at once."

He suspended his right hand balled into a fist over the table.

"When are you going to ask me about this?"

He released the projectile so that it danced on the metal surface to a tune of its own making.

"Also, when do I get my phone back?"

08

WATCH YOUR SIX

Charlie was riding shotgun when Randy pulled up to a street corner amid upscale Georgetown shops to get me. The weather had warmed, so I was waiting for him on a bench, fiddling on my phone and watching women in yoga pants.

I usually insisted on taking the Metro when we met up, but we were heading outside the city limits. I otherwise felt weird hopping into his car for walkable distances, accessible by public transport, only to park at an overpriced lot. He didn't make me feel bad when I rode with him. He was as oblivious to this excess as he was to the multi-thousand-dollar watch he slipped on every morning. It was second nature.

I sat behind the driver, and Randy screeched off before I had the chance to strap in or fully shut the door.

"Where we off to?" I asked.

"Pick up Scoop," Randy said. "He lives in Navy Yard like a damn Republican."

"Why do you say that?"

"It's where they cluster. Maybe 'cause there's not a lot of melanin in that neighborhood."

Scoop was outside his soaring, ritzy apartment building. He squeezed in behind Charlie, whose seat was pushed back to accommodate his long legs. Scoop didn't say anything, even as his knees were partially tucked into his chest. He just laid his palms on Charlie's shoulders in greeting, dapped up the open palm Randy offered, and muttered something unintelligible to me.

"Now on to God's country," Randy announced.

"You're a man of God?" Charlie asked.

"You heard Uncle Christopher. We Lancasters are cafeteria papists. Father Callahan runs in the opposite direction when he sees me walk up to the confession booth. With my brimming social calendar, he knows he's in for a marathon session."

After a stretch of quiet: "What about Chuy?" I asked.

"I don't think that particular Jesús is welcome there. I don't make the rules but apparently some sins are more unpardonable than others."

"No, I meant what about Chuy today. Aren't they coming?"

"This is a boys' trip."

"Isn't that high-key fucked up?"

"I'm respecting his identity choices, Cam," Randy said. He was lying. His grin was facetious. He just didn't want them around for what would be a deluge of cishet masculinity. It felt like I was betraying Chuy. "Besides, Chuy's anti-gun. Like virulently. He won't touch the thing. No matter how phallic. Boys and gunplay is basically a circle jerk, but he still has no interest."

Randy drove farther into Virginia than I had been, out into the rural west where the fields between houses grew exponentially longer but the time between sightings of Thornton lawn signs notably shorter.

Randy didn't slow until a sign for a gun range—two busty women in flag-colored bikinis and earmuffs framing a massive machine gun beneath the words "Size Matters"—emerged.

We parked in a gravel lot, stepped out into the baking sun, and walked up to a drab gray storefront without windows or frills but for its name, Open Fire, in giant red lettering and the "O" replaced by a gun sight.

"Hell must have no windows," Randy said.

I shot him a quizzical look.

"None of the fun places do."

The place was hot inside. The white man behind the counter had sweat stains collecting under his armpits in concentric circles like age rings on a tree. He'd be four. He wore smudgy glasses, a Velcro-band wristwatch, and a baseball cap with a ponytail that spilled out from above the adjustable strap.

He had us sign a Release, Waiver, Indemnification, and Assumption of Risk Agreement. None of us read it. I watched Scoop scrawl his full name.

"Your government name's Stephen?" I asked.

He pursed his lips in reply.

"It's a cute story, actually," Randy said, laying an arm on Scoop's shoulder and hooking it around his neck. Scoop squirmed. "Papa Blum nicknamed him Scoop 'cause as a baby boy—way past walking age—he insisted on being scooped up and carried everywhere he went. I figure it's why he's cursed with rail-thin calves. Unlike yours, Cam. Yours are substantial."

Scoop was trying to shove him off now.

"What gives? Didn't Daddy show you any affection growing up?" Randy asked, squeezing his grip, coiling his elbow around Scoop's bobbing Adam's apple.

Randy turned back to me: "His dad's a tough guy, Liz tells me. A big guy. A specimen of evolution more like our Charlie here. Big-time booster for the University of Kansas football team. Scoop grew up never missing a home game on Saturdays."

I jerked my head up.

"You followed the team closely as a kid?" I asked.

"Let him go, Lancaster," Charlie boomed.

"I came out of the womb by choice, motherfucker. Don't tell me what to do," Randy snapped. Nonetheless, he complied.

Scoop fixed the askew collar on his T-shirt.

"What's it to you?" Scoop asked, finally addressing me.

"I'm a college football fan. That's all."

His scowled face loosened, erasing its lines and hanging low in contrition.

"I was there every game but didn't pay much attention to them," he said. "Now Isla's a different story. I'm sure she can spout off the KU starting rosters for every season this century."

I chewed on the thought, trying to slow down my beating heart.

"I'll have to ask her about that sometime."

Scoop flipped out his vape pen, brought it to his lips, and inhaled.

"You can't smoke that in here, boy," Ponytail said. A steely-eyed Scoop blew white vapor slowly out of his mouth like the caterpillar in *Alice in Wonderland* and placed the cylinder back in his pocket. I tapped his chest with the back of my hand and leaned into him.

"No vaping, but he gets to dip?" I asked, pointing discreetly at the plastic bottle in the man's hand filled with brown tobacco muck. The side of his cheek had a conspicuous lump protruding under his skin.

Scoop gave in to a gap-toothed grin. He was loosening up to me.

"You boys from the city?" Ponytail asked.

Our silence was his confirmation.

"We'll get Emma Mae to help ya'll out, then."

Emma Mae was a ten. She was a pint-size, olive-skinned brunette in a formfitting tank top, denim short shorts, nose ring, and trucker hat. We boys exchanged knowing glances clear over the top of her head as she led us underground. No other customers were in the bunker, just a bear of a red-faced white man seated on a stool in combat boots—hairy navel exposed from a too-short shirt—who checked out the guns for us from the locker.

Emma Mae walked us through the loading, aiming, and firing of the handgun Charlie had selected as a starter, herself pumping out a startlingly accurate round into the right chest of the paper male silhouette twenty-five yards away.

"Is that what you do to the hearts of men you date?" Charlie asked as she transferred the weapon into his enormous hands. She only smiled. He was flexing the muscles in his arms needlessly as she guided him into position.

"Let's make a friendly wager on who's the better marksman, gentlemen?" he proposed before firing.

"What are the stakes?" I asked.

"How about the lucky fellow gets to buy the lovely Emma Mae dinner tonight?"

He didn't wait for agreement—or her consent—before pulling the trigger.

Meanwhile, the bear in boots was listening to talk radio on a prehistoric boom box, antennae erected to the heavens. The volume was maxed out so it could be heard over the ballistics. "He's also just hard of hearing now. Won't wear these," Emma Mae explained, holding up the earmuffs in her hand.

"His body, his choice," Randy quipped.

Fire. Fire.

Fire. Fire. Fire. Fire.

Fire.

"The Demon-rats are hypocritical cucks. Trying to hashtag MeToo every last one of us into social oblivion when their own house isn't in order. Makes the timing of this scandal a little suspect, if you ask me. But I'm not tripping all over myself to emancipate Judge Frederick Douglas over there. Those are his chains. Placed on him by his masters: Old Man Stevenson and his Hip-Hop Princess Kiara Jones."

Charlie's results were scattershot. All landed on the paper: accurate but imprecise.

Randy stepped up to the firing line.

"I'm used to working with a bigger shooter," he told Emma Mae as he wrapped his long, thin fingers around the firearm and winked.

Fire.

Fire.

Fire.

Fire.

Fire.

Fire.

Fire.

"I see it differently, Joe. This is an all-out war on men. And we ought to root it out before it ends up in the pussification of America. Make Men Great Again, I say. This little lady, former clerk of his, what is she even saying Jigaboo Freddy did? That he pleasured himself in front of her. But she supposedly stayed until he shot off into a cup. You have two legs, woman. Walk away. She says he also reached up under her skirt. But she accepts a recommendation letter from him and sends a glowing—some might say fellating—note of thanks back. And she doesn't end up getting that Supreme Court clerkship. What she does get is pissed. It sounds like a classic case of a girl fine with it, up until it stops working."

Randy hadn't hit the page. "Unfortunately, I'm a Yankee son a bitch. But shooting blanks ain't all bad. It means no need for birth control," he joked.

I was up next.

"You can place the eyewear over your glasses," said Emma Mae.

"That's all right," I said, folding my pair away into my pocket.

Fire. Fire. Fire.

Fire. Fire. Fire. Fire.

"It can't be coincidence that right as he's railing against the scores of baseless sex accusations persecuting the young men of America, an accuser of his own pops up. The hearings no doubt put the idea—crying rape—in her pea brain. The radical feminists got a hold of her and recruited her, trying

to tank his nomination the same way the reputations of young men are smeared on a daily basis. Now it looks like the loony left won't get to steal a SCOTUS seat before real Americans get a say and sweep in a Thornton revolution. Hallelujah! Praise Jesus."

I heard cheers behind me as my shot-up target surged toward us on the conveyor. All of the holes were in the chest, within inches of each other.

My dad had taken me shooting once when I was far too young for it. I could still smell the alcohol on his breath. I could still feel the way my hands shook out of fear of a misfire. Out of fear of disappointing him.

"Looks like our boy Cam has won Emma Mae!" Randy said. Our prize—the object—hid her blushing face behind the sweep of her hair. "There's no way Fire Crotch can do better. I've used the bathroom after him. Boy can't aim his circumcised pecker for shit."

Scoop flipped him the middle finger as he got set up.

"Circumcised?" I asked, shaking my head at the unnecessary detail.

"He's Jewish, Cam. Don't be ignorant."

Fire. Fire. Fire. Fire. Fire. Fire. Fire.

"I hear ya, Rogan. Let's see how fast the Demon-rats throw a brother under the bus. That's how they treat black folk. Drive them straight from church to the polls to collect their votes and swiftly pay them no mind afterward. Come on over to the dark side, Mammy and Pappy. At least with us, you'll get good, conservative Christian outcomes and not the Devil's agenda. But I digress. Back to the jackass party: There's no time to switch Freddy out for another brother or a hussy. They're all too chickenshit to do it in the lame duck. If they want to pack the Court, they'll have to go with the alleged pervert."

It wasn't clear at first if Scoop had penetrated his target more than once. But the gaping hole—dead at the center of the figure's forehead—was larger than ours had been and not as perfectly circular. It was the type of perforation that formed from seven projectiles tearing nearly perfectly into the same space.

The shouting, jumping, and play tussling with the scrawny Scoop—manhandled by the three-way pile-on, buried under significantly greater weight—came staggered as the realization of his feat hit us with varying delay. There was collective elation. Male bonding was a fraught exercise. It didn't often inspire complex feeling within me. But every so often—if you're lucky, if the moment is just right—it can make you feel like a kid again. This was one of those times. I felt a sense of belonging, of unbridled joy. I felt full in that hole reserved for masculine affection that my dad had left neglected since childhood. A hole as big as Scoop's seven-bullet perforation.

"Where'd the fuck that come from, Scoop?" Charlie asked, after the boy had reappeared out from the fray.

He shrugged. Even when he knew a direct answer, his shoulders seemed perennially pinned to his ears.

"Clay pigeon shooting. Since I was a boy. Did it competitively in high school, too."

"If that isn't the whitest, most elitist thing I've heard, and I'm from Connecticut," Randy said.

"Says the senator's nephew," Scoop said back.

Randy smacked the back of his head, emitting a thud, and hushed him, laying a finger perpendicular to his lips. The locker attendant had been watching us.

"You use shotguns for that—skeet shooting—don't you?" I asked Scoop.

His nod was slow. His eyes were narrow.

"You could blow a man's head square off with aim like that, couldn't you?" I asked.

Scoop flashed his gap.

"Or a woman's, for that matter. If it's close range. If you're a sick fuck," he answered.

"Semiautomatic?"

He scoffed.

"That's child's play. No need for training wheels. I can do it single shot."

"Good to know."

"For what?"

"For self-defense. Of course," I said. "God forgive my usually bleeding heart, but we probably could have used a few more guns when that lunatic assailed the next Supreme Court chief justice in open committee. I wouldn't shed a tear if a racist prick like that got slugged in the head. Just saying: we might feel safer from right-wing nuts if we were packing heat."

"As the only Republican among us, I'll second that," Charlie said. "But they're going to clamp down on security. No one's bringing guns into the Capitol."

"Just the ones already there," Randy said.

"What do you mean?" I asked.

"Like my uncle's. I know where he keeps his."

"I thought civilians were banned from carrying."

"As with everything, senators are the exception. No one checks them for weapons. He told me the same thing you said, Cam. The scare made him wish he had it with him, right there in the committee room, and not stowed away in his personal office collecting dust. A madman would have to mow down thirty staffers before he'd reach my uncle. It's of no use to him there."

"We should move it for him."

All eyes landed on me.

"It'd be the familial thing to do."

Emma Mae retrieved the firearm from Scoop.

"You ever date a ginger?" Randy asked her.

She inspected Scoop's face.

"How old are you again, hon?"

The three of us erupted into laughter. Scoop's skin turned the hue of his hair.

The pot-bellied attendant approached us with a long gun in his paw. We piped down as he held it out to us vertically. A tattoo of the Confederate flag crept out from his bunched-up shirtsleeve.

"Overheard you boys discussing shotties. One of you wanna give her a spin?"

We turned to Scoop.

"You're the expert," I told him.

Scoop gripped the barrel.

"Let's dress the target up," the attendant said. He retrieved a newspaper clipping from his shirt pocket. It was a photograph of Senator Grunwald-Santos. He pinned the image atop the silhouette's head and sent the target careening back to its faraway position.

He was trolling us, having overheard our job talk or maybe even figured out the identity—and political party—of Randy's uncle. Scoop's headshake was apoplectic.

"I'm not doing that shit."

He was offering the shotgun back.

"I'll do it," I said.

I didn't want to play into the effete Washingtonian stereotype that Joe Six-Pack had contrived of us in his mind. I found the whole thing comical. This was no big deal.

"Don't you, like, have the hots for her, Clark Kent?" Charlie asked.

I collected the gun from Scoop, walked up to the line, donned the safety equipment, and assumed the position. I steadied my aim.

"The line between sex and violence is quite fine."

Fire.

As we were preparing to leave, Charlie pulled Emma Mae aside, out of earshot. He was being touchy. Her reactions were giggly and airy. He handed her his phone. She apparently saved her phone number in it.

Scoop climbed over the barrier into the line of fire. No one else was down there shooting. He sprinted down the lane and picked something off the ground. He stuffed it in his pocket and rejoined us.

Charlie was right. The security line at the Hart Building entrance was longer than usual that next work morning. I stood directly behind a tall, striking man—product in his voluminous onyx hair, suit impeccably tailored, skin clear—who blotted me out like an eclipse. At the magnetometer, the officer had to tell him several times to remove his shoes. This was new. The committee terrorist had kept the baggie of flour in his sneaker, and so much about law enforcement was reactive.

The officer groused to me as the man—now cleared—walked away: "You'd think he'd be used to taking off his shoes before entering a room."

The man was Asian.

I didn't smile.

I tore off my own shoes. I felt cool air on my big toe poking out of a hole in my dress sock. Out of shame, I stepped through the detector in a hurry.

At lunchtime, I ran into Charlie loitering in the corner, massive hands in his pockets. I gave him the driveby head nod, but surprisingly, he pulled me aside.

"I texted Randy to meet me here. You can wait with me, if you like," he said.

I grinned. We were friends finally. Liz would be so proud.

"I have something to show you," he said, looking so giddy, he was nearly bouncing. He fetched his phone from his blazer pocket. "You know that sporty, hot chick from the shooting range?"

"The one whose name sounds like the abbreviation for mixed martial arts?"

"That's the one," he said. "Look at what she sent me."

The photo he pulled up on his phone was a nude: a headless, topless, bottoms-less, albeit closed-legs, close-up of the female form. Its beauty sucked the breath out of me.

"I'm weak. Those are some first-rate tits."

It snuck out of me involuntarily. I had wanted to express indignation, but that just didn't come naturally to me. So much of manhood was trying and failing to conform to what we knew was expected from us. Disappointment had a gender, and it had he/him pronouns.

I went full in instead.

"You smashed that?"

"Cam!" he chastised, tone sharp, mustering the offense that I could not. "Of course I did. That same night. You don't get sent this and keep it in your pants."

Randy pulled up behind us and stuck his nose between our shoulders.

"Bet," was all he said about the picture and nothing else. "You rang, sir?"

"Denton needs you to get this note to your uncle."

He held thick card stock folded in two between his pointer and middle fingers like you would a cigarette.

"Why me? I'm not Christopher's keeper."

"It's private. It's personal. He wanted you."

"You read it?" Randy's face lit up.

"No. But I'm sure *you* will. See you, Cam."

As Charlie started away, Randy spread his arms crucifixion-style and yelled out after him.

"The noble Charles James, patron saint of secrets and nudes, hosanna in the highest. *Esssspiritu santoooooo.* Amen."

Passersby turned to watch, but Randy didn't care. He flipped a hand through his shaggy hair and pulled on me, eventually slipping into an arm hold as if we were prom dates.

"Come, bruh. Let's find this little bitch."

First, he casually flipped open the note, leaving it exposed for me, and him, and anyone within a foot of us to read.

Chris, Bill's a go if you are. Fuck Sandy! It's on you.

—Scott.

"Salty," he said.

Our walk to Senator Lancaster's office was short. We moved past the lobby and to a corner office with a clear sliding front door where a bald white man with his back to us sat in his rolling ergonomic chair. He was scrolling through Instagram on his phone, swiping through pictures of hunky, scantily clad white men in fitness attire or beach wear and double tapping nearly all of them.

"Objectifying those poor boys, are we, Rossy? They're someone's sons, man," Randy said unnaturally loudly to Ross Sanderson, the keeper of the senator's schedule.

"What do you want, Randy?"

"Six-pack abs like the gentlemen in those thirst traps, but I'll settle for my uncle's whereabouts."

"The senator doesn't have time for your games today. If it's money you're after, that's what Greta's for. Go ask her."

Randy's lips tightened to the point they lost all color.

"You *flatter* me."

"I *know* you. Since you were a boy. Since my time working for your dad. Nothing's changed. Run along. Skedaddle."

"OK, boomer."

"I'm a millennial."

"Whatever. I have something to actually contribute. A personal note from Senator Denton relayed to me by his body man, specifically to me and no one else. It's urgent."

"Leave it on his desk. Nothing confided in you can be that sensitive."

Randy grimaced.

"Your disdain is noted. I'm not hot enough for you, I guess. Show him your deltoids, Cam."

My cheeks were on fire.

"Your ugliness is inside, Randy. Not on the outside. And that's what matters."

An intern poked his head in.

"Hey, Ross," he said. "Greta says voting's been extended. He'll be on the floor for another twenty."

Ross shot him daggers. Randy planted a noisy smooch on the kid's cheek.

"Jerry, you moron. I love you."

Randy flashed Ross a peace sign and walked off.

Before I turned to go, Ross bore his eyes into me.

"He will lead you straight into fire. Ditch him before he does."

Randy moved with alacrity, and I had to break out into a light jog to keep up. Inside the Capitol Building itself, we entered a room beneath the Rotunda that was brightly lit by candelabra chandeliers and had archways held up by stained-rock columns.

Randy noticed I had stalled to peer at the ornate surroundings. So grand and glitzy. And little old nothing me amid it.

"This is called the Crypt."

"Why's that?"

"Because George Washington's body is rotting down below us."

I flipped my eyes downward and felt a draft that chilled my bones.

"Just kidding. He was supposed to be entombed here, but he ordained that his remains stay at Mount Vernon. White men and their plantations, huh? So now, like the Tomb of Jesus, it's a burial ground with no body. I haven't done a Capitol tour in years, but I guess it's all still here, swishing around in the old noggin."

He diverted course to the center of the room.

"Peep this," he said, tapping his foot against a white marble compass carved into the floor. "We are standing at the exact center of the city, where it divides into the four quadrants. Right now, I'm in Northwest *and* Southeast at the same time."

He stared off at nothing in particular.

"I remember—many years ago—a black man on the Metro overheard me say I wouldn't be caught dead in Southeast. This was before gentrification, before Navy Yard was, like, a destination. He looked me dead in the eye and with a voice as gruff as gravel, he said, 'That's where the *real* men live.'"

He clicked his tongue several times.

"I nearly shat my pants."

I'd ask him why he mentioned that the man was black, but I already knew. This was a horror story, and it was the quickest way to convey fear.

He waved me onward. My hard shoes echoed on the sandstone floor.

"We need to get you some suede Ferragamos."

He wasn't joking.

But I found it funny. He was unapologetically himself.

Randy led us to the entrance to the Senate chamber. He expected me to go in. My stomach dropped to my knees; my blood turned to ice. Randy caught my feet dragging and shoved me. I came within inches of slamming into the pair of officers guarding the doors.

I recognized the tatted Hispanic one as Liz's Ernesto Gomez.

Randy addressed his older counterpart.

"I need to get a private message to my uncle."

"Certainly, Mr. Lancaster."

He stepped aside. Randy nudged me forward. The elder officer halted me with an open palm.

"Not him, sir."

I darted my eyes from him to Randy to Ernesto.

"It's all right, Vic. He's Lancaster's nephew, too," Ernesto said, giving me a friendly nod. I nodded back.

Randy looked stunned but impressed. His eyes flew briefly to the surname on my ID.

"My aunt's son," he said.

"Of course. Sorry, sir."

Randy squeezed my arm as we stepped onto the Senate floor.

"I don't know what you've been doing with my family name when I'm not around, but I'm here for it."

I knew he wouldn't mind. Very little tripped him up. I guess when you have privilege to fall back on, nothing is a big deal. In this moment, it felt nice to be unbothered like him. Unburdened like him. I wanted to be nestled comfortably in those suede designer loafers.

We strolled down an aisle of tawdry blue carpet with an indiscernible pattern, between rows of desks reminiscent of grade school situated in a semicircle. Senators—mostly old white men—milled about in clusters, whispering among themselves. Not about the vote presumably. The result had been pre-telegraphed. None of it was spontaneous. Modern American parties had killed suspense.

The chamber was small. The second floor housed a press box with a giant, swiveling camera, centered among mezzanine seating. Members of the public by the handful took turns sitting up there and watching the most deliberative body in the world do nothing. The rostrum against the back wall was high, surrounded by a charcoal marble barrier with bookish men and women—parliamentarians and such—seated behind it. Whitehurst stood at the top of it against a backdrop of drab blue curtains. He presided over the session with a gavel in his hands and a warm smile but cool gaze. He wasn't—but I nonetheless felt him—following me with his overcast eyes.

"Spotted," Randy said.

His uncle was off to one side, beside a brick house of a man—tan fellow in a tan suit and earpiece—no shorter than six-foot-six. He stood in stereotypical bodyguard fashion, hands folded in front of his junk.

We approached them, but Randy kept a distance of several feet.

"Randolph," the elder Lancaster said simply.

He turned to me, saying nothing for an awkward stretch.

"We met previously, sir."

"Yes, young man. I recognize you, even with all your clothes on."

No hint of joviality. My eyes fell to my feet.

"What's with this Secret Service–looking dude?" Randy asked.

Only then did I notice the bags weighing down the senator's eyes.

"Ever since my supposed star-turn in the confirmation hearings, threats on my life have come streaming in."

"Isn't that always the case?"

"More than usual. Tenfold. And the rhetoric is sharper. It's…specific. It's…credible."

He slipped his hand into his suit and pulled out a pocket-sized knotted rope. A noose.

"I found this tossed onto our stoop this morning."

Randy swallowed hard. He turned ashen.

"Are we in danger?"

"We'll be fine, son," he said, stepping forward, reaching out and massaging his shoulder. Randy didn't recoil. "I'm just being precautious. Asked the Senate sergeant at arms for some extra security. They'll be watching the house over the next few nights. Just 'til things die down."

"Aren't you flying back to Connecticut tonight?"

He dwelled on it for a while, then retracted his arm and pivoted to me.

"Why don't you stay over tonight, um, uh…?"

He was waving his hand, grasping for a word, grasping for a name.

"Cam."

"Yes. Right. Keep Randolph company. I would be indebted, and we have the space."

Randy rolled his eyes, but he didn't protest. He must have been spooked.

"Yes, sir. Of course."

His face moved in a way that approximated a smile before readdressing his nephew.

"We need to sit down and talk before wheels up tonight. Just you and me. Man to man."

Randy nodded. He handed him the note. The senator read it to himself, and as if the expletive on the page—*"Fuck Sandy!"*—had conjured her, Senator Grunwald-Santos appeared. She looked at Randy. She looked at me. Nothing, no acknowledgment. Not even a hint of familiarity flooded her doe-like eyes. Because I was nobody in that moment. Because I had nothing she wanted. She swept right past us to Lancaster.

"Chrissssssss." She giggled. Her hand shot to his arm. She leaned in for the kiss. He fumbled, moving left then right then left again before planting one on her cheek. I watched her hand linger on the back of his neck.

"I never did thank you for standing up for women at the hearing the other day."

"It was the right thing to do."

"The Wright news is awful, isn't it? You know, it isn't too late to switch him out for Loughlin. The White House will listen to us. They will listen to *you*."

"I wish I could be as optimistic as you are, Sandy. Americans are already early voting. The election's in weeks. If Jones loses, there's no way we ram a nominee through in the lame duck. It becomes Thornton's seat to fill. It's Wright or no one."

"Chad Thornton isn't winning. He's a clown. A sideshow."

"Now when have I heard that before? Feels like déjà vu just hearing it out loud, Sandy. He's got a fifty-fifty shot in a polarized nation. You willing to bet regaining a woman's right to choose on it?"

"Some things are worth more than that."

"Like what?"

"Our morals."

"Say you and I from our privileged perch. Abortion will always be available to our kin. Tell that to a poor black teenager in Hartford. That we stood on principle as she bleeds out in some back alley."

"The girl hasn't even gotten to tell her story, Chris. We let him get an up-or-down vote, we let him on that Court as fast as some want it, and we silence her. We silence others like her. We tell them, 'No one cares. Don't speak up. You won't ever live it down—*never*—but he gets a pass. And he might just become a Supreme Court justice one day.'"

Something clicked in his sagging eyes. His spine straightened, adding inches to his height.

"You're right. Excuse me."

He turned to depart but shooed us first.

"You boys should leave the floor. You know you can't hang out here."

On the way out, we watched him walk up to 2 Bills—seated at and spilling out of a desk chair, hand atop his cane—and whisper in his ear. The chairman nodded. Whitehurst was watching.

"She knows who I am," I said to myself, staring straight ahead and not at Randy beside me.

"Who?"

"The senator. Sandy. She *knows* me."

"So?"

"And she didn't say a word to me. Not a smile. Not a nod. Literally nothing behind her deadened eyes."

Randy laughed but didn't respond.

"Whore," I said.

Outside the chamber, Liz was chatting up Ernesto. I waited until she detached herself from his side to approach her.

"How was shooting with the boys?" she asked after pleasantries.

"Fine. Charlie made a friend."

I blurted it out like a breath I had been holding in for minutes. The sight of her and her buddy in uniform must have made me jealous. Her eyes grew small.

"OK."

The silence stewed.

"He tell you about her?"

Her smile was sardonic, almost chilling.

"If you have something to say, Cam, tug on your balls and say it."

"He slept with her. Did he tell you that?"

She looked away, flashing me her red-cheeked, enraged profile. It wasn't until she spoke that I figured out she was mad at me, not Charlie.

"What are you trying to do here?"

"I'm sorry, I just—"

"Don't be sorry. Just mind your own damn business."

I figured she'd be grateful for revealing the betrayal. You know, rejecting the bros-before-hoes edict. Doing my part to dismantle the patriarchy.

Senator Lancaster emerged from the floor, and a swarm of reporters—to the tune of clicking cameras and flashing lights—descended on him out of nowhere, like inanimate objects previously camouflaged by the baroque walls that had sprung to life. Surprisingly, Lancaster paused before the horde.

One of them stuck a microphone in his face.

"What should the White House do about the Wright nomination, Senator?"

"I know what we on the committee should do, and the chairman agrees. We ought to hear from the young lady. And from Judge Wright again, too. His former clerk has come forward with serious allegations, and they shouldn't be brushed aside—not in everyday life, and not when the stakes are this high. Judge Wright is a big fan of due process, so it's only fitting we have a public airing of the matter. This seat belongs—not to the Democratic Party, not to President Stevenson—but to the people."

He dashed off alongside his security as other questions, left unanswered, were barked at him.

Randy's eyes were misty.

I could spot the admiration softening his face, even as he fought himself—with what appeared to be Herculean effort—from breaking out into a smile.

"I'm proud of him."

That didn't last past nightfall.

I was on his block with an overnight bag strapped to my back when my phone buzzed. His text message to me read simply: he's a dead man.

As I neared the brownstone, a man hopped out of his car. He was security, and he wasn't going to let me in. The creak of the front door interrupted our back-and-forth. A darkened figure the shape of Senator Lancaster emerged.

"Let him through. He's a friend of my nephew's."

I stood taller—chest out—as I walked past the guard.

Lancaster was still blocking the doorway when I reached him. He was now partially illuminated by the glowing moon. He was unsteady on his feet, wobbling, even as an arm rested against the doorframe. He was as dressed down as I had seen him—a cashmere sweater and slacks—but one end of his shirt was messily untucked. His pompadour was flat and featured uncharacteristic strays. His eyes were raw and bloodshot. He reeked of sweet whiskey. He was drunk.

Randy's words replayed in my mind: "*He cleaned himself up. Got sober. Waited a few years. Reformed his image.*"

He was lugging his rolling suitcase behind him.

"He needs you tonight, son. He's hurting. *I* hurt him."

He pushed me aside borderline roughly and stalked off into a car awaiting him.

I rushed inside, worried I might find my friend strung out on the floor, literally injured. The senator had physically threatened him before.

The inside of the home was dark. I had to grip the walls to find my way. There were no signs of life, so I yelled Randy's name. The voice that answered was faint and mousy, but I followed it to a room on the first floor. I didn't see much but for the whites of my friend's shining eyes.

I heard the spark of a lighter. The flame drove out the darkness. It danced and so did its shadow onto Randy's sullen face. He used it to light a couple candlesticks and the end of a cigarette, which he popped into his mouth and puffed profusely. All around us were shelves of books, leather-bound upholstery, and fragrant mahogany. It was his uncle's study. I sat myself in a chair opposite his and didn't say a word. It would have felt disruptive. He would begin his story when he was ready.

But he didn't. He merely handed me a handwritten letter of several pages. He gestured with his cigarette that I should read it. I had to hold it up to the candlelight.

7-18-2014

Randolph,

I write to make amends, my boy. They say you cannot earn your way to recovery without apologizing to the ones you hurt. I am of the belief that you cannot apologize for the pain you've wrought without first acknowledging what you've done. So even as I wallow in my heartache—crying streams of tears that hit the page, threatening to streak the ink and muddy my unburdening—I know for us to move forward, we must look back. I know I must tell you about how your father spent his last moments. May God—and hopefully you, one day—forgive me.

I need you first to know that I loved Art. More than any other man in my life. More than your grandpa certainly. Grandpa Henry was tough on us growing up. He had impossibly high expectations. He withheld his love. He was never satisfied. Your father responded by excelling, compulsively seeking perfection—like Icarus—to win his approval. Win his affection. But the man had none to spare for anyone but himself. It drove Art mad, quite honestly. I was a late, unwanted, surprise baby, eight years junior to your father. Grandma Olivia had had her literal tubes tied and still I poked through, a fact my dear parents reminded me of every day. I was a rare, statistically abnormal mistake that Catholic guilt saved from being aborted. Perhaps I had a destiny to fulfill and that's why I defied nature, but whether it was for good or for evil, I could never resolve in my mind.

I responded to my father's austerity much differently than Art did. From birth, I was nihilistic and rebellious, much like you. Art saw fit to play protector and overseer. In that way, he became an extension of our father—more loving, of course, but he was ultimately not my peer. He was just another authority figure. I think my birth radicalized him, made him more serious. It ended his childhood. And it gave me license to never end mine. Here was another man, just like Pop, with sturdy shoulders and a head screwed on right who I could disappoint. It's not an excuse—just an explanation—but the pressure from both of them was less diamond producing and more shaken can of soda. I devolved rather quickly in life: no drive, no focus but girls and substance abuse. I got a thrill out of letting the two of them down. It was finally something I was good at. If I emulated them, I'd always be third best. At least at devastation, I was unmatched.

I didn't drink all that much that night. Well, I did, but I am an alcoholic. It barely affects me anymore. Art was at his best. You should have seen him: working the crowd, conversing with everyone—even the wait staff—and remembering the most obscure details about them. I hung back and sulked: moody and depressive. I wasn't angry at anything in particular. Just the usual. Just life.

On the drive back, we argued. If I told you I remembered over what, I'd be lying to you. But I know it was small. Nothing worth a damn in retrospect. It was a stand-in. I heard nothing but a lifetime of castigation and dissatisfaction from him. He no doubt heard nothing but resentment and the avoidance of responsibility from me.

I didn't want to live. I hadn't said the words aloud, but I had felt them for all of my conscious life. They were inscribed on my heart.

I sped dangerously up at first. I wanted him to see how little I cared, how little regard for my own life I held. But he just kept talking. He wasn't taking me seriously. He said I was being dramatic. He was in mid-sentence when I veered the car off the road. I just remember jerking the wheel as far right as I could. The wheel rolled and rolled, seemingly forever, never sticking. The car spun. We flew over the cliff. I don't remember landing.

When I awoke, I smelled blood, gasoline, and smoke. I had to fully knock out my cracked window to crawl out. A little fire had sparked under the hood. I saw Art: bent, contorted, and mashed up against the windshield. He didn't appear to be breathing. I worried the car might become a tinderbox. I began to back away. I sat down on wet rock, head in my hands, feet dunked into the low river stream. My phone wasn't with me. It must have flown out of my pocket from the collision.

My head hurt. I was concussed and bleeding. I wasn't thinking straight. It began to rain—pour really. I remember thinking that was good, that it would keep Art and the car from catching aflame. The rainfall comingled with tears until it choked them off. The pelting stung my throbbing head. I sought cover under a rock formation. I may have fallen asleep. I told myself if I did, I'd probably die from the head trauma, and that'd be OK. And time passed. I couldn't tell you how long, although I can recite the exact number of minutes today. 257. You know that I've woken up at exactly 2:57 a.m. several nights since? I think it's my conscience, or Art, or God, or the Devil reminding me of my sins.

I wandered out to the road once the rain stopped. I had to scale a dirt wall. I flapped my arms and jumped up and down like a madman at the first set of headlights. The woman who helped was far too kind to me. She had no idea what I had just done.

I sat with him in the ambulance. I held his hand the whole way. I'm so sorry.

Uncle Christopher

Randy was sobbing by the time I finished. It wasn't until I felt cold dampness on my cheeks that I realized I had been crying, too. We stood, and he collapsed into my arms. He shook so hard, it took considerable strength to hold him up. His wailing was among the saddest I'd ever heard. I could hardly breathe myself. My heart tightened.

"My father meant everything to me, Cam. Everything," he said. "He got me. Even though I was a handful. Now who gets me? No one. And *that* man killed him. He left him for dead. He's out here: assuming my father's life, living my father's dream, keeping his brother's son under his thumb. It's sick. It's evil. It hollows out my heart so there's nothing left inside. Just hate."

When he finally dislodged himself, he was sober.

"I'm going to murder him."

He said it plainly. It was not an aspiration. It was a promise.

"The letter's backdated," I noted softly.

"He never gave it to me. He gave out all of his Alcoholics Anonymous amends—save this one. He was too much of a coward. He kept it stowed away."

"Why give it to you now?"

He shrugged and allowed himself to spill noisily back into his chair.

"Our priest has apparently counseled it for years. Maybe the recent threats have made him confront his own mortality. He scrapped ten years of sobriety in order to do it."

He polished off a glass of amber liquor sitting beside him.

I felt awful. His uncle had laid so much on his wiry shoulders—generations of hurt and cruelty. Our guardians had no right fucking us up like this. It was as much his inheritance as the gobs of money at his disposal. I wanted to soothe him, but I didn't know how. I knew all about neglect but this level of betrayal amid great privilege was foreign to me.

I turned to the wall, giving him my back as I inspected a weathered document on the wall. It was a framed, handwritten script of the Gettysburg Address, brittle and yellow.

"... *that we here highly resolve that these dead shall not have died in vain...*"

"It's a contemporaneous copy. Passed down in my family for generations. Did you know it will last—made in 1863—longer than this 2013 Harlan Coben paperback?" he said, while the sound of him shuffling items on his uncle's desk floated to my ears. "It's the acid they put in modern paper. It literally destroys it, disintegrates it—day by day, little by little. It's called 'slow fire.'"

I flipped around and took a seat. Our faces were perfectly aligned. I held his gaze.

"You can't do it now."

"What?"

"Kill him. You'll have to wait."

His shoulders relaxed, melting into him.

He just needed to cool off. If I didn't walk him back from the brink, he might fly off the handle. Do something rash. Do something stupid.

"Wait 'til the attention dies down," I continued. "Wait 'til he and everyone else aren't on red alert anymore. And when it's time, when you're ready, I'll be there."

Randy took a drag. Tobacco air evacuated his lungs steadily.

"You'd do that for me, buddy?"

"I would. *I* get you. We're not too different you and me. We'll do whatever it takes to avenge the ones we love."

He nodded with his eyebrows. He tamped out his cigarette on his uncle's gradually decaying note.

"Now let's get ahold of that gun."

Dear #CapHillSoWhite:
My boss killed my father.

ELECTION NIGHT

Isla had her hands tucked under her crossed arms. She fluttered her fingers against her rib cage.

"Cam didn't have intention. He didn't have *personality*. He was a basic AF white boy. Haven't you all figured out by now how he fits into all of this? Because you're asking the wrong girl. I haven't a single clue. That's what *you* get paid to find out, isn't it? You can't expect me to do *your* job."

She smacked her strawberry-glossed lips every time before speaking.

"There was something familiar about him. I even brought it up with Liz. Something nagging at me. But she brushed it aside. I eventually figured that he's just a carbon copy of every emotionally stunted boy I went to school with. The strong, silent, but toxically masculine type. The boy who fools you but ends up like all the rest of the fuckboys— pardon my French. A gaslighter."

Her mouth dropped open and her eyes rolled up into their sockets.

"You want me to take an educated guess? Is this what passes for stellar police work? I don't know, why else do twenty-two-year-old boys do anything?"

She paused for a long time, as if she genuinely didn't mean for her sarcasm to be rhetorical and instead expected an answer.

"Sex. That's what."

09

THE POLITICS OF CONSENT

I was lying on my bed—bleary-eyed, staring as the red numbers on my alarm clock blurred, thinking it was too early to fade on a Saturday night—when Liz texted.

Were ciming overt, Lisa ans I.

I shot upright. Not to this shoebox for poor church mice, they weren't.

No.

**Too late inthe uber already
omw to georrgetown canpus.**

**U don't know where my dorm room
is. U don't even know if I'm home.**

**Cum get us. If not, we finds the
clostest frat party ans get roofied.
U dont want to be teh reason we get
Fred Wright'd, do u?**

Shithead roommate home.

Place a mess. I'll go wherever else.

Get rid of himn lol were drunk Cam

lol ans we want to seeee your room.

Use ur heads. See u in 20.

I slammed my phone onto the nightstand so hard it rattled.

"You've got to go."

My roommate lowered the book he was reading to reveal a furrowed brow. He was splayed out on his bed, wearing nothing but socks up to his calves, boxer shorts, and an undershirt.

"You're joking."

"I'm incapable. I was born missing a sense of humor. It was a medical marvel," I said. "Two girls are coming over. I need you gone."

I tore off the sock from his foot—gagging briefly at the stench—strode to the door, swung it open, and hung it on the outer knob.

"See."

"That's not how that works," he said, scooting out of bed. "I'm supposed to *come home* to a sock on the door. Not be thrown out in my skivvies as a preemptive strike. It's forty degrees out, man."

"I'm horny, not heartless. Take these."

I scrounged up the jeans and jacket he had messily tossed onto a chair and shoved them into his arms.

"And go where?"

"Don't you have a girlfriend?"

His frown lines evaporated.

"So you *were* listening."

I waved off his sentimentality with a flapping hand.

"That's where you should be anyway. At her place and not reading some nerdy legal thriller on a Saturday night like a beta."

"I don't sleep over hers."

I cocked my head to the side.

"She's waiting 'til marriage," he said.

"Well, make it hard for her. Pun intended. Get some form of job at least—hand, blow, rim, whatever."

"You said *two* girls. Seems awfully selfish for one guy. Can't I just be your wingman?"

I was pushing him past the doorframe now.

"I don't need one. And I don't think Becca would like that very much, would she?"

"You remembered her *name*."

"And I can find her number in the campus directory if need be. Tell her about your bright idea to tag-team some girls, sight unseen, rather than spend your night rubbing your boner into her back while she sleeps."

His body let loose its resistance.

"I prefer being the little spoon," he said weakly.

I shut the door on him in reply.

I undressed and took a quickie shower, taking care not to nick myself while shaving my balls and trimming the rest. I stepped into several pumps of cologne. I cranked out a set of fifty push-ups. I dressed commando in gray sweatpants and a muscle tank. I swallowed 50 grams of sildenafil—recreationally, of course. You had to lie and feign dysfunction to get a prescription, but it was all done online now. I snorted a crushed Adderall tablet.

When the girls texted, I tossed on a coat and proceeded to the North Gatehouse to collect them. Upon spotting me, Lisa ran and leapt into my arms, tonguing me longer and more aggressively than she had before. She tasted of mint, tequila, and French fries. My hands settled on her ass cheeks to properly grip and keep her from falling. Liz sauntered over and pinched my cheek, trailing off in melodic laughter, strutting like she was on a catwalk.

Both wore dresses far too skimpy and leggy for the weather.

I would have offered my coat but I couldn't decide to whom.

"Aren't you two cold?"

"Are you saying we're asking for it dressed like this?" Liz asked, laughing a little too hard at her own joke.

"Asking for frostbite? Yeah."

"Oh, this Frost don't bite. Not unless you ask first."

Inside my room, they got to work. I would have pinched myself to check if I was dreaming, but every one of my nerve endings was already tingling. How drunk—or how desperate to please me—was Lisa to go along with all of this? Liz shut off the overhead lights and set the lamp to dim. She found my charger, plugged in her phone, and played R & B music at an atmospheric volume. Lisa tossed herself onto my bed, wrapping herself in a mound of sheets to warm up.

"How'd you know that was mine?" I asked.

It was Liz who answered.

"It's the half with bare walls like it belongs to a psych patient."

Liz began to sway her hips and arms in a trance. I plunked myself into a chair, watching her move. But she didn't look at me. The dance wasn't for me. It was for herself. It nonetheless sent pinpricks up my leg. Her hair was in her face. Only her smile poked through the strands. Her hem rode up her thighs. She slipped off her heels and danced on bare feet.

"Pata sucia," Lisa said, giggling, before she surged forward—shedding my blankets like a butterfly leaving her cocoon—and knocked off her own shoes with a series of kicks.

She joined in, snaking her limbs, twirling around Liz as a moon in orbit. But her eyes were steadfastly on me. The blondes eventually intertwined, arms connecting, legs grazing, bodies nearly collapsing into one another—an amalgamation of skin and hair. It was tough to tell them apart. They were mirror images. They were the same person. They were mine.

I felt the sildenafil kick in.

It was Lisa who pulled me up and over. Her sight line drifted down to the outline of my erection. She was just happy I was finally responding as a man should, not caring that Liz was there, too. If this is what it took to feel loved, to feel wanted by me, so be it.

She placed me between them. I took care to face only Lisa. Her fingers stroked the nape of my neck. I settled mine on her hips. We rocked side to side. Our faces hovered within centimeters, threatening to collide. So close, my eyes crossed if left open. So I shut them. Our foreheads melded.

She lifted my shirt up and off in a fluid motion. She fondled the expanse of my chest.

"What's your tattoo mean?"

She was looking at my heart.

Liz flipped me over. Our faces were nearly level. Her gaze dipped momentarily to the ink on my chest. I felt cold—lost—in the seconds she deserted me. The warmth returned with her.

"It's Gaelic," Liz said. "Means 'fire,' right?"

I couldn't talk. No air was passing through my lungs. My head nod was faint. Lisa was stroking my back. Liz was smiling, staring into my eyes. I heard my heart thumping over the music. I leaned forward.

I had no stronger urge than to kiss her. Not even to fuck her.

It would have been my climax.

But my lips never made it onto hers. Liz shook her head softly but repeatedly, even as her thumb flipped down my lower lip and penetrated my mouth.

"Kiss your girlfriend," she said.

My frenetic heart sank.

She lifted her other hand to my mouth. She was holding a bright orange circular pill. Stamped onto its face was the word "FLY."

"What's that?"

"E."

I stuck out my tongue. She popped it on top. It tasted bitter going down.

"Give one to your girl."

I signaled that she ought to plop a second on my unfurled tongue. She complied. I turned back around, keeping the pill visible. Lisa nodded. I grabbed her hard—pressing her body up against mine, so she could feel all of me—and massaged my tongue against hers, dispensing with the drug.

We didn't separate. In the few seconds of reprieve between sloppy kissing, I was panting like a dog. I began to guide her toward the bed.

Liz was following behind us.

"Ask her," said Liz in a sultry whisper at the foot of my bed.

"Huh?"

"Ask if she will let you inside of her."

I might have ignored her. But her hand was on the small of my naked back, part of her palm grazing the top of my buttocks, and I didn't want to lose her touch.

"Will you let me fuck you?" I asked Lisa.

"Yes, please."

We tumbled onto my bed, me on top. She was grasping at me like she was drowning, palms everywhere. I peered to the side to see Liz wipe the items from my nightstand to the floor and take a seat. She watched us, her eyes large and mouth agape.

I flipped up Lisa's dress; she pulled down my pants. I rained kisses down the naked length of her and nestled myself between her legs. I buried my face in her neck. Lisa brought up the need for a condom. I turned my face to the nightstand.

Liz dug into her clutch purse and produced a golden-wrapped square.

"I'm sorry. I only carry Magnums."

She was toying with me. She was even on the verge of a full-belly laugh, amused in her inimitably smug, self-satisfied way.

I pulled the nightstand drawer out with force and groped for a condom, which my fingertips found in short order. The sharp edge of the drawer scratched her underthigh. We locked eyes as I licked my thumb and caressed the superficial wound—a raised red line—for far too long, wiping away the scuffmarks and the instantly dried blood.

I returned to my business with new verve. Lisa perceived the effort and responded in kind. She enmeshed her fingers with the tangled golden chain that was stuck to my damp neck.

As the tempo increased, my hands kept migrating to her wrists, flirting with flattening them against the mattress but losing my nerve.

"You want to restrain her?" Liz asked.

The room began to throb along to my rhythm. It was the E working through me. Rivulets of color were running down the walls. Everywhere our skin touched sang.

"Yes," I growled.

"Ask her."

"May I hold you down?"

"Yes."

The desperation in her one-word consent was arousing.

I wrapped my fists around her slender wrists—so firmly, I felt the blood pumping through her veins—and shifted my weight down to keep them from moving. I relocated my knees so that they bore down on her legs. She howled in agreement.

Throughout, she hit noticeable peaks, but with all the drugs in my system, finishing felt far off for me.

"May I choke you?" I asked.

"Good, good, good, good," Liz said. I felt the wind of her whisper tickling my ear and the warmth of her breath. She had uttered it like a mystic would a spell, chanting it, singing it.

"Yes!" Lisa answered.

I redirected my left hand to her throat and pressed. Her eyes rolled back.

I swung my head to face Liz. The redness in her face was now trailing all the way down to her breast. She was breathing fast. It was so cute, the way she breathed. Like she was leading a Lamaze class: quick soft bursts of air that made their cool way to my cheek. Her breeze was sweet smelling. Her legs began to close in on themselves. Her hands were crushed precariously in between. She was combusting.

I felt Lisa's eyes refocus on me.

"May I flip you over?" I asked.

"Yes."

I turned her over and carried on, sitting up on my knees. I freely, greedily stared at Liz. She looked back: eyes affixed, steely, almost beautifully angry. Like she hated me for making her feel this way. Only her hands moved: from her hair to her face to her neck and progressively lower.

"Lis...Lis...Lis...Lis..." was my incantation.

Or was it: "Liz...Liz...Liz...Liz..."

I couldn't quite hear anymore. The colors were too loud. Their vibrations were in sync. The blue of Liz's eye was twinkling. It was a collapsing black hole, gripping but lovely.

I felt everything and nothing at all. My body was overheated, sweaty, and exhausted. I was a furnace out of coal. I flopped down on top of Lisa, chest flat against her back, gamely still moving.

I then felt Liz's hands in my hair, stroking the back of my head—so sweetly, so lovingly. I let loose a long, unbridled grunt and finally came in violent spasms. I rolled over, as much as one could on a college-grade long twin bed. All I remembered was the lights dimming to nothingness, the door swinging open and closed, and me sliding precipitously into sleep.

That door opening jolted me awake in the morning. Sunbeams were streaming in from windows whose curtains had been left spread open. My mouth was dry, my abdomen sore. My roommate standing by the door—dressed in the same clothes as last night—was chuckling. I peeked down and noticed I was still naked, not a stitch of covers over me, and even the used condom was still latched on. I pulled on the sheets to shield myself with a corner of the bedding.

Lisa stirred, stretched, and reached for her phone on the floor nearby.

I glared at my roommate, daring him to say a word. He only flashed a smile.

"Oh my God," Lisa said, raising her palm to her mouth. She was still looking on her phone. "My abuela had a stroke. She's in the ICU."

I saw her face crumple and so did my heart. I had loved my own grandparents. I was so young when we first bonded that I perhaps recall a version of them that is rose-colored: all carrot and no stick; all sugary sweet and no medicine. But I swore mine were uniquely wholesome. Each other's first and only love. Never forsaking my father. Seeing virtue in people where there was only rot. So wholesome that I'd wonder if, in reproducing, they had selfishly hoarded all of the good for themselves and left no helping for my father. Maybe left no helping of good for me. I knew the depths of fear Lisa was feeling: adrift and helpless, dejected and guilt-ridden. Not yourself. It hurt to see her lose herself.

I comforted her as we hurried to collect ourselves. Lisa was frantically looking up flights to Miami. I was picking up discarded clothing while my roommate stayed out of it, going about his own morning. He did turn to me once, tapping his chest in the spot where my tattoo rested on mine. Perhaps emboldened by the fact that we had shared in our longest conversation the night before or that he had caught me vulnerable, coming down from ecstasy, and he felt a false sense of intimacy.

"Nice tat, bruh. Mandarin."

The following Monday, I was waiting in front of a Dirksen men's bathroom door with yellow tape across it, featuring the words "Out of Order." My clammy hands were in my pockets, and my heart was in my throat. I intermittently tapped my shoe on the ground, and the thud reverberated as a soundtrack to my shot nerves.

Isla scurried past me with airpods in her ears. She was hugging a fattened brown paper bag the length of her torso.

My hand shot out unthinkingly, grabbing her by the arm.

Isla staggered backward.

"When I saw you, I figured we should chat. I don't think you and I have had a one-on-one since we met."

Her eyelashes flickered while nothing else on her face moved.

I cleared my throat. I wanted to get her on my side. I *needed* to.

"I know you don't care for me much—"

"It's Scoop who doesn't like you. I don't care enough to form an opinion."

I couldn't help but smile. She was so blunt. She masked it so well in group settings, because she rarely said a word. But she was perennially, silently judging. When she spoke it aloud, it bordered on social ineptitude, but she was so self-possessed that it convinced me that this might actually be social interaction on a higher plane.

"You and Liz appear to be close. I see ya'll together all the time."

She was hard to read. There was a noiseless scoff and eye roll, but there was also softness and a slackening of tension that made me think a wall was coming down.

"So is that what this is about? You're trying to get into Liz's pants?"

I choked, a sputtering stalled engine.

"I'm with Lisa!"

I sounded loud, and brash, and over the top. Isla thought so, too.

"Lady doth protest too much."

She looked away, pondering, reconsidering her harshness.

"Liz is a role model. A big sister. Where I see myself in a few years. She looks out for me. I look out for her."

"Right. No doubt. You once alluded to Liz picking up strays like me. What did you mean?"

"I don't remember every damn clever thing I say," she snapped, before softening again. "But it's in her nature. She did it with me. She pulls people into her orbit. She gives them warmth. She shines her light on them. She's the sun. And we're the Plains Natives."

"Huh?"

"They worship the sun."

I chuckled. But she hadn't a hint of a smile.

"She gives, but she can take it all away, you know. She does that from time to time. Especially with men. It drives them wild. Drives them to act in ways they wouldn't normally. When her sun sets, it's cold, cold, cold."

I didn't like her tone. It sounded like she was making fun of me.

My eyes lowered to the sack in her arms.

"What's the deal with the bag?"

"It's a burn bag for sensitive documents. I'm heading to the Office of Senate Security."

I laid a hand on the bag like it was her pregnant belly and shook it. It rattled like it contained plastic. Like it contained cassette tapes.

"It's nice of them to trust an intern with that."

"I'm the office fire safety marshal. Scratch that: Liz is the office fire safety marshal, but she sends me to the meetings for her. It's bitch work, and I've got a background in handling fire."

"Oh, yeah?"

"I was the youngest Eagle Scout in Kansan history. Best fire maker in my troop several years running."

"Whitehurst lets Liz weasel out of the role like that?"

A spark ignited behind her eyes. She moved in closer, planting a hand on my shoulder. I may have even felt a squeeze, but my senses were reeling at the uncharacteristic touch. My armpits became instantly damp.

"Ohhhhhh," she said, her lips forming the letter. "He lets Lizzy do *anything* she wants."

Her smile stretched into perpetuity, running down the side of her face. She was an awful lot like Liz. An awful lot like Sandy. Mocking me for sport. Gauging my reaction. A tease.

I gritted my teeth and spoke through them.

"He must really like her."

"Oh, he *loooooooves* her."

This time, she indulged in a throaty cackle as Randy walked up to us.

"Hello, Cam. Hi, Scoop in a wig."

"Asshole."

The three of us settled into awkward silence.

"Get lost, Isla. Cam and I have to use the little boys' room."

He laid a palm on the taped-up bathroom door, swinging it an inch.

"That one's out of order," she said.

"Not for getting a blowie from my pal, it's not. Scram, and mind your own business."

He disappeared inside. I followed behind him.

He had flipped on the lights and laid his hands on top of the sink, staring at the drain and breathing heavy and hoarse. He looked like a different man from just seconds ago.

"You didn't tell her, did you?"

He cleared his dangling hair out of his frenzied eyes.

"Because she can't be trusted. She'd run off and tell Liz. Liz would tell Charlie. Charlie would tell Scoop. And eventually, the whole world would know."

"I've told no one, Randy."

His lips formed a tight line, and he nodded.

"Good boy. 'Cause I'm spinning out. Spent the night alternating between crying hysterically and typing incriminating search terms into Google. I need to be relieved of this."

He pivoted to face me and pulled down the crotch zipper to his pants. I raised my hands in alarm.

"You were joking back there, right?"

He unbuckled his slacks, reached into his briefs, and pulled out a revolver.

"What the fuck, Randy!"

"I had to get it here from my uncle's office discreetly. It'd be an obvious bulge anywhere else. And if police pat you down, they won't touch there. Now slide it into yours."

"And risk shooting my dick off?"

"The barrel's empty," he said, spinning the clicking chamber to reveal six unfilled slots. He walked over to me, pulled bullets out from his blazer pocket, and slipped them into mine. "You'll have to load it in the committee room. I'll distract Stan. You said you have a key, right?"

I gave him a curt nod before grabbing the gun, untucking my shirt, and wiping the six-shooter down with a corner of the garment. I was shaking from the shock of him sticking to his word. The gun's weight in my hands made it real.

"You're leaving your fingerprints all over it," I muttered.

"I'm not an expert criminal. I'm an aristocrat."

"Same thing."

After cleaning it, I jammed the gun down my underwear. I shivered when the cold metal slid up against my groin.

"It's a rush, huh?" Randy asked, grinning.

"Please don't remind me that this was *just* touching your bits."

"You sure you'll find a good place to hide it?"

"I'm resourceful."

"What if we later forget where? Or someone else finds it?"

"I won't. They won't."

His eyes were wide, and his breath still shallow. The color had drained from his face. He looked like a little boy again.

I sighed.

"Chekhov's gun," I said.

"Excuse me?"

"If you introduce a loaded gun, it's got to go off at some point. It's a narrative principle. We'll find it. We'll use it. Don't worry."

His eyes didn't regain their cocksure veneer.

"Hey," I said, grabbing hold of his shoulder. "You all right?"

"No, Cam. Not since the letter. I'm wrecked."

"I know. I can see that. Try to chill. This, too, shall pass."

We emerged from the restroom and walked off together toward the committee room. The gun's placement was deeply uncomfortable. I compensated by dragging my left side.

"You're walking funny," Randy said. "I know you're not used to having something substantial between your legs, but cut it out."

We didn't have to go far. As we approached the doors, I slipped the key Charlie had prepared for me into my palm. Stan was pacing the long hallway, far enough away for me to recognize his face but miss the details. Randy engaged him at the distant end, leaving me at the doors fifty feet away. I heard his raucous greeting and gave them my back, obscuring the lock with my body.

The key slipped into its hole seamlessly.

"What are you doing?"

I whirled around to face Shelly, and I yelped, allowing the key to plunge to the floor.

I doubled over and grunted—the gun digging into me—and collected the key through the pain. I shot up to catch Shelly's bewilderment.

"I was checking to see if the door was locked. For Liz Frost. Out of Whitehurst's office. She wasn't sure if it was open for a hearing today."

"You checked it by inserting an unrelated key?"

She jiggled the doorknob. It didn't turn.

"It's closed," she said.

"Of course. The lock looked half turned. Thought maybe it was just caught in between. You send an idiot intern, you get idiot work, am I right?"

She grabbed and held on to my hand.

"I hired you myself, didn't I?" she asked.

I nodded.

"Did you send a picture in with your résumé?"

Again, I nodded.

"That must have been why, sweetheart."

She tapped my cheek twice with her hand and walked off. My skin was on fire.

The condescension stayed with me long after she left. It felt heavy in my chest.

Too bad she was cute enough to fuck but not to date.

Awful, I know. For her, that is.

I didn't wait long. I reentered the key, twisted it, pushed forward, and shut the door behind me. Light filtered in from the cloakroom, casting a half circle onto the burgundy-carpeted floor.

I moved swiftly to the dais, to the spot reserved for Senator Lancaster, feeling with my hands for any drawers or compartments. None. I rushed over to the large exterior coat closets that lined the wall. I swung one open to find it empty. I stepped in and searched with my hands. A circular cutout on the backside of the closet had cable and Internet wires poking through, keeping the furniture from being flush with the wall by a few inches.

There were muffled voices and advancing shadows coming from the cloakroom. I flattened myself upright inside the closet, tautening my gut and swinging the doors closed as much as I could. The pit of my stomach was quivering. My devious mind tried to fool my body into thinking it needed to cough. I held it in. I peered through the crack to watch Whitehurst and Williams stroll in from the cloakroom together. The cavernous room carried their voices clear across it.

"You didn't run it by me, Bill."

"I don't recall when *I* became *your* subordinate. I call the shots."

"And yet you let Chris Lancaster call this one. Alcoholic, controversy-ridden, blue-state Senator Lancaster—who wouldn't know the first thing about winning a competitive race in the American heartland. The politics of this are awful."

"All of this has happened before. It's become somewhat the norm. The girl will get up there. She'll sing her ditty, shed some tears, and be heard. She isn't even white. The blowback will be minimal. He'll be confirmed, and we'll look like the good guys for not sweeping it under the rug."

Whitehurst was shaking his head.

"Those were Republican nominees. Tomorrow, a young woman will get up there and eviscerate a Democratic nominee on issues that are traditionally our strengths and turn them into nooses around our necks."

"Is winning all that matters to you, Dale? I swear I don't recognize you anymore."

"Come off it. A lot of good our morals will do us when it's a Republican chairman pushing through judges in white sheets next year. Or worse, in a couple of years, I'll be back on the University of Kansas payroll and you'll be put out to pasture, decaying on a porch in Iowa farm country."

"It's done, Dale. What would you have me do now?" Williams asked.

"Give me the gavel. The members don't respect you. They grandstand and speak out of turn. This isn't about ego. This is about saving our country from right-wing, authoritarian decline. Let me salvage what I can from the spectacle bearing down on us."

I saw through the crack in the door as Williams lifted his cane and wagged it at Whitehurst.

"Over my dead body! You'll have to kill me. Drive a stake right through this ancient, enlarged heart before I let you sideline me. And make sure I've all the way died because as long as I am breathing, as long as this ticker is beating, I will sit in that chair right there, and you will call me chairman, you arrogant son of a bitch."

"It wouldn't take much. You've got one foot—if not both—firmly planted in the grave already. They probably wouldn't even autopsy the body. Figure Father Time finally came to collect."

"Don't you threaten me. I didn't rise out of the Des Moines factory workers' unions without taking out a few knees. I will ruin you."

"How's that, old man?"

"Your office knew about the girl, Dale. She met with your staff. Didn't think I knew that, did you? How do you think that will look once the blood-sucking media sink their teeth into it? Senator Whitehurst—pro-choice savior of women in the American heartland, as you call it—sat on serious allegations of sexual misconduct and did *nothing*."

The silhouettes stopped talking and moving. Whitehurst was steeped in thought. Williams was sneering.

"You wouldn't dare leak such a thing," Whitehurst said finally. "It wouldn't reach me. I'll make some strategic firings. Blame staff for keeping me in the dark. You have no proof that I knew a damn thing."

"Test me. You're not the only one who creates and hoards evidence. I'll forgive you your youthful rebellion—*this* time. Return to your deferential, easygoing nature tomorrow, and we'll put this behind us."

Williams began his sluggish walk to the exit.

"Fine. Go on with your clusterfuck tomorrow. It's your funeral."

With Williams gone, Whitehurst shouted out a series of curses. He marched off in the same direction, tapping at his phone and bringing it to his ear. Just as he was departing, he sent a final remark blaring behind him.

"Lizzy, I'm going to kill the motherfucker."

I pulled the gun out of my crotch, filled the six rounds into the cylinder, and tucked it snugly through the hole, wedged between the wall and the closet, resting on a bed of suspended wiring.

Dear #CapHillSoWhite:

My boss is threatening to expose me.

★ ★ ★

It felt otherworldly to stand adjacent to that room the next day—my eyes trained on the doors to that closet as if I could see through to the gun I had stowed away—with a cadre of police, the country's leaders, and the whole world watching. Judge Wright would face his accuser before 13 million television viewers. Shelly reassumed her role as an intern weigh station, but she put me out of commission early, reserving a spot for me near the front of the cloakroom.

"You just watch, honey," she said in that slow, pity-drenched tone you reserved for simpletons and foreigners who don't speak the language.

Randy joined the rest of the interns this time, posting up beside me.

Others in the gang were present except Lisa, who had left for Miami. Things had felt awkward over text since our first night of intimacy, and I was ashamed that her absence felt like a reprieve. A lot was plaguing my mind, given the plot with Randy, and I just didn't have the band-width to deal with our situationship. She had a late flight to catch the night before, but she texted me an update early in the morning.

Missed my flight. SGS wouldn't quit with the last-minute requests. 😈 Still at the airport.

The day very much felt like the opening night of a play. The audience were in their seats, buzzing in conversation. The supporting cast—hoping for a breakout moment—was up on the dais, shuffling through paper, conferring with their aides. The press formed a gaggle along the wall, snapping and flashing lights like underpaid paparazzi. We were all waiting for the starring actress. Her seat was empty. Only a standard white placard with her name on it embellished her spot in center stage: "Candela Maldonado." It would be the first time the world laid eyes on her. We would not begin until she arrived and walked the sullied, government red carpet to the spotlight.

Her entry was anticlimactic. She was a relatively short Latina in her thirties who slipped in the middle of a parade of taller white male law-yers. She wore a boxy suit that tried to hide her shapely figure, and she had zero makeup. She wore her hair in a matronly bun, but two strings of curls rebelled down her face, threatening to express a hint of style and allure. I didn't know the woman, but her presentation looked alien, antiseptic, not broken in.

"Is she hot enough to harass?" Randy asked me.

"You're gross," Isla chimed in from behind.

"I'm sorry. That was the patriarchy talking."

Funny how differently liberal men talk when they think women aren't around. They're just conservatives with shame.

After hushing the horde with his gavel, the chairman made short, perfunctory remarks. He mostly listed her impressive professional accolades: summa cum laude, law review, competitive clerkships, and a big-law gig on track for partner. But nothing about why we were here. He finished hardly a minute after he'd begun, and it was her turn to tell her story, without much of a preface. Her voice was startling: higher in pitch and mousier than I'd expected it to be. It wavered as she breathed it into the microphone. She was reading from papers unsteady in her hands.

"My name is Candela Maldonado, and I do not want to be here. I fought myself long and hard to keep what I am about to tell you secret. I did what most women know to do from childhood when facing the unwanted advances of men. Brush it off. Blame yourself. Put it behind you. And I was nearly successful.

"But when I watched Judge Wright at his confirmation hearing defend a man credibly accused of raping a young woman, and do so by invoking the image of Emmett Till—a boy mutilated and lynched at the false charge of merely whistling at a white woman—I felt nauseous. It struck me that the more we keep quiet, those of us suffering through serious assault and toxic work environments, the more we will be marginalized and neglected, the less supported other brave women who come forward will feel.

"I have no great illusions about what will happen here once I am done. If history is any guide, Judge Wright will be confirmed. Other women have sat where I am sitting. They have poured out their hearts and told you their truths, and those men who hurt them still sit on their prestigious perches. I honestly have little doubt that Judge Wright will be the third, sitting shoulder-to-shoulder with them in a couple weeks' time. But even in the face of such cynicism, I know my story is worthwhile. It's in the telling that I and others like me will find our strength."

Xoxo, D.C. Gossip Girl @MakeDC51st • 10s
Oh shit. This girl sounds credible.

Candela talked about growing up on her father's cattle ranch in Southwest Kansas as one of eight children. She was of Mexican descent, but her family had lived in this country for generations, since that part of Kansas belonged to Mexico. Three of her brothers served in the US Army, based out of Leavenworth. So committed to assimilation were her grandparents that, as a little girl, her mother was struck on the wrist with a ruler if she uttered a word in Spanish. Candela always wanted to be a lawyer, so she studied hard in high school and got into Harvard, but Cambridge was cold and isolating. Her father grew ill by the end of her time there, so she went home and continued her legal studies at the University of Kansas. She worked nights to help support her struggling family. Upon graduating, she clerked at the district level in Kansas for Judge Constance Borland, who encouraged her to apply to a clerkship in DC. She was surprised when Judge Wright hired her, but she figured her hardscrabble life experience resonated with him.

"You work long, rigorous hours as a clerk at such a high level. Your job becomes your life; your colleagues become your family. I grew to respect, admire, and even love Judge Wright as a father figure. Privately, he is nothing like the staid man he presents himself to be in public. He is warm and gregarious, prone to making so-called dad jokes and being affectionate. It's why I forgave him so readily those first few times his hands grazed mine a little too long, or his eyes lingered on my body, or he would share intimate, increasingly inappropriate details about himself and expect me to reciprocate. If I called him out on it—always lightly, always politely, of course—he'd say, 'It was just a joke!' But it wouldn't take long for him to return to the line, flirt with it, and see what it took for him to cross it. It's like he was testing me, watching what I endured and pushing the line farther out each time—a lapping tide, pulling back and forward, gradually eroding the shore unnoticeably until it was too late.

"The stress of our interactions weighed me down considerably. Having to rebuff his overtures in a nonthreatening way was a second job in itself. He would ask me out on occasion, dropping the names of restaurants or wines he liked and implying that I should join him. I'd say 'no,' always rattling off an excuse about being busy with work. He would tell me, unprompted, how sore his muscles felt after a morning workout and ask me to come over and feel how strong he was becoming. He'd ask if my past boyfriends worked out and to name some of my favorite body parts on a man. After a morning gym session one time, I recall him telling me that when he and his wife were still together, she would treat him to fellatio to relax him if he felt particularly sore, and that it was a shame there was no one present willing to do the same. I just walked out of his chambers, without another word.

"He would casually throw in mention of his masturbatory habits. How, since his wife left him, he'd been abusing himself like a teenage boy—*his* words—and he gradually began incorporating references to me, how he couldn't get through a workday without relieving himself because I was around. It was all talk, incredibly uncomfortable and demeaning talk, until it wasn't.

"One late night, he walked out from behind his desk, sat on its edge—not five feet away from me—lowered his pants, exposed his erect penis, and began masturbating. I was frozen in my chair. It took embarrassingly long for me to process what was happening. And once I did, I took out my phone and stared at the screen, hoping he would see that I wasn't paying attention and stop. But I continued to hear him and catch movement from my peripheral. So I just wept. I stared at the background photo of my mom and dad, and I wept. When he was nearly done, he made sounds that prompted me to look up, not least of all because I had the alarming, skin-crawling fear that his semen might end up on me. He was that close. But he reached for his cup of stale coffee, ejaculated into it, and—out of breath and laughing—asked if I wanted to drink it.

SoccerMom76 @KarenKiley_76 • 2m
This guy's sick. He has no business sitting in
judgment of anyone, let alone women.

"The day he reached under my skirt and digitally penetrated me, I distinctly recall nothing forewarning it. That's how it always was. I even came up with a term for it: drive-by harassment. He would talk about legal doctrine at length, throw in a sexual remark, and pick right back up on the law without a blink, without a stutter. He left me without time to respond, without time to recover. That day he violated me, he said nothing relevant before or after it happened. I do recall he smelled his fingers and crinkled his nose afterward. That was when I lost it. I ran out of there in tears and vomited in the restroom. It was the humiliation that sent me reeling. I didn't feel human anymore. For the first time in my life, I remember thinking that I wanted to die.

"I lost a significant amount of weight. He noticed. He warned me that if I continued to lose fat from my breasts and buttocks, he would no longer find me attractive. I remember losing hair in the shower. I hope this isn't too personal, but my period became quite irregular, to the point that I hadn't menstruated in half a year."

Out in the crowd, you could hear nothing but errant coughs as she described staying put because there was a definitive end date. With three months left, she began counting down the days on a paper calendar in her office.

"If I could just make it 'til then, I thought, I would not have gone through all of this in vain. This was the most prestigious job I had ever held. You don't let go of that lightly.

"So when it ended, naturally, I wanted his endorsement for a clerkship on the Supreme Court. This was entirely normal. The DC Circuit is what's called a feeder court. It is by no means guaranteed, but it is a logical next step, and everyone seeks it out. And honestly, after what he put me through, I thought I deserved it. He wrote me an exemplary letter of recommendation. So I wrote him a demonstrative thank-you note in return. That is customary in my industry. I didn't want to burn a bridge with a man who would undoubtedly continue to go far in life. And I was genuinely grateful for the words he put on the page, praise I had earned that focused entirely on the quality of my work product. I didn't get a Supreme Court clerkship. But I wasn't surprised. I went to work at a big law firm instead, and my ordeal with Judge Wright was finally over.

Wright's Coffee Cup @CreamInHisCoffee • 1s
This is all awfully convenient. Como se dice
'gold-digger' in Spanish?

"I'm sure there are people out there scrutinizing my every action and inaction over the course of that year. I don't blame you. You can't come up with any criticism that I haven't already hurled at myself. I can supply you the rationale behind my decisions but that doesn't mean they were always the most rational. I don't see my job here today as justifying anything. I see my job as telling it as it is—the horrific, the unexplainable, the unimaginable—all of it. I just want someone, anyone, to know what happened to me. It's up to you what you do with that information."

The room was both silent and loud, devoid of noises except for the mechanical sounds of blinking camera shutters. The chairman looked lost, but not as he typically did, just out of words instead of out of his senses. He swiveled his head to the Democratic side of the aisle, hoping to gain some sort of nonverbal support, but all of them looked just as blank. The woman had just given a performance of a lifetime. And everything in politics was performance.

"Thank you, Ms. Maldonado," the chairman finally said. "Let me begin by commending you for your bravery. I only have a few questions. You mentioned Judge Borland. Were you aware that she testified in support of his nomination before this committee in truly unequivocal terms?"

"Yes, I am aware."

"How do you explain that and the numerous other women who have come forward to vouch for Judge Wright?"

"I can only speak to my own experience. I will say that men who treat certain women inappropriately can treat other women with the respect we all deserve. They have mothers, they have daughters, they have wives they love and adore. None of it precludes them from preying on women at a power disadvantage. As for Judge Borland, a black woman I know he revered, I'm honestly not surprised he didn't act lewdly in front of her."

The chairman bared a nervous denture-heavy smile.

"Why do you say that?"

She stared down at her hands, caught in a fit of blinking, as if she were considering declining to answer. She broke into her own curt, uneasy chuckle.

"May I quote his colorful language?"

Chairman Williams dawdled, quivering mouth open, as if he wanted more than anything to say no.

"Of course."

"He once told me that black women were for marrying, but white women were only good for fucking—and that, as a Latina, I was close enough."

Her hand shot to her mouth. She was straining to hold her eyes open, to keep from crying, but she failed. Just as tears rolled down, she immediately wiped them away with the back of her hand, as if they offended her. The chairman shuffled in his chair, ultimately leaning far back, as if he wanted to fade into it.

"I yield back the balance of my time."

That wasn't common. If there's anything senators love most, it's using up their time to speak.

"The chair recognizes the ranking member."

Senator Johnny LaRue began his remarks by rambling, stripped of his usual eloquence. It sounded as if he hadn't quite settled on a position. As a Republican, he knew he wanted to tank the president's nominee. But as a conservative, he allowed bouts of skepticism to seep through, unable to shake his bias against domestic-abuse survivors. He was two men—battling one another in public view. He finally settled on a question.

"You told us the judge groped you—"

"Penetrated me, sir."

"Right. *That*," the senator said, red-faced. Men loved sex talk, but only when they had field advantage. In this venue, with a woman dictating the terms, the senator hated it. "What were ya doing so close to him? That he was able to reach?"

She only half stifled a sigh.

"I actually remember it well. It was the day I returned to work after my father passed away. Judge Wright wanted to console me. He walked over to hug me. It was when he pulled away—as I was sniffling, as I was drying my eyes—that he reached under."

There were gasps from the gallery.

Senator LaRue found his convictions. They fortuitously aligned with his politics. Had they not, he would have found a way to lose them.

"That's just appallin', young lady," he said. "This country is going to hell in a chicken coop. I will do my damnedest to make sure that man winds up nowhere near the Court."

"The chair recognizes Senator Whitehurst."

He didn't speak right away. He sized her up, warmth in his eyes, chin resting on his propped-up hand. He flipped through a binder—microphones picking up the flurry of turned pages—and nestled a pair of reading glasses on the bridge of his nose. When he spoke, he did so through a smile. I watched him on a screen. He was telegenic. Having heard him in his seedier moments, I had forgotten how self-assured and charming he came off when the curtains were up. He had "future president" written in his eyes. It was nauseating.

"I am proud to call you and your family my constituents, Ms. Maldonado. Thank you to your brothers for their service. Your life story serves as an inspiration to us all, and my office stands at the ready to supply you with any resources or help you may need once this is over and done with. I wanted to read into the record the thank-you note you referred to. Is that all right?"

She nodded, but her face was unmoving.

As he read, he tried casting a neutral tone, but he emphasized key words along the way, seemingly subconsciously.

"*Dear* Freddy—*I am beside myself with emotion. As I write this, I am crying my eyes out, with pure joy of course, at the letter you wrote on my behalf. You are a smart, loving, kind, and* moral *man—a legal giant on whose shoulders generations of lawyers will stand—and we don't deserve you. I am a lucky gal to have spent our days—and many a* night—*talking about life and the law. I will miss you. And when the time comes for you to make history, and I know you will, I will be right there behind you, giving you my full-throated endorsement.* Yours, *Candy.*"

He whipped off his glasses.

"You often address the judge, your boss, as Freddy?"

"He insisted. Everyone in his orbit called him that outside of the courtroom."

"And you called him moral?"

"We shared religious beliefs. I knew he would like it if I said that."

"It sounds as though you often spent nights with him?"

"We worked late. I mentioned that. It was a tough job."

"But none of the other clerks were around? Particularly on the night you say he exposed himself to you?"

"The other clerks were married. They had children. They had families. I was single. I didn't have anyone waiting for me at home."

"And, as you noted, Judge Wright was single, too? Divorced at the time, right?"

This was Senator Whitehurst, the prosecutor, reliving his days as the hotshot Wyandotte district attorney. It wasn't hard to see how he might have enthralled jurors: winsome for the women and gays, strong but unimposing for the straight men. His words were scalpels, gently incising—not hacking—into her story with a finesse that was riveting.

"You OK?" Randy asked me.

"What do you mean?"

"You're sweating buckets, bruh. It looks like you're going to be sick."

I did feel sick. Like I was going to lose my breakfast. I wiped my brow.

"I'm fine."

"You thinking about the packed heat?" he whispered and formed a finger gun. I slapped his hand down.

"Yes, that must be it."

"Chill. My uncle hasn't even noticed it's gone."

I returned my attention to the cross-examination of Candela Maldonado.

Whitehurst noted that she had declined the judge's invitations to dinner, saying only that she was busy.

"Not because you were uninterested?"

"That was implied."

"Or because his request was inappropriate?"

"Women learn to turn men down gently."

"Certainly a supervisor attempting to court a subordinate is inappropriate. But it's not illegal, and it's not necessarily sexual assault. Might this have been a misunderstanding, Ms. Maldonado? If you addressed him in the manner you did in this letter, might he have thought he had a shot and been inappropriately persistent but unaware that—without a clear 'no,' without a shove, without a complaint—you did not consent to his pursuit?"

Her eyes were wide and her mouth mimed words, but no sound came out. One of her lawyers laid a hand on top of hers. She winced and scooted her hand away. It snapped her out of her stupor.

"I don't have to explicitly tell others not to pleasure themselves in front of me or not to reach under my skirt in a place of work."

"But he never threatened to fire you, right?"

"He did not."

"He never told you to keep any of this secret, right?"

"No."

"In fact, he allegedly did these things out in the open. We call the opposite consciousness of guilt—and it can be powerfully incriminating. But Judge Wright showed none of that. He acted as if he thought he was doing nothing wrong."

Her eyes were wet again.

"It's funny how being audacious about it can be a defense."

Whitehurst let the lamentation sit.

"Your time is up," Williams said. "The chair recognizes Senator Denton."

The senator was leaning far forward, putting all of his weight on his forearms, looking like a slumped marionette with his limbs spilled on the table. I half expected him to extend an arm and point his crooked finger down in castigation like God toward a meek and fingers-laced Candela.

"I'm sorry, but I'm finding this all better suited for the back pages of *Playboy* magazine and not the US Senate. Time and again, the confirmation hearings of male candidates to the Supreme Court have been dragged into the gutter, prying into the sex lives of adults instead of focusing on the law and jurisprudence. But here we are, dishonoring and debasing this country's institutions with years-old allegations. The time to adjudicate such a matter was *then*, when it happened, not now, coincidentally when the man is on the verge of reaching the height of his professional career. You are accusing Judge Wright of *rape*. Why didn't you report any of this to the police when it happened?"

Candela recoiled when he landed on the word "rape" in that singsong Southern drawl of his.

"I was in no emotional state to involve the authorities. I had just lost my father. I was scared of losing my job. I had no interest in bringing charges against the judge, or sending him to jail, or even stripping him of his judgeship. I just wanted it to stop."

"Why didn't you tell any of this to anyone?"

"I didn't have anyone to confide in. I was alone in the city. And I was ashamed of it—too ashamed to tell my mom. I would never talk to my brothers about it. Most of the clerks were men, and I didn't want the women to see me differently. I resolved to keep it to myself and never tell a soul."

"And yet here you are. Telling your mom, and your brothers, and your former colleagues, and the rest of the freedom-loving world at precisely this moment. Why now? Out of revenge? Because he dared stand for due process and the constitutional rights of the accused?"

"I should have come forward earlier. But it's daunting for victims to do so in everyday circumstances, let alone when your abuser is a prominent federal judge. I am stronger now—that's what's different."

"What's different are the scores of high-powered attorneys funded by dark money who are whispering in your ear and doing the bidding of liberal interest groups. I feel sorry for you, Ms. Maldonado. You're being used as a pawn in this hatchet job of a moderate, centrist candidate so that President Stevenson can turn around and nominate a liberal in the lame duck. You're not paying for any of these fancy-pants lawyers, are you, miss?"

"They're offering their services pro bono."

"Of course they are. You looking for a seven-figure book deal out of this?"

She audibly scoffed.

"No, Senator. I don't need money. I do all right for myself."

"I guess torpedoing this man's reputation will have to be payment enough, huh?"

"You don't expect me to answer that, do you, Senator?"

He didn't.

After several rounds of questioning, it was Senator Kelley's turn. Other than Senator Grunwald-Santos, she was the only other woman on the panel. Spectators perked to hear from an undecided female voice. But she yielded all of her time without a comment or question. The disappointment from the crowd was palpable.

Grunwald-Santos was last to speak. Her voice was firm and carried to the back of the room with power. She was addressing the witness, but she wasn't so much looking at her as she was looking into the camera.

"You come here, Ms. Maldonado, making a simple request, the same request many women before you have made and will continue to make: to be believed. We are repeatedly told it is never the right time to speak up. If it's in the moment, then it's why didn't you scream louder, fight harder, say 'no' ten, twenty, thirty times more until you lost your voice and passed out from the strain. If it's the next morning or a few days afterward, well then, you've waited too long. The moment has passed. But it's never too late for the truth. And we do men a disservice when we pretend they require a bullhorn to understand when a woman isn't consenting. We treat every allegation of sexual assault—regardless of where we are: in a court of law, in the court of public opinion, in a committee hearing to decide whether to bestow the awesome privilege of a lifetime appointment—as if it requires proof beyond a reasonable doubt. And then we define proof beyond a reasonable doubt to mean the woman has to justify her very existence, every move, every decision. The truth is that the standard doesn't matter. Because we never believe. We see the bedroom as sacrosanct, immune from public scrutiny and policing. And it's expanded to the workplace. Anywhere a man designates as sexual, the matter is deemed private, consent too blurred, the details too sordid and smutty for polite society to evaluate. I won't stand for it. I stand with you instead, Ms. Maldonado, and every other forgotten woman who has shouted into the wind to no avail. Futility will not silence us. I for one believe you."

She turned off her mike. The chairman banged his gavel.

"We stand in recess and will hear from Judge Wright when we reconvene."

Isla jammed the hand holding her phone in between Randy and me, directing our eyes to the screen with her thumb. The phone was open to Twitter, showing the tweets from the two major presidential candidates reacting in real time to the testimony of Ms. Maldonado.

Governor Chad Thornton @ThorntonRevolution • 3h
The Stevenson-Jones administration has done it again. Judge Wright is a predator. The President ought to withdraw his nomination, and let the American people decide who should fill the seat. Candela Maldonado, I believe you.

Vice President Kiara Jones @JonesforUSA • 2h
Candela Maldonado is a courageous young woman for coming forward with her truth. Her words were powerful and moving. President Stevenson should withdraw his nomination of Judge Wright. Candela, I believe you.

ELECTION NIGHT

The roommate's hands were gripping the edge of the table, white knuckling it, as if it were a precipice and he were dangling off the side.

"I know nothing about him. He kept me at arm's length—farther than that even. He was mentally down the block. Shared nothing. Avoided me. Appeared generally resentful of me. And I tried. But he's an asshole. Plain and simple."

When he moved his hands, their sweaty outlines were left behind on the metal top. He wiped the remnants away with the edge of his sleeve.

"I don't think there's anything deep about him to discover. I think that was the problem. I'm a white guy, too, but that's a new thing among white men in this increasingly multicultural society: feeling unspecial, feeling unremarkable. He probably just wanted to be seen. I don't share that white male angst. My girlfriend's Asian, you know. I studied Mandarin in college. I *get* it. I'm *down*. He just came off like another meathead, tattooing himself with a symbol he didn't understand just to seem exotic. Pathetic."

He was shaking his head, drifting in unpleasant memories.

"He must have been a secret smoker. Who smokes anymore these days? Never saw him with a cancer stick in hand. But he once came home, just a few days ago actually, late at night, reeking of smoke. And I mean the stench was overpowering. It was a cloud emanating from him. As if he had just crawled out of a burning building and barely made it out alive."

10

RUN, SENATOR, RUN!

Judge Frederick Wright strutted into the committee room a new man. Flanked only by his sons, he walked brisker, he breathed huffier, the muscles in his face—from his wide eyes to his snarled lips—were twitchier. He wasn't talking, but every bone in his body was screaming. The meek man was coming undone.

"Judge Wright, the floor is yours."

The witness had nothing in his hands.

"I would thank you for giving me this time, but I fear the writing is plainly on the wall, and I do not feel gratitude, only revulsion. I have worked hard to make it here. Labored twice as hard, and twice as long, and minded my p's and q's like a good ole boy, modulating my blackness so as to be nonthreatening, so as to be palatable, climbing the ladder ploddingly, methodically, but quietly so I can finally be accepted. So I can finally be one of you. I learned that dance long ago, as a black kid in Cambridge making do. And what has it gotten me? A public flogging. Tied to a tree and lashed down to the bone. Cast aside and tossed away. Because I am disposable. Because we are all disposable as soon as we exhaust our usefulness to you. Well, no more. I won't shuck and jive for your entertainment. I will only be myself and speak the truth.

"I did none—*nothing, zero*—of the things of which I've been accused. I categorically and unequivocally deny them. They are anathema to my being as a man, as a father, as a Christian. Simply put, they are lies.

"I wish I knew with certainty what is motivating these fabrications. I can no easier climb into the mind of Ms. Maldonado and explain to you why she has come here, now, and wedded herself to this *story*, as I can bare my own memory and show you what actually happened. It puts me in a precarious position. It is famously difficult to prove a counterfactual. And let me be clear, *everything* Ms. Maldonado has stated is indeed counter to fact."

He conceded she had a way with words. It was she, in fact, who had written that much-ballyhooed sentence in the dissent: "...the kangaroo court hollowed out but dressed up in law." She was a gifted storyteller, a spinner of fiction. He had no sexy counternarrative to tell. The tedium and monotony of legal research and writing wasn't as exciting. It wouldn't sell papers.

He pointed out that she was struggling with her mental health.

"Ah, the old nut-or-slut defense," Isla whispered to us. "There's one..."

"I was aware of the one or two attempts she made to take her own life. She was open about it, and her colleagues informed me of it, too. I advised her to seek counseling, and it's my understanding that she followed through. But she was not of sound mind or heart that year. I'm glad to see she is doing better, but the woman who came before you today is not the same woman who clerked for me all those years ago. I can't say whether she convinced herself of ugly things, whether she genuinely believes them because of the trauma that beset her, but I can tell you they have no basis in reality.

"It's also true that she developed a certain affinity for me, particularly after her father died midway through her clerkship. The effusiveness of the note she wrote is a good example. In retrospect, her attachment to me was probably unhealthy and unprofessional."

"...and there's the second," Isla said.

He apologized if he indulged her for too long, humored her far too much, left the door open for her to have misread his empathy as affection. He was her elder and employer: it was his responsibility. But he didn't want to transfer her, didn't want to punish her for developing a schoolgirl crush. He wrote her a glowing recommendation letter because she deserved it. Her work was top notch. But she was noticeably cold when the Supreme Court turned her down.

"There was a sense of entitlement there that didn't sound like the woman I knew. Like I was talking to a stranger. Like I had been talking to an *actress*."

For years, the two maintained friendly contact, checking in around holidays and clerk reunions.

"Until last weekend, that is. Until it appeared all but certain that I would be confirmed, and the radical left wing got ahold of her. I don't blame Ms. Maldonado. She is a sensitive woman trying to piece together a very rough period in her life. She has been led astray by dark and powerful forces that see her as a means to their own ends, and I pray that she be given grace, peace, and solace.

"But I do blame *them*. For dragging this process and this storied institution through the mud. And I do blame *you*. For giving them the platform to do it.

"Make no mistake, these forces are partisan. The judiciary is meant to sit above the political fray. But we have increasingly perverted it. These confirmation hearings have become warfare. Just another way for the political branches to score political points. No matter the human collateral caught in the crosshairs. I am a human being, *dammit*—"

His fist thumped down on the table, creating thunder, rattling pens, sloshing water out of the glass in front of him. A sigh riffled through him like a shudder, and his voice regained its traditionally measured composure.

"—I am not a political football. I have a family. I have a reputation to uphold. And I won't allow craven special interests to undermine all of that for a political power grab. This is more than just about a job now. This is about human decency. This is about lending mere accusation the power to tear down good people and their careers. If you cave in to it, it won't stop here. There will be every incentive to dig up whatever claim ten, twenty, thirty years into the past, however uncorroborated, and crucify humble men and women called to public service. This will all become a trial by fire, discouraging even the thickest of skins from committing themselves to the greater good.

"You debase yourselves—"

His voice cracked. His eyes were wet and gleaming. Camera shutters went off in a frenzy.

"You debase yourselves..." he tried again, before cutting himself short. "I have half a mind to just walk on out of here. Withdraw my nomination. Say, 'Forget it all. This isn't worth it. You've broken me.' But then I think of my sons. I can't have them see another black man run out of this town. See him quit. See him defeated and his head hanging low. That isn't the example I have set for them. You're going to have to vote me down. You're going to have to go on record. I've been counted out all my life. I sat here and had flour blown in my face like my ascension to the Supreme Court were a comedic bit. Like I was a fool. But I am no one's fool. I am a man of integrity and honor, and I won't back down."

He settled into his chair, noisily readjusting the microphone as the veritable period to his statement.

In the stretch of silence that proceeded, eyes gradually collected at 2 Bills. His gaze appeared unfocused, affixed to the back wall.

"Chairman," Whitehurst said.

The old man didn't so much as blink.

"Chairman!" Whitehurst tried again, reaching over and shaking him—hard. He sputtered alive.

"Huh? What? Where?"

He clawed at Whitehurst's extended hand and stared deep into his eyes.

"Judge Wright has finished his statement. It's time for questioning."

Recognition filled the elder's eyes. He tossed Whitehurst's hand aside with a sneer.

"Of course. Thank you, Judge Wright," Williams said. "I am pleased to hear you sympathize with Ms. Maldonado and do not blame her for where we find ourselves. That's big of you. I have a question..."

He scanned his papers, flipping pages in a panic.

"...but I fear I've lost my train of thought."

An aide jumped up to whisper in his ear. Eventually, he waved the kid off, sucking his teeth.

"I don't think I heard you say whether you deny the allegations made by Ms. Maldonado."

Judge Wright's eyes narrowed.

"I did, Chairman. I deny them in as strong terms as possible."

"I see. Well, I think that's important. Don't you, Dale?"

He said it casually, as if he had forgotten that he was in conversation with the country and not just a personal friend. Whitehurst didn't try hiding the confusion and disdain wrinkling his brow. Williams's lips quivered. His shining eyes moved over to his colleague, stripped of the bravado. He was the most powerful man in the room with a literal gavel in his hands, but right then—slumped over, sad, and lost—he looked every bit his age. The sight stole my breath. I felt secondhand embarrassment. The interns around me were exchanging glances and whispering to one another. I watched only him like a car accident on a backed-up roadway.

"I think you're done with your questioning, Bill," Whitehurst said. He commandeered the proceedings: "I recognize ranking member LaRue."

The Louisianan's volume and rhetoric began at a ten.

"It's always about race with you people," he said, cutting short a natural pause and adding, "you *liberals*," before groans could metastasize in the crowd. "Well, marry my niece and call me a monkey's uncle, because I just don't get it. According to that young lady's testimony, you're a race hater yourself, disparaging white women as nothing but sex objects. Whites won't get a fair shake on a Wright Court, will they?"

"That's preposterous and bordering on slanderous," Wright said. "I seem to recall a certain sitting justice calling *his* confirmation hearings a 'high-tech lynching,' and if I am not mistaken, Senator LaRue, you regularly name him as your favorite. I don't think it's coincidental that we share a skin color and similarly unconscionable treatment by this panel, if decades apart. But a member of your party nominated him, and I suspect that's the true difference. I understand the game—it isn't new—but be straight with the American people when you're playing it."

"Let me be straight then. You have disqualified yourself from continuing service and brought shame to the judiciary. I yield back."

"I recognize myself," Whitehurst said, eyeing 2 Bills, who didn't appear to protest the takeover by his second-in-command. "In the last round of questioning, Senator Denton decried our detour from the law, so allow me to try and bring us back. Tell us, Your Honor, why does the law recognize certain statutes of limitation? For the non-lawyers watching at home, that means certain allegations can't be heard once a certain number of years has passed. Why not?"

"With time, memories grow faint or become distorted. Evidence fades, is subject to tampering, or is lost. Witnesses disappear, become infirm, or die. The credibility of the matter is increasingly suspect. For all, there is a season. But most of all, the law favors finality. We can't have the threat of litigation forever hanging over someone's head. We can't empower complainants to choose without restriction when to bring charges, lest their motives be corrupt. We seek the truth but only up to a point. Eventually, the silence controls."

"And we are tasked with making a judgment here," Whitehurst said, "but we're not all operating under the same burden of proof. And we haven't even settled on whose burden it is. Is there any court in this country where the accused has to prove his innocence?"

"No, Senator."

"Right. In America, the one making the allegation is charged with proving the matter. In this case, that would be Ms. Maldonado. Proof beyond a reasonable doubt doesn't feel quite right here. This isn't a criminal hearing. So let's go by their standard: fifty percent plus one. We have her word. We have your word. Classic stalemate. But it's her burden. It's on her to bring additional proof. Has she proffered a single person to back up her claim? A friend, a coworker, a therapist? Has she submitted a single contemporaneous document that meaningfully moves the needle? A journal entry, a letter, an e-mail?

"But *you* have, Judge Wright. Included in the record is a thank-you note indisputably written by her *after* the alleged impropriety. It corroborates your position that nothing untoward happened between you two. It undermines her credibility. And credibility is important here when we have a universe of just two witnesses. We've had a litany of supporting letters and live testimony vouching for the judge's decades-long stellar reputation, a significant chunk of them from women above him, below him, and everywhere in between. The signatories have only swelled since these allegations came to light. On her part, we have an admittedly distraught and disappointed young person, put through the emotional ringer and waiting the better part of a decade to speak up. Can my colleagues honestly say, by any metric that is fair—outside of pathos, or emotive appeal, or gut instinct—that these allegations have been substantiated? That any fair-minded jurist wouldn't rule in your favor?

"And I understand we make up the rules as we go here. Advise and consent means whatever you want it to mean. But as a country, we've thought long and hard about how to resolve genuine disputes of fact. Our system, while flawed, is the best system in the free world. In that system, Judge Wright is not guilty. He is not responsible. And we cannot in good faith punish him.

"I now recognize Senator Denton."

The senator's beady eyes had turned into slits, eclipsed under the weight of fluttering eyelids. He lifted a paperback book in his veiny hands and stuck his nose mere centimeters from its pages, obscuring his face from the television audience with its spread cover. The book's title—*What We Say to Ourselves in the Dead of Night*—was featured prominently in red bold type.

"Funny you should mention fiction, Your Honor," Denton said. "I'd like to read a passage from a popular romance novel published in 1999, when Ms. Maldonado was growing up. A warning to parents: the following excerpt gets spicy."

Gertrude slammed the keys on her typewriter as Mr. Lerner dictated a missive to his loving and faithful wife. The two eyed each other from across the room, as the contents of his dictation grew increasingly lurid. She loosened a blouse button with her left hand—still typing with her right—and fanned herself in the sweltering office devoid of air conditioning. He sat at the edge of his desk, as his manhood firmed—

At this, there were snickers.

—underneath his corduroy trousers. She fled her station— and her senses—and dove to her knees. She unzipped him

and let him loose, nursing him with her mouth. When he was close, he alerted her by tapping her on the head and took the matter into his own hands. She planted her lips on the inside of his thigh. He finished in a spasm, reaching toward his glass of gin—knocking pens over in the process—and depositing his cloudy product into it.

"Would you like me to drink it?" she offered.

Awaiting no answer, she knocked back the concoction and giggled.

"You taste like danger, only sweeter," she said.

He peered over the edge of the book and was met with stillness. He set it down and leaned into his microphone.

"Pardon the smut. It's exactly the type of filth we need to ban from so-called sex education curricula. But the similarities between this story and Ms. Maldonado's account are striking. It's entirely possible she lifted the details directly from the novel or—having read it as a young girl—internalized it and, in her trauma, mistaken it for an actual, resurfaced memory. There's no way to know. And with that, I yield back."

"That was certainly...something," said Senator Lancaster, inviting chuckles, his lips sewn together in a pursed, small smile.

The hearing carried on like a match of table tennis. It was Sunday sermon for the Republicans—all fire and brimstone and wrath without the salvation or redemptive parts. Very Old Testament. Then, in a whiplash in tone, the Democrats pursued cautious but friendly questioning, tiptoeing around and massaging what was the delicate beating heart of it all. This was about sex. It was about power. Denton's softcore reading hadn't been too far afield after all. He had just said the quiet part out loud.

Senator Kelley demurred once more, forfeiting her time without comment.

Grunwald-Santos closed the proceedings. She set her sights immovably on Judge Wright. He gamely locked in on her in return.

"Some of my colleagues undoubtedly watched your forceful denial and saw strength. I didn't. I heard a screed. I saw a tantrum. This is what it looks like when a man feels entitled to something and is unaccustomed to it being withheld or delayed for even a moment. You pound your fist on the table. You yell until you're blue in the face and point fingers at everyone but yourself. And the lengths other men will go to defend you—close ranks, contort themselves and their purported values into a disingenuous pretzel, sift through softcore pornography published when Ms. Maldonado was just *thirteen* years old—it's staggering.

"Withdrawing your name from consideration wouldn't be weak, Judge Wright. It wouldn't set a poor example for your sons. It would show a commitment to healing and humility. It would send a message that this seat doesn't belong to any one person. That there are plenty of men *and* women capable of filling in, doing the job, and doing it well. Justice does not begin and end with you.

"But from what I've seen, I doubt you have it in you to step aside. You showed the American people your true self. It isn't the veneer of calm Ms. Maldonado confirmed you adopt in public. Under pressure, back against the wall, when a choice must be made between the good of the country and your personal ambition, we see how you respond: petulantly. And that man—the man we saw dissembling earlier—doesn't seem so unlike the one Ms. Maldonado described, the one preying on a subordinate because he knows he will get away with it.

"I'm confident I would approve of the overwhelming majority of your opinions. Securing your presence on the Court would advance progressive causes for a generation. Certainly I'd take a hundred Judge Wrights over a single nominee Governor Thornton might make. And yet you leave me no choice. After your performance today, I'm not even sure you possess the judicial temperament for the job. I cannot in good conscience turn a blind eye to what you did to that girl, no matter the political or ideological expediency it would bring.

"I've seen enough. If the president doesn't pull your candidacy, I will be voting against your nomination."

The committee being so closely divided as it was, Judge Wright could not afford to lose even one more Democrat.

Whitehurst adjourned the session with the rap of the gavel.

Isla shared her screen with us again. The president had spoken.

President Bob Stevenson @POTUS • 10s

Judge Wright has vehemently denied any wrongdoing. I won't be withdrawing his nomination to the Supreme Court. He deserves an up-or-down vote.

I followed the milling crowds out of the room, losing Randy and Isla as we spilled into Dirksen's halls. I let the current carry me toward the elevators. It brought me to Chuy and another of Senator Kelley's senior aides, a white man named Tom. Surrounding us were demonstrators, women with signs and raised fists who broke out into a familiar—now inversely motivated—chant: "Wright is wrong!"

A series of knuckles shot straight up and caught Chuy in the nose.

I saw their head snap backward. I sprung over to their side and laid a hand on their back. Tom had seen the blow, too. He hit the call button on the elevator car labeled "Members Only," a restriction only applicable during votes, but the public didn't know that. When the doors slid open, I pulled Chuy inside, and Tom joined as the third passenger. The screaming masses did not cross the threshold.

"You all right?" I asked in the peace of the elevator.

"Yes. Fine."

On cue, a torrent of blood plunked down from their nose, spraying their hands and hitting the ground. The stream was so dense, the splatter landed with a thud.

"Shit," Tom said, leaping and shrinking into a corner.

"It looks worse than it feels," Chuy said.

The doors opened to the tunnels. Chuy started out but slipped on the blood. They came crashing down to the floor so hard, the elevator jostled. I crouched down to a squat to help Chuy up.

"I've got wipes in the office," Chuy said.

"No!" Tom yipped, quickly stepping over to the perimeter of the car to exaggeratedly avoid the puddle at the center and blocking Chuy from exiting with raised palms. "Are you having an episode or something? You can hardly stay upright nowadays. We can't let the senator see you like this. Your condition: it's not contagious, is it? You ought to clean this up. Sterilize it. You know, *just in case*."

Chuy only blinked.

Tom backed away and left, speeding down the hallway.

I wiped up the blood with saliva and balled tissue from my pants' pocket, leaving a thin film of reddened brown behind. Chuy wasn't moving.

"Let's find a bathroom."

Chuy wasn't much help. They allowed me to guide them, looking forlorn and lost in thought along the way. I returned us to the Hart Building, where a wave of cresting voices floated up from the ground floor. We leaned over the banister to peek down at the building's hollowed-out center. Hundreds of women in pink wool hats sat cross-legged on the surface tile, their yells bouncing off the marble walls and carrying up several flights.

These were not the same women protesting Wright's abortion

221

politics last week. I spotted newly prevalent nose rings, streaks of funky-colored hair, rainbow insignia, and Birkenstocks. One sign read, "Wright is Rape." Another: "Believe Women." A third: "Chief Rapist." One woman carried a blown-up graphic of nine justices with three of their faces crossed out. Its caption read: "One-third Predators." One sign just read, "I hate it here."

Capitol police officers were securing the protestors' arms behind their backs and handcuffing their wrists. Some had to be dragged, refusing to stand, howling as they were made to slide across the squeaking floor. Batons were out. Hair was whipping. Spit flew. My heart pounded secondhandedly.

"This way," I said, backing away from the sight.

Inside the men's room, Chuy moved to the sink on their own, lathered their arms, and scrubbed them raw.

"What kind of person thinks what you have is transmissible?"

"An asshole. You should have seen the way he avoided me like the plague the week I came back from a gay cruise."

My phone vibrated in my pocket. I glanced at its face advising of seven missed calls. I answered and lifted it to my ear. I thought I was having service problems because I heard no one on the other line.

"Hello? Can you hear me?"

"I didn't make it in time."

Lisa's voice was flat.

"She's dead, Cam. My abuela is gone. I was too late."

My stomach dropped.

"Oh. I'm so, so sorry."

Chuy flipped around from the mirror to pause and face me.

"I didn't even get to see her. She was waiting for me, and she held on as long as she could, and I missed it."

No goodbye. That thought haunted me. My skin grew itchy and my chest felt leaden. I was numb.

Lisa fell apart on the phone. She was a faucet turned loose. The receiver was filled with her sobbing and errant hiccupping.

"It's not your fault."

I was reaching for the words, but it was hard to get them out past my tense chest.

"Of course not. It's that bitch's fault."

She was barreling through her words.

"Who?"

"The senator. Sandy. She knew about the family emergency. And it was still, 'Do one more thing for me. Just one last thing.' She didn't care. She never cares. Fuck me."

"No, fuck her!"

I said it like I was speaking directly to my mother. I had felt the same anger toward her once. She also had kept me from a proper farewell.

"I hope she fucking dies, Cam! I'm serious. I want her dead."

I knew the feeling. I had wanted my mom dead, too.

I listened quietly as she wordlessly cried for several minutes.

Dear #CapHillSoWhite:

My boss kept me from saying goodbye to my dying grandma.

★ ★ ★

Chuy texted just shy of midnight and asked to meet on the steps of the Lincoln Memorial, centrally located to our homes. They said they knew it was late, but they didn't have anyone else to turn to. I told them I'd be there in thirty. I rented a scooter off the street and motored the mile and a half along the moonlit Potomac. It was a cool night and the wind at my back made it cooler, but I didn't mind. I had felt feverish since Lisa's breakdown. Might have been in reaction to that, or the swigs from my flask I had taken throughout the day.

Chuy was already there in what passed for them as casual clothing: an animal print short-sleeve, capris, and leather slippers. I was in a hoodie and joggers. They were standing before the giant sixteenth president, neck craned to stare into his vacant eyes. Even this late, a few stragglers hung around, including a set of parents snapping pictures while their children slept on their shoulders and two teenagers making out in the shadows.

"Nice drip," I said from behind. They didn't turn.

"Kelley claims to share ancestry with Lincoln—d'you know that? She and Tom fucking Hanks," they said. "She's as batshit as Mary Todd, so it makes sense to me."

They turned my way.

"How's Lisa?"

"Homicidal."

Neither of us cracked a smile.

"I had a fistful of benzos in my hand when I texted you," Chuy said. "I filled my tub with warm, soapy water. I had a bottle of my favorite Cab Sav on the ledge. I was ready to swallow the blues and submerge myself. Leave this place how I prefer myself: high as all hell."

It shocked me, how close to the edge Chuy had been pushed. They said it so casually, while my anxiety soared. We can't lose them. They are a bright light in this world—a pick-me-up when everything is going wrong. So self-assured. So effortlessly funny. We depend on them to lift us up when we're down. They *had* to know that. How much they mean to us.

Their face crinkled, eyes shined, and lips emitted a short whine. I pulled them into me. They stood just a bit taller, so they bent their knees to rest their head above my clavicle.

"I don't know why you like me. I don't even like me," they said.

The solution seemed obvious: "So become someone new."

Chuy disengaged and tilted their face up to peer at me.

"Aren't you supposed to tell me to never change and learn to love myself or some greeting-card shit like that?"

I shrugged. "Hasn't worked for me."

I pulled out my flask and shook it in their face. "Let's talk about it over a drink?"

"You sure you want to swap saliva with me? You know, *just in case.*"

Their grin was sardonic, self-pitying, sad. They were still so close, I could smell the perfume wafting from them: notes of lilac and honeysuckle. I cupped the back of their warm neck and crashed my lips on top of theirs, hard. I left them there for a few heartbeats, parting them only slightly. Their own were moist, soft, and tasted of gloss, but the barely visible stubble above them scratched me like sandpaper—a new sensation. This wasn't romantic for me.

I wanted them to feel loved in that moment. I wanted them to know how close I felt to them. Even the air that separated us was too far.

When I pulled away, they leaned back in for a second kiss.

I rested my open palm on their chest to draw them short.

"That was a onetime deal, bud."

They nodded. We moved over to the top stair and sat. I kicked my feet out down several steps, elbows locked and hands down on the cold concrete. They had their knees tucked into them. The reflecting pool unfurled before us was pitch black. The Washington Monument on the other end was a towering spear stabbing into the starless sky.

"Senator Kelley knows I have MS."

"I didn't tell a soul, Chuy."

"I know that."

They sipped from the flask. Their face contorted.

"Is this gasoline?"

"Pretty much. It'll put hair on your chest."

"No, thank you. I pay hundreds a month to get it lasered off."

I took a slug. "Why would anyone care if you have MS?"

"Small-minded, uninformed people who worry I'll go limp or have a seizure in front of constituents. You know, go full eyes rolling back into my head, foam streaming out my mouth. Like you see in the movies. She knows, and she thinks less of me for it," they said.

"How?"

"Must have seen my medical file."

"Isn't that illegal? A HIPAA violation?"

"You seem to be under the impression that things like laws and rules apply to them. They don't. Besides, I waived it for her—specifically her and only her. Unthinkingly. I signed something when I was a kid starting off in her office years ago. It was strongly encouraged, if not an implied requirement for getting the job. Her son has a rare auto-immune disorder. And HR sold it to me as an easier means to get sick leave approved and mental-health accommodations, should I need it. I have a history of panic attacks. My therapist recommends I take a day off every month for self-care, so I figured it'd be a good idea to let the boss have access to my medical history. These were progressives—I didn't think I had any stigma to worry about."

"You think she told others?"

"We had an interaction at the Capitol Hill Club. Just days after the Wright scandal blew up."

"Isn't that place for Republicans?"

"Yes. I had to choose a place to bartend for my sommelier midterm. I butched myself up for it and everything: wiped away the nail polish, no foundation, dressed as plainly as Charlie—"

"And myself?" I was baiting them. My smirk gave it away.

"No, sweetie. You're on another level. If you hadn't just kissed me, I'd call you *violently* straight."

My body tensed. I pivoted. "What was she doing there?"

"Meeting with Senator Denton. Just the two of them. Over oysters and lobster. A real meal of the people, you know? I served them their wine. They were making some sort of deal over the Wright nomination. She wanted something in return for a 'yea' vote."

"A bribe?"

"Horse trading. You really are new to Washington, aren't you? Not like money directly in her pocket. Pork for California. Some sort of transportation project. Probably a new freeway, like we need another one of those. Denton's the ranking member on Approps. He can make it happen."

"You think that's how she'll vote? The only other woman on Judiciary. Based on funding a highway somewhere?"

"Kelley'll do whatever is in her personal best interest. Full stop."

"And if Grunwald-Santos found out?"

They snorted.

"She'd kill her herself, don't you think?"

"Not if you get there first."

They looked away.

"What did she tell you, Chuy?"

When they turned back to me, only seconds later, there were fresh tears in their eyes.

"She didn't do it in front of Denton. She pulled me aside. Said she wouldn't feel comfortable with me continuing to serve her or anyone for that matter. 'Not when you might have a flare-up. You understand?' she asked, but it didn't feel much like a question. I agreed to go home. I felt really awful. Like maybe she was right, and I was being insensitive for even feeling offended. Like maybe I was just damaged, and I had to learn to accept that.

"She said this one last thing that stayed with me. 'Don't you think everyone in the office has a *right* to know?' It was their right to know, not mine to tell. I actually nodded. I felt insecure about the whole thing, and I didn't know how else to respond. Others have been treating me differently even before Tom's meltdown. I thought I was being paranoid. I never would have imagined she would go and do it. Just spread it like a harmless office rumor. I mean I can't sue, can I? My parents have political careers of their own to worry about. And someone down the food chain always takes the fall. Maybe Tom would go down, but not Kelley. So I thought about dying. It's always the white noise in the soundtrack to my life. Growing up like this—identifiably queer—it's always in the background. When I'm feeling really low, it resurfaces. It seemed like the superior solution to just quitting. Maybe they'd feel sad? Feel responsible? I'd like that. I'd want them to think they'd killed me.

"But they would just move on, wouldn't they? No one cares longer than a day. Guilt is temporary in Washington."

They finished off the flask and wiped their lips off with a sleeve.

"I've been meaning to ask...do you run, Cam?"

"I can run. I've got strong legs."

"You may want to try Rock Creek Park. It's beautiful there. Particularly between five thirty and six thirty in the morning. The trail by Broad Branch. Just stunning. And who knows? You might just run into someone. Someone who could use a scare."

Dear #CapHillSoWhite:

My boss told everyone about my secret disability.

★ ★ ★

I awoke in a fog when it was still dark out. I was dehydrated. My throat was scratchy. Crusts had formed in the corners of my eyes. I threw on sweats, laced up my running shoes, and sprinted the four and a half miles to Rock Creek Park in under thirty-five minutes.

I slow-walked the trail cratered by sheets of towering rock and along a bubbling tributary underfoot. The ground was swathed in red and yellow foliage, and the air was dense; it filled the cavities of my lungs.

On mornings like these, the climate couldn't figure out what season it wanted to be. Bugs zipped and stuck to my face as if I were a windshield. My boozy sweat must have attracted them.

I was there to go sightseeing. See if I could spot a certain senator. Send her a message. That's how our representative form of government works, right? We have the right to petition for a redress of grievances, and oh, did Chuy and I have some grievances to sort out.

Nearly no one was around. That made the sight of movement downhill easy to spot. It was like I had conjured her with my mind. Her name, Kelley, had been on my lips on a whispered loop before she appeared. It made my heart giddy and my mouth dry.

I lay in wait for her in the trees. Her oversized Berkeley sweatshirt, and her Lycra leggings, and the details of her face began to fill in as she neared. She was alone. She looked small, unimportant. Here, she was no one but a middle-aged woman in frumpy clothing, open to the elements, vulnerable to wildlife.

I let her pass and counted out the seconds to ten Mississippis. I then followed behind, matching her pace to maintain our distance. Far enough not to rouse suspicion.

Close enough for her to feel me.

The chase peaked my adrenaline. It shot up my legs and settled in my groin.

I began to kill the space between us. She was a magnet, drawing me near. I pounded pavement harder. My strides were longer, more graceful. More lion than gazelle. This close, I could see her neck was thin.

When I pulled up to her eight o'clock—the length of two, maybe three prostrate bodies away—my eyes swung to her right. We were heading uphill. The fall was growing in distance and danger. It wouldn't take much. Just a little shove.

She sensed me, and I could see her body tense up. She pivoted her head to catch a glimpse. Once. Then, a second—this time a smidge longer. Not a third. That would be staring. That would be rude. Plus, I wasn't black.

I drew parallel to her. I matched her bounds. We hit the earth at the same time.

She looked at me again.

I lunged at her.

She came to an abrupt stop. So did I. Her sneakers skidded on asphalt. She yelped. There was horror in her eyes. My hand landed on her shoulder. I didn't push. I tapped.

With my non-offending hand, I shoved a fiver in her face. A Lincoln. "You dropped this."

She hadn't.

Out of breath, startled, and speech lodged in her throat, she accepted it nonetheless.

I unleashed a fit of coughs into the air and my open hands. She recoiled.

"I'm sorry. I'm very, very sick. Say 'hi' to your son for me."

I took off and didn't look back.

Liz charged into the intern cubicle the next morning and flipped the television on.

"Kelley's announcing her vote on the floor right now."

As the senator began speaking, Liz reached for my hand.

"The tenor of our politics has never been coarser. This country is divided, and there are forces on both sides—the right *and* the left—that use terror to advocate for their causes. The number of threatening messages relayed to my office has skyrocketed. I want you to interrogate what role you have personally played in raising the temperature. I want you to make a conscious effort—with your family and with your friends, in your schools and in your churches—to tamp down this rhetoric. Before someone ends up dead.

"I won't bow to ugly pressure like this. I won't allow the politics of hate to color my judgment. I won't blindly follow what others say my gender demands."

"She's voting for the bastard," Liz interjected.

"Women are not a monolith. We think for ourselves. I came to this decision after careful, reasoned contemplation, evaluating all of the testimony put before us, as well as the credentials and experience the nominee brings to bear.

"I will be voting to confirm Judge Wright. There is no question the man is qualified for the position. The boy from Inglewood, California, has indeed come very far. Our highest Court ought to reflect the diversity of our people, and his ascension will be an inspiration to countless young boys and girls across this land. I will not stand in the way of that. Not when this nominee is as superlative as everyone says he is."

"Not everyone," Liz said.

Senator Kelley seemed to intuit the reproach.

"I do not take the allegations from Ms. Maldonado lightly. They cause me great concern."

"Senator Kelley: Always concerned. Never does a damn thing about it. Spineless," Liz muttered.

"She should be heard. She should be taken seriously. And she was. That's what we do in America. We listen to both sides. But there was nothing—outside of her word—to corroborate her claims. I won't just choose one side over the other. Not based on sympathy. Not based on some purported loyalty to womanhood.

"Judge Wright has expressed remorse, and I believe he has learned his lesson. I have no doubt some will refer to me as a gender traitor or a political shill. Let your voice be heard and loudly, but do not pair it with a raised fist. Now will be a time for healing. That is my prayer for this great nation. A republic—if you can keep it."

Liz had her arms crossed, and her fingers were digging into her skin, leaving imprints. She was staring at the screen but speaking to me.

"You agree with her, don't you?"

I scoffed.

"What makes you think that? I never say shit."

"Because you're a man."

She was doing that thing she does, and I wasn't in the mood for her prodding. It didn't feel sexy at the moment. And isn't that the reason I put up with her jabs the way I did? Because it lit my thighs on fire.

"I'm agnostic," I said.

"What a privilege."

11

GANG OF H8

Half of my body and face were spattered with blood when Chuy swung open their front door. I was wearing a clear bloodied poncho over a full suit.

"Dad on a rainy day at Disney World? Carrie as prom *king*?" they asked.

"Patrick Bateman," I said, lifting the toy ax in my hand. "You know, *American Psycho*?"

"If looks could kill."

At midnight, it would be Halloween. Isla and Scoop would also turn twenty-one. Chuy was hosting the costume birthday party at his sprawling home in Alexandria. All of the Hill's young staffers had been invited, not just the Democrats, not just the core eight of us—everyone. It had been billed as epic, as a suburban rager worth the cost of the Uber to get there. Chuy didn't disappoint.

From the doorway, I could hear a professional DJ spinning records and see the pumpkin-foliage décor mixed with traditional birthday fare.

Chuy's getup was obvious. They wore a blond wig, red lipstick, pumps, and an iconic white dress, a flowy number single-strapped around the neck with a kinetic skirt ending just below the knee.

"You're Marilyn."

"With a beauty mark this gorgeous," they said, signaling beside their lips, "it's either this or Cindy Crawford."

Chuy pulled the door wider away to reveal Liz beside them: same outfit, hair pinned up, miming the pose of holding down her rising dress above an imaginary sewer grate.

"Jinx," she said with a squeal and a wink.

"Now this has me sexually confused," I joked.

The Monroes giggled.

"Speaking of sex, do you stare at yourself in the mirror while having it and flex like your character?" Chuy asked.

"Oh, he doesn't do that," Liz said, purring.

"Why do you say that?"

She wiped my cheek with her thumb and sucked the dyed corn syrup off it. Déjà vu.

"'Cause his 'O' face ain't the prettiest," she said.

I finally noticed the person standing behind her that whole time. Charlie wore a plain suit—the same black jacket, white shirt, and red-or-blue tie combination he sported every workday. I lifted an eyebrow.

"It's a couples costume," he said gruffly. "I'm JFK."

Pinned to his lapel was a button that read: "Kennedy '64." Militantly minimalist.

"Lisa still in Florida?" he asked.

We had kept in textual contact, but our phone calls had dropped off.

"Prepping for the funeral, yeah," I said.

Inside, a respectable crowd had formed, but the space wasn't brimming. I joined the others in the living room doubling as a makeshift dance floor. Isla wore a floor-length red frock and a white bonnet.

"Handmaid?" I yelled over the music.

"Amy Coney Barrett," she corrected.

Randy would have looked like a monk in his plain black robe if it weren't for the scythe he carried in his hands.

"A little on the nose, no?" I asked him out of the others' earshot.

"It's for easy access when I score later tonight."

He lifted the hem above his waist to flash the side of his bare ass.

"Dude." I shielded my eyes belatedly. For effect.

"King of the underworld but not underwear, eh?"

He chuckled at his own joke.

Scoop looked like an English schoolboy.

"Cam's definitely a Hufflepuff," he said to the group.

"I don't know what that means," I said. "Never read the books."

"What kind of antisocial head case doesn't know *Harry Potter*?"

"The kind that gets laid, Red," Randy said. "I don't know who in their right mind dresses as Ron fucking Weasley for their twenty-first birthday. No one wants to fuck Ron Weasley."

"Cam's a Slytherin who doesn't know it yet," Liz said, laying her arms lazily across my shoulders. "Or he's just really, really good at hiding it."

I smelled alcohol emanating from her pores already.

"I need another drink," Charlie announced, pulling Liz away a little roughly toward the kitchen.

"Careful, or I'll go Lee Harvey Oswald on your ass, Jack," she told him in a just-sweet-enough chirp.

I leaned into Chuy.

"Marilyn's had a fair amount to drink," I told them.

"And this Marilyn is trying to catch up. I want whatever the hell she's having," they said.

"Hey," I said, locking eyes although I could see nothing but shine. "You OK?"

They mulled it over, incisor tearing into their bottom lip, before nodding.

Chuy had lost some of their glow since the other night. It weighed on me.

"Blood brothers, remember?" I said.

I reddened my right hand with spatter and offered it to them. They accepted it with a smile.

"Para siempre."

The party picked up precipitously. The home filled out with people, white mostly. Randy was guzzling. I stuck to clear liquor and soda water. Fewer calories. We were standing by the bar as he refilled his cup yet another time.

"I'm thinking we lay off my uncle. At least for a while."

He wasn't looking at me. He spoke it into his cup.

"Your anger's fading."

"No. Never," he said. "He's just been doing the right thing lately. Slowing down the whole Wright coronation. People are counting on him."

"You want Wright voted down?"

"You don't?" he asked. "I'm a hoe, Cam. Not a hypocrite. Besides, it's what my dad would've wanted. I'm sure of that."

"Too bad he isn't around to cast a vote himself," I said.

He winced.

I pulled in so close, he could no doubt feel my breath.

"You sit in your anger, Randy. Let it fester. Let it grow. Let it metastasize, wrap itself around your heart, and squeeze until you cannot bear it. And then, only then, do you make up your mind. That's when you make your move. That's when you'll truly be free."

I didn't want him bottling up his emotions. Pressure finds release whether the time is opportune or not.

There was that pall of uncharacteristic sadness in him again.

I didn't pull away. I gripped the back of his neck. He was so warmed by the touch, he purred. I nodded. He nodded back.

"Who hurt you, Cam?"

He smiled, jokingly, but it faded just as soon as it came.

I lingered in my heartache.

"Just *being* hurts enough."

"Randolph Lancaster!" a white man shouted, although he had already moved within feet of us. He sported a country accent, blue jeans tucked into leather boots, a double-breast-pocketed wrangler shirt, a black rancher's hat, and a mustache. He shook Randy's hand.

"Carlisle Bucky," Randy greeted back. His smile was tight, lacking warmth. "This is Cameron Leann."

We were all using full names. Like proper networkers.

"Congressman John Mustard's Office," he said, offering me his hand. Name, then occupation. Right.

"Senate Judiciary. Majority," I said, following convention.

"Oh, wow. Busy time for you, then. Exciting time. I'm thinking of making the switch over to the Senate myself. Shall we exchange business cards?"

"I'm just an intern."

"Today's intern is tomorrow's chief of staff. Besides, no one who's a good friend of Randy's is *just* an intern."

Randy laughed.

He pulled a card from his wallet and handed it to me. Carlisle Bucky was, indeed, the congressman's chief of staff. He didn't look much older than Randy.

"Bucky's from Texas," Randy said.

"Dripping Springs," he said, exaggerating his twang.

"This isn't a getup, by the way. This is how he always dresses," Randy added.

"Stereotypical AF," Bucky said, hands up in surrender. "Down to the pickup truck parked outside."

He waved us over to the window. Bucky pointed out the soot-ridden, flatbed truck propped up on massive tires in the driveway. He pulled out his phone from his shirt pocket, unlocked it by bringing it up to his face, and tapped on a bright green app. The car roared alive—engine purring, headlights beaming.

"Remote start," he said.

When we turned back around, Randy was gone.

"You dressed as a blood bath, Cameron?" he asked, winking.

I nodded along, although he was wrong.

"Kind of like what's happening in that committee room, amirite?"

"Oh, I don't know. I think Wright comes out alive."

"Whoa! Am I getting some insider information here? What has the senator's nephew been telling you about the kingmaker's thinking?"

"The opposite, actually. He thinks he'll shoot him down."

"So what brings you to the contrary view?"

"Well, he's a man, isn't he?"

Half of his lips shot upward. He liked that.

"But by the grace of God go I," he intoned.

I sipped from my drink, the first swig in a while.

"You don't dress up for Halloween?" I asked.

"Nope. Never did. 'Cause of that God fella I mentioned."

I loosened my tie, unfastened a pair of shirt buttons, and flashed the golden cross hanging from my neck. He did an emphatic double take.

"Mark of the beast in this godforsaken town," he said. "You sure you're not an 'R'?"

"I don't have any appreciable politics other than self-interest," I said. It felt good to be honest. I could let my guard down with him. He was like me. "What about you? You want Wright voted through? The natural political order is turned upside down on this one."

"Nah. I don't. It's not the president's seat to fill."

"Excuse me?"

"He didn't legitimately win the last election."

Not entirely like me.

"Oh, well, now you've lost me. Did you help storm the Capitol that one time?"

He bared his teeth, but I wouldn't call it a smile.

"You opposed to patriots rising up against an out-of-touch government that no longer represents them?"

"Not necessarily. Opposed—offended even—by the harebrained way they went about it. In daylight. On camera. Broadcasting who and what they represent on flags with big, bold lettering. Where's the finesse in that?"

"Finesse? In a fight against tyranny?"

"In violence of any sort. If it's the message that's most important, fine. I guess bang your pots and pans as loud as you want straight to a maximum-security penitentiary. But if it's the kill you're after, be surgical. Be covert. Come correct."

The features on his face danced.

"You're strange, you know that? You sure don't sound like a Dem."

I shrugged.

"A Wright Court won't regulate the bedroom. Or a woman's body. That's good enough for me. I just want to fuck without consequences."

Bucky lifted his cup in a toast.

"Amen," he said. "Ultimately, that's all us men want."

I clanked my cup with his.

The clock struck twelve, and the house lights came on. There was singing and the slicing of cake. Liz had a sway to her while she was standing. Her eyelids were half-moons drooping down. I focused on the throbbing vein branching down the side of her neck. My own blood grew hot under my skin.

She hadn't chatted me up all night. I missed her attention.

I poured her a drink and approached when she was unattended.

"What's this?" she asked, slurring.

"Water."

"Nope."

She tore it from my hands, stalked over to Bucky, and shoved the drink into his chest.

"Stay hydrated, cowboy!" she howled, before returning to my side.

"You ignore me all night and now reject my offering?"

"I don't need you to rescue me, Clark Kent."

"You don't call me that," I noted. "Are you mad at me? From the other night?"

"You'll need to be more specific."

"The night of the threesome—um, sort-of threesome."

"Again," she said toothily, "more specific."

I grunted. She was playing cat-and-mouse with me like always. It frustrated me. She relaxed her body. Her hand darted to my forearm.

"I wasn't there, honey. You dreamt me up. Conjured me like it was a sensual séance. That, and you were tripping balls."

"You play with me. It's like you hold me under water, give me just enough air before driving me back down again. I can hardly catch my breath. It's exhausting."

"Then why do you keep coming back for more?" She was beginning to look more sober.

"Because I'm obsessed with you, and you know that."

She gasped. Her tiny hand flew over her mouth.

"You're mocking me?" I asked.

The sharp corners of her eyes wilted.

"No. I'm genuinely surprised to hear you have feelings for me. Do you even have feelings?"

"I avoid them as best I can."

She laughed and then looked away.

"You're not obsessed with me, Cam. You said it yourself. You won't hurt someone for me. Maybe only yourself. And that's not enough."

There it was, her games. I caught her chin and turned her to face me. She took a deep breath.

"I lied. I love hurting people."

"And the wolf sheds its sheepish outer layer."

"That's all a matter of perspective. Peter Pan is just a guy in tights kidnapping children from their beds, and Captain Hook is the good guy trying to stop him."

"Weird take, but OK."

She pulled out her phone and began scrolling. Its glow lit up her face but deepened the shadows hollowing out her eyes.

"Have I bored you?" I asked.

"No. I just need you to hurt my boyfriend for me."

"Huh?"

"I came across this a few hours ago. I don't think his name's out there yet, but it's only a matter of time. It doesn't seem like anyone's told him about it."

She flipped her phone so I could read a tweet.

> **Luke Russell @PolitburoLMR • 3h**
> **Late breaking: 'Senator Denton Caught Berating Driver**
> **in Racist Tirade.' Hear the audio exclusively here:**
> **https://www.politburo.com/news/senator-berates**
> **-driver-in-racist-tirade.html**

"This is going to crush him," she said.

"Liz!" I snapped, shaking. "Why haven't you told him?"

"I'm drunk," she said. A tear materialized out of nothingness and ran down her face. "And I can't watch how he takes it. I won't."

"Why me?"

"He trusts you."

"No, he doesn't."

"Yes, Cam. He does. You were there with him."

She didn't need to explain. I knew when she meant.

"Now?"

"Before he hears it from an enemy and not a friend."

I needed to prove myself to Liz. Show her I was courageous and reliable. I marched over to the bear of a man. He sat on the arm of a couch, looking like *The Thinker*: pensive, sinewy, and every bit carved of bronze. Maybe he knew. He was already a defeated man, slumped over and camouflaged by the black. I felt great pity and shame for openly coveting his woman.

"Not feeling the party?" I asked.

"Not feeling being made into a cuck. Watching my girlfriend throw herself at every swinging dick here."

My nose twitched as if it had picked up a foul stench. My sympathy fled me. I was disgusted and jealous of how entitled he sounded. I understood that women weren't property, but—if this one *had* to be anyone's—I wanted her to be mine. I didn't call him out on it, though. Men don't do that to other men.

I went in for the kill instead.

"You know she lied to you."

He stood up and towered over me.

"How so, Clark Kent?"

"She *has* tried out the whole open relationship thing. Once."

I thought I finally had something to lord over him. But his grin made me recoil.

"Oh, she told you about that?"

"Not the details. Just that she had," I said. "You told me she hadn't slept with anyone else."

"I lied."

I must have looked flustered. I came for the king and missed. How pathetic.

"So, she didn't hide it from you?"

"We did it together."

"You had a threesome!?"

I nearly shouted it.

"I wouldn't call it that. Two of us didn't touch. By design. On purpose."

"Liz didn't let you touch the other girl?"

"Who said it was a girl?"

He sat back down. I was stunned. Begrudgingly impressed. He hadn't struck me as the type. I pulled out my phone.

"I have something to show you. And you're not going to like it."

I searched for the article and handed it to him. He read it silently. The changes in his face were subtle but noticeable. Everything flared just a tad. His hold on my phone had transformed into a grip. When he was done, he looked up at me as if to ask, *What's next?*

"You want to hear it?" I asked.

He nodded.

"And you want to do something about it?"

Again, he nodded.

"Then let me gather the others. I know where we can go."

I pulled everyone into Chuy's art studio. With the door closed, the music was muffled and only the thrumming of heavy bass rattled the walls. We kept the lights off. Plenty of moonlight crept in from the floor-to-ceiling windows.

Charlie was leaning against a table with his arms crossed when I hit play.

"Sorry I'm just returning your call now. My nigger driver forgot to relay your message. You know, that [bleep] kid? I swear, these mud people are more hassle than they're worth. But you gotta hire 'em these days, I guess."

Charlie didn't react. Scoop was bouncing.

"That asshole!" Scoop said. His voice was quivering.

"What did they bleep out?" Charlie asked.

"I think it's your name," Liz said. She was beside him, looking lost and not touching him, which was unusual. "Looks like they didn't use your name in the article, either. Kept you anonymous."

"That won't last long. Your job's public record," Chuy said.

On cue, Charlie's phone lit up.

"DC number, but I don't recognize it," he said.

"Don't pick it up," Liz said.

A voice mail notification popped up. He listened to it.

"*Washington Post*. Seeking comment," he said flatly.

"I'm pressed," Scoop said. I couldn't quite see tears but I thought I heard sniffling. "What can we do?"

"His place is nearby," I said.

A few heads turned to me but only briefly. After I spoke, Charlie kept his focus trained on me.

"You think reporters will be camped out at your apartment?" Randy asked.

"I don't know," Charlie said.

"Then you and Liz should stay over. Maybe for a few days even," Chuy said. "There's plenty of space. Just gather your thoughts. Lay low for a while."

"I can't. They're voting on Wright this weekend. I'm picking Denton up from the airport tomorrow," Charlie said.

"Wait, he's in North Carolina?" I asked.

He was still looking at me. He nodded.

"So no one's at his home?" I asked.

"So what?" Scoop barked.

"So I think Cam is proposing we pay it a visit," Charlie said.

"And do what?" Isla asked.

All eyes were on me now. I loved that they looked to me for mischief.

I walked over to the giant wooden cross leaning against the wall. I ran my palm down the length of it. A splinter penetrated me. I left it there.

"The senator talks like it's the 1950s," I said. "I say we send him a message straight out of that era."

We resolved to wait until the party was in its dying gasp before

Charlie and I would head out to the Denton estate, sans jacket and in rolled-up sleeves. Everyone else would stay behind.

"Why you two?" Scoop asked, jealous.

"We're the strongest," Charlie replied.

In the meantime, we all danced. We didn't talk. We didn't drink. We just swayed our bodies and stared into each other's knowing eyes, a slight smile tingeing our lips. We now shared in a secret. It was thrilling and nerve-wracking, and it bound us to one another.

The logistics weren't entirely clear to me until I surveyed the final stragglers closing out the night. Among them was Bucky Carlisle, passed out face up on the couch: legs askew, snoring, and hat sliding off to reveal significant balding.

"Odd," Randy remarked. "I thought he was a teetotaler."

"Check this out," I told Charlie.

I removed the phone from Bucky's shirt pocket, held it up to his face, unlocked it, and tapped the green app I had seen him open earlier. His truck engine turned over.

The boys plus Chuy helped carry the cross to the flatbed. We fastened it down with a rope. The girls loaded the car with canisters of paint thinner. Chuy gave us disposable gloves so we wouldn't leave behind fingerprints in the car. I drove us over. It was my idea after all.

The plot of land was pitch black. Just the silhouette of a home against rolling greenery steeped in shadows.

"No security cameras?" I asked.

"Not in the yard. Drive right onto the grass."

I bypassed the driveway and pulled into the field with the headlights off. I didn't come to a stop until Charlie told me to do so. In my rearview, the home was a small pentagon that I could blot out with the tip of my thumb. We sat still and silent for a long while, staring out at the landscape. I pressed my gloved ring finger, pricked by the splinter, into the steering wheel so I could feel some pain.

"He ever call you that word in person?"

"He didn't need to," he said. "I heard it in his tone."

"Why'd you stay?"

"Sometimes you seek approval from the shittiest people. So you don't feel so shitty yourself."

"You still want to do this?"

"I'm not second-guessing. I'm just processing."

"Then we'll sit here. Until daybreak if we have to. Until you're ready."

I surprised myself by reaching out to touch his forearm. He surprised me by leaving it there. As much as we competed, I wanted him to know I cared for him. And I did, especially in this moment. He wasn't alone.

And so we sat. I couldn't turn the engine off. I had no way of turning it back on. Its vibrations were comforting and sleep inducing. I dozed off. I didn't wake up until I heard the car door slam. I caught Charlie moving toward the back. I sprung out of my seat and joined him. Without exchanging a word, we fell into a sort of choreography, intuitively knowing how to help the other out.

We dug into earth with our hands. His tore through it like a shovel. A palette knife helped keep the hole perfectly rectangular, just wide enough for the base of the cross to fit snugly. We made the slot deep enough so the cross wouldn't keel over. We laid down the wooden structure to douse it in paint thinner. We huffed a whiff of the intoxicant. My brain smarted.

When we had soaked it, so its brown camouflaged into the black, we erected it, grunting and fumbling it into the slot. I climbed onto Charlie's shoulders and put weight on the horizontal beam to secure it in.

We had to rile ourselves up before setting it alight. We bumped chests and roared.

A rush of blood coursed warmly beneath my skin. There was a tingle in my toes and fingers—dancing nerve endings—that sent me floating above ground. Our cavorting was a talismanic ritual that shook off any lingering inhibition. We were drunk off our zealotry.

Using gas lighters, we met the crucifix with fire.

It was swallowed faster than I'd anticipated. Even as I felt the heat singeing the hair from my arms and its flickering blue-orange light blinding my eyes, I continued applying flame to the body. Charlie had to wrap his arms around me and pull me back, as smoke the smell and color of a tar pit emitted in plumes straight into my face.

We tumbled down to the ground, rolling several feet away.

We watched it burn. From our knees. Out of breath and laughing. We felt untethered to the earth and drifting among the stars.

When we saw lights flicker on in neighboring homes down the road, we scampered into the truck and sped off. I could hardly tear my eyes from the rearview sight of the smokestack floating high, blocking the stars.

Dear #CapHillSoWhite:

My boss is a racist prick.

By the time we returned to Chuy's home, the adrenaline rush had worn off, and the two of us were wrung out. Liz had been waiting on the porch. She didn't say a word, but her pursed lips were asking a question.

"It is finished," I said.

We made our way to the bedrooms. She led a sullen Charlie into one. I wasn't paying attention and nearly followed them inside. She laid her hand on my chest to stop me. There was a slight smile on her lips. Maybe it was a sneer.

I turned around, found a vacant room, and slept—alone.

It was Saturday. Just three days before Election Day. The Senate office buildings were sparsely filled. Senators had their skeleton crews with them: a junior staffer for menial tasks, a chief of staff or legal counsel, maybe a press person for messaging. That was it. As a lowly intern, I had not made the cut. In fact, I had still been in my sleeping clothes, settled into a corner of my bed with my laptop tuned to live coverage, when Randy called.

"I'm picking you up in fifteen," he had said. "We're watching the vote from inside the committee room."

"I'm not working. I won't be let in."

"The fuck you won't. You're with Randolph Lancaster, soy boy. Wear a jacket."

This time, Randy wasn't relying on name alone. As we pulled up, he handed me a glossy VIP pass identical to the one he wore around his neck.

"Compliments of Uncle Douchebag," he said, eyes rolled into his skull.

The committee room itself looked trimmed down. There was less spectator seating. Not as many reporters and photographers had been invited. The Democrats no doubt wanted it to be a muted affair. A loss in the vote would represent a significant failure for the party just 72 hours before the country voted. A win wasn't cause for raucous celebration, either—not with liberals threatening to sit the election out and independents reportedly wary of partisans pushing through a tainted confirmation with the clock winding down.

Randy and I sat in the front row, hugging the far-right aisle. It brought us level with Grunwald-Santos. She looked on edge. Wright wasn't present, likely watching his fate from the White House with his team. From the gang, I caught sight of only Charlie, by the door, and Liz, by White-hurst. I hadn't seen either of my friends since the party. Charlie was stoic, as always. Liz was slumped in her seat. Her mascara was slightly streaky. Her eyes were puffy. She had a bad case of the jitters.

"Doesn't leadership already know how your uncle's voting?" I asked.

"No," Randy said. "He was still undecided as of last night."

"I thought these things were choreographed in advance."

"Not always. Sometimes—just sometimes—there's magic."

Chairman Williams called the session to order. One by one, in their assigned turns, the senators speechified before casting their votes.

When Whitehurst voted aye to advance the nomination out of committee, as expected, Liz shot up from her seat and walked out of the room.

Her boss didn't flinch.

When Denton fiddled with his microphone, the limited cameras in the room went off in a flurry of flashes. Before his bigoted screeching had hit the public airways, there was talk of him second-guessing his support for Wright. His party was unified in opposition. A not insignificant segment of the center-left had taken to the streets in protest. It had felt less and less savvy to stick his neck out for a doctrinaire liberal who many despised across the political spectrum and secure a win for a lame-duck president from the other party. Charlie had put it this way: "Why exactly am I shilling for this negro again?"

But the scandal had made a "no" vote impossible. Denton had put out a brief statement apologizing for his lapse in judgment. He had hugged Charlie (*literally*) and every notable black Republican—of which there were few—so close, you'd think he hadn't compared their skin to filth. He now wanted it all over him. In no universe was he voting against the country's putative inaugural black chief justice.

His voice was small when announcing his aye vote. You couldn't imagine him using it not long ago to foot-stomp the reading of pornography into the official record.

The hush was palpable—nearly stinging—by the time we reached Lancaster. I felt the muscles in the body sitting beside me tense up. Randy was looking down at the ground beneath his feet. At hell. Maybe wishing it'd swallow him whole.

"My brother Art once told me to do nothing that requires you to hold your nose," Lancaster said.

Randy's head snapped upward, eyes affixed to his uncle.

"He taught me to be proud of my choices. To be resolute. You can wrestle over a decision. Be contemplative and sober and deliberate. But once you choose a lane, do not be squeamish about it."

Randy grunted. The unfortunate choice of words—it was Uncle Christopher's failure to choose a lane that killed his father—appeared to pain him.

"So, today, I won't be equivocating or rationalizing. I will be full-throated. To put it bluntly, I do not believe Ms. Maldonado."

Microphones picked up gasps from the gallery.

Randy deflated in his chair. His spindly hand covered his eyes.

"I do not think being declined the privilege of a seat on the highest court in the land—its chief seat, in fact—is particularly onerous. It's a reasonable accommodation that a sexually abused woman be kept from having to see her harasser sit in such a prestigious post for a lifetime and make literal life-and-death decisions for women and their families. His opinions, when in the majority, will be final—done *with prejudice*. There will be no relief, no review, no recourse after him. But that does not mean I find *every* allegation of sexual assault credible. The standard cannot be no standard at all. It cannot be 'believe always' without scrutiny.

"And I simply do not believe Judge Wright did what Ms. Maldonado claims that he did."

I heard the cracking of Randy's knuckles as he balled his fists.

"This isn't a gut feeling of mine. Just facts. No emotion. No speculation. For instance, fact: No other woman has come forward to impeach Judge Wright's character. Fact: Ms. Maldonado did not tell another soul about what happened to her until a few weeks ago—not her friends, not her family, not the pages of her diary. Fact: She penned a fawning note of thanks after the purported assault, and she maintained friendly contact with her alleged harasser for years. Again, we can analyze why that is, but her plain written words speak for themselves. They tell their own story. They tell a different story."

His nephew was shaking his head.

"It doesn't even sound like him," Randy whispered to me. "Like he's a puppet, and it's Whitehurst who's got his hand up his ass. It's almost word for word what that slick greasy-haired asshole argued at the last hearing."

"Why parrot Whitehurst?"

"Because my bastard uncle's been bought off. It explains the about-face. If he was going to do this—make a full one-eighty—he had to come out strong. He had to call her a liar."

He redirected his attention to the senator.

"The facts do not fit the story Ms. Maldonado recounted to us. If I'm being fair, they contradict it. With pride over the historic nature of his achievement, I will be voting in favor of Judge Wright both on this committee and on the Senate floor."

That was it. The air had been drained from the room. Even Grunwald-Santos failed to summon her typical theatrics when prefacing her vote in opposition. The chairman capped it off by casting the deciding vote. Judge Wright had eked out a victory. Three strikes of the gavel brought the matter to a close, and senators filed out to join the full Senate in what everyone knew was pro forma now.

I rushed off to find Liz, adrenaline filling my legs like lighter fluid, but she was just outside the committee room, blending into a corner.

My hand hurtled over to her soft underarm, before my rational brain had even ordered it to move.

"You OK?"

"I'm fine," she said, steely-eyed, but she hadn't pulled away from my touch. "Nothing twenty-four years of lived womanhood hasn't prepared me for."

"You're taking this hard, though." I was trying to be comforting.

"I'm taking this personally."

Her eyes were wet again. My heart was in my ears. I had never seen her so shaken nor so vulnerable. The bravura she wore like a second skin had slinked off. To see her—the *real*, raw her—made me feel light-headed.

"There's something more to this," I said, leaning in, bringing in my second hand to hold her other arm. "Who do you need me to hurt?"

"The man who loves me can handle that."

"That can be me."

"That can also be him."

I felt Charlie's presence behind me. I didn't turn to face him until I felt his giant hand on my neck. But it didn't feel menacing. It felt reassuring. It was almost a caress. I didn't let Liz go when I looked into his expressionless face. His face held neither hostility nor affection. Perhaps, at most, resignation.

"It's been an emotional morning, Liz," Charlie said. "Let me take you home."

She peered into my eyes with her sad ones, patted me on the cheek, and left in her boyfriend's embrace.

I retired to the intern cubicles, where I knew I'd be alone. I sulked in front of the ancient television set and watched as history was being made. By afternoon, it was official: Freddy Wright, the accused sexual harasser, was chief justice.

Liz sounded like a dream when I answered her call late that night. I was awaking from one myself. When we hung up, I could not recall what she had said exactly. But I knew she wanted me over. Right then.

The last time she had summoned me on a dying Saturday night, I had resisted. Not this time. Not after what it had led to before. Not after hearing how she sounded on the other line now: scared.

I dressed myself in a sprint and ordered a car to take me to her.

The front door to her apartment was already open a sliver. I knew Lisa wouldn't be back from Miami until the following afternoon. I let myself in. The shared spaces were dark, but her bedroom door was outlined in golden light. I walked over to it, as my breathing, my pulse, and my prickled skin were on high alert.

Was this some sort of trap? What an odd thing to think. I disposed of the thought as fast as it had cropped up.

I wrapped my hand around the knob—hotter than I imagined it'd be, how they warned you it might feel if a fire awaited you on the other side—twisted it, and pushed forward.

I stood in the doorway for a while, adjusting to the sight. Charlie was there, standing by the window. His massive black body took up so much of the frame, it was hard to pull my eyes away from him at first. Everything that orbited him was dwarfed in comparison. He was not himself. He was not composed. He was huffing. Teetering on hyperventilating. So angry he could cry. His chest swung in and out like an accordion.

Liz was a heap of limbs on her bed. Fresh and dried tears adorned her face. Her ocean blue eyes were wild, adrift, refusing to focus on any one spot for too long. Her hands were claws, curved and drawn.

I must have moved toward Charlie aggressively. I didn't feel myself do it. Liz put herself between us, pinning her hand to my chest as she always did to draw me abruptly short with an intimate touch.

"Not him," she said, voice soft through gritted teeth.

I scoured her eyes for answers.

"Whitehurst?"

I followed her eyes to the bed, where they landed on an old-school cassette tape player I hadn't noticed. I could read the label through the clear tape deck. I had seen it once before: "Burn after Playing." She pushed play. Her eyes never left mine as it rolled, as if all that mattered in the moment—in the world—was my reaction. That made me warm from the collar down.

It played a symphony of instruments building to a crescendo. At first a single noise: Rustling. Just rustling. Frantic. Panicked. Of clothing? Of clothing. Then it was joined gradually by a second: Panting. Breathing. Rhythmically. Exercise? Sex? Sex. Layered on top of that was a third: Grunting. Staccato. Male, but indiscernible. Like stabbing. Like a dagger. Like thrusting. Then a fourth, before a clear song emerged: The word "no." So faint at first. Interjected as neither a verse nor the chorus but an off-handed refrain, cacophonous with the music. The other sounds just grew louder to compensate, drowning it out. Also: "Stop." Still a whisper but louder. Said firmer. More frequently. Time was running out. And: "Please." A string of all three, so mumbled, so jumbled, they merged into one word.

Nostopplease. Pleasestopno. Nonopleasenostop. Pleasepleasestopno. Stop. Stop. Stop.

The only word to accurately depict how I felt inside was "full." Turmoil was bubbling up inside of me. There was barometric pressure coalescing in my lungs. I felt the way a teakettle shook in the seconds before popping. The intensity with which it all came spewing out of me was startling, even—*especially*—to myself.

The tears that sprang to my eyes fell hot, burning hot. I let out a husky and garbled wail that lurched up from my diaphragm.

Liz's eyes flared. Did I detect satisfaction—almost ecstasy?

"You recognize this?" she asked of the tape.

"I get it."

She shut off the recording and her hand flew to my cheek. Charlie watched with no discernible change in posture.

"You going to bring this to the police?" I asked.

My voice struggled to get past my boa-constricted chest.

Liz and Charlie shared a glance. She flipped around and walked to the window, looking out at the city and not at me.

"It won't go anywhere," she said. "It never goes anywhere. Not against the powerful. And I wouldn't want to put myself out there like that anyway."

She paused.

Charlie slipped behind her and wrapped his arms around her top half, eclipsing her entirely from me.

"It's messy, Cam," she continued. "It wasn't always like that. It didn't start off that way. Just that last time. When it was ending. When I began feeling used. When the full weight of the power imbalance came crashing down on me. He reacted aggressively to me pulling away. So I made a habit out of secretly recording our interactions those last few times. As insurance, I guess? As a taste of his own medicine? Never imagining I would capture *this*. Never imagining he'd stoop to *this*.

"But it just wouldn't look right from the outside. I had invited the affair. Some might say I pursued it. If Candela had to contend with just one contradictory note, well, I'd have plenty. And months and months of my continuing to work there."

Charlie hugged her closer. I began to feel like a voyeur. I backed up slowly to the door.

"Why are you—the *two* of you—coming to me about this?"

I must have sounded accusatory. She rolled out of Charlie's arms, leaving one hand entwined with his and reaching the other out to me. I allowed her to hold my hand, interlacing our fingers and not just touching palms. Linking the three of us as one.

"I figured you'd know what to do. You always do."

"Is that it? I'm just here to hatch a plan?"

"No! I wanted you by my side. You and Charlie both. Because I trust you."

I looked past her at Charlie. He pulled closer to us.

"You care about Liz, Cam. I know that."

Our eyes locked for a lifetime before I nodded, and he did the same, breaking the trance.

"You're ready for what I have in mind?" I asked. "It's dark."

The two of them shared a laugh.

"We know," Liz said, stroking the back of my hand with her thumb. "You're not fooling anyone, Free-Stater. We know what lurks beneath you. We're ready for it."

"We'll have to involve the others," I said.

"All right, but I don't want to be the one to tell them what happened to me. I don't want to speak of it ever again."

"We'll take care of it," Charlie vowed.

"He's not a good man. He's a mother fucker," she said.

She turned her face up at Charlie, and he dipped far down to lay his lips on hers. She turned the peck into something longer, deeper.

Again, I began moving toward the door, but she was still holding my hand. She wouldn't let go. She disconnected her mouth from her boyfriend's.

"Stay. It's late. Spend the night."

I swept my eyes toward the single bed. She followed my gaze, then looked at me and nodded. She flipped around to reengage Charlie in kissing. But our hands were still linked. She squeezed mine and yanked me closer.

I stood behind her, shaking. My mind and heart were racing. The latter won. I closed in.

I settled my free hand on her hip and lowered my lips to the nape of her neck. She let go of my hand and sent hers to the back of my head, rolling her fingers through my locks.

She lifted her face upward to moan.

It gave Charlie and me the opportunity to meet eyes. We didn't speak, but we exchanged a silent agreement.

We killed the lights.

I slept soundly that night. But I dreamt of the recording. Over and over again. A detailed regurgitation of it. How my mind had glommed on to it so easily, etched it into my mind's eye so accurately, was a mystery. But it haunted me all night.

Dear #CapHillSoWhite:
My boss raped me.

★ ★ ★

The moon hung high in the night, out in Chuy's backyard. We arrived from all over the city. Lisa came almost directly from the airport, making a pit stop at her apartment to drop off her bags and freshen up. On Chuy's porch, I greeted her coolly, maybe on purpose, maybe that male urge to nonverbally express what could easily be put into words: *I'm just not that into you.* I'm sure she noticed, but she didn't say anything. I hadn't been diligent in maintaining contact since the passing of her abuela. She must have felt it coming.

Liz was intentionally late. I gathered the inner circle—Lisa, Chuy, and Randy—to recount the sins of Dale Whitehurst. Lisa's hand flew over her open mouth. Chuy turned pallid. Randy was mute.

"We're going to do something about it," I said, drawing them near in a huddle, arms slung around each others' shoulders in a ring. "Something violent."

I paired it with a wink and a nod. There was a degree of innuendo I wanted to maintain with these three. For plausible deniability, I suppose, but without any real concern for the plausibility part.

They were on the inside but not as inside as Liz, Charlie, and me. We were the nucleus. It was clear from the night before that we shared everything—our intentions, our bodies even.

"Can we count on you?" I asked.

Lisa nodded, not meeting my eyes. She was on the verge of tears. She was emotionally wrought from weeks-long grief. And maybe, just maybe, she knew how much Liz meant to me and allowed herself to feel more aggrieved in a bid for my fading affections.

"Of course," Chuy said, breaking the circle to hug me.

Chuy always had a strong personal bond with Liz. Before Chuy met me, she had been most sensitive to their identity struggles. And I knew they also cared a great deal for me—they would follow me down, down, down.

"Anything you need, brother," Randy said.

He just looked lost.

They all knew a thing or two about wanting your boss dead. Hate had already taken residence in their hearts. Like all Hill staffers, right?

Charlie was off in another corner of the home handling the delicate matter of Isla and Scoop. Isla adored Liz; Scoop adored Charlie. But they were kids. Kids with none of the jaded animosity of permanent staff. They formed the outer circle. I imagine Charlie convinced them that this was all just meant to scare Whitehurst. Send him a message. And they were too young, too stupid, too self-involved, too enamored to think otherwise. I didn't talk to them or pay them mind that night. They hated me. I would only shake their commitment to the plan.

When Liz appeared on Chuy's doorstep, Lisa lost it. She wrapped her arms around Liz and sobbed upon seeing her. In their long sad embrace, the blondes became indistinguishable.

Chuy met their forehead with Liz's.

The hug Randy saved for her was limp-armed and fleeting. The sentimentality of it appeared to make him nervous. He was unlike himself: quiet, failing to wisecrack, deadly sober. He wouldn't look any of the women in the eye. Especially Liz.

I pulled him aside.

"I'm just very upset," he said. "It's been an awful October."

"You're not getting gun-shy on me, are you?"

I cracked a smile, but I meant it.

"We do whatever it takes to avenge the ones we love, right?"

He had already crossed the line into homicidal ideation, even as emotions drove him to vacillate about it wildly. And he was sure Liz's abuser had manipulated his uncle against the one thing that compelled Randy to spare his life: justice for Candela. For all his toxic philandering, Randy was a dyed-in-the-wool progressive. Candela had softened the ground. But this time, with Liz, it hit too close to home.

In the end, I had taken up arms for him. He was now willing to do the same for me, for us.

The air outside was crisp. The eight of us donned jackets, sat around a blazing bonfire, and shared a joint. Just like we had that first night, months ago.

We were light on details. It was more about bonding. Sharing in trauma. Rallying around a cause. You don't go to war without pumping up morale. It was Chuy who brought out the papier-mâché Whitehurst. The *año viejo* from Chuy's native Ecuador. We could have burned all six. That's how much we hated them. But Dale Whitehurst would suffer a singularly macabre fate. He deserved special treatment.

I tossed him into the fire.

Everyone cursed, and cheered, and spat, and danced. The chemicals holding the doll together produced thick black clouds of smoke that billowed from his disintegrating body.

I stuck my face into the smokestack's path. I wanted his innards all over my skin.

Randy had to pull me away from it. I was coughing and laughing wildly.

"You're going to suffocate yourself, you sicko," he said, humorless.

I saw the fear in his eye. His fear of me. Of what he finally saw in me. What they all finally saw in me.

I was an animal.

Liz didn't look scared. She looked content.

I knew it. She was the same as me all along.

12

TINY TRAGEDIES

*You can tell the greatness of a man by what
makes him angry.* —Abraham Lincoln

Now's about the time I come clean. My real name is Cameron En-lai
Lian, and I came to DC to kill Senator Dale Whitehurst.

I wasn't born with bloodlust. That came later. At first, I was just a
boy. A boy learning how to become a man.

I had one good role model. And a really, really bad one.

By the law of averages, I should have turned out just fine. Then
again, I was never good at math.

My nai nai awoke every Sunday morning before church to the fra-
grance of freshly clipped white lilies in a glass on the dining room table,
compliments of my gong-gong. Strands of blinding sunlight stabbed
through the windows, revealing a trillion dancing particles. The scent
of scallion pancakes wafted in the air. The Taiwanese elderly couple
split the corner of the table, seated in silence, his veined hand draping
hers. He wore his suit and hard shoes. She wore a floral dress to her
ankles and pearls. They were beaming: at everything and at nothing in
particular. On my way to the bathroom—inexorably late and slinking
in my pajamas—I'd steal a longing glance at the couple adrift in one
another.

My single mother—the blond white woman seething in the corner—watched with disdain. She was a foreigner in her own home, ungifted in the language of love.

I tried to set my alarm early and catch my gong-gong on his way out. See how he pulled off this magic trick. It took a few times. I was always too late. But one time, when the sky was still black and the groaning of floorboards was the only sound, I intercepted him at the door.

I still wore my onesie pajamas, ruffled hair, and sleepy eyes.

He sported those kind eyes of his and that perennial smile.

He collected me in his arms, saying nothing, and stepped out into the night. I nestled my head in the crook of his shoulder. He was fond of pointing out to me ordinary things and reciting the Mandarin equivalent in his soft and smooth accent. He did so again on this early-morning walk. I listened but didn't repeat any of the words back. He always ended his lesson with "kiss," planting one atop my head, cuddling me close, and tickling my ribs.

My squirming was purely performative. "No" meant "yes."

He led us to a yard behind a farmhouse on yawning acreage and up to a conservatory. To me, it was just a glass house with pretty flowers in it. We entered through the back. He slipped out a tiny flashlight from his pants pocket and lit the way to the lilies. From his other pocket, he produced tailor's scissors and cut off a fistful of stems.

"Is this stealing?" I asked.

"It's an arrangement," he said.

Back home, Gong-gong lifted a finger to his lips—forming a cross—and let out an exaggerated hush.

"Never tell."

Next time the landowner, white-haired and white-skinned, came into my grandpa's shop for an alteration, he didn't pay. Gong-gong showed me the bill. He had scribbled down "debt paid" where the dollar amount would go.

Gong-gong was always there for me. My father, his prodigal son, was not. He came around sparingly. My father, En-lai Lian, went by Eli, and he was like no Asian man I had seen in the media. I adored him for that.

He arrived one hot summer afternoon when I was six, after months of absence, as my school bus pulled up to our home to drop me off. He was on his motorcycle, kicking up clouds of Kansan dirt into a whirlwind. The sight and wail of his needless revving pulled my classmates toward the windows to gawk at my father: unshaven, oily hair hanging to the jawline, decked out in sleeveless leather and cowboy boots.

It was the shape of his eyes that drew the most curiosity.

One white boy, Chaz, called out at me as I sprinted off the bus to tell me he didn't know I was one of *them*. A racial slur rolled off his tongue like nothing.

I stared at him and his snaggletooth smile for a while.

I don't even remember being offended.

If anything, I remember realizing for the first time that I could pass.

"Dad!" I shouted, running into him and wrapping myself around his bottom half.

When he pulled back and squatted to my level, he was chuckling.

"Call me Eli," he said. "All my friends do."

He sized me up.

"You've grown," he said. "You're going to be solid like your old man. Not soft like Gong-gong."

Eli whisked me off on his bike. He didn't advise anyone inside that he was taking me. My arms didn't reach all the way around but I dug into him, clutching on to his sides with a firm grip. I was riding blind because his wide back blocked my sight. I inhaled leather the whole way. Every sudden movement came as a surprise. I was trembling and sweating at the same time.

We stopped for a six-pack of beer.

Two women at the counter were enamored of me. Eli called them girls, and flashed them a toothy smile, and got all wiggly.

"He's so cute," one said.

"Mixed kids always are, aren't they?" said the other.

"Oh, he'll be quite the skirt-chaser," Eli said, winking.

It didn't look like they liked that.

Our next stop was an open field, where blue expanse met green with nothing in between but miles of horizon. He plopped me down on a flipped loose tire, cracked open the tab on his beer—emitting a sigh in both the man and the can—and gurgled so long, his Adam's apple bobbed and rivulets of bubbling yellow ran down his chin. He lay out on the ground, arms folded behind him, hands cradling his head.

We caught up. I was overjoyed at hearing his voice, at just being near him. He asked about school. Mostly he asked about Mom.

"What does she say about me?"

I looked away to summon the nerve.

"That you're a dirt bag."

He became a snake in the grass, hissing.

"Ah, well, she's a bitch."

I smiled out of nervousness. I asked him where he'd been. I tried to say it nonchalantly but my voiced cracked. I wanted the explanation to be a good one. I needed it to be.

"On the road. All over. To see and be seen."

That felt unsatisfying.

He rolled onto his side, stuck his hand into his vest, and pulled out a gun.

"You're old enough now to learn how to use this."

He arranged three of the empty cans on tree stumps lined up dozens of yards away. He sat with his legs spread in a V and tucked me in between them in the same formation, my back against his torso. He sandwiched the pistol in between my tiny hands and encased them in his larger ones. We extended our straightened arms and pivoted the muzzle to the can farthest left.

"How's your vision?" he asked.

"Perfect."

"*You* aim. *You* pull the trigger. When you're ready."

My hands were shaking. His steadied mine. My palms became increasingly slippery. The metal was heavy in my grasp. I heard his beating heart, regular like a metronome, so unlike mine, overwrought in my bird chest.

"I don't want to."

"What does that matter? Do it anyway."

I sank my teeth into my lip until I felt pain. I shut one eye. I aimed. Fire.

It was scary loud. I felt kickback, despite the bracing stability of my father, who hadn't budged. I hadn't hit anything.

"Again," he barked.

I let loose a whimper like a whinnying horse.

Fire.

"Again!"

Fire.

"Again!"

Fire.

The ping of the can knocked off its perch relieved my steel-drum heart. Eli leapt to his feet and pumped a fist in the air. I jumped up and hooted alongside him.

"Good man," he said, hand in my hair.

He squatted again, making our eyes level. He set his spread palm against my sternum, covering nearly half of the terrain of my torso. The warm touch elated me.

"That voice inside, the fear, the one telling you not to pursue your wants, your desires, that's the boy within. A man has no use for that voice. A man tells it to shut the fuck up."

From the moment we got home, Eli was greeted to Mom's yelling.

"I oughtta call the police and report you for kidnapping!"

"He's my son, too, Joy."

"Your fatherly contribution began and ended with that regrettable thirty-second deposit I was too drunk and too stupid to turn down."

"Such grace. Such class."

I stowed away in Mom's closet, the farthest from the kitchen where the tempest was brewing. It was where I hid from the world. I had swiped her cigarette lighter and began compulsively rolling the igniter with my thumb, watching the flame it produced flicker in the dark. I hovered my open palm over the fire, snatching it away only when the pain—pleasurable at first— became unbearable. It distracted me from the pain I felt inside. It wasn't long before the screaming match migrated to the bedroom. There was still daylight out. Through the spaces between panels on the door, I saw my parents stutter-step and fumble onto the bed: yelling and kissing, kissing and stripping, stripping and moaning. I felt numb all over, detached from the scene before me.

I poked my head out early on. See if I could slip out unnoticed.

A shirtless Eli was sitting up against the headboard and facing me, fingers interlaced behind his head, relaxed, like I'd seen him on that grassy plain. Mom was dipped down at the apex of his spread legs, bobbing up and down like that Adam's apple of his.

He saw me and grinned. He lifted a finger to his lips curved cartoonishly upward, shushing me softly.

I retreated into the darkness and watched the whole of it.

Position after position, he was mean to her.

"You're a slut. A whore. Good for one thing and one thing only."

Insult after insult, she reveled in it.

"I'm *your* slut. I'm *your* whore. All yours. Only yours."

I didn't understand it at the time. I felt only shame.

I watched until the man came. That's when sex ended, I learned.

Later on, I wouldn't let my mother kiss me good night. She didn't know why. I guess I didn't, either. Maybe I still don't. Maybe it was budding misogyny. Maybe my father wanted me to see her exactly how he did. Maybe that was his greatest revenge.

Eli was gone by morning but had literally left her with child.

Mom prayed for a girl. She didn't shy away from telling me why.

"I can't have two of him running around."

In other words, two of *me*.

I saw her cry at the gender-revealing ultrasound and the nub of a phallus it revealed. No tears of joy for Joy.

I was allowed to name him. I chose a character from Bible study: Nathaniel. That made my gong-gong smile.

"That means 'gift from God,'" he said.

Was Eli God in this instance? That was already one of his many complexes.

For a middle name, Nat was given my grandma's maiden name, Po. Eli wasn't present for the birth, so I got to be in the delivery room. I was old enough to feel no jealousy or competition. From the time I first met Nat—screeching, purple, bloodied, and featuring monolid eyes more like Eli's than my own—I knew I loved him. I knew he was mine, and I had to protect him.

As a boy, he attracted more than his fair share of bullying.

He was shorter than I had been. Scrawnier. More identifiably Asian.

A pack of older boys tailed him on the playground one day, singing "ching chong" and other made-up, vaguely East Asian gibberish while slanting their eyes with the tips of their fingers. I cussed them out. They were apologetic. Only because they knew me from school, and I was nominally well liked.

"I'm sorry, man. We didn't know you two were family."

When I wasn't busy being my brother's keeper, I spent an inordinate amount of my days thinking about sex.

I can't remember a time I wasn't a sexual being. I don't know if I blame my father. I think I was just born that way. Even before I could get erect, I'd recurrently press my penis into the mattress and feel a jolt of nascent pleasure until it lulled me to sleep. I remember praying for a girlfriend long before that was viable or even desired by boys my age. A teacher at my Christian school found a little girl and me playing "show me yours, and I'll show you mine" in the bathroom, before I had learned the words to label either.

Gong-gong was unfazed.

"He doesn't know what he's doing."

"Of course he does," Mom said. "He's his father's son."

Television had an accelerant effect on all of that. I didn't see any Asian male sex symbols. All of those were white.

But I wanted to be more like them. I wanted girls to want me.

So I began working out at an early age. Eli had left weights strewn about in the garage, collecting dust from when he was a teenager intent on bulking up. During one of his brief cameos, when I was eleven, he showed me how to use them. He was thrilled with my burgeoning interest.

"I've given up on Nat," he said. "I think he'll end up a fairy, don't you?"

My brother was just four years old at the time. I glowered in response.

When training legs, Eli noted—with undue pride—that I had strong calves.

"Daikon legs," he said, flexing and slapping his own. "I didn't pass down many of my genes, but you got that Mongolian trait from me."

In truth, I had always noiselessly walked on the balls of my feet, building up my legs. I liked the concept of sneaking up on others.

"Tell your mom to put you in soccer," Eli added.

I chose football instead. It was more American. And according to the TV shows raising me, it drew the most attention from girls.

I wanted the letterman jacket. I wanted to win the big game. I wanted to get blown under the bleachers.

Mom let me play, but I had to take piano lessons to balance it out.

That lasted only a few months. Not because I wasn't good at it. My instructor told me otherwise. I had a penchant for recognizing and remembering long sequences of notes. Strong echoic memory, she called it.

But what was more cliché than an Asian kid playing the ivory keys?

"I don't want to be a pussy," is how I put it to Chaz, by then my teammate and best friend.

"You are what you eat, Keanu," he replied. Others began calling me that. I didn't mind. Girls were always fawning over Keanu Reeves.

But not over me yet.

By thirteen, I had a crisis of faith. I stopped taking communion. I'd pick up the cracker from the circulating plate, and when the pastor said, *Do this in remembrance of me,* I'd fake bringing it to my lips, only to drop it under my shoe and crush it to pieces. I broke the body of Christ. Not literally—we were Protestants, not damn papists—but symbolically nonetheless. There had to be a ring of hell reserved for that.

My prayers were growing angrier. I began incorporating ultimatums. I told Chaz that if God didn't make a way for me to lose my virginity soon, I'd become an avowed atheist.

"How can a God of plenty exist but be sparing in this one critical way?" I asked.

"Unless He's a girl," Chaz said, shrugging.

One stereotype didn't come naturally to me. I held no academic promise. I had trouble paying attention in class. I could always dream up something more interesting in my mind.

"Did you hear that, Cam?" my teacher would inevitably say.

"Huh?"

"It was called the Kansas-Nebraska Act, leaving the question of slavery open to the settlers of each territory. Bleeding Kansas, as we were known before statehood, was rife with violence. Free-Staters flooded the area, and from the very start, our constitution banned slavery in this great state. That *will* be on the test. Get your head out of the clouds, son."

Once I heard it, I remembered it. But I seldom heard it on the first go.

There was a time when I was fourteen—and doing little else than masturbating and lifting weights 'round the clock—that Eli got his shit together. He turned in his bike for a Buick. The college dropout got a job, but he wouldn't say doing what. I was still living with Mom and my grandparents, but Eli got an apartment in the city, close enough to host his sons after school on certain weekdays, but never on weekends. Those were his high holy days.

All we knew was that he was around, and he had spending money, and he wanted to see us semi-regularly. It drove Mom up a wall, but he was playing house, and that was enough.

Eli got me a copy of his key. He didn't like picking us up from Christian school.

"Those hypocrites never accepted me. All they know is judgment."

"What about Gong-gong?"

"He's the worst one of them all," he said. "Doesn't say a fucking word. Judges merely by deed. Just lives his life perfectly as this shining example meant to make you feel like shit in comparison. What kind of a sadist does that?"

So Nat and I walked the twenty blocks, hitched a ride with older friends, or splurged on a cab when we had a scheduled visit.

Eli must have forgotten we were coming that last time.

The sky was one massive cloud of charcoal gray. We made the precarious walk anyway, eyes floating upward every few steps, daring God to make it rain.

We arrived at his apartment still dry, slipped the key into its groove, and let ourselves in to a living room littered with empty beer cans, tossed clothing—some woman wear—and congealed food. That wasn't too concerning. He had never kept his place or himself tidy. But a few frames had been knocked off their shelves, a painting or two were askew, a streak of hot sauce ran down the wall above where the bottle lay thrown on its side, and a table had been flipped over. Oldies music from the nineties played faintly from speakers plugged into a laptop computer.

I thought I heard muffled noise coming from the bedroom.

The door had been left ajar.

"Stay here," I told Nat.

I crept toward the room on my toes. A cold sweat dampened my temples, under my arms, and the soles of my feet. The nerve in one of my eyes was on the fritz, twitching out of the corner. By the time I reached the bedroom, my breath was short, the hairs on my arms tall, my heart rate high, and the moisture in my mouth low.

I pushed the squeaking door open.

No one was inside. Balls of sheet were tangled on the bed. They were stained. Mostly what looked like clear, faintly yellow liquids dried over. Some blood, like a paper cut's worth. The nightstand had candles with streams of wax frozen in place—as well as whips, chains, furry hand-cuffs, a prescription bottle, and a Holy Bible.

I approached and picked up the bottle: temazepam, it read.

I heard a stirring again. It was coming from the closet.

I eyed its shut door. Time wasn't operating on its usual schedule. I felt lethargic and bogged down, an invisible weight bearing down on my chest.

There was no scenario by which I didn't open that closet door. It was predestined. It had been scripted in the story of my life. It was inevitable.

I don't think my legs moved of their own accord. They were being pulled over. The brass knob was a magnet.

I swung open the door in one fluid move. I didn't want to lose my nerve.

The woman tied up on the other side must have been caught by surprise.

She yelled past the ball gag in her mouth at a decibel level—and for long, oh so long—that knocked me backward. High C-sharp. I heard a second scream join hers, and I thought it was mine. I had to feel my lips with fingers numb to figure out that my mouth was still shut.

I turned around and saw that Nat—eyes filled with horror, the kind that gives you the shakes—was watching the woman in bondage: naked but for rope circling her wrists and ankles. There was dried blood in her hair, by the temple, where damp strands clung to her skin in the pattern of a spiderweb.

It wasn't 'til she tried to roll out over to us that I picked up my brother in my outstretched arms and ran out of there.

I set him down and caught my breath in the kitchen, mulling over our next steps. I had every intention of leaving her there, finding a way home, and never speaking of this again. But the seven-year-old beside me, leaning up against the wall for support, was red-faced and badly hyperventilating. It didn't take a long look at him before a twinge in my heart set me straight.

Begrudgingly, I called 911.

The police found her, drugged, along with brick after brick of sealed narcotics.

In the ensuing year, Nat and I were largely shielded from the legal process, but not those first few weeks. Those first few weeks we had to tell the same story over and over and over again.

They always asked us the race of the captive.

"Black," I would say, a tiny part of me angry that it mattered. I hated race and its prevalence.

Mom—who hated Eli most of all—oddly used the fact to defend him.

"Eli isn't even into black girls," she said.

Prosecutors were treating the matter seriously. It was an election year for the Wyandotte district attorney, who was seeking a promotion to national office. Toward the end of it all, approaching resolution, we were told there was a nonzero chance we'd need to testify at trial, against our own father. But Eli didn't want to put us through all of that, I was told. He accepted over a decade in prison instead. That sacrifice was the high point of his fatherhood.

Nai nai sank into depression. Gong-gong was resolute.

When I was on the cusp of sixteen, Gong-gong drove me out to a vacant lot to help me practice for my driver's license exam. Before we switched seats, he shut the car off entirely, inhaled a belly of air, and exhaled noisily, staring out in front of him.

"I failed your father," he said. "Spoiled him here, in America, like he never would've been back home. He was never the same after he flunked out of college. I was never quite sure why, but *something* happened there that set him on this path: living only for himself and no one else."

He gathered my hand in his and bore into my eyes.

I don't know why, but I felt myself tearing up. His warm gaze was the sun, blinding me. His touch was dry and reassuring.

With his free hand—showing a dexterity that amazed me—he unclipped the golden chain with a cross charm dangling from his neck and dropped it in my palm.

"Go to college, my love. Take this with you. Graduate. Make something of yourself. It's my only wish for you," he said. "Eli is your past. He is not your destiny."

With two strong fingers, he tapped me repeatedly on the chest—where my beating heart lay—and intoned the Mandarin word for "fire," not "heart."

"Tend to that fire. Don't let it die. Burn bright."

He meant everything to me. I couldn't break his heart. In him, I saw the man I could become. The man he deserved for me to be. It finally felt within reach.

Grades alone weren't going to get me there. But football might.

I poured every bit of myself into the sport—making the varsity squad my junior and senior years, becoming a utility player who Coach could put in anywhere without complaint, leaving them all in awe, not of my talent but of how hard I went at it every minute of the game.

When I met with scouts my senior year, they were bowled over by my stamina and resourcefulness, but they couldn't quite find a place for me. One scout caught me punting balls during practice. Coach often asked me to punt to the receiving team in games—a not-so glamorous role—because my legs were more developed than those of other teenage boys, and I didn't bitch about it.

The man must have seen something he liked.

"Welcome to the University of Kansas," he told me with a big grin and a hearty handshake. That's how I became a kicker at a Division I program.

Jayhawk fandom was unrivaled in town. On the last game of the season, I finally got that blow job beneath the bleachers. Stacy Greeley wanted a piece of the stud heading to Lawrence to play ball.

Her service featured a lot of teeth, not much depth, and she kept stopping to remove errant hairs from her mouth. But it was sufficient.

I pulled her hair at one point. On impulse.

She jerked her head up and snapped at me. I apologized and kept my hands behind my back for the rest of it. After I completed, she appeared disgusted, but I didn't care. I felt dominant, powerful, validated. Not unmanly. Not "Asian." It was the feeling I had long been searching for.

Becoming toxic was a small price to pay for becoming a man.

As my sexual proclivities darkened, I blamed the media. I was just overcompensating because of how passive they made Asian men out to be. I liked that better than the possibility that my father's deviant genes inhered in me or, worse yet, that all men had a deep, dark underbelly that only civilization kept in check.

In college, sex became a constant. Even early on when I was riding the bench. Football as a status symbol was enough. Alcohol sure helped. So did the training rigors of a top-notch program and its effect on my body. I did all right for myself.

I got in minor trouble one time after a hookup my sophomore year.

We met at a frat party. She was sober. I wasn't. I didn't recall much of it the morning after. I know we returned to her dorm room. Her roommate was sleeping, at periods snoring. I tried to get her to agree to sex acts of decreasing seriousness with increasingly less pushback. The negotiation ended in a hand job. I didn't spend the night.

By morning, she had reported the incident to her resident advisor.

My coach was the one to inform me that the girl said she felt pressured. That I had insisted.

"Isn't that just called flirting?" Chaz asked me.

I didn't understand how the active party could be the one violated.

"I literally just lay there," I told my coach.

He blew it off.

"It won't make it to the Ad Board," he said. "It's one of the tamer ones I've heard. And I've heard plenty."

He chuckled and slapped my back.

The girl withdrew the complaint within days. I heard her roommate didn't dispute the facts, but her concluding sentiment—which she shared openly with administrators and gossipers alike—killed the matter: "What's the big deal? We've all regretted bad choices in the morning."

I also met Katie at a frat party. But Katie was different. I liked Katie.

She walked up to me while I was in a huddle with my boys. That can be intimidating to girls. She just tapped me on the shoulder and launched into conversation. Katie always went straight for what she wanted. That was her superpower. That was her downfall.

She had olive skin, dark eyes that were probing—even in the dim lighting—and the right side of her lips curved naturally into a half smile. As if everything she heard brought her sarcastic delight.

"You're Cameron, right?"

"Cam."

"That's not on your birth certificate, is it?"

"No."

"Then I'll call you Cameron. As your parents intended."

It felt like negging. In my experience, only douchey guys like myself did that. I had never seen a girl try her hand at it and fail so fantastically. It was endearing, so maybe it was working.

Plus, I had snorted a line of coke earlier so I had some pep in me.

"And you? What should I call you?"

"I'm Katie."

"Isn't *that* short for something?"

"Nope. Just Katie."

"All right, Just Katie. Do we know each other from somewhere?"

"Doesn't everyone know you?"

"Ah, so you're a fan of the team?"

"Not really. But we have class together."

"So you've been checking me out in class?"

I smiled wide, winked, and leaned in. Her natural smirk was unmoved.

"You're hard to miss. You sit with the meatheads who barely fit in their chairs. It draws some attention."

"Not me, though?"

"You fit in your chair."

A buddy of mine turned to lay his weight on my shoulders and interrupt.

"That's 'cause he's a kicker!"

Like a Greek chorus, he said his piece and whirled back around.

"There's kicking in football?"

"You really *aren't* a fan."

She peered down and pulled a strand of her hair behind her ear.

"So what's this fixation with names about?" I asked.

"They're important. They're the first element in forming your identity. They have meaning."

"What's mine mean?"

"I can look it up." She pulled out her phone and, with speedy thumbs, popped my name into a search engine. What she read made her thick brows stitch together. "Crooked nose."

"Ouch. How's mine?"

She reached out and ran her pointer finger down its slope.

"Good. Handsome."

I felt my pulse down in my groin.

"There's a Spanish word that is close-sounding to your name. I'm Latina," she explained. "It's camarón."

"What does that mean?"

"Shrimp."

She laughed.

"Are you calling me small?" I was play-frowning.

My buddy whipped around again.

"He *is* Asian! You know what that means," he howled, lifting his pinky finger suggestively. This time, I socked him—firm but not incapacitating—in the ribs. He turned away, rubbing his side.

"You're not that short," she said, squeezing my arm. She let it linger there. "And you're definitely not small."

Our smiles faded and our stare was long.

"What's Katie mean?"

My voice passed through faintly. It was hard to speak. The air had been sucked out of me.

"Pure."

"Does the name fit?" My eyebrows were dancing.

"Well, I *am* a virgin."

"Oh, shit," I let loose reflexively. "You religious?"

"Yeah."

"So you're waiting for marriage?"

"Not necessarily," she said, shrugging. "Actually, it's why I came over. It's what I noticed in class."

"What?"

"This."

She nudged the collar of my shirt down and pulled out the lock and pendant around my neck. I felt a rush of heat to my face.

"I'm blushing."

"You've been pink in the face this whole time. It's acetaldehyde. Asian flush."

"You knew I was Asian? Before my buddy said it, I mean?"

Again, she shrugged.

"With a name like Lian?"

Katie and I began dating not long after we met, near the tail end of my sophomore year. One month in, we became exclusive and Instagram official, without having done anything more than heavy petting. That restraint made me feel particularly upright and moral. Like I wasn't all bad. Like I was worth redemption. We went to church together. We studied for finals together, and she helped pull my grades up. Over the summer break, I met her family and she met mine. Nai nai didn't leave her room. But Gong-gong was pleased. And Nat liked her.

Mom was cynical.

"Don't go knocking her up," she said, plunking a bunch of free, clinic-handout condoms onto my open palm.

"We're not having sex," I said, teeth clenched.

She raised her eyebrows to the heavens.

As sticky season rolled on, it became more difficult. The heat and thinner, skimpier clothing didn't help. We didn't have the privacy of our dorm rooms, and neither of our family homes was conducive to such a thing. But I had never felt such burning. Arousal was an oxymoronic condition: a feeling so good that, at the same time, demanded to be ended immediately. We were just so inseparable, bodies mere inches and thread counts from each other all day. And no amount of praying was warding it off. I'd drift off into fantasy right in front of her, some of it troubling: slamming her into a wall, pinning her down, immobilizing her limbs, squeezing her throat until her eyes shut.

I read about it online. The impulse didn't seem as deviant as I had first thought. Lots of men—lots of women, even—appeared to like it.

I convinced myself I felt this desperate only because I loved her. The longing was deeper and fiercer than anything I had felt for a stranger, passerby, or fling. It wasn't mere lust. It was that and so much more.

Katie was reluctant but not opposed. She took to the study of the subject like an academic. She read how more and more Christians of our generation were rationalizing a more *libertine* lifestyle, focused on monogamy and long-term commitment over the artifice of a marriage license. She rejected out of hand the wink-and-nod technicality of millennial Christians who had declared all orifices but the ass markers of virginity. Or so-called soaking, where you put it in but don't thrust. If she was going for it, she was going all in. It was her way.

Midsummer, we made the decision to have sex.

I insisted she get on the pill. I didn't want a layer, however thin, between us, hampering the sensation of our first time.

I rented a hotel room for us on the outskirts of town. I pulled out all the cheesy stops: rose petals on the bed, a bottle of champs on ice, R & B playing off the phone. We fooled around a bit, and I could feel how tense, how frigid she became at my touch. We actually took showers, separately, to calm our nerves and freshen up before consummating.

She didn't want anything to drink, so I polished off the bottle while I waited. Then, it was my turn to rinse off the pre-guilt.

When I emerged, I didn't even bother getting dressed. I scooted into bed naked and pressed myself up against her. She had seen and felt my body before, but her response this time was new: stiff and distant, far away.

I would forever hold fast to the fact that I asked before entering. Like a gentleman.

"Are you OK?"

"Yeah."

With that, we delved into our listless lovemaking. For the whole of it, she dissociated. I imagined it hurt—because she winced and she bled—but aside from that, she was frozen. We would occasionally catch each other's eyes, but even as she looked at me, she was unfocused and lost in thought. It lasted long, very long, likely because I had had so much to drink that my nerve endings were dulled and delayed. I think that made it worse for her.

I didn't react as I thought I would. At first, I was put out and considered calling the whole thing off. But it wasn't long—as I felt her lifeless body beneath mine—that I sensed a tingle under my skin. I actually liked that she was unmoving. My breath came in faster. My thrusts were deeper. I rolled my head back farther and grunted louder. When I held her arms down above her head, I felt how limp her wrists had become, and I came. I remember crumpling on top of her, catching my breath while she barely breathed at all.

We cuddled. We didn't talk. We prayed. We feel asleep.

We rented that hotel room three total times over the break. We had sex each time. She grew increasingly looser, but only slightly, and I could see it was taking a great deal of energy for her to muster even that bit amount of engagement.

"Do you think you can stop moving entirely?" I asked at one point during those attempts. I liked her better dead still.

She was affectionate and loving in our everyday lives. We were becoming increasingly closer and more connected. It was just during sex. She was almost petrified, paralyzed by the act itself—not by me.

She spent those last few weeks of summer with her parents in Mexico. Her pastor father baptized her over there in a lake. We reconnected at school at the start of our junior year. We didn't spend too much time together at first and certainly not overnight. We were both busy. She had her extracurricular commitments, including the pro-life student group she headed. And other than pining after Katie, I had filled the summer days with football. I was named the backup to the backup kicker in the preseason. And the schedule as soon as the term began was grueling: two-a-day practices, daily weight training, regimented eating and sleeping, and of course, the bright lights on game day.

That first home game against a lowly reputed rival featured a string of bad luck. The first-string kicker tweaked his ankle in the third quarter. The second-string kicker appeared concussed—hobbling on his legs like a newborn fawn after a delayed and brutal hit drew a penalty—and had to leave the game to undergo protocol.

I was put in the game in the fourth quarter.

It was surreal. The roar of the crowd resounded in my chest, how it feels when the bass in a car is turned all the way up. It drowned out any independent thought I might have. I operated purely on instinct. I was outside of myself, watching and not directing my own actions. It was spiritual, the closest to God I'd ever felt.

I punted a few balls when it was our turn to defend: a pair of touchbacks, an inoffensive performance.

We were down late. The offense had marched down the field but fell just short, bringing up a fourth down within field goal range with only seconds to go on the clock. The fate of the game lay on my shoulders. We won or lost by my hand.

That meant the eyes of tens of thousands in the stands—and a camera beaming my image nationwide—would be trained on me, and only me, in this moment of high pressure.

I remember how my skin crawled as I trotted out to the thirty-yard marker.

I felt preemptively sad for myself. That so much of my self-worth was wrapped up in this. That so much of the self-worth of the grown men watching—from the newly inculcated to graying alumni—was wrapped up in this. The expectation was stifling.

I mimed the sign of the cross, marched in place, ran up to the ball, and kicked.

Wide left.

There was a collective, audible release. An ocean of disappointment crashing loudly onto me. And then there was blackness because I cannot tell you what happened in the hours that followed. I was awake—moving, breathing, living—but just barely. My brain all but shut off. I had receded, shrunken into myself. I was on autopilot.

I know I was put on so-called "suicide watch" for a few days afterward. That was precautionary. That was customary. I had no designs on killing myself. But isn't it awful that the burden was so great and the feeling so common that there was a formal structure already put in place for athletes who biffed the big game?

I wasn't suicidal, but I *was* depressed. Friends were avoiding me. There were no congratulations or high fives as I strolled down the halls of campus—only stares and whispers. Gong-gong called to check on me, show me he still cared. He suggested I return home and commute to class for a while. I turned him down. I shouldn't have.

On the last night I would spend with Katie, I was still in a funk. I was having trouble sleeping, so I texted her late on a school night, past midnight. She let me in to her dorm room. I slipped into bed with her. I think she was half-asleep. I pulled her into me, but she was fussy. I distinctly recall the twin feelings that inspired in me: annoyance and eagerness. It made me all the more determined.

The little strength it took to subdue her added to a sense of power.

And I had felt powerless for days at that point. I hadn't felt like a man.

"Be a good whore and do as I say," I said, but it didn't sound like me. Just something I had heard in a porno once.

She reached for her phone, and I thought she was setting her alarm. I took it from her hands and laid it on the nightstand.

The removal of her pajamas was noisy. They weren't slipping easily off her squirming body. I had to unbuckle my own pants.

She was tensing herself. Making her compliant became a seamless part of the choreography. She was saying nothing. Just jerking her muscles in spasms that I quelled with my weight and an ironclad grip.

I had to pry her legs open.

The sex was strenuous. It was taking increasing effort to hold her shifting body down. I broke out into a sweat. We were both breathing and grunting loudly.

I heard her small voice. So tiny, a murmur. I can't say I registered the words. There was blood rushing in my ears, but I understood them to be protestations. I won't say otherwise. But I was full bore ahead. It was physics—momentum—and there was no stopping now.

I didn't think I'd last very long anyhow. I tried hard for it to end, per her wishes. I had to spit into my hand and transfer it to lessen the friction.

Her pleas were coming in louder, faster. It was breaking my concentration. It wasn't helping. So I put my palm over her mouth to muffle the sound. I just needed a few more seconds, and it'd be over.

I stared into her eyes those last few thrusts. She had quit moving, speaking. She looked frightened. I came, and I dismounted.

We didn't cuddle. We didn't talk. We didn't pray. I fell asleep.

I heard her get up in the night to go to the bathroom, and she wasn't there when I awoke in the morning.

Within twenty-four hours, I found out Katie thought I had raped her. Coach shared the news with me. All of my blood—ice cold—pooled at my feet. My heart was in my throat. I nearly collapsed.

"But she's my girlfriend," I said.

Coach didn't seem as dismissive this time.

"You're suspended from the team pending an investigation, Cam."

I tried reaching out to her. She had her number changed. Her father threatened my life before hanging up on me. I was warned by the school to stay away. So I stopped. We crossed paths on campus a few times. There was panic in her eyes when they caught mine. I became so nauseous at the reaction, I fought to keep my food down. My friends were supportive, but any hang featured a chorus of insults hurled at Katie and women in general. It didn't make me feel better, only guilty. And I wasn't guilty. So I stopped hanging out.

Gong-gong again offered that I come home. For a second time, I rejected him. We hadn't spoken about the allegations in any meaningful way. We only talked process. But I heard the pain in his voice over the phone, and I could imagine the way it would manifest on his lovely wrinkled face, and even that was too much. Seeing it in person might've killed me. It would have made the whole thing feel real. And it wasn't real. It was a misunderstanding. So I stayed away.

It took nearly the year for the Administrative Board to meet on my case. Being away from Katie had been torture. I wanted to be near her, but even the thought gave me the shakes. I met with a defense lawyer, the same one who had represented my father in criminal court.

I told him what happened. It was the first time I had run through the night's events with anyone. I was foggy on the details. He listened quietly with his hands folded in front of him, before nodding and putting away his papers. Was that all? Were we done?

"Say a tenth of that. We'll write something down. No one should ask you anything. Just say you two were sexually active for months, she vocalized regret at having sex before marriage, you did it in secret—particularly from the judging eyes of her father—and she consented every time, including the last. That's it. Anything else can be incriminating if you get charged," he said, standing to go.

"I thought you said criminal charges are unlikely."

"They are. With these facts? Even if she's willing, the district attorney will kill it. But you can never be too careful."

"So I have a good shot at staying in school?"

"I didn't say that," he said, laughing. "What are you, again? A third-string kicker, right?"

I nodded. "Why does that matter?"

He didn't answer.

"Stick to the script. If you get in trouble, just repeat lines from your sheet of music. Don't improvise. Be one-note."

"I thought they couldn't ask me anything."

"It's a free-for-all in there, kid. I don't even know who sits on the board outside of the university president. It's secretive as all get-out."

"Won't you be there to object?"

"Oh, I'm not allowed to speak. I can whisper in your ear if you freak out."

He was at the door, holding it open, tapping his foot, glancing at his watch.

"Will Katie be there?" I asked.

"Son," and this he said with pity, dropping down to a baritone and placing his hands on my shoulders. "You're never seeing Katie again."

"But I love her."

His eyes became small.

"You don't do what you did to people you love."

It was the cruelest thing anyone would ever say to me. It wrecked me.

My gut was quivering on that morning I sat before a council of white men seated behind a long table on the auditorium stage. I wore my father's old suit. I was squeezing my hands together so tight, I drained the color from them.

I read my statement of five sentences, tops.

The microphone whined as I shoved it away from me, and all of us in the room sat in silence. The men glanced at one another in a series of nods that traveled in wavelike fashion down the row.

The man to the left of center—black coif, thick sideburns, tanned skin—motioned to the stenographer in the corner. He mimed slicing his throat. He was telling her to kill the record. Her fingers went still.

A burly man seated at the end of the firing squad spoke first. His name, per his placard, was Buddy Blum.

"You play football, son?"

I looked to my lawyer. He indicated it was all right.

"I was recruited to play, sir. Here on scholarship."

"You haven't started a single game, though?"

"No, sir."

"You attended the sexual assault talks required of all freshmen, didn't you?"

"Yes, sir."

"And you attended the sexual assault programming specifically required of our players, didn't you?"

"Yes, sir."

"So you were aware of the high level of respect we demand our players show their women, right? We teach our boys not to be aggressive with them, don't we?"

"I'm not an aggressive person, sir, and I didn't disrespect Katie."

"She says that you did, son. Is she lying?"

"No." It shot out of me just as my lawyer's hand reached for my arm. I kept my eyes on my questioner. "Katie doesn't lie. She's just mistaken.

I was mistaken. There was a miscommunication. But I didn't mean to hurt her. I love her."

"Were you thinking of the team at all, son? And the shame this would bring to it? To us all?"

I dipped my head down, chin to chest.

"I'm sorry."

The man who had cut off the reporter spoke next and last. His name, per his placard, was Dale Whitehurst.

"This is your second allegation of misconduct, young man."

"That was withdrawn, sir."

"But it was filed, and it's on record."

He let it sit for a beat. I couldn't look away from him.

"I understand you can't afford to stay in school without football."

"Probably not."

"Did you really think you'd be allowed back on the team?"

"After this misunderstanding?"

"After your performance."

"On the field? You mean one blown kick?"

His smile was wide. Perfect, pearly, straight-set teeth. He twirled his thumbs—one, two, three revolutions—before speaking again.

"Your father is in prison on sex charges, isn't that right?"

"What the hell does that have to do with anything?" I shot up to my feet. The chair screeched beneath me. My lawyer grabbed my arm— hard. It had only been seconds, and I had barely noticed my own transformation, until I felt my breath coming in heaves, my shoulders had been squared, my teeth were bared, and my face was hot.

His puckered smile was small this time.

"You're right. Certainly no flashes of aggression I can tell."

There was light laughter from the panel.

"'You can tell the greatness of a man by what makes him angry.' My hero, Abraham Lincoln, said that. Tell me: is this making you angry, son?"

The flop back down into my seat was the longest fall.

I was summoned back a week later. Whitehurst read the verdict.

"We convene this session of the Administrative Board to decide the matter of Katie Galindo—and the record will redact her name—versus Cameron Lian on allegations of sexual assault in violation of the student code of conduct. In compliance with Title IX, we have taken the testimony of the complainant and the accused, and we have reviewed the available evidence to render a sound judgment. We find you, Mr. Lian—by a preponderance of that evidence—responsible in this matter. We hereby rescind your scholarship and formally expel you from the university indefinitely and effective immediately."

Gong-gong made space for me at home. This time, I couldn't refuse.

We didn't talk that night. He opened the door for me, nodded, and retreated to his quarters. Mom was in rare form. She was all tears and moans and constricting hugs and sloppy kisses. She guided my head onto her lap and put her hands in my hair, stroking the back of my head—so sweetly, so lovingly. It was nice, however out of character. I dozed off into sleep in that position.

My mother was mothering, finally, but this was just her way of gloating. She had been vindicated. Eli's corrosive genes and influence had struck again.

I was aimless for a couple of years after that. I picked up odd jobs, but nothing stuck. I slept in late. I got high and drunk and did a not-so-great job at hiding it. Gong-gong insisted I apply to another college and finish my degree. But whenever I got to the question—*Have you ever been found responsible for a disciplinary violation at any educational institution you have attended from the ninth grade forward, whether related to academic or behavioral misconduct, that resulted in disciplinary action? If so, please explain.*—I always put the application away. I didn't know how to talk about it.

Ages twenty-two, twenty-three, twenty-four, twenty-five came and went. Nothing changed.

I had a bad bender one weekend. I rented a cheap motel downtown to recover, away from the prying eyes of my family. Nat, now eighteen, was in town from college. He wanted to see me. I didn't have it in me to get out of bed, so I allowed him to visit me in my disordered room and condition.

The way he navigated the disarray and the look of alarm in his eye were familiar. I had seen it when we had stumbled onto our father's skeletons. A single glance sent me to the depths. I tried to make small talk, even as I felt myself sinking.

"You have a girlfriend yet?" I asked. "Or a boyfriend? Whichever."

He looked terribly embarrassed.

"No. I'm not focused on things like that. Just my studies."

He had to have caught my eyes shining. I hadn't felt joy like that in a long time. It was the feeling of hope, a feeling that had eluded me all my life.

"Good man," I said. "You're going to be solid like Gong-gong. Not soft like Eli."

It took me a long time to finish my thought. And even when I did, my voice wavered.

"Not soft like me."

When he left, I began drafting my answer to that elusive application question. I furiously scribbled it on napkins. I transferred the words to the online form from my phone. All that was left to do was hit send. When I was done, I walked to a local tattoo parlor. I chose the Chinese character for "fire"—just four strokes—and had it inked permanently above my heart. It had been listed incorrectly under "lucky," although they looked nothing alike.

"Drunk sorority girls get that one all the time," the artist told me.

I would never show it to Gong-gong—he wouldn't approve—but it was a way of carrying him with me. To hear him, and not Eli, and not myself, when facing a fork in the road. It turned out to be timely.

A call from my mother awoke me that Sunday morning.

She was shouting into the receiver.

"It's your gong-gong! They shot him dead, Cam! Dead!"

The owner of the plot of land housing the conservatory had himself died weeks before. Gong-gong hadn't been told. His son inherited the home, the land, the greenhouse—everything. His father hadn't before mentioned his arrangement with Gong-gong. It wasn't written anywhere. All of it had been verbal.

That morning, as Gong-gong had made his stealthy way onto the land, the son had grabbed his shotgun, rushed over to meet the intruder, and—within close range—blew him away. Square in the face.

I didn't get to see his body a final time. Mom had him cremated— incinerated by fire, turned into nothing—with startling speed.

"He was unrecognizable, Cam. In no shape to be seen," she pleaded.

I felt every emotion doled out by God at Creation. My rage was instant. It competed with overwhelming sadness that lodged itself in my throat. And then there was guilt. Oh, so much guilt. I didn't know what to do with my hands but claw at myself until I drew blood. I felt his loss physically within me, like an organ had gone missing. Like I no longer had a heart. It had died along with him. I finally found the words to reflect the ugliness I felt inside.

"I don't fucking care! I would have felt him! I would have held him! Like he held me. I would have said my goodbyes!"

My throat was vibrating so hard at the volume of my anger. The words felt heavy on the way out. I was vomiting them out. They began deep down from the gut. My eyes were burning, and there was snot running down my nose.

"You're scaring me, Cam."

"Good, you fucking whore! You should be scared of me. *I'm* scared of me," I yelled. I had chosen between the two: the rage had won out over the grief. "You did this to wash your hands of him. You only care about yourself. I hate you so much, Mom, and I've always hated you. I can't stand the look of you. And I will never forgive you."

Nai nai died of natural causes six days later, before next Sunday morning. Before she could miss her lilies. Her heart just stopped beating.

We met with the same godforsaken lawyer who had represented Eli and myself.

"The State isn't proceeding with charges against the shooter," he said. "Castle doctrine. He was in his own home. On his own property. You have a right to defend it, including by using deadly force. You have no duty to retreat. It's a complete defense. You can't go to jail. That's Kansan law. That's the law across the country honestly."

"But my grandpa wasn't doing anything wrong. He had a right to be there," I said.

"Not since the previous owner died. I know your grandpa didn't know, Cam—and it's heartbreaking—but his permission died along with the father. By all accounts, the son didn't have a clue."

"He shot him in the face. He didn't even give him a chance to explain."

"It's gruesome. It's a tragedy. But no jury would convict."

"Can't the district attorney at least try? Can't he bring charges? Plead it out to *something*."

"Neil Whitehurst? I don't think so. The man has aspirations for higher office. He doesn't sign off on losing cases like these."

I scooted to the edge of my seat.

"What was that name? Whitehurst?"

"You're thinking of Dale Whitehurst, the senior, the senator who served as a regent at your former school. Neil's his son and handpicked successor as the district attorney. The senator's actually the one who prosecuted your pop. The Whitehursts are careful, restrained Democratic politicians. In deep-red Kansas, you gotta be. They go after guys like your dad. Not like the one who shot your grandpa."

I paid Eli a visit in custody to explain all of it to him. The burden fell on me. Mom would never go. And I had forbidden Nat from seeing him. Although I had a feeling Nat had been paying him secret visits anyway. He was never good at lying like I was. But he was a man now, and I didn't push the matter.

I hadn't seen Eli in some years. I had fielded some of his calls home here and there, engaging in conversation mere minutes long, but I hadn't made the trek in person for a while.

Through the glass, he looked bigger. Working out every day will do that for you. He looked scarier. Same greasy hair, same unruly facial hair, but there was something new in his eyes. He had the look of a man who had dropped the pretense. A man who had come into his own. He had the confidence of the devil himself.

"Dale Whitehurst's a fucking asshole," he said after I was done explaining.

"I wish I could kill the fucker myself," I said, sneering.

"So why don't you?"

Our eyes met for all of eternity. It felt like a game of chicken. I looked away first. He always did win.

"Because I don't listen to every stupid idea that pops into my head like you do," I said.

He hissed, flashing his teeth and mocking me with that goofy smile of his.

"Haven't you figured out you're no better than me, boy? Only a thin pane of glass separates us. I'm in here and you're out there by mere circumstance. The sooner you resign yourself to that, the more at peace you'll feel. Be a man. Don't just get fucked. Do some of the fucking yourself. Sit in your anger, and do what it is you feel deep down."

I ended our session prematurely.

"Stay away from Nat," I warned.

I turned twenty-six shortly after Gong-gong passed. I reached out to a former teammate who had shown an interest in politics while we were in school. I lied and told him I had completed my degree elsewhere. I told him I was thinking of working in Congress.

"That's great to hear, Cam. You were really railroaded with that assault bullshit back in the day. It'd be nice to have a perspective like yours—a true victim's perspective—up there on issues like that. You should apply to intern. That's how you start off. I did it myself right out of school."

"Won't they do a background check?"

"Oh, God, no. Not for interns. Literally the most junior staffer in the office hires them. There's, like, no vetting. Just send your résumé. Besides, is there even anything on your criminal record? Weren't you, like, never charged or arrested for any of that?"

"No press, either. Can't Google it. I was a nobody. No one cared."

"That's awesome, man."

I researched the senator and came across the details of his mentor, Senator Bill Williams. I wanted to be close but not too close. I drew up my résumé in a day. I subtracted four years from my age. I attached my picture to it. Before I snapped it, I picked up an old pair of Nat's glasses and threw them on. I had read somewhere that the Clark Kent effect was real. The last thing I changed was my last and middle name. I made them more white sounding.

I worried that last bit was internalized self-loathing, and not just strategy. Maybe I wanted to disown everything to do with my father. Even as I had resolved to become him.

I hit send, and I waited. I thought about Katie. I thought about Gong-gong. And I sat in my anger.

13

BLEEDING KANSAS

Before you embark on a journey of revenge, dig
two graves.   —Confucius

We planned the assassination seated at a round table in a corner of Charlie's favorite Chinatown restaurant, chomping on egg rolls and scallion pancakes, listening to faint Color Me Badd, Maxwell, and Bell Biv Devoe in the background. It was the night before America voted. It was late, and the restaurant was empty.

A young woman—hostess-cum-waitress-cum-janitor-cum-short-order cook—was flipping chairs on top of tables, eyeing us with the impatience of a worker trying to get home. I strained to hear her complaints in Mandarin to the older woman, her aunt, ostensibly helping her close up shop but actually just dozing off behind the counter.

We were loud, she said. Inconsiderate also. But she suspected nothing.

"I'll run through our roles," I said.

"Have you ever heard this man speak as much as he has tonight?" Randy quipped. The group chuckled and smiled. I was truly one of them.

I carried on.

"First, Lisa gets us in."

"All of your names are already on the guest list. Plus a last-minute addition—"

"—the target—"

"Yes, Cam. The 'target,'" Lisa said, quelling a smile. "SGS asked me to strike his name, but she won't notice that he's back on. How are we sure he'll even show up?"

"I've cleared it with his scheduler," Liz said. "He'd otherwise spend the night at home with the wife and kids, and he'd do anything over that. He's coming."

"Second, Chuy gets him drugged."

"Whitehurst will order a scotch. Macallan. Neat. That's his go-to," Liz said.

"I'll be working the bar," Chuy said. "The boy I offered to cover was relieved. No true politico wants to be slinging drinks on Election Night. I'll mix the crushed-up pill Cam got me into his drink when he's not looking."

"How exactly is it that you have access to last-minute roofies, Cam?" Charlie asked.

"My roommate's a perv," I lied. "Use the amount I precut. Just enough to get him woozy."

"Say less. We don't want him passing out. Not yet," Chuy said.

"Third, Liz gets him over to the committee room."

"I've spliced a previously recorded call from Denton," she said. "I'll call DJW's phone from a blocked number and hit play. 'Meet me in the committee room,' he'll hear him say. Then I'll hang up."

"And Denton won't be at the party to muck it all up," Charlie said. "He declined the invite. Wants to lay low as he's persona non grata with just about everyone right now."

"Fourth, Randy gets rid of security."

"There's no coffee place open that late in the area, Cam. I checked. How am I supposed to slip Stan the cinnamon?" Randy asked.

Lisa dug into his forearm and her eyes grew wide.

"The senator's carrot cake," she said.

"Huh?"

"2 Bills loves it. SGS is baking a sheet for him for the party. Correction: *I'm* baking a sheet for him for the party. She pretends she does her own baking, but it's all me. The recipe calls for cinnamon. I'll make sure there's enough in there—and masked by something stronger, anise maybe—to put him out of commission for a while."

"How do we know he'll accept a piece?" Scoop asked.

"He will," Randy said. "Dude's got a sweet tooth."

"Fifth, Charlie lures him inside."

"I'll unlock the door and leave it open a crack. Flip on the cloakroom light. Sit in Denton's chair but swing around, giving him my back. He'll think it's him," Charlie said.

"Sixth, Scoop gives him the scare of his life."

"Why does it have to be me?"

"Because of your aim, Scoop," I said.

"But I thought we weren't shooting anyone."

Charlie, Liz, and I communicated with our eyes.

"You are shooting him in the back," I said.

"What?"

"They're rubber bullets. Isn't that right, Randy?"

"Yes, we switched the bullets out for blanks," he said, casting me a dour look.

"We can't afford to miss and hit a wall," Charlie said. "He'll spin around and identify us. We don't want to hit him in the head or near a vital organ. That might seriously hurt him. We need him to topple over. We need to incapacitate him. We need to be precise. Your freakishly accurate talent gets us there."

Scoop—slowly, reticently—nodded.

"Seventh, Isla creates a distraction."

"A fire ring," she said. "Right beneath the sprinklers. Have them and the alarm set off. Clear out the whole building."

"What about the security cameras?" Scoop asked.

"I have a friend on the inside: Officer Gomez," Liz said. "He told me in confidence that the cameras in that wing undergo a maintenance reset between exactly eleven thirty-four and eleven thirty-seven p.m. every night. We have an awfully short window to get in and out of the committee room."

"So what will *you* do, Cam?" Isla asked.

"I'll run interference. Resolve any hiccups—and there *will* be hiccups. The important thing is that we can't text whatsoever. No calls, either. We play our roles, assuming the person before us did theirs. And we do not unilaterally abort, or we risk leaving one of us hanging out to dry. This is the last time we'll talk about this. Ever. Amongst ourselves. To our families. To the pigs. Ever."

I stuffed the last pancake in my mouth.

There were solemn nods all around.

"Now, let's get out there," I said as I chewed, "and have the best fucking night of our lives."

I arrived to the Capitol on Election Night early and alone, wearing my ill-fitting beige suit. Only one entrance on the Senate side was open. The offices in the building were dark and vacant. I stepped through the metal detectors and didn't trip off the alarm. The guard additionally waved me down with a wand.

I walked to the Senate Reception Room in the Capitol Building proper, eschewing the underground shuttle. For a long stretch, I contended with no noise but those of my own intrusive thoughts and the faraway meowing of a cat. On the way, I stepped over canisters of white paint, one lidless, left against the wall. I noted the time it took to calmly walk from Dirksen, where the Judiciary Committee room was located, to the double doors leading to the party.

The intern posted at the threshold checked off my name and ushered me inside.

The room was moderately sized but incredibly ornate. It felt intimate, cramped. Constantino Brumidi's art decorated the ceiling with pastel portrayals of cherubs, Roman warriors, and maidens draped in flowing garments. The upper walls boasted milky pale figures that leapt out at you. Chunky gold moldings lined the borders, arches, and corners of the room. A chandelier hung low, nearly cutting the space in half. There was a giant mirror behind the bar, and the floors were hard and shiny with the busiest of patterns. All of it hurt my eyes.

Among the relics, a 120-inch projector screen had been set up against a wall, playing live coverage from MSNBC.

The crowd was light at first. The polls in Washington, DC, were still open. Senator Grunwald-Santos was holding court at center, greeting the big names as they piled in. She wore her hair up, a formfitting green dress cut just below the knee, and big, sparkly jewelry across her plunging neckline. Her husband—tall, lean, and dashing—stood by her side.

They looked like a political mailer come to life. Youthful and attractive. Vibrant and in love. Interracial and nonthreatening. But like all of politics, it was a front.

Chuy was behind the bar in their bartending smock.

Lisa fluttered up and down the room in floor-length gold—looking like one of the room's fixtures come to life—alternating between her boss on one end and the help on the other.

I melted into the loudly adorned wall, idling on my phone.

When the polls closed on the East Coast, the projector screen was unmuted and the voice of the anchor played thunderously in the antique room.

"As polls close in Florida, the news desk can project that, as expected, its governor, Chad Thornton, will win the state's thirty electoral votes. His first big haul of the night."

Grunwald-Santos led the crowd in tepid jeers.

"We are able to project also expectedly that Vice President Kiara Jones will win New York and its twenty-eight electoral votes."

The crowd mustered a half-hearted cheer.

Randy arrived in a tailored tuxedo. He had tied up the hair usually in his eyes into a little manbun. Senator Lancaster, also in a tux, waltzed in behind him. The greeting between him and Grunwald-Santos was cold and swift.

"You and your uncle rode here together?" I asked.

Randy hadn't said hello, just plopped up beside me on the wall and acted coolly, as if we were strangers. The sweat from his hands stuffed into his pockets was seeping out and discoloring the fabric. I could see his gut quiver.

I reached out and laid a stabilizing hand on his shoulder.

"We did," he said. "It was the most awk limo ride of my life."

"You two talk about his vote on Wright yet?"

"Not one word."

"Talk about your pops?"

"Never, Cam. I know I'm a pussy, but the minute he opens his mouth about my dad, knowing what I know, I'm putting a bullet in it. Bet."

The top of the hour brought more poll closings. It was "too early to call" in Iowa, but Michigan was "too close to call," a bad sign for the vice president's home state.

Charlie joined the festivities next. He wore his traditional monocratic work ensemble.

We ordered drinks at the bar shoulder to shoulder.

"What can I get you gentlemen?" Chuy asked.

"Vodka soda," I said.

"Beer," Charlie said, pointing to a domestic bottle.

As Chuy poured, Charlie and I didn't turn to one another as we spoke.

"You came alone?" I asked.

"Of course."

"And the boss?"

"At home in his pajamas, drinking straight from the bottle. Right where I left him."

"What'd he think of the Halloween lighting we left in his yard?"

"He thinks someone's trying to kill him. But he can't decide if it's a white supremacist angry at his vote for Wright or a woke liberal angry at what he called me."

"So he's essentially asked you to move in and guard his life, that it?"

"That's the idea. Take a bullet for his sorry ass."

"Does he realize he brought the danger in under his roof?"

"No, I don't think he does."

Senator Kelley appeared in a purple pantsuit. How bipartisan.

"She's giving high-powered lesbian chic realness," Chuy whispered to me.

"But she's no ally, is she?" I asked.

"Big facts. The hypocrite."

She didn't greet Grunwald-Santos at all, bee-lining to Lancaster's side instead and clinging to him throughout the night as a buffer.

Another hour, another announcement.

"No surprise here. Despite a stronger showing than usual for the Democrat, Ruby Red Kansas remains in the Republican column. We can now project its six electoral votes will go to Governor Thornton."

I spotted Isla and Scoop enter. They wore matching dark blue suits that fit faultlessly on their svelte bodies. His was accessorized with a silk pocket square and greased-back hair; hers with black pumps, heavy rouge, and hair extensions.

He strode his way to me immediately with a nervous gait, despite my tries at warding him off with eyes of stone.

"There's too many people around," he said.

"All in this room, and none anywhere else. It was so dead silent on the way here, my mind was playing tricks on me. Thought I heard a cat."

His eyes bulged.

"Demon Cat? We're doomed to fail."

"I'm sorry?"

"The ghost cat that haunts the Capitol. You saw it. Only bad things happen when it appears. Like, presidents die, you know? JFK. Lincoln."

"I didn't see it. I only heard it," I said. "And 'bad' is a matter of perspective. The enemy gets a vote, too. You should head off. Wait in the wings. Your nervous energy won't do us any good."

I slipped him the extra key to the committee room.

He lingered, stomping his foot and emitting a short whine, before leaving.

I felt a knot in my belly when Liz and Senator Whitehurst made their way in—together. The pair looked like a dazzling May-December couple. She was elegant in black and pearls. He looked expensive with his designer suit and blinged-out watch.

"Did you know she was coming with him?" I asked Charlie.

"Nope. You?"

"Not at all."

When 2 Bills arrived, there was a fuss in the crowd and guests began to line up to greet him. He was wearing his old, misshapen suit and leaning on his cane, as always. Grunwald-Santos skipped the impromptu line, gave him a kiss on each cheek, and slowly guided him to the cake in the corner. I walked over to eavesdrop.

"I know how much you like my carrot cake, Bill," she said.

"Wonderful, Sandy. Thank you."

"Lisa, get him the first piece," she said in the tone of a neurotic mother.

As Lisa cut the cake, Whitehurst approached, with Liz by his side.

"Bill, Sandy, good evening."

"Dale," Sandy said through a pained smile. "I didn't think you would make it."

"The invitation came a little late, but I wouldn't miss this fete you threw for yourself."

"Right," she said, wrinkling her nose at Lisa before turning back to him. "And I see you left Emily at home and brought this lovely young lady instead. Have some decorum. This isn't the House of Representatives!"

He made no attempt to hide the rolling of his eyes.

"She's just an aide, Sandy."

"That hasn't stopped many a powerful man before."

Liz turned red. Whitehurst dropped the forced smile and opened his mouth to no doubt deliver a tongue-lashing, but another ripple gripped the crowd, making heads turn. I looked over to the doors to see that a sloppily dressed and unsteady-footed Senator Denton had just sauntered through.

"Your favorite GOP punching bag is finally here!" he announced to everyone and no one in particular.

"What the hell is he doing here?" I heard Charlie mutter to himself behind me.

"Get rid of him," I whispered back.

In seconds, Whitehurst and Grunwald-Santos had swarmed Denton. Liz and Charlie followed. I floated to the outskirts of the ring forming around him.

"Sir, how did you get here?" Charlie asked, laying his large hand on his back. Denton squirmed away from the touch.

This close, I noticed that he wore fuzzy, Scrooge-like slippers on his unsocked feet.

"I do know how to drive, Charlie boy."

The slurring of his words bordered on comedic.

"I wouldn't call him 'boy' if I were you," Grunwald-Santos warned.

"Shut up, bitch," Denton said.

Onlookers gasped. Whitehurst grabbed him forcefully by the arm. "Scott, you're making everything worse for yourself. I'll take you to your car."

"He can't drive. He's drunk," Grunwald-Santos said.

"Then I'll drive him home myself," Whitehurst said. "It's clear I'm as welcome here as he is."

"No!" Liz blurted out.

All eyes turned to her. The senators looked stunned at the outburst. Aides were always invisible—hanging on the periphery, barely on the same frequency, buzzing just beneath the surface—until they weren't, until they brashly made themselves known.

"What I mean is: you don't have to leave, Senator," Liz said, voice shaky and eyes down low. "Charlie here's my boyfriend. He's Senator Denton's body man. He can find him a safe way home."

Whitehurst took a half step back and eyed Charlie down. The information appeared to catch him by surprise. Perhaps she had never before mentioned a boyfriend.

"Yes, Dale, please. Stay," Grunwald-Santos said. "I was being facetious. I'm sorry. Keep Bill company. I know he'd want you here. Let this young man take Scott home."

Denton, newly half lidded and mumbling, allowed Charlie to escort him off with uncharacteristic ease. I drew close to them as he was leaving.

"I'll get him in an Uber," Charlie whispered to me.

"And if he resists?"

"I'll break his legs."

Back by the cake, as an oblivious 2 Bills was digging into his piece with gusto, Lisa was handing Randy a slice. Others were already in line for their own.

"Take it. Before it runs out. Go now. It's almost eleven," she told him.

Minutes later, an announcement cut through the chatter, sucking the air out of the room.

"Every poll has now closed in the contiguous United States. We can project that the vice president will win the fifty-four electoral votes from California, the home state of now-Justice Frederick Wright, whose nomination Vice President Jones opposed. We can also now predict that the vice president will win the popular vote by several million over Governor Thornton, a feat every Democratic nominee has achieved in the last thirty-two years but for one cycle.

"Even still, the Electoral College chooses our president—not the people. Our news desk is now confident that the vice president has lost her home state of Michigan to Governor Thornton. That puts him marginally ahead with only a handful of swing states left undecided, including a surprisingly tight contest in Iowa."

Whitehurst and 2 Bills were conferring with Liz hovering just steps behind.

"Night's looking bad," Whitehurst said.

"We're on the brink of losing our democracy," 2 Bills replied.

Liz drew closer.

"Need a drink, Senator?" she asked.

"Good idea," Whitehurst said.

"I can get it for you."

"No. Everyone here already thinks we're fucking," he said, stressing the vulgarity and scrunching his face with disgust. Her eyes flared open in reply. "I'll get it myself. You able to drink, old man?"

"Of course," 2 Bills said, trilling his lips like a horse. "I'm a prehistoric creature but not dying. I've got the liver of a Tibetan monk."

"No offense. I just don't know what kind of pills you're on."

"The full complement, son. But that's even better. I'd love to just knock myself out tonight."

Whitehurst led 2 Bills to the bar. Liz slipped out of the room with her phone in hand. Isla trailed her. I moved within earshot of the men.

Whitehurst ordered his Macallan, neat.

2 Bills was dawdling in choosing. Chuy got started on the one order.

"It might not be too bad if Thornton wins—"

Chuy turned around. The tumbler in their hand was shaking.

"—and we hold on to the Senate. We can investigate the shit out of the Nazi fucker—"

Chuy dug into their suit pocket.

"—and maybe impeach him right from the start. You and I, we'd be even more influential with a divided government," Whitehurst said.

Chuy produced a baggie of powder. Looking down at their hands, they didn't notice the mirror was reflecting the furtive move to the people behind. Whitehurst was staring straight at it.

"We will be doing no such foolishness, Dale—"

I was desperate. I leapt forward.

"Senator!" I shouted, jamming my hand forward in greeting.

Whitehurst pivoted toward me, away from the mirror. Nothing on his face moved but for a twitch in the corner of his mouth.

"It's a pleasure to meet you. Cameron, sir," I tried again.

He clasped my hand and didn't let go. He stared me down unbearably long. I felt my palm touching his dampen. I wanted to look away, but I was paralyzed. I searched for recognition in his eyes.

"Cameron what?"

I hesitated. Our hands were still linked.

"Leann, sir. Cameron Leann."

Had he remembered, I suspected I'd feel relieved. Either it'd put an end to this all—finally, somewhat blessedly—or I'd just lunge for his throat and squeeze the life out of him right there, right then. See it as my last waning opportunity.

"Pleased to meet you," he said instead. "But the chairman and I were talking. It isn't very polite to interrupt."

"I'm a friend of Lizzy's." It shot out of me without thought.

"Oh," he said, softening his posture. He gave the largest smile, making up nearly the full width of his face. "She's a special girl, ain't she?"

I smiled back tightly. My eyes had no levity.

"Yes, sir," I said. "I'll let you two get back to it. My apologies."

He hadn't let up his grip. I had to withdraw my own hand.

When he whirled back around, Chuy had already set the senator's drink—now laced with sedatives—on the bar top. Whitehurst wrapped his hand around the glass.

"Oh, that smells great," 2 Bills said. "Pungent. Strong. Just what I need."

"Take my drink, Bill. It's yours."

"No need! I'll pour him another," Chuy said, voice elevated, hands flying wildly to prepare a second.

Whitehurst ignored them. He shoved the drugged drink in 2 Bills's hands.

"Bottoms up," he said.

The elder senator knocked back half the amber liquid in a single gulp. He made a noise of exaggerated refreshment afterward. The senators stepped away once Chuy poured a second, which Whitehurst accepted as his. I walked up to the bar.

"We just roofied an octogenarian," Chuy said.

"Don't sweat it. It doesn't matter. So the target won't be as compliant. Guns are the great equalizer."

I kept an eye on the pair. I saw when Whitehurst picked up his phone. He was on it for seconds. He peered down at it curiously when he hung up. I neared them again, bringing Lisa along for cover. We moved our lips soundlessly at one another, trying to listen in.

"Whitehurst's telling him to go to the committee room with him," Lisa said.

I had been more focused on watching 2 Bills. His eyelids were intermittently floating shut. His breathing was shallow. He was leaning heavily on his cane and, eventually, on Whitehurst himself. He was teetering on his orthopedic shoes. He was fading, and it had to be apparent to Whitehurst. And, yet, he kept talking about taking him to meet Denton—not home, not to the hospital, but across the sprawling complex.

Whitehurst offered him sips from his drink. The chairman's own was now empty.

"I think he thinks 2 Bills is OD'ing, and he's not doing a damn thing to save him," I said.

Whitehurst led him away, out of the room. I grabbed Chuy.

"We got to go."

They put up a placard noting the bar was closed.

"I'll stay here for now," Lisa said. "Make sure SGS doesn't flip out about the interruption in service. I'll meet up soon."

We caught up with the senators at the Capitol subway. The car was empty, awaiting passengers, but Whitehurst bypassed it, leading a sluggish 2 Bills by the arm down the long pedestrian path instead.

"He's making the old man walk his way back. Why?" Chuy asked.

"I don't think he wants the subway attendant to see the shape he's in. They're going to arrive late," I said.

The time was 11:22.

I grabbed the open bucket of paint I had seen earlier.

"We'll need this," I told Chuy.

We hopped onto a subway car and ducked down when we whizzed past the senators. We were going to make it there first.

Down the hall and around the corner from the Judiciary Committee, we saw Stan still there and upright, plate of cake in hand and three-fourths of the way done eating. He looked healthy, upbeat.

"It's taking too long to affect him," Chuy said.

When it turned 11:34, I surged forward, unthinkingly—just knowing something had to be done—but Randy, approaching from the other side, beat me to it. Randy opened his mouth to say something to Stan, but nothing came out. The officer spoke first instead.

"Randy, thank God you're back. Think you can stand here for a few minutes? I need to use the bathroom, and it's sort of an emergency. No time to call for backup."

"Sure, bud. However long you need."

He waddled off.

We all met at the doors: Scoop and Charlie. Chuy and myself. Liz and Isla. No sign of Lisa yet.

Scoop unlocked the door. I found the two black half-spherical cameras poking out from the ceiling at each end of the hall.

"These things are turning back on any minute now," I said to whomever was close enough to hear.

I doused them in white paint. A fair amount splattered back onto the ground, sprinkling my hands and clothes.

We spilled into the darkened committee room. Someone turned on the cloakroom light. Another powered the television—set to election coverage—and turned the volume all the way up. I heard the groaning of Denton's chair on the dais. I shoved Scoop into the closet and closed its door behind him.

"The gun's through the hole," I said.

I heard him scrambling.

"I can't find it."

"The gun or the hole?" I asked.

He didn't reply. I opened the closet door and stepped in. There were voices and footsteps coming from the main entrance, so I froze, leaving the door open with Scoop and me squeezed inside. Through the cracks on the hinge side, I saw Whitehurst and 2 Bills enter the darkness.

The elder was moaning, draped around Whitehurst's shoulders

and fumbling on his feet. Before reaching the center of the room, 2 Bills rolled out of Whitehurst's arms and collapsed onto the floor. He flung his cane toward the dais. Whitehurst crouched to his knees, but it wasn't clear what he was doing. He wasn't saying anything, and he wasn't panicking, making only slight movements that produced no sound.

I dipped my hand into the crevice, felt around for cool metal, retrieved the firearm, and pressed it flat against Scoop's stomach.

"Now!" I whispered.

He shook his head.

I thumb-cocked the hammer to the revolver. It made a clicking sound.

"You must."

I transferred the gun into his hands. He turned away from me, staring at oak paneling and not moving. As Scoop was dragging his feet, our window was closing, and my heart was in overdrive. I was operating on pure desperation and adrenaline.

I shoved Scoop out of the closet. Hard. He stumbled out and tapped the trigger in the commotion. The bullet erupted out—drowning out the voices droning on the television—and hit a wall. Whitehurst leapt to his feet. I saw Liz and Isla emerge from the cloakroom. Randy and Chuy jumped up from behind the dais. Charlie swung around in his boss's chair. Hands over my throbbing ears, I stepped out into the room.

"What is all of this?" Whitehurst demanded.

Scoop lifted the gun with both hands and aimed it at him. Whitehurst wiped the anger and bewilderment off his face. His frightful eyes widened. His mouth dropped open. His palms flew level with his face in surrender. He shrank into himself, looking small, and unmoored, and contrite—for what, he had no way of knowing.

Scoop circled his target, holding him in his gaze, coming to a stop when he was between Whitehurst and the exit. His hand was steady, even though the rest of his body was trembling in full revolt. The skilled marksman's hands knew better than to succumb.

Whitehurst scanned the room at the faces of the twenty-somethings surrounding him.

"Lizzy? Sweetheart," he said.

I saw her swallow hard whatever excuse she had lodged in her throat. She had progressively made her way to Charlie's side.

"Do it now, Scoop," I said. "He's seen our faces."

Whitehurst swung his gaze over to me.

"I'm not an idiot!" Scoop yelled. "You lied to me. This gun is lethal."

"Good thing it is. You have a gun pointed at a sitting senator. *You.* That's aggravated assault with a deadly weapon at the very least. There's no turning back now, kid. Fire the rounds and save us all."

We were all projecting our voices over the loud programming.

"Don't listen to him," Whitehurst said, voice calmer than the panic besieging his eyes. "I won't tell a soul, son. I promise. You end this here, and it's nothing. No one gets in trouble. Just put the gun down, please."

"Time's almost up, Scoop," I said, illuminating the screen to my phone in his direction. "Shoot it."

I heard someone entering the room. We all turned to look. I expected to see Stan.

It was Lisa. She stopped short at the doorframe, taking in the scene.

"Run, Scoop!" Isla shouted.

Scoop let the revolver fall from his hands. It hit the carpet with a thud. He whipped around and charged toward the exit, colliding into Lisa and bringing them both down. Whitehurst had his eyes on the gun. He started toward it. Liz backhanded Charlie in the chest.

"Do something!" she yelled at him. "For me!"

Charlie ran after Whitehurst in long bounds that covered the room. Still, the senator was going to reach it first. On his way, Charlie bent down and grabbed hold of the chairman's cane.

Whitehurst had his back to him. In a crouch, the senator gripped the gun, stood, and turned around, but Charlie had already drawn the cane, swinging it with such force, I heard the wind it whipped up over the buzzing of the television.

It struck Whitehurst in the jaw. Blood sprayed from the point of contact. The gun flew from his hands. Isla was shrieking.

He was still on his feet. Charlie whacked him with a second blow. This one struck his temple. More blood.

He was on his way down. He struck him a third time, vertically, on the top of his skull. I could see the life drain out of him. It was instantaneous. His body plummeted to the ground like a rag doll. Charlie, breathing heavily, stood over him. He started crying immediately.

Lisa and Scoop watched from the doorway.

I was stunned but elated. I had visualized this moment so many times but wasn't sure it would come to pass. A burden was finally lifted, and I could breathe again. Pure relief.

We should have run, but we were glued to our spots. Lisa got up and even shut the doors, as if that flimsy barrier could shield us from the contempt of the world on the other side of it.

I drifted over to the body and knelt before it.

I saw Charlie huddle to Liz's side, where Randy, Isla, and Chuy had gathered, looking like hollowed-out shells of human beings. Nothing substantial behind the eyes. Just weakness.

At least I was going to savor the moment. I coated myself in his blood. I stared into the face of death. I liked what I saw. I saw a piece of myself, one that had always felt dead.

"...*The news desk is now able to project the winner of the presidential election. Having netted Iowa's six electoral votes by a razor-thin margin, we can declare that the forty-seventh president of the United States will be Florida Governor Chad Thornton. It is predicted that the election of the conservative Republican—who ran on a platform of instituting a national abortion ban, removing mention of race and homosexuality in schools, and creating a voter fraud police force—will draw protests in the tens of millions in the coming weeks. Experts predict a sizable portion of those planning to march hadn't even bothered to vote."*

I felt a presence hovering above me. It was Liz.

I stood up to face her. She wiped some of the senator's blood from my cheek with her thumb. She put it in her mouth and sucked it dry.

The men in long guns burst through the doors.

Words flew out of me impulsively.

"They made me do it."

14

CHAMELEON

Once made equal to man, woman becomes his superior. —Socrates

She was born Elizabeth Marie Frost, but everyone took to just calling her Frost.

"Liz sounds like a bottle-blond airhead giving handies off the side of the road," she once said. "Elizabeth is regal."

Her mother, Rain, had grown up in a conservative commune in Kansas that the federal government raided in an episode that didn't draw as much attention as the standoff in Waco. The leader of this sect shot himself in the head at the first sign of law enforcement camped outside the property line. Rain was liberated at eighteen years old. She met the older, established heir to a successful meatpacking company, Robert Frost, then thirty-four years old, and the two married later that year. He had seen her as a rebound from the loveless, sexless, childless marriage to his college sweetheart that had just ended. She saw in him an authority figure, the only model of love she had ever known.

She gave birth to Elizabeth, their only child, on the same day she turned twenty. Geminis both. Frost came out of the womb with balled fists—so tight, it impeded her blood circulation—and a full set of hair: locks of chocolate brown, just like her mother.

Rain took a sharp turn from her past life. She shed her religious upbringing, associating all of it with the years of abuse she suffered, and became an "avowed militant feminist," her words. She kept her maiden name. She spelled "women" as "womyn," both socially and professionally. She organized, marched, and raised funds in support of sex workers or against genital mutilation, both a world away and here at home, including the foreskin removal of newborn boys. All within her affluent cul-de-sac community. She maintained a sex-positive home, handing out condoms to visiting children as early as grade school.

"You know, white feminism," Frost would describe it with a smirk.

Rain's own sex life matched her free-spirited talk. Robert had grown up a Unitarian Universalist, a liberal tradition focused more on tolerance and acceptance than any particular creed or formal belief system, so he didn't mind.

It was a not-so-well-kept secret that Frost's parents were swingers. But they never explored on their own. Always together. And no one was invited into their bed twice. Those were the rules. Sometimes, Robert only watched. Other times, he would participate. Frost recalled a revolving door of couples or single men or women staying overnight at the home. Mornings weren't awkward. At the breakfast table, the little girl would chat them up and show off her prized possessions like these were her new friends. It made her sad when they never returned.

She didn't have a problem speaking to adults like peers.

In the second grade, Mrs. Halstead directed Frost to stand for the pledge of allegiance. The seven-year-old ignored her.

"Do you hear me, young lady?"

"Yes, I do."

"Then why won't you listen?"

"Freedom."

Robert sat her down that evening to talk about her behavior.

"Why didn't you stand?"

"She didn't say 'please.' You're supposed to say please, right, Daddy?"

He chuckled and lifted her onto his knee.

"I never want you to shy away from speaking up. There's power in your voice. Others will try to take your power, try to silence you. Because some think girls aren't supposed to speak. So, for them, you speak louder and more often. Wherever they say you don't belong, insert yourself. Make your presence known. Sound good?"

She nodded.

"But be strategic. Obey authority when you can stomach it. Strike when there's advantage. Don't go to battle with nobodies. Like poor Mrs. Halstead. Do as she tells you. Until it matters. Until it's important to you. OK?"

"OK."

"I love you, Elizabeth. My dad never told me he loved me. I want it to be different between us. You hear me? I love you."

And Frost loved her father back.

Rain, however, inspired ambivalence in her. Her mother was over-bearing, particularly when it came to monitoring her child's development. Nothing was private for a woman intent on making sexual education a feature of everyday life. It forced Frost to grow up faster than she otherwise would.

Frost got her period early when she was just eight years old. She knew what was happening. By then, her mother had demystified the process in great detail. Frost would come to believe the stress and pressure of anticipating it so young had triggered its early onset.

She locked herself in the bathroom with an exasperated Rain on the other side.

"Let me in, honey."

"No! I want Daddy."

"He won't even know what to do."

"I don't care. Get me Daddy."

He dashed to her side. She let him, and only him, tend to her. He was there when she needed him. Reliably present.

There was a string of days he was gone, though. She never forgot them.

It was the first time her mother had a friend over while her daddy was away. It was the first time she saw the same friend come more than once.

He was tall and strong. Tan for a white man, not like her daddy, who was pale. Full head of jet-black hair. Pronounced dimples. A masculine presence that took up great space, even what he wasn't using. It was his energy. It felt heavy, enveloping, like heated air on a chilly evening.

She hadn't chatted with him those first two mornings. Daddy wasn't there, and it just didn't feel right. On the third day, he approached her as she was drawing on the coffee table. He sat on the couch within arm's reach of where she had spilled herself onto the floor.

He wore an undershirt, slacks, and bare feet, hair on the knuckles.

She remembered how widely he spread his legs while seated.

"What are you drawing?"

"A gun."

She felt him lean in closer to peer down at the sketch.

"Oh," he said. "Like a toy of yours?"

"No. This is a real one."

"Now, where have you seen a real one before?"

"Like the one my daddy keeps loaded in his nightstand. For when strange men make their way inside the house. To blow them away."

She heard him clear his throat.

"That's not very ladylike, is it?"

She shrugged.

"How about I tell you my name? So I won't be a stranger anymore," he said. "I'm Dale."

She didn't offer her own.

When Robert returned, Frost let it slip that Rain had had an overnight guest. She wanted to punish her. Women punishing women; it would be a recurring theme in her life. But it was Frost who ended up most bruised. Robert didn't take it well. He tolerated his wife's libertine streak only when he could take personal advantage. He collected his things, packed his bags, and left—for good.

He remarried unnaturally soon. Robert was a serial monogamist like that. His third wife bore him three children in two-year bursts: a boy, a girl, and another boy. Frost would spend sporadic weekends at their house. It was at her dad's new house where—at thirteen—she had sex for the first time. She hated the phrase "losing your virginity." You weren't losing anything. If anything, you were gaining knowledge—of good, of evil—like Eve and the apple.

She couldn't remember a time she wasn't a sexual being. It predated learning of her parents' unorthodox sexual arrangement. Before she was old enough to recognize it as predatory, she would—nearly indiscriminately and without warning—cup and release boys' privates as she ran around the playground at recess. She developed an early affinity for pornography, despite learning from the prevailing culture that it was a solely male endeavor. Her tastes were rather hardcore and exclusively man-on-man, a preference that led her to believe she was violently heterosexual. There was something about a man dominating another man—as brutally and as roughly as she wanted—that felt safe and unproblematic when a woman wasn't involved. In public, for socially acceptable thrills, she took to carrying a romance novel with her everywhere she went. She loved reading; it was like mental cosplay. Try on someone else's life for size. She read *What We Say to Ourselves in the Dead of Night* as a teenager after having found the timeworn book among her mother's things.

From Tommy, the boy who deflowered her—*that* euphemism she did enjoy for the pure comedy of it—she learned of goodness.

He was a tall, skinny, seventeen-year-old emo kid she desperately wanted: black-painted nails, cartoonishly wide-legged jeans, black mascara, and all. But he was weeks away from becoming legal, when Frost would overnight transform into jailbait. So she worked hard at seducing him on a tight schedule. She invited him over to her dad's place one weekend the summer after he graduated and before she started high school.

Robert looked thoroughly bemused by the otherworldly boy standing before him. But he allowed his daughter to retreat to her room with him. He allowed her to close and lock her bedroom door behind her. He allowed them to remain there, uninterrupted, for the fumbling, unwieldy sex they went on to share. He allowed him to leave an hour-and-a-half later without a cross word or look but a handshake and a "good night."

In the act, Tommy had been sweet, and nervous, and self-conscious. He had said all the right things, including an "I love you" that neither of them accepted for truth but rather as a means of building comfort. He had eagerly devoted time to sex-adjacent activity aimed at pleasuring her, and it had gone well.

Frost ended up on her porch afterward, staring wistfully up at the Kansan sky. Robert joined her.

"Do you now think I'm as big a whore as she is?" she asked her father.

Her stomach dropped at the flash of horror in his eyes. She had never seen him so pained. He had been at the door, but seconds later, he was crouched down by her, swaddling her in his arms, holding her head to his chest, and rocking.

"You're your own woman, Elizabeth," he said. "Making your own decisions. Hopefully, not bound by the bullshit double standards that men have created. You make your own choices about sex, and loyalty, and love. And I trust you will make the smart ones."

He still loved her.

But as the demands on him from his new family grew, the weekends Frost spent with her father dwindled. He wasn't all that present anymore. She had teenage things to attend to anyway.

Tommy had fallen for her. In those weeks, he showered her with rides to the mall, candy, and gifts. She doled out sex, noting how the prospect of it—alternatingly withholding and bestowing it—motivated men to action. She felt no shame about it. She enjoyed the sex itself, and how men responded was none of her concern and, moreover, outside of her control.

Tommy had developed feelings, but she hadn't, and she told him as much when he turned eighteen. He cried and complained of feeling used.

"How can you have sex with someone and feel nothing?" he asked.

Ask men since the dawn of history.

From Pete, the boy who impregnated her, she learned of evil.

She met him in the summer before college at dance camp. As mother and daughter grew increasingly distant, Rain sent Frost away to overnight, weeks-long camps during breaks from school. Frost and Pete were counselors. The boy two years her senior was the perfect amount of effeminate, stocky but lithe, boasting curly black hair and light eyes. He was one of only a handful of heterosexual men there, so he was in high demand.

"You Jewish?" was her opening line upon approaching him in the ballroom.

"Huh?"

"The curls. I figured you might be Jewish."

"No," he said, wrinkling his brow. "I'm Roman Catholic. Italian. Pete D'Amico."

"Oh. Right."

"You're Liz?"

"I go by Frost actually. Or Elizabeth. Never Liz."

"I think I heard some of the kids call you Liz. Must have been on accident."

"By accident."

"Yeah. That's what I said."

"No, you said, 'on accident.' It's 'by accident.' I hate that."

He wrinkled his face at her and narrowed his eyes. He broke out into an unsure smile.

"What you reading?" he asked.

Elizabeth Frost: perennially with a book in her hand.

"The Secret History."

"What's it about?"

"A group of friends that conspire to commit murder."

"Oh. That's intense."

"You want to blaze up?" she asked.

His eyebrows picked up.

The two found a secluded spot in a field and shared a joint under tall grass. He ended up talking a lot about himself: insecurities about his masculinity, his lack of ambition, his divorced parents and broken family. Frost didn't find it all that charming, but he was sufficiently sensitive, so she let him feel her up under clothes that first time.

Days later, she ignored him. It wasn't a tactic—she had had her fill of weepy Pete and his gab sessions—but she soon recognized it stoked a fire in him predicated on nothing more than her aloofness. He otherwise knew and seemed to like very little about her.

"Men are hunters," she told a girlfriend. "You make them give chase, and you're all they see. But like dogs that catch the car, they have no idea what to do once you give in."

After a week of courting, she let Pete catch the car. The two would sneak off during work hours and squeeze in a quickie wherever they found the privacy. All of Pete's sessions were quickies regardless of the time constraints. He wore condoms, but ones too big that fit his ego but not his penis. Two or three ended up lost in the process, and he would humiliatingly poke around in there when he was done, trying to fish it out, before she slapped his fingers away and left to do it herself in private.

The two left camp "dating" and planning to reconnect but no one brought up exclusivity or used the terms "boyfriend" or "girlfriend." Frost was beginning at the University of Kansas in the fall.

She met Katie Galindo moving into her dorm. Frost and the junior shared a communal bathroom alongside eight other girls living down the same hall. Katie's parents helped move her in, and the middle-aged couple—warm smiles and vibrant eyes, like the light of Jesus flowed within—made it a point to knock on doors and introduce themselves to the girls sharing space with their beloved daughter. They wore posh, perfectly unwrinkled clothes and held hands like a pair of lovestruck teenagers.

Their interactions with the girls ended always with the same question.

"And I just have to ask," Mr. Galindo would say, "do you know Christ the Lord as your personal savior?"

"Know in a biblical sense?" Frost asked, not able to help herself.

She felt shame at the smart-aleck remark even as it emerged from the depths of her dark heart.

In the mornings, Frost would stagger late into the bathroom for a shower and pass by Katie as she applied the finishing touches to her face in front of the mirror. Katie appeared to exclusively wear skirts, with her blouse or sweater neatly tucked into the waistline. She combed her long, shiny hair over and over, standing at various distances and angles to ensure not a strand was misplaced and her beauty was accurately reflected from every vantage point. There was an intensity to her that sped your heart rate up at merely watching her.

Katie and Frost didn't talk, but they exchanged glances. Always cursory. Always Katie who looked away first. Frost imagined her parents had warned her about the heathen girl down the hall.

Frost saw her at the extracurricular fair as the freshman swept past the tables lined up in the gymnasium. The banner taped to her booth read, "KU Right to Life," in which the "t" doubled as the Christian cross. From a distance, Frost was captivated, eyes glued to her as Katie beamed at and conversed lightheartedly with friends. Perhaps it was the incongruity of the macabre topic juxtaposed with the trail of laughter and chatter that floated out of Katie's beautiful mouth. Perhaps it was the knowledge that Frost's period was way late and the sneaking anxiety that within her womb grew that pink, coal-eyed, alien-adjacent collection of cells prominently featured on cardstock behind her.

Katie's boyfriend drifted into frame. It was the first time Frost laid eyes on him, but she saw the way he kissed and held her. He wore the trappings of a football player, which fit all too perfectly with what she had imagined for the immaculately put-together, fetus-loving Katie. Frost noted that he was cute and, from the jersey on his back, that he had an Asian-sounding surname.

Amid a sea of positive pregnancy tests littering the bathroom floor, Frost called Pete.

"It's mine?" he asked, near tears.

"Yes."

"You flushing it out?"

She paused, blinking back rage.

"Yes."

"Good. Let's go Dutch. I'll Venmo you."

Frost drove herself to the closest abortion clinic in the state on a Saturday afternoon. A throng of protestors lined the periphery. She sat in her car, hands clutching the steering wheel, past late for her appointment. She exited when a critical mass of them appeared distracted by their phones. Few of them stirred when she flew by them. They held their signs, and stared at her with shiny, sad eyes, but they were silent and solemn. Maybe on the way out—when she was no longer an expectant mother but a murderer—would they cast their stones.

A hand grabbed gentle hold of her arm. Frost whirled around to a pamphlet shoved in her face.

"Choose life."

It was Katie, surrounded by friends, enmeshed in the crowd. Up close, within inches, newly aware of each other, they exchanged blank stares, unable to scrabble together the words. As usual, Katie looked away first, shrinking from her and back to her friends' side, firm hold on the anti-choice literature.

Frost would have preferred a sermon, as if Katie cared, as if she were worth saving. Instead, it felt like Katie was embarrassed for her. Like she had nothing to say to women like her. Like Frost was a lost cause.

She collected herself, strode into the clinic, got her pills, and left.

In the hours of bleeding, cramping, and crying that followed, Frost called Pete. No answer. He texted immediately after the missed call.

It done?

Yes.

She got a Venmo notification afterward for half the cost of the procedure, like they were splitting a check at dinner. The cheery ding of a bell on her phone and a thumbs-up emoji—the only text he put in the memo line—cut through the morosity.

She called her dad next. He sounded busy and out-of-breath—corralling his trio of kids at the zoo—but satisfied and content. Like he had everything he needed. Without her. She ended the call quickly without revealing its purpose.

"You sure you're all right, Elizabeth?"

He had to have heard it in her voice—the way that it trembled and cracked and collapsed under its own weight. But the question was largely rhetorical. He didn't have the time for an emotionally wrought digression.

"I'm good. Promise."

The final text from Pete came not long thereafter:

> **This thing between us is getting a little serious for me.**
> **I think we should stop seeing each other? Best of luck,**
> **Frost. ✌️ Fun times.**

Her roommate, dressed in all blue, returned that night to find her still in bed.

"Big loss tonight to a shitty team. A nobody kicker choked on a layup of a field goal."

Frost would go on to regret the procedure—not just days but years and a lifetime later. Her head understood its necessity: how she avoided being tied to a deadbeat, saved her career before it had begun, and cleared the path for an unburdened young adulthood. She wasn't religious, she hadn't felt a connection with the clump of cells that was a part of her for just a blink in time, and she sure as shit would never vote to take the choice away from others. But her heart forever hurt. Progressives weren't supposed to feel that way. It engendered a glut of guilt. With certain women, she would volunteer having made the choice as a teenager.

"You must be so happy you went through with it?" they'd ask.

"Oh, yes. Completely."

She would then excuse herself to go cry.

The night a shell-shocked Katie burst into their shared bathroom in her disheveled nightie had been one such time. Frost was finishing up, drying her eyes in the stall where she had sought refuge from her roommate's prying eyes. She stepped out and Katie flew in, shaking, drawing near the sink and the large mirrors.

Frost peered at her but only briefly, locking her sights on the door instead and intending to sweep past. A familiar touch on the arm stopped her.

"I need help."

Katie had her back hunched over and was clenching her legs together.

"I think my boyfriend raped me."

"You *think*?"

Katie recoiled.

"I didn't want it. I never want it."

"He's done this before?"

"Yes. I mean, no. I gave him permission before."

Frost had a hard time seeing Katie as a wounded bird. Here was a girl who saw herself as a cut above the others, a culture warrior shaming mortal women for spreading their legs and deigning to control their own bodies. But that night, she looked no different than any other godless woman, holding in the semen her Christian boyfriend had pumped inside of her like the rest of them. She would end up flushing the early components of a child just like Frost had.

"But you didn't want it this time?"

"No."

"Why not?"

"It's a sin."

Frost gave in to a smirk and pulled her arm away. Her judgment came swiftly. She washed her hands.

"You lost me there, sweetheart. Take a shower. Go to bed. The Lord and His castigation will be there come morning if you still crave it."

Frost was shocked at how unfeeling her voice sounded. Clearly, so was Katie. She physically reacted to the words like a blow, turning sallow, twisting her body away, and hanging her head. There was a coal of sympathy alight and deep within Frost's gut. But she snuffed it out. Her reservoir of mercy was dried up, having spent it all on herself.

Frost saw the boyfriend a second and last time in the morning, down the hall, emerging from Katie's room alone. He looked oblivious. He wore an undershirt that bared his arms and the top of his chest. A golden cross was hanging in the gap of his clavicle. Frost was frozen at her own door, watching him but trying not to make it obvious. When he walked by, without slowing, he turned his head to her and winked.

"Mornin'," he said in a low register.

For months, whenever Frost caught sight of Katie, her eyes lingered. She was convinced she was seeing what her haunted conscience wanted her to see. Frost became obsessive over every detail. There was the weight loss. She saw bone poking through skin in places she hadn't before. There was the loss of color—in her cheeks, in her lips. In those rare times they shared a bathroom—because often, Katie would leave at the first sight of Frost—she watched that same entrancing hair-combing routine. Except this time, clumps of hair would fall out. Katie didn't even flinch. She just kept combing, dead in the eyes. Frost would ask her friends for updates: Katie's grades were cratering. Her parents were recommending pulling her out of school. The school's investigation was in bureaucratic delay.

Frost expected she might be summoned to tell her story. It kept her up at night. She didn't think she could put to words how callous she had been. She replayed the scene so often in her mind, she could recite and reenact the lines as if it were a script. Down to the lighting. Down to the ambient noise. Down to the look in her eyes. When Frost shut her own to go to sleep, she saw them. Two pools of brown despair.

But Frost never approached her. The shame was paralyzing.

Katie disappeared those last few weeks of the school year. When Frost found out her parents were moving her out of the country for good, back from where they had emigrated, she drove out to Katie's home address hours away. But she was too late. The house had new residents by the time she arrived. She didn't get to make amends.

On the last day of class, Frost found a bulky envelope in her campus mailbox. It contained a letter and an old-school cassette tape. The tape was labeled: "Burn after Playing." She read the letter first. It wasn't addressed to anyone.

My therapist said it would help to write a letter to the people I hate. But I won't give Cameron the pleasure of hearing from me again. And Dale Whitehurst won't even read it; probably just some low-level staffer of his, and she would trash it after she did. So I'm left with you.

I'm supposed to let go and forgive you and forgive myself and all that bullshit in this letter. But I won't be doing that. I want you to feel bad. I want you to hate yourself like I hate you.

I'm sure you think that you and the disregard you showed me fall low on the list of things on my mind. But it's at the top actually. I think about it all the time. I can't let it go. I was at my most vulnerable. I needed to know I hadn't invited it. I needed to know I wasn't inventing it. That I wasn't misunderstanding something fundamental about men, women, and the rules of sexual engagement. That I reserved the right to say "no," always and forever. But you gaslit me. I know the term is overused, but it's exactly what you did. You made me question my own trauma. That was inhumane. That was unpardonable.

You're probably wondering what a powerful man like Dale Whitehurst did to earn my wrath. Well, he was no better than you. Sure, he led the charge to expel Cameron. But that was low-hanging fruit. Cameron had embarrassed the football program—on and off the field. Sacking him helped them score the political capital to do nothing when athletes of actual use act in the same ways. You think if Cameron were a high-producing quarterback that the Ad Board would've done a damn thing? That Dale Whitehurst would've cared?

Early on, after the fog of self-doubt had cleared—a fog you helped create—and I was intent on pursuing criminal charges, Whitehurst called me into his office. It was just the two of us. He told me that he used to be the district attorney. That his son was the current district attorney. That no one would believe me. That Cameron had sent an infamous "U up?" text. We all know what that means. That I had let him into my room, into my bed in the middle of the night. What had I expected from a 21-year-old boy? I couldn't be that stupid. He told me they would use my Christian faith against me. That I was just a girl crying wolf because I had sinned and didn't want anyone to find out. That he was my boyfriend, and we were sexually active, and I had consented every time before that. What was he supposed to think I wanted? He wasn't a mind reader.

A quiet expulsion was one thing. A criminal prosecution was public. It'd make the school look bad. It'd make the football team look bad. And I'd lose. It was selfish to put everyone through that. Did I mean to ruin that young boy's life? Hadn't I loved him, even a little? Where was my Christian compassion?

I never even presented him with the recording I made, the recording I now gift to you. It occurred to me that it didn't matter what proof we have. They never believe us. We could have DNA. It can be video recorded. He can confess. It won't matter. Because men aren't prepared to be held to account for what happens in the bedroom. Period.

Through that lens—where women are conniving liars looking to take good men down—how could I even explain that I unlocked my phone, frantically tapped on the voice memo app, and hit record right before he initiated sex? How could I explain that I had felt something was very, very wrong from before that night and that it made me nervous? That it made me record the affair, just in case? How do I explain not calling 911 instead, or my parents, or a friend if I was so scared? Why didn't I tell him about the recording to get him off of me? Surely that would have gotten through to him if my pleas did not.

Rape is the only crime in which we demand that victims act perfectly rationally. In which we ask victims to explain themselves instead of the perpetrator.

Too little evidence, and the case is weak. Too much evidence, and it's a setup. Either way, women lose.

Dale Whitehurst is spineless. He brought me back to that moment in the bathroom with you. He killed my spirit. He killed my sense of hope. Sometimes I wish that he and every other man so petrified of false allegations be personally treated to them. How delicious would that be?

I'm leaving this place. A fresh start will do me some good.

I converted the audio file into a cassette tape so you could have a physical copy. Nothing digital. I don't want this to get around or wind up anywhere official. That isn't the point. I'm gone, so it won't matter. I just want you to have it. Maybe because, deep down, I still want to prove it to you. I want you to believe me, believe that it happened. How sick is that? That I still care?

Bye, Frost. Fuck you.

Frost forced herself to sit through the recording—that first time and over a hundred times more. She held on to it as a grisly keepsake.

Frost couldn't get out of bed for days. She felt weak inside. Sore, not unlike the aftermath of her terminated pregnancy. Just like then, she felt she had lost something. Something integral to her. The thing that made her feel human. She would stare at the mirror and shake and curse at herself until she was red in the face.

"You're worthless!" she'd say with so much conviction, it frightened her.

Woman's inhumanity to woman was the worst kind of sin.

And then, one day, something clicked. The men who fucked up weren't doing this. They didn't wallow. They didn't self-reflect. They didn't care. The world kept turning for them. But if they couldn't regret on their own, she would make them regret. She would make them feel loss.

She could not make it up to Katie. But perhaps she could make it up to herself.

In three more years, she had earned her degree and, unemployed, was visiting her father, watching television with him on the couch. A commercial for the reelection of Senator Whitehurst played on-screen. Her dad grumbled to himself and flipped it off in a huff. It was a sign.

Frost volunteered for the campaign the next day.

She felt purpose for the first time in years. Hers would be a different type of public service. She would gain the trust and confidence of bad men. She would lie in wait. She would find the perfect time to strike. Then, she would strip them bare and reveal their ugliness for the world to see.

She was unusually devoted for an unpaid aide. She was the first to arrive and the last to leave. She signed up for the most unenviable of tasks. She poured all of her energy into helping the senator keep his job. Higher-ups noticed. It impressed them. Some made it nasty.

"She's probably just another Whitehurst groupie," Frost overheard one unmarried, middle-aged white woman say. "We get a few young girls like her every cycle, practically in love with Dale."

Her good work did earn her a brief meeting with the senator after he won in a landslide. He wanted to thank his most ardent supporters.

"I'm Dale," he said, as if that weren't apparent.

She slipped her hand in his.

"I'm...Liz," she said. She wanted to be a new person. Like a character in one of her books.

"You've got tiny hands, Lizzy. Is it all right if I call you that? I had a dear aunt Lizzy who I adored."

"Of course, Senator. You can call me anything you want."

"We're going to be filling positions in my Washington, DC, office. We could use hardworking Kansans like yourself over there. Might that be of interest to you, Lizzy? You'll get a lot of face time with me."

"Oh, that sounds wonderful, Senator. An absolute dream really."

She moved out there, worked hard, made friends—many of them men, many of them lovers—and climbed the social ladder. She was oh so great at networking.

"It's called being a slut," some hateful women said behind her back.

Liz, as she had newly taken to being called, didn't mind. It felt smart. Transcendental. These other women were still operating under the rules of the patriarchy. Liz was making her own rules. She was rewriting the playbook. She was forgoing no advantage. And she was getting what she wanted, and that's all that ever mattered. She was, without shame now, finally her mother's daughter.

Charlie James caught her eye at work. The incongruity of the large black man shepherding the small white senator down the halls drew her attention. She asked a coworker of his about him.

"He's a snack," the girl said, swooning. "Big-time college football star. Did the NFL combine and everything, but never got drafted.

Wasn't good enough, I guess. He's from a well-connected family plugged into North Carolina GOP politics. I think there was some sort of sex scandal with him but nothing came of it. And I only ever see him with blondes, though. Sorry."

Liz read up on Mr. James on Google. Lots of praise. She had to get to page 10 of the search engine results to spot the one or two articles addressing the controversy. He was accused of sexually assaulting a girl. It went nowhere. He went on to be considered for the Heisman Trophy. None of the stories ever mentioned what happened to the girl. Her name wasn't published. It was hard to track down. Frost found it eventually in the comments section. An anonymous keyboard warrior had doxxed the girl's identity, calling her a gold digger looking to cash in on the rising star's future fortune. The top result for her name was an obituary. Years later, she had killed herself.

Liz didn't know how, but she figured Charlie might be useful. Be the fall guy whenever she needed it. Be the muscle in her vengeful scheme. Kill two birds with one stone. Sex and love made men do wild things.

Liz dyed her hair blonde that night. She found out where Senator Denton's next big event would be, wore her sexiest red dress, and arranged to run into Charlie. She saw the look in his eye, and it was over. Hook. Line. Sinker.

In that tour she led, she hadn't recognized Cam at first. She kept staring when she spotted his familiar face amid the crowd. It wasn't until he spoke up in an affectedly deep tone—"Free"—that it hit her: a wave of panic and nausea that she squelched behind a saccharine smile.

"Rock chalk, Jayhawk."

To her credit, she tried baiting him into remembering her. At first, it was just fun.

He lied about his age.

"You look older," she told him.

He was whitewashing his ancestry.

"You have Chinese in you, Cam?" she asked him.

He was pretending to be someone he was not.

"You can come here and reinvent yourself. Become an entirely new person," she said to him.

He never seemed to grow suspicious. He grew attached to her instead.

He didn't hide his ambitions particularly well, either.

"Then why don't you kill them?"

The suggestion had first come from Cam's lips. That was helpful.

Her teasing soon became a test. If he was going to prove himself as useful as Charlie, she had to be sure he didn't know what she knew.

She tried on the vanity glasses he was faking as prescription.

"These aren't helping at all," she mused to him.

As much as he called himself white, he seemed to speak of whites as others, like the bros wearing shorts and sandals in the winter.

"Your people, no?" she asked.

"No," he responded.

She left Katie's tape out, visible for him to easily spot in case he had seen it before. In case, despite her letter, she had sent him one after all. He said nothing.

"I *know* you. Trust me," she told him.

Isla's Jayhawks knowledge threatened to crater the whole thing. Liz had to throw her off the scent.

"He looks like someone to me. The name rings a bell, too. Someone on the depth chart at KU maybe?" Isla asked her.

"Oh, I know who you're talking about. Went to school at the same time as him. Completely different person," Liz said. "You know all those meatheads look the same."

Liz needed Charlie emotionally vulnerable. She had met Luke Russell fortuitously at that bar with Cam. She cultivated that relationship and leaked the audio to him of Denton colorfully bad-mouthing Charlie. She had caught it on one of her tapes.

When Cam professed his infatuation with her, she knew he was all in.

She never explicitly put the fabricated accusation against Whitehurst to words. That was intentional. She only intimated it to Charlie and Cam, and she never even hinted at it in the others' company. She played the tape to ensure Cam was solid. To see if he was double-crossing her or if it would finally dislodge something in the back of his mind. She had to know right then—before the police got involved—that he wouldn't unearth her secret motivation.

"You recognize this?" she asked him point-blank after playing it.

Love, rage, stupidity, or all three had blinded him. He had no clue he was listening to himself violating his own girlfriend.

She had actually revealed to both Cam and Charlie her true motivations for the Whitehurst plot.

"He's not a good man. He's a mother fucker," she told them. Two words. Not one.

You hear what you want to hear.

She asked Ernesto to do her a favor.

"The morning after the election, no matter what, e-mail this name and picture anonymously to the authorities," she instructed him. "Do not tell anyone about it ever. Just do it, and forget about it."

Her father had dutifully shipped her a copy of her yearbook. Cam had been expelled too late in the year to be scrubbed from it. She texted Ernesto a screenshot for the entry under "Cam E. Lian."

"Isn't this that Lancaster kid?" Ernesto asked.

"He's never who he says he is."

Police now had their motive in glossy black-and-white: expelled football screwup, alleged rapist, and son of a convict puts a hit out on the man who ruined his life. The jury would love that. Ripped from the plot of a soap opera.

Investigators asked her whether she and the senator had an improper sexual relationship. After it was clear that Charlie and Cam weren't being let go, their lawyers—who were in an information-sharing agreement—insisted that she be confronted with her alleged cries of rape.

"Absolutely not," Liz said. "I would never allege anything like that because it isn't true. I was very good friends with Emily, the senator's wife. Ask her. She would know. I never had sex with the senator—consensual or otherwise—and if either of these men, with whom I *did* have a sexual relationship, grew jealous of the fatherly affection he showed me, well, that's on them. Not me."

"What about this tape you supposedly played them?"

"I'm baffled by that. All lies. How does someone record their own sexual assault? That just doesn't happen. They know I recorded lots of conversations for the senator. That's probably where they got the idea. You can listen to all of them. You won't find anything remotely like what they're describing."

"And you'd be willing to testify to that in a court of law? Against your ex-lovers?"

"Of course. These men are killers and dangers to the general public," she said. "There is one issue, of course. My lawyer says I'm still exposed, given the lies those two are spinning. I want to help, but he won't let me do that unless I'm granted immunity from prosecution. Is that something you're willing to give me?"

The others corroborated that, on second thought, they never did hear about the assault from Liz directly. And certainly no one talked about a taped recording of it.

Liz had successfully cried wolf.

She felt bad for the guiltless members of the gang who caught a case. She hadn't quite thought that part through. But Cam was the brain, however little he possessed of it, and Charlie was the body, all he was ever good for anyway. They were the government's targets. The rest would flip, plead out, and avoid serious jailtime. The feds needed their testimony.

The authorities weren't sold on flipping Liz. She was so central to it all, and the lower-level plotters with exposure of their own could make a solid case against her and the boys. She had credibility issues that made her a shaky witness without bringing something more to the table.

"Oh, and one more thing," she told them. "I own tapes proving the chairman of the Senate Judiciary Committee, Bill Williams, explicitly traded votes deregulating the semiconductor industry for cash and the promise of building a chip plant in Iowa. I can get you those. You bring me on board with full immunity, and I testify to it all. I'm all yours—body and soul—for the foreseeable future."

Now that was a deal the feds couldn't pass up.

She walked out of the FBI field office a free woman. She set up a small fire on the rooftop of her apartment building, burning Katie's tape and letter as the brightly lit Capitol Building loomed distant in the background. She wondered if the story and mention of the perpetrators had hit the international news cycle. Maybe reached Mexico and a certain ex-pat who might find the news delicious. She hoped so. She'd sleep easier imagining it had.

Men get what they deserve. Hashtag: Yes, all men.

ACKNOWLEDGMENTS

My earliest and most ardent dream was to publish a novel. I don't know that as a young boy I could have wrapped my mind around the thought of a second. It has come to pass only because of you:

> My sister, my hero. My loving mother. My steadfast father. My brilliant Brooksie, who feels so deeply all the feelings in the world, and little Walker, so joyful and sweet. I will take every opportunity—use up barrels and barrels of ink—to tell you all that I love you.

I cut my political teeth on Capitol Hill as a kid straight out of college. It's a brutal and beautiful place, boasting its own awful and awe-inspiring culture. This book is my (gruesome) love letter to it.

After a decade away, I returned to serve as investigative counsel to the House Select Committee to Investigate the January 6th Attack on the United States Capitol. I am grateful to Tim Heaphy for bringing me on board, and I am indebted to my team and friends—Soumya Dayananda, Bryan Bonner, Damon Marx, Percy Howard, and Jon Murray—for trusting my judgment, input, and mediation skills when debate got heated. Thanks to James Sasso and Sean Quinn for the long hours we spent choreographing the summer hearing I was fortunate enough to co-lead with Soumya, and thanks go to Sandeep Prasanna, who recommended me for an adjunct professorship at Georgetown Law to keep me busy in my downtime. As counsel, I got to grill witnesses—a Senate-confirmed secretary, inscrutable Secret Service agents, military leaders, police chiefs, and a big-city mayor—and got to write a chapter and a couple of appendices for the final report.

It was fun. And together, I like to think we did good, good work on behalf of the republic.

From a legislative fellow to chief of staff, my Hill journey has been a winding road. My latest stop with Congressman Glenn Ivey—a kind, smart, and earnest public servant—has been a joy (you are nothing like the horrible bosses depicted in this book!). I am humbled every day for the opportunity you gave me to work for the American people.

So many of you threw your enthusiastic support behind me when my debut came out. It warmed my heart to see family and friends filling out the seats at Books & Books in Coral Gables for my first fancy-pants, in-person book talk. A few of you really leaned into trying to get my book out there—Lucero Ortiz, Mirla Urzua, Evelyn Lilly, Yomari Chavez, and John Dey—and that meant so much to me. This go-round, I had new contributing editors Seema Mahanian and Lyssa Keusch to help me refine my vision. Much appreciated.

Every one of you who bought and read my last book has earned my lifelong affection. Perhaps none more than seventy-five-year-old Harry Lejda from Sophia, North Carolina—where there are "more cows than people"—who wrote to me and said, "Keep writing fiction; you are so good at it."

Thanks, Harry. Onward. Upward.

ABOUT THE AUTHOR

Robin Peguero spent seven years storytelling to juries for a living, most recently as a homicide prosecutor in Miami. An Afro-Latino and the son of immigrants, he graduated from Harvard College and Harvard Law School. He has written for the *Miami Herald*, the *Harvard Crimson*, and the *Harvard Law Review*, and he served as a press spokesman in the US House, a speechwriter in the US Senate, and an investigative counsel on the House Select Committee to Investigate the January 6th Attack on the United States Capitol. He is currently an adjunct professor at Georgetown Law and chief of staff to a member of Congress.